Play Dates

By Leslie Carroll

PLAY DATES
TEMPORARY INSANITY

Play Dates

Leslie Carroll

AVON
TRADE

An Imprint of HarperCollins*Publishers*

PLAY DATES. Copyright © 2005 by Leslie Carroll. All rights reserved. Printed in the United States of America. No part of this book may be used or reproduced in any manner whatsoever without written permission except in the case of brief quotations embodied in critical articles and reviews. For information address HarperCollins Publishers Inc., 10 East 53rd Street, New York, NY 10022.

HarperCollins books may be purchased for education, business, or sales promotional use. For information please write: Special Markets Department, HarperCollins Publishers Inc., 10 East 53rd Street, New York, NY 10022.

FIRST EDITION

Designed by Elizabeth M. Glover

Library of Congress Cataloging-in-Publication Data

CIP Data

Carroll, Leslie Sara.
  Play dates / by Leslie Carroll.
    p. cm.
ISBN 0-06-059606-6
1. Divorced women—Fiction. 2. Mothers and daughters—Fiction. 3. New York (N.Y.)—Fiction.   I. Title.

PS3603.A77458P55 2005
813'.6—dc22   2004016091

05 06 07 08 09 JTC/RRD 10 9 8 7 6 5 4 3 2 1

For Irene

My deepest thanks to Carrie Feron and Lucia Macro at Avon Books for their creative and incisive editorial vision, and to my wonderful agent Irene Goodman for her constant inspiration; to my dear friend Gail Matos for being my daily correspondent, cheerleader, and constant lifeline to the rest of the world during the writing of this book; to Rebecca Scarpati, Joan Sloser, Jan Leslie Harding, and most especially to my sister Nicole Gruenstein for sharing their maternal wisdom and humor; to Bruce Belland for his generosity, despite the fact that his lyric ended up on the cutting room floor; to den farrier for putting me in touch with Bruce as well as for his myriad wonderful insights; to Brian Vinero, NYC tour guide extraordinaire; a wink to Sakamoto-san; and a nod to my late grandfather Carroll Carroll. He knows why.

Chapter 1

"Zoë, honey, please put those down. You're only six years old."

"I'm six and three-quarters."

"I'm sorry, sweetie. Six and three-quarters. Yes, you're a big girl, now. Still, you can't wear high heels to second grade."

"I want to look like MiMi."

"You'll have plenty of time to look like your aunt MiMi," I cajole. "*Believe me*, you don't want to rush growing up."

"Yes, I do."

We've been hunting for the perfect pair of school shoes for upwards of half an hour. My linen dress is clinging to my body like a limp dishrag. This has to be the hottest Labor Day on record. You could fry an egg in the middle of Broadway. It's so muggy outside that we could have *waded* up to Harry's Shoes, which must be the craziest place in the city to have to visit on the last shopping day before school starts. It's mayhem in here. The decibel level is even worse than a Saturday afternoon at PlaySpace. Honestly, I don't know how the salespeople cope. The management must give them a free hit of Prozac when they punch their time card.

I think the mothers and merchants of New York City will breathe a collective sigh of relief tomorrow. I sure know I could use a break. I've spent every day this summer with Zoë. It's the first time I've ever had to care for her 24/7. I lost both husband *and* housekeeper in the divorce. Hilda had been Scott's mother's housekeeper at one point, so her loyalty was to the Franklins. I've had no one to pick up the slack, so I could catch a catnap, find twenty minutes for a manicure, or—God forbid—go to lunch with a girlfriend.

Zoë, looking like a wilted daisy, comes over to me complaining of the heat and humidity. "I'm sticky," she gripes, pushing limp bangs off her forehead with a grubby hand. I open my bag, whip out a Wash'n Dri, mop her brow, wipe her hands, and pin up her hair with an elastic and a clip.

"Blow," Zoë says, and I purse my lips and generate a gentle Mommy breeze, cooling the nape of her neck and her face.

Brimming with purpose and bustle, a tall woman with one of those year-round tans, forty-something and looks it, practically tramples a knot of preschoolers to get to me. She's nearly out of breath. "Who do you work for?" she asks abruptly.

"I don't understand," I reply, caught completely by surprise.

"I've been watching you from across the room," she says. "I'm sorry. I thought you spoke English. I wanted to know who you work for."

"Who do I *work* for?" I'm still not getting it. Maybe the intense heat of the day has baked my brain.

The woman slips into the cadences one uses when they think they're speaking to someone either dreadfully hard of hearing or from a country whose gross national income wouldn't cover the cost of an August sublet in the Hamptons. "It's so hard to find someone who—you know—well, speaks *English*. And is well-groomed—and—you're so good with the little girl." She unsnaps her Fendi "baguette" and withdraws a slim leather card case. "If you're ever unhappy with your present situation, please

do consider giving me a call. Xander isn't much of a handful."
She points out a small boy about Zoë's age with an unruly mop
of brown curls, banging together two Yao Ming-size Timber-
lands as if they're a pair of orchestra cymbals.

Oh, good Lord. I get it now. "You think I'm an *au pair*, don't
you?" I ask the older woman. She looks so smug, I decide that
the most delicious way to set her straight is through indirect
communication. Besides, a smartass remark just isn't me. My sister Mia is the one who excels at the witty rejoinder. "Zoë,
sweetie, please let's settle on something. *Mommy's* going to pass
out in a few minutes if we don't get away from this crowd." The
child has a way of totally zoning out for some reason whenever
we go to a shoe store. I guess it's why I postponed the school-
shoe shopping expedition until the last possible moment.

I'm trying not to let her see how exasperated I am that what
should have been a half-hour excursion is turning into a day
trip. And in this heat it's not easy. Ever since her father left, I
feel guilty when I get angry or lose patience with her. The divorce was rough on both of us and I'm unused to being the dis-
ciplinarian. More than that, I'm uncomfortable with it. My
own parents are uncharacteristically non-neurotic. Actually, I
suppose their loopy progressiveness is their own form of dys-
function, and not having grown up in a strict household, I
haven't a clue how to run one, even when discipline is clearly
called for.

My now-ex-husband Scott was able to handle his dot-com
CFO responsibilities from home much of the time, so while I
took a full course load at Columbia and got my bachelor's degree in art history during Zoë's first four years, it was Scott who
heard our daughter say her first word ("Da") and whose hands
she let go of when she took her first cautious, halting, baby
steps. Zoë worships her father and has been blaming me for the
divorce, even though it was Scott who decided to walk away
from the marriage several months ago.

My cell phone vibrates. It's my friend Sue. "Where are you?" she demands accusingly.

Well, no reason for her to cop an attitude, just because we haven't been in touch for a while! What have I done to her? "I'm at Harry's trying to find Zoë some school shoes she can live with. What's the matter?"

"Oh . . . nothing. Just that I've been sitting here at Farfalle since one thirty. I'm on my third glass of Pinot Grigio and the waitstaff is making me feel particularly pathetic for having been stood up. At first I thought you must have been held up in transit, but—"

"Hold on, Sue." I cover the phone and turn to Zoë. "You can have the lace-up or the ones with the buckle." Shit. I was supposed to meet Sue for lunch today. We've had this planned for ages, but the dry-erase board got Bolognese sauce on it, so we had to wipe it clean and I guess I didn't remember the date with Sue when I went to write down all our activities again. The collateral damage was that the appointment also got wiped clean out of my mind, so of course I didn't arrange for baby-sitting.

"I am so sorry," I apologize. "I completely forgot. Please don't hate me. It's been a bit insane lately." It's hard to continue the conversation while keeping an eye on Zoë, and the cell phone connection is dreadful. I'm becoming one of those people who yells inanities into her phone. Tales that can wait to be told at another time. One of those people for whom boiling oil and melted lead is an insufficient torture. "Sue, let me call you when we get home, and maybe we can set something up for . . ." *Sssssssshhhhhhh.* The connection goes dead. *Next year. Maybe.*

Aargh!

So, here I am, trying to keep things light to disguise my frustration. "How can you hate shoe-shopping and be my daughter?" I tease.

"*Daddy* hates shoe-shopping and I'm *his* daughter, too.

They're divorced," Zoë volunteers, for the benefit of anyone within earshot of the girls' shoe department. "Daddy left her for an older woman."

Where did hell did she get that phrase? Oh, right, she hears me use it all the time on the phone when I'm venting to Mia or to my female friends—like Sue—whom I hardly find the time to see anymore, even though they live across town.

"Well, dear, it's usually the other way around," Xander's mother mutters, loud enough for me to hear. She has an edge to her that I find instantaneously unpleasant. Maybe it's just me and I'm having a bad day. I'm sure this woman with the cancer cabana tan and the meticulously highlighted blown-straight-to-within-an-inch-of-its-overprocessed-life hair is a very lovely human being, despite the fact that she is quick to assume that a young woman in charge of a child must be its grad-student nanny. Evidently, she must have read too many celebrity tell-alls.

By this time, Xander has wandered over to his mother. She covers his ears with her jeweled hands. "Men are pigs," she hisses sororally. She sizes me up some more and then extends her hand. "I'm Nina Osborne. So, you're her *mother*. Fascinating. You don't see too many your age these days. It's . . . so retro."

I shake Nina's hand. "Claire Marsh." My own name tastes unfamiliar on my tongue. "Sorry, it takes a little bit of adjustment. I was Claire Marsh and then I became Claire Franklin, and it's so recently back to Marsh again that I"—I'm babbling here—"the judge only signed the decree a few weeks ago allowing me to go back to legally using my maiden name."

"How long have you been—?" Nina looks at Zoë and stops herself, deciding that the "D" word is a dirty one to say in front of my child, who has, herself just used it in a voice loud enough to carry in Yankee Stadium.

"Memorial Day. Fitting, huh?"

Nina points at herself with a manicured talon. "Last Valentine's Day. Can you believe it? How's yours coping?"

I watch Zoë's little fingertip caressing a pair of size 6½B Steve Madden platforms despite my previous attempt at admonishment. "Wishing she were an adult. I think she feels really out of control of things. I try to keep her busy so she doesn't have too much time to mope. I'm hoping all the distractions will help her get past the divorce so she can begin to move on."

"You're so brave," Nina says, eyeing Zoë.

"I don't know about *that*," I say, trying to laugh off the pain I still feel at having been abandoned. "It's not like I had a *choice* in the matter."

"I mean you're so brave not to care about children's fashion," she clarifies.

So that's why she was sizing up my little girl dawdling by the funky ladies' shoes in her Children's Place sportswear. Her son is wearing Ralph Lauren chinos and polo shirt. Zoë and I are clearly N.I.O.L.D. (Not In Our League, Dear).

Horrid woman.

"Xander is acting out," Nina confides, no longer feeling pressured to sugarcoat her son's behavior. "He really misses having his dad around. The jerk. Robert, not Xander. In fact I'd be the happiest woman in New York if I was able to find an *au pair* who could handle him. Xander, not Robert. *Robert* did that himself quite nicely."

I do the math and surmise why Nina is now on the prowl for a new nanny. I corral Zoë and bring her back into the children's department, steering her to a table with various navy and black oxfords and Mary Janes. "Okay. Pick something," I sigh. "Please. I'm not kidding." I turn to Nina. "If an *au pair* works for a married couple, what would you call a nanny working for a single parent? An *au seul*?" She doesn't appear to appreciate my efforts at levity. At least I'm amusing *myself*. Anything to try to retain a sense of humor this afternoon.

Zoë tugs on my skirt. "They're boring," she complains. With a desultory motion she pushes the sample shoes around on the table as if they were an unwanted plate of peas. "They don't have a style."

They do have a style, actually. Boring. The kid happens to be right. Still . . . "They're not supposed to be stylish, Zoë. They're school shoes."

"Why can't this year be like first grade? We didn't have to wear uniforms last year."

"Well, The Thackeray Academy, in its infinite wisdom, thinks that by the time you get to second grade you should concentrate on your schoolwork instead of showing off."

"Oh, is Zoë at Thackeray?" Nina asks. "Xander, blue or black. *Not* brown!" She looks at me, her face at once grim and woeful. "Xander's colorblind. Like his father." She leans over and whispers, "I just hope he never inherits Robert's male-pattern baldness." Notwithstanding her previous confession about Xander's "acting out," Nina seems displeased that in such a public place her son has demonstrated something short of sheer perfection. "Xander is transferring to Thackeray this year. He was at Ethical Culture for his first two years, but after Robert took up with Gretl or Britta or Caressa, or whatever the heck her name was—"

Xander pokes his mom. "Ula. Her name is Ula," he says angrily. I get the feeling the kid kind of liked Ula, too.

"Ula," Nina repeats acidly, elongating the first syllable of the nanny's name as though she is in extremis. "*Ula*—and left us high and dry, Xander began acting like Dennis the Menace on speed. So, I wanted to find a private school that wasn't quite as permissive. Xander needs structure. Thackeray's insistence on uniforms from the second grade on somewhat eased my mind."

I vividly remember the academy's much-vaunted "discipline." The notorious Marsh sisters were the scourge of many a Thackeray educator from preschool through twelfth grade. There was nothing that Mia and I thought we could get away with that we didn't try. And for the most part, our parents found our teachers' exasperation to be a source of mild amusement. This was in the pre-uniform days and long before marriage and motherhood would round off most of my edges. About five years ago, when parents of scholarship kids made a huge fuss about the undue focus on brands and labels (people like Nina Osborne being Exhibit A), the Thackeray administration decided to take drastic steps to remedy the situation. Zoë has been enrolled since kindergarten, and she's right—they don't make the preschoolers through first graders wear uniforms. Actually, it's more of a uniform *suggestion*, though it conjures up images of cold war fashion. Nikita Khrushchev for Kids R Us. There are a number of prescribed outfits, all in shades of blue and gray, and the kids are permitted to exercise their creativity by making their daily sartorial selections from this rather limited pool. Like Zoë said about the shoes: boring! But now I'm finding myself somehow grateful for the regulation. Now I'm a single parent. Now I'm watching every penny.

I admit that for her first couple of years, Zoë owned more French fashions than I did. Her wardrobe tells the story of the financial state of affairs during my marriage. She wore Oilily and the Dior Baby imports. When our savings started to dwindle, we moved on to Shoofly and Space Kiddets for toddler togs, then to Gap Kids and Gymboree, and now it's Daffys, Old Navy, and Children's Place. There is no Wal-Mart in Manhattan.

And now I'm going to have to find a real job for the first time in my life. It probably seems weird for a twenty-five-year-old New York woman to be saying this, in this day and age, but straight out of high school I went from my parents' home into marriage and pregnancy, not actually in that order. Then I attended Columbia while Scott worked from home and minded Zoë. During the dot-com boom, I didn't need to work. Since I graduated, I've been in the—some believe—enviable position of full-time mommy for the past couple of years.

But what else am I good at, which, while I bring up baby, will bring in the bucks? I studied art history because it interested me, not giving much thought at the time to needing to use the knowledge as anything more than playing amateur museum docent to friends and family. Without a master's degree, I can't get a teaching job, and going to graduate school at this point is about as likely to happen as getting blasted by a comet while standing in the middle of Times Square or finding a man who won't leave me. As Hilda the housekeeper is no longer in the picture, flexibility is key. I'll still need to be able to collect Zoë from Thackeray every day and escort her to and from the myriad after-school activities to which she is committed, most of which, like the lion's share of her stratospheric tuition, are now funded by her doting grandparents. Sometimes I wish they lived in the city. Their physical assistance would be as valuable to me as their generous financial aid.

I can't help noticing that Nina is staring at me. In fact she's been sizing me up during our entire conversation. I feel like a microbe.

"You're so . . . so *perky*." Funny, I've never felt less so in my life. "You remind me of someone," she adds. "That actress from *Legally Blonde*."

"Is that good?" I ask her. Her expression looks like she's got a hair stuck on her tongue. I guess Nina's got image issues with perky blondes. I take an educated guess at Ula's hair color.

"I'm still trying to get used to seeing someone so . . . well, such a young mother. I had Xander when I was thirty-eight. I'd done everything I'd planned: college, grad school, total immersion in the corporate culture, golden parachute, married well—the works—and the only thing I had left to fulfill was my biological destiny."

Her biological destiny? I've never heard that one before!

"Who does she see?" Nina asks.

"What do you mean?"

"Her therapist. Xander's isn't working out. And I thought,

since Zoë was going through divorce issues, too, that you might have found someone you're happy with. Xander's been seeing a Freudian, and the last thing he needs to hear right now is that he's got issues with his mother."

How did I end up living in a world where six-year-old children routinely see psychotherapists? "We . . . we're managing on our own," I tell Nina. "And, to be honest, I don't know of anyone. I'm sorry I can't be of any help."

She looks amazed, but elegantly covers her discomfort at having so boldly exposed her son's emotional shortcomings to a mother with—how could it be possible—a kid who is relatively sane, or at the very least, not in need of professional counseling. She switches her focus to a stunning pair of pumps, she excuses herself, and saunters over to admire them. I note the designer name emblazoned in raised gold letters over the warmly lit display case. Illuminated with its own pin spot, the sample pair resembles a priceless treasure—like something from the tomb of King Tut—in a climate-controlled, vigilantly guarded room at the Metropolitan Museum.

My mouth begins to water. *If only . . .*

But not anymore. Those are trophy-wife shoes, and that's no longer my life. Making sure Zoë's got everything she needs is my priority. A new pair of Stuart Weitzmans can wait. Besides, when am I going to wear them? When I take Zoë to that horridly overheated bikram yoga studio on Saturdays? Or ballet class on Wednesday afternoons? Or the kinder karate program she begged to try this year?

I convince Zoë to settle for a pair of navy T-straps, promising her that maybe next year I'll allow her to wear the grown-up-looking slip-ons that she clearly prefers. I do admire the fact that she's already developing her own sense of style. Even if it usually means that she wants to dress like a grownup. Or like her aunt Mia, who, for a woman about to turn thirty, still dresses like a rebellious teen, in precipitously high platforms, low-riders, and belly tees.

Tomorrow. Tomorrow Zoë will start school again and I can begin the job hunt. I've been unable to focus on it, what with her being home all summer, and the divorce so new, the hurt so raw for all of us. This would have been the first year she'd have gone to camp, but given the upheaval of our lives, it didn't seem like the right thing to do. My parents offered to foot the bill if Zoë really wanted to go. But I chafed at the idea of accepting any more charity from them and thought it would ease the transition into single parenthood if Zoë and I spent the summer together.

My mom and dad sent a check anyway. I insisted on it being only a loan. They didn't want me to have to job hunt during the summer. There were too many drastic changes already. They convinced me that there'd be more time to look, and, hopefully, a better market, after Zoë went back to school.

I did take her to a couple of the municipal swimming pools—both of which she pronounced "icky"—and I thought she might like it if we went out to Coney Island. But the long subway ride made her cranky, the amusement park overwhelmed her—too noisy—and she was scared to set foot in the ocean. We spent a few weekends at my parents' house in Sag Harbor, where she got to play with their Irish Setter and visit a quieter beach on the Long Island Sound. I think that was the last time I've had the chance to exhale since early August.

We're having to learn to cope as a twosome, Zoë and I, and it hasn't always been easy. Maybe I should log onto Amazon and see if they sell something along the lines of *The Complete Idiot's Guide to Single Parenting.*

• • • • • • • • • • •

Dear Diary:

This is the last good day of my life. I'm starting second grade tomorrow. My teacher, Mrs. Hennepin, is the meanest in the world.

Mommy had Mrs. Hennepin when SHE was in second grade and
Mrs. Hennepin hated her. There are two second-grade teachers at
school. My Aunt MiMi had the NICE second-grade teacher but
she's not there anymore. Mrs. Hennepin is still there. Mommy
says she's a dinosaur. There is a different nice second-grade
teacher now, but I didn't get her. Mommy tried to get me switched
into the nice teacher's class but Mr. Kiplinger who is the headmaster said no. He said if he did it for Mommy he'd have to do it
for everybody. Mrs. Hennepin looks like Alice in Wonderland from
my video but she is really old. She has blonde hair and wears
white hairbands a lot. I think her head would fall off like Nearly
Headless Nick if she didn't keep it on with her hairbands.

    This diary is a secret. Daddy went away and Mommy cried all
the time. She went to talk to a lady who told her to make a diary
because it would help her feel better. So I'm doing it, too. Mommy
used to not get mad at me so much. We had more time to play
when Daddy was around. We had a nice housekeeper named
Hilda. She wore blue bedroom slippers to do chores and stuff and
picked me up at school sometimes and took me to the playground.
But now we don't have Hilda anymore so Mommy has to do everything. Mommy hates the playground so we almost never go there
anymore. It's okay because I like to color and watch videos but I
like the playground, too. I like climbing the monkey bars and I like
the slide, except when it's really hot outside because then it burns
my tushie.

    I wish I could help Mommy. She always looks sad. I was in
first grade and then I had graduation and then Daddy moved out
of our apartment before the summer started. The place he worked
for, even though he worked at home, went out of business last
year. He got really angry because it was hard to get a new job. He
and Mommy fought a lot. Daddy yelled. He yelled "money doesn't
grow on trees!" I have never seen money growing on trees, not even
in Central Park. There are so many people in New York, maybe
they took it all a long time ago and there's only leaves now.

Then Daddy got a job. He went to work in a restaurant and he fell in love with the lady who runs the restaurant. Her name is Serena Eden. She's really skinny and has dark hair. She only eats foods that aren't cooked and she's old like him. Not like Mommy. Mommy looks the same way she did in the picture we have when she married Daddy. Daddy was a teacher at Thackeray in the Upper School. I'll go to school there when I'm older. Mommy was in his computer class. Then after she had her graduation they fell in love and got married and had me. Mommy looks like my Barbies, too. My Aunt MiMi is four years older than Mommy. Mommy's hair is blonde. MiMi's hair is almost black and she sometimes has an earring like a little dot in her nose, and more than one earring in each of her ears, but she dresses more like my Barbies than Mommy. She wears really fun clothes and fun shoes and fun hats. I like to go over to her house because we play dress-up. She lets me wear any of her things, except stuff she calls "vintage." Her real name is Mia but I call her MiMi because Mommy said that was her nickname when she was little. When she wanted something she would yell "Me! Me!" So people started calling her MiMi.

She's really fun. And she has a fun job. She puts makeup on models and movie stars and she gets a lot of free clothes because of her job. Sometimes she gets really nice presents from people who are happy at the way MiMi made them look. And she lets me play with her makeup when I go to her house to visit. MiMi is more fun than Mommy now. Mommy got grumpy when Daddy went to live with Serena Eden. He comes to pick me up on week-ends to take me places. He tries to be her friend but she doesn't want to talk to him. He came to take me to the planetarium and he told Mommy she would be happy again if she started to go out on dates. Mommy looked like she was going to cry.

I saw her looking at grown-up party shoes today when we went to Harry's to look for school shoes for me. They were Cinderella shoes. When I get older, I want shoes like that, too. We met a lady named Nina who is really mean-looking. She has a son named

Xander who is my age. Nina was looking at the shoes, the kind like MiMi wears with very high heels. Mommy was looking where Nina was looking and I felt sad because she looked like she wanted the shoes. Maybe wearing shoes like MiMi would make Mommy act more like her, because MiMi is happy and making jokes all the time. MiMi is my favorite person in the world because she is funny and she lets me dress up and put on her makeup and she doesn't scold me. I don't think Mommy is funny like MiMi. Mommy only tells me stupid knock-knock jokes.

• • • • • • • • • • • •

"Hal's history," I told Claire. She's the best shoulder to cry on; if there's anyone who knows about bad breakups, it's my sister Claire. Her spouse left her for an older woman, for Chrissakes. Like some sort of midlife crisis in reverse. Scott just walked out on her and their kid and took up with the owner-manager of Eden's Garden, the eatery where, after his dot-com company tanked and they ran through most of their savings, he got a job doing the books.

Serena Eden, who weighs, like, twelve pounds, and whose skin shines like glow-tape under a blacklight, glommed onto the uncooked food fad and is making a killing in undead food, though I would have thought her type wouldn't even kill a carrot because they believe it was a much-respected mystic in a past life. Maybe it's not some weird vegan thing about murdering livestock and produce. Maybe it's about having a healthier colon, or something. Whatever. The food is gross either way you slice it. Serena Eden serves "meat" made out of chopped nuts and has the nerve to charge fifteen bucks a plate for it. Call me opinionated, but I don't trust anyone who isn't an omnivore.

Come to think of it, I don't trust too many people, period. It's safer that way. And, quite possibly, if I want to totally depress myself by analyzing it, one reason why I'm still single and unattached as I slide precipitously toward my thirtieth year.

Back to food. I'm a total carnivore. That's why I was so attracted to Hal. We met on the Fourth of July at a bash in Hampton Bays hosted by my friend Gina who has a share there. Hal was doing his macho men-with-tongs thing over the grill and it was lust at first sight. Now, when I look back, maybe it was the sirloin I was salivating over. I went straight up to him and said I liked the marlin tattoo on his right bicep. "Nice ink," I think I said. I'd had three beers and felt pretty proud of my opening line. In spite of what my folks think of my so-called bohemian lifestyle—which I come by honestly, having a former Beat Generation poet as a dad and an offbeat dress designer for a mom—I'd never dated a man with a tattoo, although I have my own—a unicorn—just above my right ankle. The unicorn would have freaked my grandmother. Nana would have said it meant I couldn't be buried in a Jewish cemetery. Stuff like that is why my dad became an atheist.

After the barbecue, Hal and I hopped on his motorcycle and sped over to the Central Pine Barrens, where we snuck in through a gap in one of the fences and fucked like bunnies amid the wildlife.

Hal's greatest talent was that he knew where—and how—I liked to be touched without my drawing him a road map. This, of course, immediately qualified him to be my sexual soul mate. I thought I'd finally arrived at the end of my hunt-for-the-perfect-boyfriend. Last stop. Everybody out at Montauk.

That's my holy grail. A real, full-time boyfriend. But so far, I've done lots of research with little reward. If we're all created equal, how come some people have so much luck in the love thing while the rest of us—the un-loved—seem doomed to roam the earth like the un-dead—ever searching, never resting, until we find The One?

So spring has sprung and my summer fling has flung. Fourth of

July to Labor Day. Some track record, huh? *Two* months. Wow. Now that I'm doing the math, I'm discovering exactly how bad I am at this mating game. It's not that I'm super-picky, like Gina, who once dumped a guy because he had a thing for Adam Sandler flicks. I just have laughably bad luck with men—the kind of lifelong losing streak that makes me want to stay away from Las Vegas.

"What happened?" Claire asked me. She'd just dropped off Zoë for her first day of second grade with the dreaded Mrs. Hennepin. I'd managed to avoid being in her class—my first and last luck of the draw—but Claire suffered through her shit eighteen years ago. For some reason, that woman had it in for my baby sister. Claire's changed a lot since we were kids. She used to be a hellion, like me. I am still, in some ways. But how bad, really, can a seven-year-old kid be? I think Claire was the only second grader in the history of Thackeray to be assigned detention.

Claire had just told me that Zoë sat down on her butt right there on the pavement and refused to go in. The kid threw a full-fledged tantrum. Everyone was staring. Claire said she never felt more powerless as a parent. Zoë wouldn't budge an inch. Parked herself on the sidewalk and screamed her lungs out.

"You'd think Mrs. Hennepin was Torquemada," I said.

"She is," said Claire. "Which only made it harder to deal with Zoë. I had to be the bad guy and get her to go inside, when, in fact, I agreed with her. We tried to get her switched into the other class as soon as we received the teacher assignment, but Thackeray wouldn't do it. They're as stubborn as Zoë."

It wasn't 'til Ashley, one of Zoë's friends, came by, all upbeat, with her dad and her Powerpuff Girls knapsack, that my niece agreed to set foot inside the school. Note to self: arrange to meet Ashley's dad, if single. I like the Powerpuff Girls. They kick butt.

"Mia, are you there?" Claire said. "I just asked you what happened with Hal?"

"This was a new one," I told her. "He thought he was allergic to me. Said his skin broke out in hives whenever we were together."

"You're kidding!"

"I wish."

"I never liked him!" Claire said supportively.

"*Now* you tell me!" Unlike me, whose love life has been more like a landslide, Claire was always rock-solid in the relationship department. It was a bit weird at first that at age eighteen she married her high school computer teacher, Mr. Franklin, who's fifteen years older than she is, but he was definitely a hottie, and everything was great between them until he lost his job and hit crisis mode. A bit early for mid-life, in my opinion, but who knows? Maybe he plans to drop dead at eighty.

"So, I guess it's time to get back on the horse," I told Claire.

"Maybe you need to go solo for a while," she suggested gently.

I thought about it. She's been making a lousy go of that, herself, so it's interesting advice, coming from her. On the other hand, although she's not doing too well in the recent divorcée department, she hasn't been out there looking for love. She's really not ready, anyway. Of course, she hasn't had the time, either. The way Claire's life is structured these days, *Zoë* has a better chance of getting a date on a Saturday night. And the way *mine* is, Zoë, who is a total social butterfly, will be eighteen before *I* find a husband.

Claire focuses her every waking minute around Zoë. For the sake of her psyche, she has *got* to get out of the house. I don't mean so she can meet men. That can come later, when she's emotionally up for it. For now, she needs to do it for herself. To that end, I had an idea. An old pal of mine, Gayle Struthers, comes into town from Texas next week. She'll be here for just a few days, and, since she's never been to New York City, she wants to see it all. Crammed in, nonstop. I asked Claire to join us.

"Be a tourist for an hour or two," I urged her. "C'mon, it'll be a kick!"

She hemmed and hawed. "But I've got Zoë and she needs to be taken to school and picked up every day and then she's got ballet on Wednesday . . . or is that Saturday? No, Saturday's yoga. I'm breaking a sweat just thinking about it. And Zoë's teacher's a bit of a zealot. I'm not sure I like the altar in the room, with the bikram guy's photo surrounded by little candles. I think I prefer nondenominational exercise, at least for children. And we were going to sign her up for that Museum Adventures program for kids because she loves to do art projects, so I thought she'd get into going to all the museums with other kids her age and learning about the paintings, and you should have seen her the other day. She came home from school with this picture she made that was all drizzles and dribbles and she said, 'Look at my Jackson Pollock!' She's such a precocious little—she remembered the style and the name of the painter because she used to sit on my lap when I was studying and look at my art books with me and point to the color reproductions with her finger and ask 'What's this?' 'What's this?' It was—"

"Whoa, there, honey! Now, repeat after me: A Claire who takes good care of *Claire* will be a *better* Claire who takes care of *Zoë*." She refused to repeat the little mantra, but she got the point. Still, she insisted that she wouldn't be able to join me because it was her one chance this week to grocery shop in peace. Zoë has zero tolerance for supermarkets. I know this from personal experience. My niece has a particularly short attention span for stuff she doesn't like to do.

"Look, Zoë will be in school while we're off sightseeing with Gayle. We'll work around your drop-off and pick-up schedule. Even your grocery schedule. Okay? You need to get out and have some fun. Do something on your own. Remember what the rest of life is all about." Reluctantly, Claire agreed. I felt like I was performing an act of tough love to get my sister to do something—

anything—for herself. Granted, this excursion is *my* idea, but still . . .

Claire rushed me off the phone. It was time for her to head over to Thackeray to pick up Zoë and bring her over to kinder karate. The kid's really picking it up fast. Gives some real credence to the "get 'em while they're young" theory.

. . . .

Dear Diary:

I hate Mrs. Hennepin. She's stupid and she dresses like a little girl. They should make HER wear a uniform and see how she likes it. Everybody in class looks so boring. Why couldn't they pick pretty colors if we all have to dress the same? I would pick yellow. Yellow and orange. And maybe pink. But a real bright pink, like the color of one of MiMi's lipsticks. Not a pink that's for babies.

Mrs. Hennepin read the names of everyone in her class. When she came to my name, she said, "Zoë Marsh Franklin. Are you going to be as much trouble as your mother was?" I thought that was a mean thing to say. There are two best parts of second grade. One is that Xander Osborne, the boy from the shoe store yesterday, is in my class. I don't think he likes girls, though. I don't think he likes anybody. He acts kind of angry all the time. I like him, though. And I was nice to him even when he wasn't nice to anybody else. And my friends Ashley and April and May are in Mrs. Hennepin's class too. April and May are twins but they don't look alike. April has dark hair and May has blonde hair. And their chins are a different shape. Their mom's name is June. I think that's funny.

The other best part of second grade is that Mrs. Hennepin said that she wants us to practice writing, so she wants us to write things down every day. Xander said, "You mean, like a diary?" All the boys laughed. They said that diaries are for girls. I asked *her if we have to show her what is in our diaries because I thought they are supposed to be secrets.*

When Mrs. Hennepin looks at me, she has a fish face. She doesn't look at the other kids that way. I'm going to be the best at writing. That way, maybe she won't hate me.

Chapter 2

Well, Zoë's been in school for a full week and so far I've only gotten two notes from Mrs. Hennepin. In the first, she made a big deal out of Zoë and her little girlfriends calling her Mrs. Henny Penny behind her back and giggling about it. I laughed that one off. Besides, *my* generation called her that, and I bet every class before and since has done the same, so it's about time she got used to it. Kids will be kids, and there's much worse they could call her. Thank God they probably don't know that the woman's first name is Regina. I sound like my father—New York's poet laureate at the time—who, faced with the same note brought home from school in *my* sweaty little hand, wrote back to Mrs. Hennepin reminding her that Henny Penny was a famous literary figure and urging her to accept the compliment graciously. His response earned me two weeks' detention. And she wasn't even impressed by getting his autograph.

I seem to be forever planning my life around other people; and nothing my sister ever schedules works out exactly according to plan. To do anything sociable with Mia is to embrace Murphy's Law.

I realize this right after I drop Zoë at school, so I phone Jennifer Silver-Katz, the mother of Zoë's best friend Ashley, to see if she can take Zoë this afternoon.

I can hear in Jennifer's elongated sigh that this would be an imposition. "We were going to take Tennyson for a lip wax."

Tennyson, Ashley's older sister, is *ten*.

"I guess I can try someone else," I say, dejected and disappointed, wondering which mom might be more responsive at the last minute. I should have thought of this sooner. We get booked up pretty quickly days, if not weeks, in advance, if my own dry-erase calendar is any indication of the norm.

"Well, I suppose I can swing it," Jennifer says, "if Zoë doesn't mind sitting around Bumble and Bumble while Tennyson has her treatment. She can sit there with Ashley and look at the pictures in *Vogue*. But," she adds, drawing out the word, "I'll need you to do me a favor on Wednesday and take the girls from school to ballet and bring Ashley back with you. It's our anniversary."

"Oh. Congratulations."

"Thanks." She sounds less than thrilled. "Oh—and that's my day for snack, so you'll have to pinch-hit for me there, too. This year two of the girls are on Atkins and Miss Gloo says that three of them are lactose intolerant. So no cheese and crackers. And of course, no sugar or processed foods. But you know that. So, you'll pick up Zoë by five today?"

I assure her that I will and hang up. This gives me thirty-seven minutes to 1) phone the school to let them know that Jennifer—she's on my "okay to pick up" list—will be getting Zoë after school today; and 1a) ask them to send a note up to Mrs. Hennepin so she can tell Zoë to go with Ashley and her mother this afternoon; 2) do a week's worth of grocery shopping, get it home, unpack it; and 3) get to midtown to hook up with Mia.

When I meet Mia and Gayle at the appointed place for the

start of the sightseeing tour, Gayle gives me a big hug like she's known me all her life. Gayle is very tall, very blonde, and very loud. In fact, she's exactly how I'd pictured her.

Mia met Gayle a few years ago when some hotshot designer flew her out to Houston to do the makeup for a trunk show he was doing at Neiman Marcus. Gayle is a rich, childless housewife with scads of disposable income, as demonstrated by her head-to-toe designer ensemble, so I'm guessing Mr. Struthers is in oil.

"Well, I'll be damned!" she crows. "So you're Mia's baby sister! Aren't you just the cutest l'il thing!"

I'm not *that* little, certainly much bigger than a "bug's ear," which was the next thing out of her mouth, but most women I know are significantly more petite than Gayle. We board the bright yellow "Trina's Tours" double-decker faux London-style sightseeing bus for the four-and-a-half-hour, full-city excursion and clamber up to the roof, where we're completely outdoors, so we can better enjoy the view. With the plethora of competing tour companies to choose from, Mia confesses that she selected Trina's because it's run by the mom and pop team of Bubba and Gladys Taylor, a pair of native Georgians whose brochure proclaims, "We all loved the Big Apple so much, we just *had* to worm our way in!" Trina herself is the couple's overweight, sullen daughter, a twenty-something who is the company's receptionist-cashier. Not the best first impression, but the Taylors appear to be doing quite well for themselves, so I bite my tongue.

Mia thought Gayle, being a Texan, would relate to the city sights presented with a distinctly Southern flavor. Gayle, however, explains that there's a world of difference between Texas and the South, and only Yankees think the two are somehow synonymous. Mercifully, her annoyance with us non-Dixie chicks passes as quickly as a cloud scudding in front of the sun.

"Are you psyched for this?! Because I'm psyched!" She hollers. "Here, hold these for a spell." Gayle reaches into her voluminous leather hobo bag and pulls out three plastic cups, which she hands to Mia. "Okay, you hold tight to those, now," she urges my sister, then dives back into her handbag, and drags out a large thermos. "We are going to partaaayyyy!" she warbles at top volume. I ask her what she's got there. "Margaritas," Gayle replies. "My own secret recipe. No adventure is complete without 'em." Gayle unscrews the plastic cup that serves as the thermos cap and pours each of us a round.

It's 10 A.M.

I haven't had a drink this early in the day since my honeymoon.

So, here we go.

As the bus lurches away from the curb in a cloud of squirrel-colored exhaust, a young woman climbs up the stairs, grabs the microphone and cheerily welcomes us. Her name is Kathie—with an *ie*, like Kathie Lee, she emphasizes with a giggle, then apologizes if she's disappointing any of "y'all" but she's not going to give us the Southerner's guide to New York.

"Good thing," Mia mutters sourly, then returns to her Margarita. "This is more than enough for me." Evidently, Gayle's lesson in regional whatever went in one multi-pierced ear and out the other.

"I am a native New Yorker, now," Kathie says proudly. Then she proceeds to tell us that although she hails from Raleigh-Durham, she completed a "very prestigious" acting program in "my old home state of North Carolina," (which she pronounces dropping the r's so that the first word comes out "Noth" and the second one sounds like "Ca'line-ah,"), "but I am proud to say," she adds, beaming, "that thanks to my theatrical training I have completely lost my regional accent."

"Not. Or she'd better return her diploma for a refund," Mia grumbles.

"Well, she's perky, anyway," I say brightly.

"She's making my teeth hurt," Mia says.

We head up Eighth Avenue and round Columbus Circle. Kathie starts explaining the differences between uptown ("noth") and downtown (smiling broadly, "south"), then points out Central Park to our right ("designed by Frederick Law Olmstead and Calvert Vaux in the nineteenth century"—so far, so good; she's got that right). We stop at 72nd Street.

"Ladies and gentlemen, if you look to your left, you'll see the famous Dakota apartment building. Now who can tell me what happened there?"

"They shot *Rosemary's Baby*," I yell out, emboldened by Gayle's tequila.

"They shot John Lennon!" Mia screams.

"Damn asshole did it because he was in love with Jodie Foster, didn't he?" Gayle asks loudly. "Fool didn't even realize she was a les—"

"And on your right, Strawberry Fields," Kathie says, having cranked up her volume so that it drowns out Gayle's editorial comment. She starts to lead the bus in the Lennon-McCartney classic. Gayle shoves her margarita cup into my hand and starts playing air guitar and shaking her blonde mane to and fro like she's having a mild epileptic seizure. As we continue uptown, past the Museum of Natural History, all three of us are in tears, weeping dolefully for John.

This maudlin display of sentiment necessitates a refill. Gayle pours another round as we motor through the 96th Street transverse, heading toward Fifth Avenue and the East Side. Enroute, Kathie explains that Fifth Avenue is the dividing line between the east and west sides of Manhattan. Coming out of the transverse, the driver makes a right on Fifth and we begin to shake, rattle, and roll down the section of the avenue known as Museum Mile.

As we get to the Guggenheim Museum, the trouble begins.

"Ohhhhh, the *teacup* museum," Mia sighs. "That was always my favorite, growing up. It still is, I think."

Mia's much more into modern art than I am. I prefer the old masters and the Impressionists. Although, in college, I studied everything from the cave paintings at Lascaux to Andres Serrano's "Piss Christ," my taste pretty much runs out post-Picasso. With Mia, the weirder the better. I think she claims to admire really strange stuff just to get a rise out of people.

"This unique building, which many people think is shaped like a giant teacup, is one of the most famous museums in the entire world," Kathie tells the tour. "The inside is one giant spiral, just like if you started to peel an orange in one go. If you stood at the top of the ramped floor and dropped a marble, it would roll all the way down, down, down, right to the bottom!"

"Imagine that!" Mia says.

"The Guggenheim Museum was designed in the mid-twentieth century by Andrew Lloyd Webber—"

Jesus Christ. Superstar. I can't believe what I just heard. "Frank Lloyd Wright!" I call out, correcting her. How can she not know the name of probably the most famous American architect in the world? And she's a tour guide for goodness sakes!

"I didn't know Andrew Lloyd Webber was an architect!" Gayle says, genuinely impressed. "When did he have the time to build it, between writing *Cats* and *Evita* and *Starlight Express?*"

"No! He didn't," I tell Gayle, leaning in so she can hear me. There's a lot of traffic down below, a considerable amount of superfluous horn honking, and a bit of wind here on the upper deck. Our margaritas are sloshing around and I'm starting to treat my cup as if it contains some precious elixir. I'm going to be a real sight when I redeem Zoë from Jennifer Silver-Katz.

"Oh, I've heard of him," Gayle says, when I mention Frank Lloyd Wright. "He did that house in Pennsylvania . . . Running Water . . ."

"Falling Water," I whisper under my breath. (What can I say, I was an art history student.) "Yes, that's the guy!" I add, clinking cups with Gayle.

"You know, I did wonder about Andrew Lloyd Webber," she says, her tone low and confidential. "Although it sounds like the inside of the museum is a real lot like the set for *Starlight Express*. At least the Houston production."

It gets worse. Kathie points out the glorious (and really famous) Gothic–style St. Patrick's Cathedral (Roman Catholic, on Fifth Avenue at 50th Street, right across from Saks Fifth Avenue—another landmark, at least on *my* version of the tour), referring to the church as the Cathedral of St. John the Divine (Episcopal, and located on Amsterdam Avenue, just north of 110th Street).

I grab Gayle's thermos and empty what's left of the margarita mixture into my cup.

We reach 42nd Street. Kathie refers to the location of the main branch of the New York Public Library as having been the site of the former aquarium. "AQUEDUCT," I shout, trying to be heard above the din and now feeling that it's my civic duty to set the tourists straight. I begin to wonder if she's not just making it all up, having a joke on the lot of us. She's a performer, after all, delivering her lines with earnest cheerfulness, acting as familiar with New York geography as she is with her own name.

As we get down to 23rd Street where Fifth Avenue and Broadway cross each other at the landmark Flatiron Building, I'm having a hard time containing myself. Kathie points to the Flatiron, New York's very first skyscraper, then tells the tour, "If you look closely, you can see that this building also has a highly unusual shape. It's a triangle! It's a triangle because this building is where that terrible tragedy, the Triangle Shirtwaist Fire took place, burning all those little immigrant seamstresses to death." Boy, is this girl mixing up her local history! The only thing preventing me from jumping up and grabbing the mike

out of Kathie's hand and strangling her with the cord is that the
tequila has shot straight to my brain, and the minute I try to
stand up on the moving tour bus my stomach plummets to the
floor and my legs feel like barely gelled Mr. Wiggle dessert.

Nearly five hours later, we're back where we began, at the
Trina's Tours office. Kathie's got the gumption to expect tips,
thanking everyone for coming, and, with her hand out, in case
we miss her point, telling the tourists that she's "always de-
pended upon the kindness of strangers." Mia sets the girl
straight, telling Kathie that Bubba and Gladys should can her
ass for ineptness and send her packing back to Belle Reve.

I'm seething, too, and I can't help sharing that with Mia and
Gayle. First of all, I feel that Gayle got ripped off by getting a
tour of New York that was only about 40 percent accurate. The
sightseeing tour was the first thing in ages that I've done without Zoë, or that's not in service of my daughter's social agenda.
And I feel gypped. "This is your idea of getting me out of the
house?" I ask Mia. I'm mighty cranky.

Defensively, she puts up her hands. "How was I to know?" she
says. "I'm just as pissed off as you are. I thought tour guides had
to be licensed."

"Maybe she crammed for the test and after she passed, she
just forgot most of it," Gayle volunteers, peering into her empty
thermos. "I'm that way with math. They taught me a bunch of
stuff in school that all sounds like a foreign language to me now.
Algebra? Forget it! Co-sign is what you do to a bank check."

Mia giggles. Mia rarely *giggles*. It must be the tequila. "All
right, you two," she says, "I'll make you a deal. I'll find out if
Happy Chef is giving one of his Chinatown tours before Gayle
goes back to Houston. That'll show you what a *good* sightseeing
trip can be!"

Happy Chef is Mia's "requisite gay best friend," as she likes to
put it. He's a gourmet chef, a "master baker" (more giggles) and
a fully credentialed New York City sightseeing guide. Before I

dash up to West End Avenue to fetch my daughter from the Silver-Katzes, Mia phones HC and learns that he'd be happy (of course—he's the Happy Chef) to add us to his roster for the following afternoon.

When I come to collect Zoë, I am greeted by a red-faced, puffy-lipped Tennyson Silver-Katz, her pugnacious little sister, and their mom, who reminds me—twice—that it'll be payback time at Wednesday's ballet lesson.

Zoë makes me a present of the little bud vase she's made out of clay and decorated in her art class at school. She insists I buy a flower for it right away, so we stop at a Korean deli on the way home, where she becomes frustrated that all the single blooms are long-stemmed red roses. She wants hot pink. A gerbera daisy meets her stringent criterion, so I buy the pre-wrapped bunch of three and we return home, playing Lines and Squares, a game I taught her from one of A. A. Milne's volumes of poetry for kids.

At dinner, Zoë and I discuss our respective days. Mia and I grew up doing that. In the Marsh household, we all went around the table sharing with one another what we did that day. You see, "Fine," was an unacceptable answer to "How was your day?" No monosyllabic responses for the Marshes, unfortunately for Mia. With a dad who's a poet laureate, iambic pentameter was more like it.

When Mia and I didn't want our parents to know what we'd been up to, we became very adept at making things up. We invented a secret signal, which would indicate that we were about to tell a straight-faced whopper, but as we grew older, we discovered that blackmail was a very useful tool. When sibling rivalry was in its fullest swing, and we couldn't even trust each other, we would just lie outright and neither of us would know whether it was true or not. Our parents, idealists that they were, insisted on an environment where the channels of communication were open and free; but honestly, would Mia really admit that after receiving a particularly miserable math grade she'd taken a nip of Sake from the bottle she kept hidden in her high-school locker? Would I dare share that I'd cut gym for the third time in two weeks to make out in the deserted science shed on the roof with tall, dark and handsome Neil Forlani, the first boy in my class to shave? I knew that science shed like I knew my own name. Better than I ever knew science, that's for sure.

Of course there came a time when Mia and I began to wonder if our parents invented tales from time to time as well.

Tonight, Zoë was going first. I used to encourage her to go first all the time, saying the youngest had to go first, (which is how we did it when I was growing up), but she decided that wasn't fair (Why didn't I ever think of that?), so now we take turns.

"Mrs. Hairpin gave me a note for you," she tells me, then jumps up from the table to hunt for it at the bottom of her yellow knapsack. "You're gonna have to be class parent sometimes. You get assigned it. Everybody has to." She thrusts the note into my hands.

I open the envelope to read a form letter. It could have been worse. There could be a personal note written at the bottom like *my* mom used to get from Mrs. "Hairpin." There was always some sort of second-grade infraction of which I was invariably guilty. Talking while on line for the cafeteria. Whispering in class. Passing notes during math. Giggling. Existing.

I sigh, relieved. "So are you getting along any better with Mrs. Hennepin?" I resist using one of the students' nicknames aloud, figuring I'd be setting a bad example. When I was in her class, the woman had been called "Mrs. Henny Penny," "Mrs. Hairpin," "Mrs. Hatpin," "Mrs. Henne-face"—and kids who knew about turtles called her "Mrs. Terrapin"—though nothing *too* awful could really be done with her last name. At least we hadn't thought of it yet. Not so for poor Mrs. Lipschitz in fourth grade. And Mr. Dong, who taught chemistry in the Upper School.

"She still hates me." Zoë shakes her head emphatically. "And yesterday she called me *Claire* by mistake." I laugh. "It's *not* funny!" Zoë insists, her eyes beginning to fill with tears. "And she doesn't want me to make my Zs the way you showed me. In script. She wants me to print them."

I take a deep breath. "Why?"

"Because she says we're not supposed to start learning script until the spring. But I can write script *already*."

"Tell you what," I say, "we'll keep practicing script here at home."

"But I want to do it in *school*." Her eyes brim with tears. "And Mrs. Heinie-face won't *let* me."

Silently, I award her cleverness points for "Heinie-face." Why didn't we ever think of that one back in my day? It's so obvious! But back to the business at hand. How dare this woman hold my daughter back? For some reason most of the parents have always adored her, so Mrs. Hennepin will un-doubtedly remain in her second-grade classroom until the day she suffers an embolism at the blackboard. "Okay, then," I tell Zoë, "go ahead, write script in school. And you know what?"

"What?" she sniffles, wiping her nose with the back of her hand.

I give her a dirty look and she picks up her napkin, cleans her hand, and wipes her nose properly. "This is what. I'll deal with Mrs. Hei—your teacher, if she sends another note."

My daughter beams. A gap-toothed smile that melts my heart. She's proud of herself for getting her way. For being ahead of the class. For feeling very grown-up. "And how was *your* day?" she asks in perfect imitation of my own singsong de-livery of The Question.

"Well, I went on a tour of New York with your Aunt MiMi and her friend Gayle."

I provide a few more details, omitting the tequila, which is now no more than a memory, and Zoë scrunches up her face. "Why did you do *that*?" she says, as though I am a total idiot. "You *live* here." I explain that Gayle doesn't live here, she lives far away, and MiMi thought it would be fun if I joined them on the sightseeing tour. I can tell from her expression that Zoë is not quite satisfied with my answer. "Then why didn't you and MiMi give her the tour? Why did you have to get on a big yellow bus with a stranger giving it?"

She's got a point. So I tell her that tomorrow MiMi and I will be taking Gayle to Chinatown on a walking trip with MiMi's friend Happy Chef. This is a bad move. Practically catastrophic. Zoë bursts into spontaneous—and spectacularly loud—sobs, as though she'd left her favorite toy (Baa, a cuddly lamb, now significantly less woolly than he was when my parents gave it to her for her first birthday) on a subway.

"What's the matter, honey?" I reach out to stroke her hand, but she dramatically yanks it away, placing it in her lap.

"I want to go!" More wailing. The words themselves are a slurred mess of tears and fury and betrayal.

I try gentle pragmatism. "You'll be in school, sweetie."

"No!" Zoë repeats her demand. "And I don't *want* to go to school. I *hate* Mrs. Hennepin. And I already know script!"

I didn't realize she'd find such a convenient excuse for her cursive precocity so quickly. I should have known. Mia and had I tried similar tactics whenever possible. Now come the attempts to reason with a six-year-old; that there are more things to learn in second grade besides the ability to make curly letters.

She's worked herself up to full-fledged hysteria. "You. Never. Take. Me. Anywhere," she sobs, each word choked with torment.

"Zoë, you know that's not true," I soothe, then launch into a litany of her after-school and weekend activities. I do nothing *but* take her places. Ivy League pre-med students have a lighter program.

"But. I. Want. To. Go. With. You. *Tomorrow*!" she wails, a tacit concordance that Mommy is right, at least on some level. She hurls a Belgian baby carrot as far as she can toss it. It bounces off the wall opposite the dinette table and lands on the kitchen counter.

"All right, that's it!" I take her by the arm and lift her off the chair. "In your room! Now!"

"Nooooooooooooooo." She's struggling to release my grip.

"Time out, Zoë. We do not throw food." I manage to get her into her bedroom amid a sea of protests.

"I want to watch Ariel," she whimpers.

"No. No video tonight."

The bawling increases. "But. I. Want. To."

"Tough. Do you have homework from Mrs. Hennepin?" She nods and wipes her sniffles away with a bare arm. I hand her a Kleenex. "Ladies use tissues," I say, sounding like . . . who? My mother—Tulia—never talked like that. She let Mia and me act like hoydens in the privacy of our own home, until we figured out on our own that such primitive behavior wasn't the way to get what we wanted. But I've got no male authority figure to back me up here. My parents formed a mutual support system, a safety net I no longer have. If Mommy couldn't handle us, she'd turn to my father, arms akimbo, and plead "Brendan, it's your turn." And Daddy, who never, ever raised his voice, would speak to us so softly and steadily and sternly, his deadly placid manner far more terrifying than any amount of yelling and screaming, particularly since, from an early age Mia and I had recognized that high volume was a sign of parental weakness. This doesn't seem to work with Zoë. Not since I've become a single parent, anyway. I think I used to be pretty good at being a mom. Now I feel like a slumping major leaguer who's being forced to try a whole new batting stance.

I hate this. I hate fighting with my daughter. I don't want her to grow up resenting me. On the other hand, I've got to be the one to rule the roost, or chaos reigns.

"I'll be in to check your homework in one hour," I tell Zoë firmly, then close the door, leaving her to her own video-less devices. I return to the breakfast nook and pilfer the remaining baby carrots from Zoë's plate. No more wasting food in the mini-Marsh household.

•••••••••••

Dear Diary:

Mommy is being mean to me. I hope she snoops and reads this so she knows that I think she's being mean. She's going to China Town with MiMi tomorrow and they won't take me. I have to learn the times table with Mrs. Heinie-face instead. We have to draw a chart to make our own times table and fill in all the numbers. She gave us up to five for homework today. Mommy helped me make the chart with a ruler because she's better at making straight lines than I am. Mine are wobbly and they don't look pretty and Mrs. Heinie-face will give me a bad grade if the lines are wobbly. Who cares what five times ten is? I hate math and I hate Mrs. Heinie-face and I almost hate Mommy. I don't want to do any math. Ever. For homework we also have to write a story about a good memory we have and draw a picture to go with it. I don't know what to write about but I like to write stories and I love to draw and I know that Mommy and Daddy and me will all be in it and we will all be happy.

•••••••••••

"Did we ever give mom and dad the silent treatment?" I ask Mia, as we trundle along Canal Street behind Happy Chef, bound for the heart of Chinatown.

"I did," Mia reminds me. "You could never shut up long enough."

"Thanks. Zoë's being sullen. She's punishing me for being the mother. For insisting that she go to school today instead of playing hooky and joining us."

Mia laughs. "I would have let her come along. Tell Mrs. Henny Penny to get over it. Life experience is more important than a day of second grade."

I consider her point, which isn't a bad one, but that's the kind of stuff that works in a two-parent household with a good cop/bad cop system of checks and balances. For every "sure, why not-er," you've got a "stop-wait-don't-er." With Zoë, these days, all I seem to do is "don't-ing." When do *I* get to be the good cop?

We've got a nice little group for Happy Chef's Chinatown food tour. Me, Mia, wild-and-crazy-Gayle, and a delightful couple from Colorado, Bud and Carol Tate. Bud's a Mets fan, believe it or not, so I take an immediate shine to him. And Carol throws pots—I mean, she's a potter, not someone with a violent temper—so we've got some common ground in art appreciation. Zoë, who loves playing with clay, would throw a fit if she knew. Although she's got her own ceramics activity after school today. I check my watch and realize I've got only a little over two hours before I have to pick her up at school and then drop her off at Our Name is Mud to make pottery with one of her friends from the Museum Adventures program.

Gayle seems to be the kind of person who would get along well with anyone. She's refreshed her tequila thermos this afternoon, but Happy Chef, a.k.a Charles, reminds her that everyone but me will be walking for nearly four hours and the pit stop locations may have negligible sanitary conditions, so Gayle stashes the thermos in her purse, after graciously offering everyone a round, nonetheless.

As we head across Mott Street, I catch a whiff of something

delicious that smells like frying dumplings, become immediately hungry, and ask when we'll hit the first tasting stop, whereupon Charles leads us to a tiny shop on the one-block-only incline that is Mosco Street. The Fried Dumpling House, fittingly, sells only fried dumplings. The shop is smaller than my bathroom. Mia looks at the place and quips, "You'd have to leave the store to change your mind."

As our tour progresses and we are treated to more of the native tastes, sights, and smells of one of the city's oldest and most exotic neighborhoods, I become increasingly impressed with Happy Chef's range of knowledge of the area, its history, and its culinary treats. As I say goodbye to everyone, needing to skip the end of the tour so I can get up to Thackeray on time, I tell Gayle that this is the polar opposite of yesterday's tour with Mason-Dixon Barbie.

"You shoulda heard Claire," Gayle crows to Charles, stretching my name into a sizeable diphthong. "She kept correcting the tour guide. She really knows her stuff!"

Mia corroborates Gayle's testimonial. "Add this to your 'what I do well' list, Claire. Why don't you try to get a job as a tour guide?" she asks me. "You'd be a natural."

"I'd be happy to coach you," Charles offers. "So long as you stay out of Chinatown!"

· · · · · · · · · · · ·

A Happy Memory

by Zoë Marsh Franklin

When I was little, Mommy and Daddy took me to the circus every year. I was scared of the clowns because they were noisy. When I was five we got seats right in the front and a clown came over and honked a horn at me. He made me cry and Daddy bought me cotton candy to make it better. Then we were all laughing, Mommy and Daddy and me, because there were other clowns who weren't noisy with little dogs dressed up like people and the dogs were smarter than the clowns and it was silly. And it was so fun.

And then the man with the elephants came over because, before, he saw I was crying. He had a baby elephant named Lizzie. The man gave me some peanuts to feed the baby elephant. He said that elephants have feelings just like people. Like when another elephant dies they get sad. I liked feeding Lizzie so Mommy and Daddy bought me a whole bag of peanuts and Lizzie ate them all before the circus started.

The man said if we came to see him after the show was over he would give us Lizzie's auto graph. So at the end of the circus Daddy and Mommy took me back to see the man with the elephants and he gave me a piece of paper with an elephant footprint on it. And he said in case I forgot who the footprint belonged to, he would write Lizzie on the piece of paper.

I still have the paper with Lizzie's footprint and her name on it. That day when we went to the circus was one of the funnest times I ever had with Daddy and Mommy. Here is a picture that I drew of all of us with the elephant man and Lizzie and my pink cotton candy. We are all smiling, even Lizzie.

Chapter 3

My kid sister has become an inspiration. Her search for a fun yet flexible job has been like a kick in the butt to get my own life in order. Time for me to enter the twenty-first century. They didn't start up the computer science classes at Thackeray until the year after I graduated, so I never learned that stuff in school. I'm one of those techno-challenged people with a fear of heavy machinery (which is why I don't drive a car), and a severe distrust of things that can think faster than I can. I do *own* a computer, at least. Typing I can do, e-mail I have mastered, as Claire would say, "to procrastinatory perfection." And I now prefer it to just about every other means of communication, but for the most part, "software" remains a mystery. It sounds more like the kind of stuff you'd find at a Macy's semi-annual white sale. Software. Fluffy towels, thirsty terry bathrobes, and sheets with a 400-plus thread count.

I'm a self-taught kind of gal. That's how I became a professional makeup artist. I liked to play with eye shadow. I hung out at a lot of clubs in my not-so-misspent youth. Over time I formed a network of social connections that led to a lucky break that turned into a tidy living. No complaints there. But I'm thinking down the road of marketing my own line of cosmetics, although at this stage in the game, or maybe because I always tend to think visually, I mostly dream of the packaging. It's a play on words of my name. *Mia♥more* makeup. Or maybe I should move the heart. *Mi♥amore*. Happy Chef would swear to the fact that I can spend days just trying to figure out which graphic looks better. I guess it depends on whether I want to look self-aggrandizing—or Italian.

I could ask Claire for help, but she's so swamped with Zoë and stuff that she doesn't have a minute. So, I've started to teach myself Excel, to learn how to make spreadsheets and other things that left-brain types are good at.

Speaking of Italian, I just met a guy on a shoot for a repeat client. I do the makeup for the runway, trunk shows, and print ads for a hot designer named Lucky Sixpence. He—or she—is English, maybe Scottish, I'm never quite sure. Nor am I sure about Lucky Sixpence's gender. For those who remember the eighties, fondly or otherwise, Boy George is the closest I can come to explaining Lucky Sixpence. Lucky struck it rich creating affordable versions of the latest trends for the calorically challenged, which is about ninety-seven percent of the female population. You have a poochy tummy but want to wear a rhinestone-studded belly tee; your ass—as my Gran used to say—is "six axe handles across" but you crave a pair of low-rise boot-leg distressed snakeskin jeans; you want to dress like Courtney or Britney, Lucky's your man—or woman. Lucky prefers to be referred to as "she."

When I first met Luca and he pointed to his chest to introduce himself, I thought he was saying "Lucky" in his sexy Italian accent. But he calls the designer *Cara Fortuna*—"Lucky Dear"—so the confusion about the name thing was quickly cleared up. I liked his deep-set, sad eyes and three day stubble, the way his hips swayed in opposition to the movement of the spare camera dangling from his neck and the fact that I didn't understand a damn thing he said (except "boo-dee-fool, bebe, boo-dee-fool"), but it sounded great. Like he was making love nonstop.

He called me *Cara Mia* and I couldn't resist him, though I admit it didn't occur to me to try. Luca was the opposite of Hal: Euro-trashy and verbal (though unintelligible). An injection of Italian culture was just what the doctor prescribed. And I'm a big fan of self-medicating.

I sent my assistants home, and was the last to leave Luca's studio after the shoot. Deliberately, I was taking forever to pack up my stuff, when he touched my arm and said one word to me—*aspetto*. Since his eyes had a pleading look in them, I figured he meant "stay." Somehow he rigged his lights and filters so we could watch ourselves make love, like we were shadow puppets on the filmy white screens. It was wildly erotic, but now I know why some celebs hate seeing themselves on film. I could stand to lose a pound or two or I'll be wearing Lucky's duds before I know it.

We smoked a joint and after some gentle but insistent per-suasion (did he not know he was shooting fish in a barrel?) Luca cranked up the stereo—Italian pop superstar Michele Zarrillo—and convinced me to pose for some photos, using only a filmy scarf as a prop. I pranced, danced, and twirled like Salome near-ing her finale as Luca kept up a stream of chatter. He used the word *bellissima* a lot. I felt like Marilyn Monroe.

And I couldn't wait to tell Claire about my new conquest.

"You did *what*?" she said. She was all but clucking her tongue.

"Don't be so fucking judgmental."

"Do you have to curse?"

Her reaction surprised and disappointed me. Since when is Claire Marsh a prude? "What happened to the kid sister who took as many risks as I do?"

"She had a kid of her own almost seven years ago. Then her husband walked out on her. Risks are a luxury she can't afford to take."

"Risks are a luxury she can't afford *not* to take."

Claire didn't respond to that. She returned to the subject of Luca and the photos. "How do you know what he's planning to do with them? For all the Italian he was spouting away, he could have told you in chapter and verse exactly where he was going to post them on the Internet. Mia, you were doing soft-core."

"Oh, please! Art shots. Purely for our mutual amusement. It's just me in the pictures. And about three feet of blue silk."

"For a woman on the verge of thirty, you can be appallingly naïve."

"Hey!"

"*Selectively* naïve, then. You believe what you want to believe. Particularly when it comes to men."

"Ouch. Are you sure you're not really talking about *Claire*, Claire?"

"Double ouch, okay? It's like you're a perennial child."

"And you're becoming a perennial mother. Claire, listen to yourself. I don't need 'stop, wait, don'ts' from you. Save it for Zoë." I'd snapped at her, without meaning to, but somehow I'd felt baited. There was a terrible silence from the other end of the line. I didn't want to apologize. There was nothing to be sorry for. Not as far as my baby sister was concerned, anyway. "I think . . ." I said, weighing my words to make sure I sounded kinder about it, "that if you had stuff of your own to focus on, you wouldn't feel compelled . . . wouldn't have the time . . . to . . . to meddle."

"Meddle?" I could hear that Claire was pissed. "You think I'm meddling?"

Okay, so maybe it didn't come out as kind as I'd meant. "I phoned you to tell you about Luca. To share. Girl stuff. Because you're my sister, so, silly me, I thought you'd be happy for me— or at least entertained by my latest guy exploit—as you like to put it." My words began to pick up steam. "I didn't ask for your knee-jerk view. Or request a seal of approval from Miss Perfect, former trophy wife. I think you spend so much of your life these days in conversations with a second grader that you've forgotten what it's like to talk to an adult."

Cradle phones convey what a cordless never can. I heard a deliberate click and the line went dead.

•••••••••••

I made a list of what I think I'm good at. Retail. Design. History of art. Not much call for that one, unless you've got a masters or a Ph.D. And I've gone on a few job interviews that I arranged around Zoë's schedule. So far, here are Claire Marsh's stats: 0 for about 10.

To break it down, Retail: Ralph Lauren and Abercrombie and Fitch liked my "look," but a five-day week on the sales floor didn't allow for leaving before 3 P.M. to collect a child from school and I've got no one to watch her on weekends. At one store, the personnel manager, like me a woman in her twenties, refused to believe that I actually had a child. It was just beyond her scope of comprehension. She laughed and said that was the first time she'd heard that one. What "one"? I asked her. "The kid excuse," she said. "Look, I know everyone wants to quit work early so they can get out to the Hamptons before the traffic becomes murder."

Design: No openings for artists, but I can't afford to be too selective, so I interviewed to be the receptionist at a computer graphics company, but the same issue raised its six-year-old tousled blonde head. Besides, spending hours on the phone was never my thing, even when I was a teenager. And the computer folks, though they were also my contemporaries in age, were like, from another planet. I thought I'd relate to them, having aced computer science class, but I couldn't have been more mistaken. They seemed to regard *me* as the alien, for being a mom, for living in Manhattan north of 14th Street, and for having clean hair.

I'm more than a bit desperate. I've got maybe three months of savings left. Scott's always on time with his child support payments, but they don't cover much. The last thing I want to do is go to the First Bank of Daddy and Mommy. They already help a great deal with Zoë's Thackeray tuition. And if they hadn't bought this apartment at the ridiculously low insider price when the building went co-op, and then passed it to Scott and me after we married, Zoë and I would probably be living in a cardboard refrigerator carton on the edge of Central Park. My parents have always been supportive, but it's more than a matter of my pride to consider them as my court of last resort. I'm supposed to be a grownup with a family of my own. I'm supposed to be able to handle this. But I'm scared. I've never had to be on my own. And with a young child to raise alone.

I take a deep breath. I'm okay, I try to assure myself. I can do this. Except that right now, I'm finding it easier to believe in Santa Claus, the Tooth Fairy, and the Easter Bunny.

I need a job. The sightseeing-guide idea appeals to me. It could be flexible, and creative—to a point, as long as one sticks to the facts. Plus, I'm proud of my city, and I love meeting new people, which I rarely get the chance to do, anymore.

I engage Charles a.k.a. Happy Chef to coach me on the test, which is supposed to be a real toughie. No Mickey Mouse questions like "Who is the George Washington Bridge named for?" He hands me a bunch of books on local geography and history, and tells me to start reading *Time Out* to get a finger on the current pulse of the city. With my main focus being Zoë, I've been so out of touch that, except for knowing where to schlep a grade schooler with a short attention span—and the locations of the major landmarks that every native New Yorker has encoded into his or her DNA—I haven't a clue about what's out there all around me. Bands, galleries, hot spots, anything cultural that's going on beyond the confines of my neighborhood might as well be happening in Cleveland. Charles would be far better off asking Zoë.

He tells me that the road to guide-dom isn't the cream puff it used to be. After too many complaints about the dissemination of fraudulent information, New York tour guides must now be licensed by the Department of Consumer Affairs. They administer the 150-question exam, which is a carefully guarded secret. But Charles still remembers a lot of the questions from the test he took, which he promises won't be too dissimilar from the one I'll be taking.

" 'The House that Ruth Built,' " he says, firing a sample question at me.

"Easy. Yankee Stadium."

"What train line takes you from Inwood in upper Manhattan all the way out to the Far Rockaways in Queens?"

"The A."

"Good girl," Happy Chef applauds.

For extra credit I hum a few bars of "Take the A Train," but then he asks me a question about Brooklyn and I am completely stumped. I haven't a clue what avenue, once known as Swedish Broadway, is now one of the main arteries of the Arab community. How arcane can these people get? I give Charles a blank look. "Atlantic Avenue," he says. "Don't forget that you need to know about all five boroughs of the city, not just Manhattan."

I blanch, becoming anxious. Maybe I didn't have such a great idea after all. I think I know my hometown pretty well, but this isn't the old "meatball down the plate." "Are they going to ask me that one?"

"They might. They asked me. It was one of the ones I blew, which is why I remember it."

"I can't do this," I sigh. "I thought I could, but I can't."

"Sure you can," he urges energetically. "I'll give you an easy one. 'How much does Shakespeare in the Park cost per ticket?' " He rattles off three prices and a fourth option: none of the above.

I give him a funny look. "D. Nothing. That's a trick question. It's free."

Happy Chef grins and makes ding-ding-ding sounds. "Bonus round. Who drank himself to death at the White Horse Tavern and where is it located?"

"Dylan Thomas. Hudson Street in Greenwich Village. See, that's the stuff that appeals to me. The human interest stories. The tortured souls." I'm now beginning to get back into it. "Hey, maybe I can get my license and then give a tour of Macabre Manhattan, with Halloween coming up." This sounds more Mia's speed than mine, but she did urge me to take risks. Even though I was really pissed off at her for saying so and hung up on her.

I embellish my tour idea, running the concept past Charles for his approval. "You know, I could hit all the places where people were murdered or killed themselves. Dylan Thomas. Sid Vicious at the Chelsea Hotel." I feel my voice rising, my delivery becoming dramatic. "Madison Square Park, where the original Garden used to stand and where Stanford White was gunned down in his own rooftop restaurant by the insanely jealous Harry K. Thaw—because the lecherous White had been passionately knocking it off with Thaw's wife, the famously sexy chorus girl Evelyn Nesbit—and it became like the O.J. trial of 1906 or whenever it was. Thaw got acquitted, too," I said, shaking my head. "Oh, and of course, the murder every visitor to the Upper West Side wants to know about: Mark David Chapman's assassination of John Lennon right in front of the Dakota."

I'm getting into this idea more and more. At least I know I'd get it right. Not like Kathie from Trina's Tours, who, in referring to the tip of Manhattan in an electrifyingly wrongheaded remark, claimed that "it's called the Battery because it's where the center of power used to be in the early days of the colonies, and where the power brokers still are today, over at the New York Stock Exchange." Obviously she got her job before they toughened up the test, or as Gayle had surmised, forgotten everything she'd ever learned for it.

"I think you'd do really well at this," Charles says. "You'll be a very popular tour guide, too, particularly for European crowds. You've got a real understated glamour. It's very Grace Kelly. Just wear all your old Prada and Calvin and Ralph Lauren things and you'll be perfect." I begin to relax until he casually adds, "There's more to qualifying than looking beautiful and passing the test, though. You need three character references, witnessed by a notary, and none of your references can be from relatives. One can be from a friend—I'll be happy to do it—and one should be from a former employer."

Uh-oh. I've never had an employer.

"And one should be from some who's known you forever."

Eek. Someone who's known me "forever" who's not a family member. I'll have to think of something. Scott has known me sort of forever, at least since I was in high school. I can't do it, though. Asking my ex-husband for a character reference is asking for pain.

· · · · · · · · · · · ·

Dear Diary:

I'm writing this in school because Mrs. Hennepin thinks I'm writing something else but I finished it already. All of the other kids in my class are having snack. But not me. Mrs. Hennepin said I couldn't have juice and cookies because I was bad during recess. I was only playing in the park with Xander and then he got mean and threw sand at me. It's HIS fault and he gets to have snack and he even gets DOUBLE cookies and I don't. Mrs. Heinie-face never does anything mean to the boys. She is like the bad witch from The Wizard of Oz *except that her face isn't green. I wish I had some water to throw on her so she would melt and then maybe we could get the nice second-grade teacher instead.*

The other kids were laughing at me and they made fun of me when Mrs. Heinie-face made me sit in the back of the class and write I'm sorry over and over again until snack is over. Even Ashley made fun of me. And April and May don't want to talk to me because they think it will get them in trouble, too. They're not my best friends anymore. I don't have any more friends. I don't have a tissue. I don't want Mrs. Heinie-face to see me crying. That will make her more mean. I know it. I wish Xander would be my friend. I thought he was beginning to like me, especially since he said he would play "house" with me at recess. We had a really good time, too. And then he got so mad at me.

Why is every person in the whole world mad at me? Xander and Ashley and April and May and Mrs. Heinie-face and even Mommy.

I'm sorry I'm sorry I'm sorry I'm sorry I'm sorry I'm sorry I'm sorry I'm sorry . . .

....

It's been a long time since I've had to take a test. I feel like I'm back in school again, facing the SATs. Time may march on, but some things never change. I threw up before the test then, and I did the same thing this morning. Couldn't even keep down coffee and orange juice. Zoë was so adorable. She got up from the breakfast table—after first asking to be excused—and then lugged the two-liter bottle of ginger ale from the refrigerator, plunking it down at my place with a gushy thud.

"You give *me* ginger ale when *my* tummy is upset," she said simply, then climbed up to fetch a glass from the cupboard.

She's delicious. This is what it's all for. We've got some rough sledding ahead, but I couldn't imagine a Zoë-less life.

The New York City Department of Consumer Affairs is down near the tip of lower Manhattan—the Battery. I start giggling to myself thinking about Kathie at Trina's Tours and the Battery as the power center of the city. I conjure visions of the Energizer Bunny rolling down Wall Street thumping away on his little drum. Kathie's catalog of errors gives me a boost of confidence. Happy Chef has prepared me well. Most of these questions aren't too hard. At least many of them look familiar. They're all multiple choice, so I keep telling myself that the right answer is in front of me. All I have to do is select it. The Swedish Broadway question is, in fact, on today's test, so I know I have that one right.

Good Lord, someone's cell phone is ringing. "Nadia's Theme," no less. Don't people know enough to turn off their phones when they enter the testing room? Do they have to be in touch with the rest of the world every millisecond of the day? How can I concentrate? How are people expected to . . . ?

Oops.

Braving forty dirty looks, I reach down and plunge my hand into my purse, which is vibrating noisily, if melodically, at the base of my chair.

I flip open the phone and answer it. "Hello . . . ?"

It's Mrs. Hennepin. I feel my stomach clench. "Is something wrong?" *Of course something's wrong, Claire, or she wouldn't be calling you in the middle of the school day.* "Is Zoë all right?"

"Yes, she is, Ms. Marsh. Physically, anyway. I'd like you to come over to the school for a conference. Right away, in fact. I know you're not working now, so—"

I try to keep my voice down. "Can't we speak at the end of the day when I come to pick her up?" I look down at my test. There are a hundred and fifty questions and I'm on number sixty-three. "I'm kind of in the middle of something right now."

The test monitor approaches my chair. "I'm sorry, but you'll have to take that outside," the civil servant says.

"Oh, right. I'm so sorry." I get up from my chair, while I'm still listening to Mrs. Hennepin explain why she needs to speak to me sooner rather than later. The kids just went into Ms. Bland's art class and then they've got science with Mrs. Peabo, so she's got a couple of hours free while her charges are in the hands of the specialty teachers.

I've got the phone nestled in the crook of my neck, my purse on my shoulder and I grab the test with my left hand and start to leave the room.

"You can't take the test with you," the monitor says. "You gotta leave that in the room."

"But I'm not finished."

"Don't matter to me. You can't take the test outside the room. That's the rules."

"But how am I supposed to . . . ?" The monitor shushes me and cautions me to keep my voice down. I'm disturbing the other test takers. "See, my daughter's teacher is on the phone. I'm not trying to cheat, if that's what you mean, and this is not a social call, it's—"

"I don't care what it is," the monitor interrupts. "But you can't be bringing the paper outside this room." This formidable young woman definitely takes her job very seriously. She means business and I get the feeling that if I cross her, she'll put me in a headlock, if necessary. Or sit on me.

My stomach is tying itself in bigger knots and Mrs. Hennepin is still on the phone calling into her end, "Ms. Marsh? Are you there?"

"So, what am I supposed to do?"

"Are you talking to me?" I hear Mrs. Hennepin ask.

"It's up to you," the monitor says. "You can finish the test. Or you can talk to your friend—"

"I told you, this isn't my friend!" I say, shaking the cell phone at her. "It's my daughter's second-grade teacher."

"I don't care if it's the President of the U-nited States. You wanna take the call, you take it *outside* this room. And you can come back and take the test again on another day."

"Then I have to pay the fee again, don't I?"

The monitor nods. "Every time you take the test, you gotta pay." I frown. What a rip-off. "Hey, girl, don't you look at me like that. I don't make the rules. And you gotta leave the room or everyone here's gonna file a complaint against me. I got four mouths to feed. I can't afford to be losing my job."

And I can't afford not to have one either, but Zoë takes precedence over everything. I tell Mrs. Hennepin I'm on my way, snap the phone shut and rip my partially completed test into strips, dumping it into the waste paper basket on my way out the door. Oh, well. So much for knowing what avenue was once known as "Swedish Broadway."

Chapter 4

To save some money, I take the subway up to Thackeray. A cab from the Battery would have cost me well over ten dollars. We need that for groceries. A monthly Metrocard is a godsend for people on a tight budget. You buy the card, then ride all you want for the next thirty days.

I anxiously stride in to the school's administrative offices, all clustered at the end of one corridor on the first floor of the building. The parent-teacher conference room is a small, uninspiring rectangle, adjacent to the principal's office. It looks the same as it did years ago. The same maple wood doors, the same musty smell, the same inset frosted glass windows lending the false appearance of accessibility, that look like they haven't been cleaned since Eleanor Roosevelt went here for one semester.

Just as I am about to rap on the glass—I know from experience if a small hand knocks on the wood, you won't be heard—the door bursts open, nearly knocking me across the corridor. Nina Osborne, her tanned skin flushed, her eyes aglow like some mythological beast we might have studied in Miss Imberman's fifth-grade class, bears down on me for the second time in as many months.

A teacher passes us, prompting Nina to alter her demeanor

and lower the volume on whatever it is she plans to say to me. "You're a heathen!" she spits through gritted teeth. "I've heard that about the Marsh girls. You're legends in this school. And obviously, the apple didn't fall far from the tree!"

Oh, God, does she have to resort to clichés? My father would be appalled. He used to forbid us to use them, saying that well-educated people can choose their own words; they don't need to stoop to shopworn phrases.

"You should be ashamed of your daughter's vocabulary," Nina continues.

I wonder what happened that caused this . . . this *tempest in a teapot.* I try to suppress a smile. Where's the fire? The big emergency? Did Zoë finally slip and call her teacher Mrs. Heinie-face? But how would Xander Osborne be involved? Maybe she encouraged him to do it, too.

"You think this is funny?" Nina challenges.

Frankly, I'm relieved. If this whole hullabaloo is about words, then I can breathe easier. It means Zoë's okay. I can stop thinking the worst.

"Oh, good, Ms. Marsh, you're here." Mrs. Hennepin pokes her head out from behind the door. Nina stalks down the hall without another word. "Ms. Marsh, do you have a minute?"

How passive-aggressive can a person get? "I have as many minutes as it takes," I say, trying to sound calm; and as soon as I step inside the room, my anxiety returns tenfold. Suddenly I'm Zoë's age, and in trouble for one thing or another. The faces of my teachers with their myriad little vendettas over the years waft through my mind, an army of invading specters from my childhood. Okay, I was not the best be-haved student in the history of Thackeray, but that's sort of relative. I didn't destroy property or draw blood. Suddenly I realize one reason why I never considered graduate school. The academic atmosphere. Instructors as punishers instead of nurturers. The narrow behavioral expectations. The tsk-

tsking whenever a child asserts her independent nature and colors outside the lines.

I'm shaking. And I don't know whether it's from anger or from fear.

The parent-teacher conference room is arranged to appear informal. There's a mahogany credenza but no desk. Two chairs and a sofa are arranged "conversationally" around a low coffee table decorated with a simple vase of cut flowers and a few magazines, ranging from *Highlights* to *Psychology Today*. I scrunch into a corner of the sofa, where I feel safest. Across from me, the two armchairs look as though they've hosted a lot of butts over the decades. I'll bet my parents wore their own dents into the cushions.

"Ms. Marsh," Mrs. Hennepin says, simultaneously addressing me and appraising my body language. "Do you still chew your hair?" I'm too stunned and humiliated to offer an answer. Apparently, the hag has a memory like an elephant.

"So," she continues, her thin lips pressed together between phrases, "Do you know why I asked you to come in this afternoon?"

I shake my head. "Well, not two seconds ago Nina Osborne tore into me for my daughter's vocabulary. I try my best not to use swear words at home, and Zoë knows she needs to be more creative with her language. Her grandfather is a poet, you may recall . . ."

"I remember your father very well, Ms. Marsh. This is not about the use of *foul* speech." Her lips press together more tightly; her mouth has become a thin slash, rimmed white with determination.

"I'm so relieved," I reply, wishing I had a net for the butterflies in my stomach. My past and present meld uncomfortably; the lines between Claire the child-up-shit's-creek and Claire the parent-called-on-the-carpet-for-it have blurred completely. "It's . . . nice to hear that my daughter is incorporating the lessons she learns at home into her behavior at school." As I look at Mrs. Hennepin, I realize that she has nothing of the divine spark about her. No sense of warmth or humor. What the hell is this woman still doing molding the minds of six- and seven-year-olds?

"As your father is a writer, you of all people, Ms. Marsh, must be perfectly aware that words don't have to be swear words to inflict lasting damage," Mrs. Hennepin says. Then she tells me what transpired during the class recess period at the playground in Central Park that morning. Zoë and Xander Osborne were playing "house" in the sandbox, making "hamburgers" with sand they had dampened with water from the nearby drinking fountain.

"What's wrong with 'house'?" I ask Mrs. Hennepin. "Kids have been playing it since the Ice Age. And if you do it right, it can be a lot more fun than hide and go seek!"

Clearly, my nemesis does not appreciate my nervous attempt at levity. "They weren't married."

"Huh?"

"Zoë and Xander weren't married."

She's got me totally confused. I try to channel my mother. What might Tulia have said? "Of course they aren't married, Mrs. Hennepin. They're still six years old. I've told Zoë she has to wait until she turns seven, at least. I still don't understand where the problem is."

"Xander and Zoë were playing 'house' in the sandbox, but they weren't married. They weren't husband and wife."

I think about this for a moment, trying to suss out what Mrs. Hennepin seems to be telling me. "Well, I'm recently divorced, so I can understand why my daughter might have wanted to play the game that way. In the past several months she hasn't had such a great experience of husbands and wives playing 'house' for keeps."

"I appreciate your efforts at pop psychology, Ms. Marsh." Mrs. Hennepin steeples her fingers and gives me a long look. With her blonde bob and her puff-sleeved dress, she looks like the world's oldest Sunday schooler. "Here's the *situation*." She makes the word sound like a code red emergency. "Zoë said something to Xander. In the sandbox."

I shrug. "What could my daughter have said to the little boy that was so terrible?"

"She asked him to elope."

I let this sink in. Then I begin to laugh, nervously at first because I don't quite know what to say, and then my laughter changes tones, morphing into a relaxed hilarity because of the *situation*'s sheer silliness.

"I really don't find the humor in this, Ms. Marsh."

"Of course you don't," I say, stifling another giggle. "It's *very serious*."

"It *is* very serious," Mrs. Hennepin says. "After Zoë asked him to elope with her, Xander Osborne tossed sand in her face—"

"Is Zoë all right?" I interrupt, jolted back to earth.

"She got a little sand in her eye, but we rushed her to the infirmary and Nurse Val rinsed her eyes. She's fine."

Nurse Val—Betty Valentine—is another Thackeray mainstay who has been at the school since the dawn of time. She is universally beloved, cheerfully aware that scads of kids over the decades have faked illnesses—particularly during gym classes—just to enjoy her tender ministrations (we loved it when she put wintergreen-scented towels on our stiff necks), her soothing voice (more like a chirp, actually, as though there was no problem too big for her to solve), and her affable companionship. I briefly wonder if she still smells like cinnamon-flavored Dentyne.

"What kind of morals do you have and what sort of words are you teaching your daughter?" Mrs. Hennepin wants to know. "Where does Zoë hear words like 'elope'? And more to the point, how does she happen to understand them?"

"Oh, in my family, we're very big on only using words we

comprehend the meanings of," I assure the teacher. "And when we don't know the meaning, we either ask or look it up in the dictionary. My guess is that Zoë first heard the word *elope* when she asked her father and me to tell her all about how we met and got married. And if you're interested in getting into a discussion of morals, you'll have to excuse me, but I have better things to do with my time."

Mrs. Hennepin's face turns ashy gray. "You Marsh girls have always been a handful," she says, her voice constricted. "And, clearly, the past eighteen years has changed nothing. This is not a joke. Xander Osborne ran away from the class and climbed a tree. We had to call for the shop teacher, Mr. Spiros, to come coax him down."

I don't quite follow the logic, if indeed there is any, of calling for the wood shop teacher, other than that he probably knows more about trees than any of them, with the exception of the grade-school science teacher, Mrs. Peabo. "Mrs. Hennepin, are you telling me that my daughter's use of the word 'elope' is the cause of another child's misbehavior? Because I refuse to accept that. I've met the boy in question, and in my experience, he's not exactly what you'd call a model child. Did you scold Nina Osborne for being a bad parent, too?"

"It is my responsibility, whenever there is an incident that involves my students, to speak with their parents individually," Mrs. Hennepin sighs. "But we appear to be going in circles. I've said my piece and can only hope that you'll speak with Zoë about what kind of behavior and vocabulary are appropriate to a second-grade classroom setting."

She starts to rise, as if she's just made the decision that this little *tête-à-tête* is *fini*, but I stop her with my voice. "Hey! Zoë didn't do anything wrong. She didn't say anything vulgar or anything weird, except that the word *elope* is probably not on your second-grade vocabulary list. And I'm proud that my daughter is verbally proficient. Now, if Xander Osborne freaked out, that's his problem, not Zoë's. And his mother's issues, not mine."

Mrs. Hennepin smiles. My argument is having no good effect. "You're entitled to your opinions on how other parents may see fit to raise their offspring, but I strongly advise you to look to your own actions, Ms. Marsh. To teach Zoë what is appropriate behavior and what is inappropriate for a second-grade student."

She sounds like a broken record. "This is ridiculous!" I slam my hand on the sofa cushion and become momentarily distracted by the resultant motes trapped in a sunbeam streaming through the mullioned window. I have to go over Hennepin's head on this one. "I want to discuss this with Mr. Kiplinger," I say.

"Mr. Kiplinger is a very busy man, Ms. Marsh."

I point to the phone on the credenza. "No doubt. Nevertheless, I want you to ring him and tell him to take ten minutes out of his hectic fundraising schedule to speak to an alumna and the mother of one of his students."

Reluctantly, Mrs. Hennepin dials two extensions in succession, requesting each party to join her ASAP in the parent-teacher conference room. After an awkward few minutes, during which neither one of us feels the slightest inclination to indulge in small talk, the principal enters the room with Mr. Mendel, the guidance counselor and school psychologist. Mrs. Hennepin cedes her chair to Mr. Kiplinger, a tweed-and-elbow-patches type who gratifies his vanity by preferring to be referred to as "Headmaster." Thackeray Academy is steeped in anglophilic pretensions. As another example, they refer to grades seven through twelve the way the English do—as "forms" one through six.

"So, what seems to be the fuss?" Kiplinger asks. His British affectation has grown more pronounced over the years. I happen to know he grew up in the Northeast Bronx. We rehash today's Playground Incident. You would think we were discussing the Bay of Pigs. "Well," the headmaster says, shooting his cuffs, "if

Regina Hennepin found it an imperative to speak with you regarding your daughter's conduct, and she feels there's a question of morals to be addressed as regards behavior you seem to find acceptable from Zoë, I must accede to her judgment. She is, after all, your daughter's teacher. She sees Zoë every day—"

"And I don't?!" I'm ready to explode, although I fear my fighting Thackeray's equivalent of City Hall may do my daughter more lasting harm than good.

"Mrs. Hennepin is a valued member of the faculty, of the Thackeray family. She has decades of experience in evaluating the appropriateness of a six-year-old's behavior." Kiplinger insists on going to the mat for his teacher, as—I suppose, objectively speaking—he should. I resist the impulse to suggest that Mrs. Hennepin has been at it for *so* long that creeping senility may be a factor here. The headmaster gives the floor to Mr. Mendel, a balding, bespectacled nebbish in his mid-thirties.

"Ms. Marsh, are there problems at home?"

I blink a couple of times. "What do you mean?"

"Well, there's no way to put this delicately, but your family has gone through a sea change since last semester. Your daughter comes from a broken home—"

This is too much. How dare this little creep! "Look, Mr. Mendel, I don't know where you come off trying to psychoanalyze my life. Zoë is a perfectly normal, if somewhat precocious, little girl. *She's* not the problem child, here. Why aren't you asking Nina Osborne why her son has such a violent temper? Why he throws sand? Every *toddler* knows it's wrong to throw sand at another child!"

"But they do it just the same," Mr. Mendel says, peering at me through his thick lenses. "And boys will be boys."

"Is that all you can say?" I'm appalled. And, evidently, friendless in this room. "How many of my tuition dollars go toward your salary?" I demand of Mr. Mendel. "So you can spout . . . aphorisms . . . instead of dealing with the situation at hand?" So much for Thackeray's attention to discipline. I look Mr. Mendel right in the myopic eyes. "So. The way you see things, I'm an unfit mother with questionable morals because my daughter happens to have an advanced vocabulary for her age, while the class bully was just 'being a little boy.' Have I understood you correctly?"

"Ms. Marsh, there's no reason to become upset," Mr. Kiplinger soothes, ineffectually playing the peacemaker.

I turn on the three of them. "I don't want you to tell me what *I'm* doing wrong as a parent. I want you to tell me what *you're* going to do to keep a genuinely disruptive child in line. My daughter uses a big word. Xander Osborne throws sand at her. He could have *blinded* Zoë, for God's sake!"

The educators exchange glances and the two men rise. "You're very emotional right now," Mr. Mendel tells me in the kind of voice one would use when speaking to a mental patient. "Why don't you go home and think about our discussion, and when you feel ready to talk to Zoë, remember, we're credentialed and we're here to help."

Yeah. You're *going to be a better mother than I am*, I was thinking. They leave the room. I'm seething with rage and frustration. True, nothing has changed in eighteen years. It's still all *my* fault.

Mrs. Hennepin folds her hands primly in her lap and looks at me, cocking her head like a spaniel. "Now, is there anything *else* you would like to say?"

The events of the day flash like the Times Square news zipper across my brain. "Ermm . . ." I begin tentatively, trying to keep my hands from anxiously fluttering, "I guess this might be a bad time to ask you for a character reference."

• • • • • • • • • • •

Dear Diary:

Mommy wasn't mad at me after all. I was afraid she would be, because she had to stop taking the test to go come to school

*to talk to my teacher. But Mommy even let me watch a video
after we went over my homework. She said Mrs. Heinie-face
overreacted. When I asked her what "overreacted" meant, she
said it meant that Mrs. Hennepin and Mr. Kiplinger and Mr.
Mendel made too big a deal out of it and acted silly. Mommy
made me promise to tell her if Mrs. Hennepin says anything
more to me about when I asked Xander to elope. I think Xander overreacted.*

*After my video, Mommy brushed my hair for me 100 strokes
like her mommy did for her and Mia and like Granny Tulia's
mommy did for her. That's one of my most favorite things. I'm
glad Mommy wasn't in a mean mood. I was afraid she would be
after meeting with Mrs. Hennepin and that she would punish me.
But she was like my old Mommy. She even told me a dumb
knock-knock joke.*

Knock-knock.

Who's there?

Doya.

Doya who?

Doya wanna hear another dumb knock-knock joke?

• • • • • • • • • • • •

The world of the gainfully employed would like to welcome
Claire Marsh to its ranks. I passed the sightseeing-guide test the
second time around, snagged my three character references,
thanks to Happy Chef and a couple of old friends, including an
art history professor I'd briefly T.A.'d for until he located a willing and qualified grad student. Regina Hennepin had declined
to help me out, and I regretted my moment of desperation, as
it left me in a position of weakness with the old bat.

With my scores in hand I do a little homework, stopping by
the Times Square visitors' center to snag a fistful of brochures
from competing sightseeing companies. One in particular jumps

out at me: Go Native! Tours, which advertises that it hires only native New Yorkers as guides. I phone them, get an interview, and am hired on the spot. Apparently, the holiday season, which officially starts on Thanksgiving, is a peak time for tourism. They'll be needing extra people, so I'm in! My very first real job. I'm delirious.

I flip open the cell phone and call Happy Chef to let him know that Go Native! was impressed by my "understated glamour." Then I dial Mia to share the good news.

"What's up? My hands are full of foundation."

I've caught her in the middle of a gig. Well, I guess the same will be said of me, starting tomorrow. I apologize and tell her about my job.

"Great news! Gotta run, though. I'll call you later," she says, then hangs up.

I'm feeling so good about my very first job that I agree to take Zoë to the playground after school. Normally, I hate going there. I find it boring because I can't do anything except watch her. I'm way too paranoid to just sit and read a book while she plays, or to become involved in a conversation with another parent, because I'm afraid if I look away for one second, she'll either get stolen or go *splat* like the kid in *Kramer vs. Kramer* and I'll never forgive myself. Zoë has no idea that this is why I don't like the playground. I think she thinks it has something to do with dirt.

I'm a lot younger than the other moms on the park benches. In some cases we're practically a generation apart and they rarely seem inclined to include me, which is just as well. They gather in clusters. It's very clique-y. In the past, Zoë's had playground dates with some of her friends; when their nannies took them, Hilda would bring Zoë, and when their moms took them, I'd go along, but I never could relax when I was keeping only half my attention on Zoë and devoting the rest of it to my own "play date" with the other mom.

But today I wanted to give Zoë a treat so I bit the bullet, and here I sit, kicking back and watching her shoot down the slide for the forty-seventh time. This is not hyperbole. I've actually been counting.

"Mommy, will you push me?" Zoë runs over to the swings.

"I'll be right there!" I go over to her, step behind the swing, and give it a few gentle pushes.

"Harder. I can't go high when you push it like that."

Reluctantly, my pushes grow a bit more aggressive.

"Nooo. Harder. I said *harder*."

"You know, you can go as high as you want when you pump." I remind her how to kick her legs for maximum propulsion.

"I like it better when you do it."

She seems a bit sullen this afternoon. "Is everything okay, Z?"

She begins to cry. "I don't want you to go to work."

I'm distracted for a second when a little boy I don't know shouts "Ula!" He's been shoved down the slide by a much bigger kid, an older boy who seems to derive great joy in sending a smaller kid crying to his nanny. Ula whips out the Kleenex and a wet towelette and immediately plies her young charge with a healthy snack (a box of raisins), while stemming the flow of tears and gently checking for any sign of bodily injury.

If this is the Osbornes' ex-Ula, she is a dish indeed. No wonder both Robert and Nina went nuts over her in their quite disparate ways. But if this is now Robert Osborne's Ula, how come she's still a nanny? There's a nosy part of me that's dying to go over and chat with her.

"Mommy, are you listening to me?"

I slow down the swing and stroke Zoë's hair. "Sweetheart, I have to go to work from now on. I'm still going to try to be with you, though, as much as I can."

"But who's going to pick me up from school?"

"I will, sweetie. Most of the time. And if I can't be there, we'll work something out with Ashley's mommy or with April and

May's mommy or with the mommy of another one of your good friends. And . . . maybe even MiMi can pick you up sometimes."

MiMi is apparently a magic bullet. "Really?" Zoë asks me, beginning to calm down.

"Really," I promise her, speaking for my sister, in absentia.

"I want to go back on the slide, now."

"Not until he's decided he's had enough. You see him?" I ask Zoë, pointing to the playground bully.

She nods. "Unh-huh."

"Well, he just likes to be mean to other kids, and I know you want to play on the slide, but I don't want you up there when he's there." This is another one of my big fears about going to the park with her. The big bullies who get away with menacing the smaller children on the equipment. There are a lot of things for which I will march willingly into battle, but when it comes to situations like this, I'd just as soon avoid confrontation. And the emergency room.

Ula is now back among the other nannies, *au pairs*, housekeepers, and otherwise non-parental caregivers. I notice they appear to be snubbing her a bit. True, she looks like a swan amid a bunch of ducks, but beauty alone shouldn't be grounds for ostracism. Maybe they know she's a homewrecker.

The nannies themselves are sub-clustered by geographical and ethnic points of origin. From one bench wafts the cadences of thick Irish brogues; from another, the musical lilt of the Caribbean. Other benches, too, host representatives from additional regions, both domestic and foreign. A United Nations of nannies.

One of the Irish caregivers is a nice-looking young man whose name is pronounced "Bree-an." Brian is ending up, so I'm overhearing, in much the same predicament as my Hilda did. Divorce spells the end of his job. His colleagues are eager for all the juicy details (do *au pairs* have to sign confidentiality agreements?) But mostly, they want to know what effect his employers' divorce will have on his immigration status. Brian fears getting deported.

"Aren't you chilly?" I ask Zoë. The sky is turning dusky. "Mommy's a little chilly. Let's head back so we can start your homework before dinner."

"Okay." Reluctantly, she begins dragging her feet toward the entrance to the park.

"C'mon, slowpoke. Wanna race?"

"Unh-unh. I'm tired. I don't feel like running around anymore."

"All right. But we've been here a long time. I want to get home before it really starts to get dark out. Okay? What do you have for homework today?"

"We have to . . . we have to . . . umm . . . we have to make a natural habitat."

"For what?"

"We can pick. We can do fishes or we can do lions or we can do bears."

"That's quite a big range of habitats to pick from, Z. How about we do teddy bears and just make a model of your bed."

"Very funny, Mommy."

There's always a trade-off. Or a sacrifice somewhere down the line. My Go Native! work schedule is such that I won't be able to make it to Zoë's class's Halloween party, which starts at 11 A.M. on Halloween itself. Both of the Thackeray second-grade classes—and their parents—are participating, so it's quite the event.

She's hysterical. "You promised," she sobs.

"I know I did, sweetie, but that's before I got my work assignments for this week. I have to work until two thirty. They were very accommodating when I told them I need to pick you up from school every day."

"What's 'accommodating'?"

"It means that they very nicely gave me a work schedule that fits around your school day." I start at nine thirty and work until two thirty on weekdays. Beginning the week before Thanksgiving, they'll give me weekend tours as well. Then I'll really have to hold Scott to his end of the bargain. I'm sick of his excuses for not being able to see Zoë on a Saturday afternoon or on Sundays.

She starts to wipe her nose with her forearm, then catches my eye and reaches for a tissue. "Can't you call in sick on Halloween?"

"I think that might be suspicious." She looks at me quizzically. "They just might get the funny feeling that I'm not telling them the truth. Especially since I wouldn't be sick the day *before* Halloween."

"So, be sick the day before."

I chuckle at this. "Then how will I make any money to take care of us? Besides, I could get in trouble for pretending to be sick or for asking for time off just a few days after I started working. You don't want me to get in trouble and lose my job, do you?"

"Yes."

"Yes?"

"Yes. Because I want you to come to my school Halloween party." She's refusing to wipe away her tears, opting to let them roll dramatically down her rosy cheeks.

"We'll have a really fun Halloween together afterwards. An official Halloween with trick-or-treating and everything in the evening. You can even wear something different from what you wear to the party. You can have two costumes and dress up as whoever you like."

"Hermione," she sniffles. "I can just wear one of my school outfits. And we can make a red and yellow Gryffindor robe." But she's still not sold on the compromise. "Everybody's parents will be at the party," she insists, bursting into tears again. "And they'll all make fun of me because my mommy isn't there."

"They'd better not or I'll come beat them up," I say, trying to get Zoë to smile. I fail.

"Come beat them up on Halloween, then."

I don't know what to do. I feel miserable. "Zoë, sweetie, Mommy's about to cry, too. Let's try to solve our problem together, okay? Like big girls." She nods, sniffling some more. "Should we see if Daddy can come to the class Halloween party?"

She shakes her head. "Nuh-uh. He *hates* dressing up and costumes, remember?" We think about it for a few moments. Zoë's taking my suggestion quite seriously, her earnest little tearstained face really giving the situation her full attention. I try not to let her see how intently I'm watching her. Suddenly, the dark cloud passes and she breaks into an adorable grin. "I've got it!" she announces gleefully.

           • • • • • • • • • • • •

Excel isn't getting any easier, but I've thought a lot about *Mi♥amore* cosmetics. I blend so many colors and products anyway when I work, I might as well start my own line. And socially, I need to spread my net wider, since everyone is a potential customer. I used to turn down gigs if the pay wasn't great or if I had to get up too early in the morning. I don't do that these days. And I'm headed to kind of a cool one. Zoë's class is having a Halloween party. That's Claire's crowd and they have bucks. The downside is that I have to spend two and a half hours facepainting forty-two second graders on a sugar high. The flipside is that their parents are encouraged to chaperone them, so it's a prime opportunity to scope out the eligible dads. I've dated enough men with piercings. There, I might meet one with a portfolio instead. And there's this, too: in my line of work, an unattached straight man is about as rare as a pink diamond. On second thought, bad analogy.

Boy, I'd forgotten how well Thackeray spends money. I guess the parents want to see their dollars at work. Right now, those bucks have been invested in blacklights, acres of faux cobwebs, and full-sized puppets of witches and ghouls. There was even a cauldron of something steaming, sending chilly wisps of smoke drifting across the classroom. I know that dry ice costs a damn fortune.

At first, I couldn't spot my niece amid the purple gloom. She found me first, making her presence known by launching herself into me, grabbing me around the waist. "MiMi!" she yelled, trying to be heard over the recorded haunted-house sound effects. Then she dragged me around the room, introducing me to everyone. Mrs. Hennepin was in a good mood; she thanked me, glad I was pinch-hitting for Claire. Someone must have spiked her cider.

They brought up the lights so I could work my magic. I figured it would be more fun for the kids if I showed up in a costume, so I dressed as a witch—my idea of one, anyway—which was a bit more Elvira-ish. Long black wig, tight black mini, black fishnets, lace-up patent-leather spike-heeled boots, also black, of course. The pointed black hat was a concession to tradition.

I set up shop at the end of a long table. I'd also forgotten how low everything was in grade school. My butt was practically on the floor, my knees up near my chin. I opened my paint box, laid out the colors and the brushes, and was ready for business.

Zoë muscled right to the front of the line. "MiMi is my aunt so I get to go first," she announced, her tone of voice suggesting no alternative. She plopped down in front of me. "I want a mermaid," she said. "With blonde hair."

"Hey, I like that," I said, pointing to Zoë's necklace. It had been fashioned out of a chain of blue plastic beads and Pepperidge Farm Goldfish, strung together and shellacked.

"Mommy made it," Zoë proudly said, "to go with my Ariel out-fit. A school of fish . . . because I was going to wear it in school!" She giggled. "And see this?" she added, pointing to the real scal-lop shell that hung like a pendant from the center. "We found this on the beach last year near Granny Tulia and Grandpa Brendan's house. A seagull dropped it."

"It's great," I said, admiring it again. "Your mommy's really clever. You know, she used to make jewelry out of all sorts of things when we were little. We would have fashion shows at home and *our* mommy would put together the outfits and Claire would do great stuff with all kinds of bangles and neck-laces—we were too little to wear earrings, then—and your Granny Tulia would let me play with her makeup. We called it playing 'runway.' "

Zoë pouted. "I wish we could play 'runway' now. I mean at our house. Mommy doesn't have time to play stuff with me anymore. I only get to play dress-up when I go to your house. Can I come to your house soon?"

I nodded. "You bet!" I finished Zoë's mermaid, painting the fishtail so it followed the curve of her jaw, the fins sprouting right in the center of her chin.

"It tickles," she giggled.

"Sit still. I can't work when you wriggle."

"Okay," she sighed, and wriggled some more.

Mrs. Hennepin passed by the table, a Dixie cup of orange soda in her hand. "You Marshes all have such artistic tempera-ments," she observed.

"You say that like it's a bad thing," I replied, ready to loan her my witch's hat. I finished up Zoë's mermaid and sent her off to snag me something to eat, while I got to work on her friend Ash-ley, who has a thing for butterflies. My niece returned with a paper plate loaded down with a chocolate cupcake frosted in the most garish shade of orange I've ever seen, a few fistfuls of Cheez Doodles, and a bunch of orange jelly beans (the only other color they had was black and Zoë knows I don't like licorice, another trait all the Marshes share).

"Oops, forgot the chocolate," she said, then skittered off in the direction of the mini-Hershey bars.

Ashley fluttered away from my table to join her, although I warned her not to touch her face, because the paint wasn't dry yet. Not a minute later, while I was creating an ugly scar on the face of mini-pirate Xander Osborne, Ashley ran up to me in tears with smudged cheeks.

"Fix it," she wailed.

"Fix it, *please*," I corrected.

A mother, eavesdropping, beamed at me.

"Fix it now," she insisted. She gave Xander a push, nearly toppling him into my lap. Good thing my brush was nowhere near his face.

"Go away! It's my turn," Xander said, shoving the little girl. Ashley lost her balance and ended up on her butt. I was surprised at what a scrapper this blonde fairy princess was. She scrambled to her feet and grabbed Xander by the bandanna he was wearing on his head, an Upper West Side interpretation of a buccaneer's do-rag.

They were going at it like two alley cats. I laid my paints and brushes aside and tried to separate them, but I realized I was getting the worst of it, buffeted by both sets of tiny fists in their attempts to clobber each other.

"Hey, that's enough!" A large male arm clad in blue serge swooped down and collared Xander, lifting him out of the fray. "We don't hit girls, son," the man scolded, yanking the boy to one side.

Ashley looked around the room—for her mom, I guess. When she didn't see her, the kid threw herself on my mercy. "He pinched me! And he pulled my hair, too!"

I crooked my finger at her, like I was going to tell her a big secret. She leaned forward while I took up the paints again to repair her butterflies. "I won't tell if you don't," I whispered.

"Don't tell what?" Ashley whispered back.

"That you started it," I said. "You've got a mean right hook."

She broke into a huge grin, showing a gap between her front two teeth. "I take boxing after school," she lisped, then hopped away to find Zoë.

"You handled that really well." Xander's dad extended his hand to me and pulled me out of the pint-sized chair to my feet.

"You weren't so bad, yourself," I said, noting the strong jaw-line and the thick, dark—though receding—hair just beginning to turn an elegant shade of pewter around the temples. "I'm Mia Marsh, by the way. I'm Zoë's aunt. The little mermaid over by the popcorn."

He shook my hand. "Robert Osborne. And . . . you've met my son, Xander. So, if you're hungry for something more substantial than sugar later in the day, how 'bout I take you to dinner?"

Chapter 5

"You are coming here for Thanksgiving, sweetheart?" my mother asks, the response a forgone conclusion. We gather at the family clapboard in Sag Harbor *every* Thanksgiving. The East End of Long Island, particularly the little seacoast villages, have a New England-y atmosphere that feels especially appropriate to the observance of all things *Mayflower*-y. "We know you don't have much to spend on a party for yourself this year, so your dad and I thought we'd make a birthday bash out of it." Growing up, I felt that being born around Thanksgiving was inordinately unfair because I never seemed to get a separate celebration of my own—though Zoë probably has it even worse. She was born on Christmas Eve. I've always had to share my special day with Pilgrims, Native Americans (weren't we *all* native after the first generation of Johns and Priscillas?) and other assorted travelers making the annual trek over the river and through the woods to Grandmother's House. An added inequity was a birthday dinner inevitably composed of turkey and all the fixings, as opposed to a celebratory meal of my choice. At least a homemade, frosted layer cake, topped with buttercream roses—my favorite part of the confection—usually replaced the requisite pumpkin pie.

Although, in Tulia's favor, our holiday visits to Sag Harbor are more akin to a weekend in Wonderland. The most traditional thing about my parents is their Federal-era home, bearing a discreet plaque from the local society for historical preservation, the house itself a relic of a young and idealistic nation.

"I've already invited Mia. She asked if she could bring a date. Is that all right with you?"

"Mia usually brings a date to Thanksgiving," I say. "Why should you need to vet it with me this year? Although, if it's that Italian photographer who took the Marilyn pictures of her, he might not really get into the spirit of the holiday. We might have been better off inviting him to Columbus Day dinner or to Garibaldi Day, if there is one."

"Garibaldi Day," my mother muses. "It wouldn't be such a bad idea to celebrate that some time. After all, we've embraced Bastille Day and *Cinco de Mayo*. We could all show our solidarity by wearing red shirts. Though the puffy sleeves would be a tough sell in menswear."

That's my mother the garment designer talking.

"Anyway, she's not bringing Luca. The photos are lovely by the way. Have you seen them? Very soft focus." Only Tulia Marsh could find a way to condone her daughter's foray into photo-erotica. "Clairey, the reason I'm asking you in advance about Mia's date for your birthday celebration is that he's the father of one of Zoë's classmates." I try to absorb these words. Thackeray was never Mia's bailiwick, even when she was a student. "Clairey, are you there?"

"Yeah, I'm still here," I mumble.

"Oh. For a minute there, I thought I'd lost you. Well, provided whatever's going on between them lasts for another three weeks, she'll be bringing a man named Robert Osborne to Sag Harbor."

Robert Osborne. Where have I heard that name? Oh, God. Oh, no. My brain is assaulted by an onslaught of what-ifs, none of them good. The last I heard of Robert Osborne, he'd deserted his prize of a wife, Nina, for something very young and very blonde with the exotic kind of name often attributed to Swedish porn stars. Maybe that's why I saw Ula at the playground a week or so ago with a little boy. If Robert dumped her, too, of course she'd need to find another nanny job, although a good reference from her most recent employer might have been a tough ticket. I have immediate visions of Robert bringing his holy terror of a son along for the holiday, followed by nightmares of an enraged Nina showing up on my parents' landmarked doorstep, then proceeding to hack us all to death with my father's beloved Hoffritz carving knife. "Ummmm, Mommy?"

"Yes, sweetheart?"

"I'm not so sure it's a good idea. I've met the former Mrs. Osborne. She's a force of nature."

My mother emits a musical little sigh. I can just picture her repeatedly running her hand through her still naturally dark hair, streaked with one equally natural slash of white. This is her customary reaction when faced with a dilemma. "Well, you know your father and I have always let you girls forge your own paths in this world. We've never told you when we thought something might be a wrong turn and have always trusted that you both will figure out when something isn't working. You and Mia have a strong center. Sooner or later, if you decide the detour isn't worth it, you'll return to that center and head off in a different direction." My mother should be writing map text for the American Automobile Association. "So, maybe Mia will break up with Robert in the next twenty-one days or so. And if she doesn't, I'll just make sure not to set out the good crystal and we'll all have an adventure."

No wonder I'm a confused parent.

"Is Daddy around?" I ask.

"He's working on your birthday poem. You know how he can get when he's deep inside his head."

"Yeah. You need to send spelunkers after him. It's okay. I'll call him later to say hi." I smile, maybe a bit smugly, thinking how lucky I am. How many people grow up with a poet laureate penning a special creation for each of their birthdays? Brendan has promised that by the time Mia and I hit forty-four and forty, respectively, he'll have enough to publish an anthology. We girls aren't too sure how we feel about that.

I say goodbye to my mother and dial Mia. "Before I head off to give my movies-made-in-Manhattan tour for Go Native! we need to talk," I tell her.

"So talk."

"What's going on between you and Robert Osborne, and why didn't you feel it was important enough to share with me?" I ask, miffed and still incredulous.

Conspicuously omitting a full response to either question, she says, "I met him at Zoë's class Halloween party."

"Thanks to which she is only eating orange food," I mutter. This is true. Ever since the party, she has refused to eat anything that isn't orange in color. Thank God it's fall, because at least orange things are somewhat seasonal. We're okay with carrots, yams, oranges, of course, and mac and cheese, as long as I add a bit of paprika to make the pasta an acceptable color. Otherwise, it's "too yellow." Most vegetables and all meats are an obstacle I haven't been creative enough to overcome. Tomato sauce has been deemed "too red," and convincing her to eat a chicken breast coated with an apricot glaze turned into negotiations worthy of the King David Accord.

"Don't blame me for the orange food," Mia says. "Robert? Okay, I do take responsibility for that. I don't know how long it will last, though. Do you know he sends his dog out to the Hamptons on a special bus? It's called the *Petney*. Swear to God, I am not making this up. Seventy-five bucks one way. The Jitney for humans costs half that. His terrier doesn't like too much open air and Robert likes to drive out to East Hampton in his two-seater Jag convertible. When he's not saying how 'different' he finds me, all he does is talk about himself. I have to come up with new ways to make him shut up."

"I'm sure you'll think of something. If you live that long. Mia, do you know anything about Robert's ex?"

"It's not exactly a subject we discuss."

"I told Mommy Nina Osborne is a force of nature."

"You discussed my new lover's ex-wife with Mommy?" she asked, appalled. Suddenly, I was thrown backwards into a vortex, revisiting years of tattling on each other's most egregious transgressions, usually involving members of the opposite sex. Wait a minute. *Lover?* It's only November 6th. She just met him on Halloween. I guess there's something to be said for their fling to have survived Election Day. Robert must vote Democratic. "Claire, how could you?"

"I *had* to. Tulia called to invite me for Thanksgiving, which, as usual, she's turning into a double celebration. Since it's *my* birthday, she thought she'd be courteous about it. So she told me you were planning to bring Robert. Not Xander, too, I hope."

"He'll be with his mother. They're going to Thanksgiving dinner at Donna Karan's."

I react like this is not a strange thing. For Nina Osborne, it's probably an annual ritual. The image of soon-to-be-seven-year-old Xander tearing up the place and the designer presenting Nina with an itemized bill for damages at the end of the meal fills me with a bit of sadistic glee.

Oh, God, we've got Xander's birthday party coming up. Nina's leased out some plum real estate at Chelsea Piers, hosting an ice hockey party for more than three dozen second graders. Semi-supervised violence on razor-sharp blades. Perfect. At least she didn't rent the Temple of Dendur. I can just picture Xander and friends running amok among the Metropolitan Museum's Egyptian antiquities.

"Well, this should be an interesting Thanksgiving holiday," I tell Mia. "Maybe Mommy can stitch up some lovely bulletproof vests for all of us."

"I think you're overreacting," she replies. "Nina doesn't even know about me and Robert."

"Can you keep it that way? What about Xander? How many six-year-old boys, particularly troublemakers, grasp the concept of discretion?" I check my watch. If I don't hightail it right this minute, I'll be late for my tour. "Anyway, it'll be my birthday, but it might be your funeral if Nina gets a whiff of this. She already detests me. All she needs to learn is that her ex is knocking it off with my older sister. And what happened to his Aryan-looking *au pair*?"

"Nina had her deported."

Wow. And why am I somehow not surprised. So, did I see a different Ula or the same one whose days were numbered? "Mia, I don't mean this quite how it's going to sound, so I apologize in advance, but I'm surprised he thought you were his 'type.' You're not even blonde!"

"Maybe that's why he says I'm so 'different,' " Mia muses. "I guess I'm off the menu."

"Dead meat, most probably. I've got to dash. We'll pick this up later, if you want to."

"Good. Because I want to run something else by you."

"About Thanksgiving?"

"Yes," Mia says. "And Zoë. Catch you later." She's the one who ends the call, leaving me with another shoe dangling. And a busload of tourists waiting for their "Location, Location, Location!" sightseeing tour.

· · · · · · · · · · · ·

Dear Diary:

I am going to meet the Powerpuff Girls! MiMi got me on their float for the Macy's Thanksgiving Day parade. She got a job

doing the makeup for the star who is going to sing on it, and they
said they needed little girls to ride on the float with her, so MiMi
asked if I could do it and they said yes. The Powerpuff Girls are
my favorite television show. I told everyone in school about it.
Xander and the boys didn't care. April and May are happy for
me but Ashley is acting funny. Mommy said she might be jealous.

I know a secret, too. MiMi has been going to dinner and movies
with Xander's daddy. Xander doesn't know and Mommy and
MiMi made me promise not to tell him. I asked why it was supposed to be a secret and they said it was because Xander's mom
Nina can be a real meanie. I know this is true because Mommy
said she wasn't nice to her the day Mommy had to see Mrs. Hennepin. I wish I could sic the Powerpuff Girls on Nina.

MiMi said we'll have to wake up really early on Thanksgiving morning, like when it's still dark out. I can't wait. It's going
to be one of the ~~funnest~~ best days of my life. Even better than
my birthday, maybe. Then, after the parade we get to go to
Granny Tulia's and Grandpa Brendan's house in Sag Harbor
for dinner. I talked to Granny Tulia on the telephone and asked
her if she was going to have orange food and she said yes. We
are going to have Marsh-mallow sweet potatoes, which she always makes special for Thanksgiving. And carrot pennies. And
pumpkin pie.

Xander Osborne's birthday party is next week and it's a
hockey skating party. I wish he would have a birthday party like
April and May had over the summer for all the girls from our
first-grade class. We went to see Beauty and the Beast, which is a
Broadway play. We even got to bring our moms. Then after the
play ended, we got to go back to say hi to the actors and each of
us got a poster that was signed by them. I thought the girl who
played Belle looked prettier on the stage than she did in her regular clothes. She looked older in her blue jeans. And her hair
wasn't even reddish brown in real life. It was dirty blonde like
April and May's mom June. If I had dresses like Belle I would

wear them all the time. Her yellow one is my favorite because yellow is my favorite color.

I'm really, really, really bad at ice skating. I went a couple of times with Mommy and Daddy to the place with the gold statue and the big Christmas tree and to the skating rink in Central Park because it isn't far from our house and my feet wobble too much no matter how tight I make my skates. I fall down and I don't like it. And it's too cold. Hockey is too fast and it's scary and I don't want to do it. And I can't even wear a pretty dress to the party if I have to play ice hockey. Mommy said I didn't have to go to the party but I want to invite Xander when I have a party for my birthday in December and if I don't go to his party he won't come to mine. And Xander is one of the people I want most to be at my birthday party.

• • • • • • • • • • • •

I have to admit I enjoy being a sightseeing guide. Especially since my Go Native! boss seems to welcome my input on tour ideas. In fact, the movie-themed excursion was my idea; and, so far, "Location, Location, Location!" has been one of their best sellers. Even in the middle of November, my buses are packed with people scrambling to grab the upstairs seats first. To catch a better glimpse of the Dakota and the Empire State Building, they're willing to sit outdoors for two hours braving some pretty chilly, damp weather.

This morning I had seventeen people from the High Point, North Carolina Jaycees, eager to see where Meg Ryan and Tom Hanks finally hooked up in *Sleepless in Seattle.* Last week, a bunch of librarians from Vermont wanted to see where the little bookstore around the corner in *You've Got Mail* was located. This afternoon, I've got a gaggle of grandmothers who specifically requested that I show them where the famous "orgasm" scene from *When Harry Met Sally* took place. Maybe I should rename my tour "Meg Ryan in Manhattan."

Boy, can those ladies move in their orthopedic shoes. I stand back while they jockey for position on the upper level of the tour bus, swatting at each other with purses and umbrellas like the Ruth Buzzi character on Comedy Central's *Laugh-In* reruns. We chug downtown, and when we get to the Empire State Building stop, knowing that they're Meg Ryan buffs, I begin my description of the landmark with the *Sleepless in Seattle* reference. However, I make the cardinal mistake of underestimating my audience. These ladies know their movies. One of them waves her umbrella to get my attention. "Don't you ever watch the old pictures? What about the classics? What about *An Affair to Remember*? All three versions."

One of her cohorts begins to argue with her. "There weren't three versions of *An Affair to Remember*, Myrna."

"Yes, there were, Helen. You don't know what you're talking about. The other two were called *Love Affair*, but only the one with Charles Boyer and Irene Dunne was any good. The one that looker, Warren Beatty, made with his wife—that was pure dreck."

"*Affair to Remember*? What about *King Kong*?" one of them calls out. "The original *and* the remake with Jessica Lange."

"That remake was dreadful," another pipes up. "Now, *that* was dreck. That girl couldn't act her way out of a gorilla's palm. Now, Fay Wray . . . *there* was a real actress!"

"Well, I like Lange," the *King Kong* fan insists, holding her ground. "She was very good in *Frances*. She got robbed at Oscar time."

"What, robbed? She got one for *Tootsie*," interrupts her friend.

"*Tootsie*, schmootzie," Lange's champion retorts. "That was a consolation prize. Now *Frances*—there was a part to die for. That girl acted her little heart out in that picture."

Can we see where they filmed the soap opera in *Tootsie*, they ask me.

"Well, it's in the wrong direction from where we're headed," I tell them, wondering if it's even okay to spontaneously deviate from the itinerary. "It's way over on the West Side. One of our local television stations used it as a studio for several years, but there's nothing to look at. Not very interesting." They ponder this and put it to a democratic vote. *When Harry Met Sally* wins, hands down, so off we go to Katz's Deli on Houston Street.

Snacks at Katz's are part of my tour. Midway through their complimentary tongue—which the staff thinks is a hoot to give to the "orgasm tourists"—I hear my cell ringing. It's Nurse Val up at Thackeray. Zoë's been throwing up ever since lunch and the nurse isn't sure whether it's just a tummy bug, or if it's food poisoning.

"She's running a fever, too," Nurse Val says, "and I don't think it's a good idea for her to stay here in my office until the school day ends, in case she's contagious. I gave her some children's Tylenol, which should begin to reduce her temperature, but she really should go home as soon as possible."

That's that. I have to head uptown ASAP. These ladies—my tourists—are all grandmothers. That means they were once mothers. They'll understand. "I'm so sorry, but I've got an emergency. My daughter got sick at school and I need to fetch her right away," I tell them, genuinely apologetic. I know I've only been working a few weeks, but I've never had to abandon a tour and I'm not at all comfortable with the idea. Still, my poor little girl is retching her guts out. This isn't a task a mom delegates.

"You mean you're going to leave us?" one of my charges asks, her voice quivering with disbelief.

"Right after the *orgasm*?" another asks very loudly, her face a study in betrayal.

I stammer another apology and explain that there are only a few more stops on the "Location" tour anyway, and that Frank, our trusty bus driver will take good care of them and bring them safely back to the Go Native! depot. Given no alternative, they say good-bye. "Your boss will hear about this, young lady," the Lange fan threatens.

"And don't expect any tips!" adds the *Tootsie* lady.

How soon they forget. I look at my group of blue hairs and shake my head, wondering where their children are now and whether they even bother to send Christmas cards.

It would have taken me a month to get from the Lower East Side to the Upper West on mass transit, and time being of the essence, I hail a taxi. I ask the cab driver to wait with the meter running while I run inside Thackeray to get Zoë. "I've heard that one before," he grumbles. "Fugeddaboutit, girlie." I let out a sigh of frustration and a couple of choice curse words, pay the un-sympathetic bastard, lowballing him on *his* tip, and he lurches away from the curb, practically before I've set both feet on the pavement.

I race upstairs to the nurse's office to redeem my daughter. The poor kid is a pasty shade of green. I acknowledge this when I give her a hug.

"I know. I look like Oobleck," she whimpers into my neck. "Yuck."

"We're going right home, sweetie," I assure her. "Did Nurse Val take good care of you?"

Zoë nods and manages a half smile. "And she gave me a lol-lipop to make my tummy feel better. But I couldn't finish it." She fishes a half-eaten orange lollipop, haphazardly replaced in its cellophane wrapper, from the front pocket of her knapsack. At Thackeray, when they know they're going to send a kid home in the middle of the day, the teacher has all their personal be-longings brought to the nurse's office so the child doesn't have to return to the classroom to gather them up.

"Well, it's been a long time since I've seen you up here, Claire Marsh," Nurse Val says. Her smile is the same warm crescent of red although she's let her carrot-colored hair go yellow-gray. I give the woman a hug. She's lost a few inches in height. I remember when she was so much taller than I was, even in my high-school years. She still smells like cinnamon Dentyne, though. "Your Mommy was one of my best customers," she says, giving Zoë a wink.

"Were you sick a lot, Mommy?" my daughter wants to know.

"Sort of. I discovered I was really allergic to volleyball. And basketball."

"I seem to recall you were allergic to swimming, too," Nurse Val chuckles.

"But you love swimming, mom."

"I love it now. But back then, all the chlorine in the pool made my hair turn green," I say, helping Zoë on with her shoes.

"But we have to wear bathing caps," the little pragmatist chirps, wriggling her foot.

"Yeah, but I was allergic to bathing caps, you see. They gave me a headache. Hold still, please, or you'll have to go home barefoot."

She holds up her unshod foot. "Not barefoot. Socked," she says, insisting on the last word.

I get Zoë home and into bed, all tucked in, curled up like a little angel with Baa nestling in the crook of her arm. I give her a glass of ginger ale and then she asks for a story, so I read *Goodnight Moon* for the umpteenth time, the familiarity providing a sort of kid-lit comfort for both of us.

"I'm not tired," Zoë says, her lids heavy with sleep.

"That's okay. You don't have to fall asleep if you don't feel like it. Do you have any idea of what might have made you sick today?" I gently ask.

She nods her head, which surprises me. I hadn't actually expected an answer. "Lunch."

"Lunch?"

"Unh-hunh."

Now I'm concerned about food poisoning. Except that she was the only kid who appeared to have come down with anything. "Did you eat anything that tasted funny?"

"Unh-hunh."

I try to stay calm, keep my voice soft and as soothing as possible, despite my anxiety. "Would you like to tell me what it was?"

"Vanilla ice cream."

I can't think of anything *milder*, except perhaps Cream of Wheat. Can ice cream, unless it's been sitting out and melting, go bad? Get rancid like milk? I'm no food chemist, but somehow, I doubt it. "Mommy isn't so smart all the time, Zoë. Do you know why the vanilla ice cream might have tasted funny and gave you an upset tummy?" She rolls over, like she's going to sleep. "Zoë? I asked you a question, sweetheart."

"Unh-huh," she responds, rolling back. I wait for her answer. She gives a sheepish little smile. "I had to make it orange."

"And how did you make it orange?" I'm wondering what they had sitting around Thackeray's Makepeace Cafeteria that was within easy access.

"Salad dressing." I make a face. She makes one back. "It was really gross."

"I can imagine, Z. But I still don't know how it would make you sick."

"Because I ate it," she says, looking at me like I'm an idiot. "Xander dared me to finish it all."

I try not to laugh, because she really is sick and she still has a fever, which is most likely coincidental. She'd probably been coming down with something anyway. Flirting. That's what it had been all about. When I was in second grade, Willy Pearson smeared Jell-O on my hair to get my attention. He sure got it. It wouldn't wash out or brush out and I had to chop off chunks of my beloved blonde curls. With Mia, it was Rob Bartholomew, who always stood in line behind her so he could smell her hair

(I guess he had a thing for Herbal Essence). And, so she'd notice his existence, he drew a picture of a monster on her favorite pink denim jacket. While she was wearing it. Tulia's second-grade crush, Tom Milliken, routinely tied her shoelaces together. Our Gran's dark braids were repeatedly dipped in the inkwell of John Oakes, who sat behind her.

"I want to go to sleep now," Zoë says drowsily. I kiss her forehead. It's still too warm, but it isn't time for another dose of Tylenol. "Kiss Baa, too," she adds.

I comply, kissing the top of the lamb's head. "I'll be in to check on you later," I whisper. "Sweet dreams."

"Okay," she mumbles softly, then turns over onto her side, nestling the bedraggled stuffed animal against her chest. I tiptoe from her room, leaving the door open just a crack in case she calls for me.

It's 8 P.M. and I'm sitting at the table in the breakfast nook, poring over *Time Out*. It's important for me to keep up with current cultural events. My tour-bus patrons are always asking me for theater and restaurant recommendations and information on other local points of interest, from the commonplace to the arcane.

I look up from the magazine for a moment. Zoë is sleepily shambling into the room in her little cotton tee-shirt and underpants. She's dragging her yellow knapsack like it's a little red wagon.

"I have homework," she says.

"Are you sure you need to do it tonight, since you went home sick today?" In my era, if you went home with a fever in the middle of the day, you weren't expected to do your homework for that day. You got a dispensation so you could recuperate.

Zoë nods. "It's a special project for Veterans Day."

"But you don't have school on Veterans Day, sweetheart. It's a holiday. The school is closed."

"I know that," she replies, like I'm slow-witted. "That's why it's due tomorrow. We've had it for a week."

I regard the look of evasion on her face. "Zoë, are you telling me that you've had to do a Veterans Day project for a whole week and you're just going to start it now?" She nods. "We've talked about this, Z. What have I told you about waiting until the last minute?"

Her lower lip begins to tremble. "Don't scold me. I'm sick."

"You're sick because you did a silly thing today," I say gently.

"Well, I have to do my homework even when I'm sick or else I get a U," she tells me. "That's the rules." Boy, they don't cut these kids any slack. "I have regular homework, too," she adds.

By the time I supervise her math homework and quiz her on her spelling words (brownstone, chocolate, exercise, and digital), it's nine thirty. Although she spent the afternoon sleeping off the effects of her tummy trauma, it's still way past her bedtime of seven thirty—a number that is more theoretical than actual, because of the amount of homework second graders get these days and the fact that we're often not even home until 5 P.M., given her after-school activities schedule. Then you have to budget time for a healthy dinner.

"We still need to do my Veterans Day project." Zoë emits a huge yawn. She's a dozen years too young to prop up with caffeine in order to pull an all-nighter. Her school day begins at eight in the morning, and eight thirty on Fridays, for some inexplicable reason. Honestly, does Thackeray really expect these kids to fast-track it for Harvard when they can barely stay awake in class?

"Okay, then. Let's buckle down. What's the assignment?"

"We have to make a memorial."

"You—you have to—what?"

"A *me-mor-ial*. It's a sculpture or a building that is supposed to honor all the soldiers that died in wars and all the ones that fought in wars and didn't die and came home."

I smile at her definition, despite my increasing ire. I think the task is in poor taste. It's too advanced for six- and seven-year-olds, whose comprehension of death, destruction, disfigurement, and dismemberment should properly be limited to the programming on the Cartoon Network. I have no problem with second graders learning about patriotism and valor and a respect for our nation's veterans. My objection is with their asking the kids to design something related so specifically to death.

"Let's make a plan here," I sigh. "First of all, do you want to make a memorial for veterans of one war in particular, or for all wars?"

She shrugs. "I don't know."

"Well, pick something."

"All wars."

"All right. Good choice. Now, do you have an idea in mind of what you want it to look like?" Zoë rubs her eyes and yawns again. These kids have most likely never *seen* a memorial. "Well, there are lots of different types of memorials. The ones to veterans sometimes look like a statue—usually it's of a man; sometimes he's on a horse, and he's holding an American flag or something. And sometimes it's an eternal flame."

"I want that. An infernal flame."

"*Eternal*, not infernal. Eternal means 'forever,' so that's a good sentiment for a memorial." I think for a moment. "Infernal means 'fiery,' actually. 'Blazing.' "

"So, what's wrong with an infernal flame?"

"Nothing. It's just redundant."

"What's 'redundant'?"

"Saying the same thing twice in a row. Let's stick to 'eternal' for the flame, okay?"

She thinks about this for several moments. " 'Twice in a row' is redundant."

"I love you, Zoë. You're absolutely right. Very good! Now, let's make an eternal flame before the sun rises."

Finally, as the clock nears midnight, we have our memorial. I've insisted that she do most of the work herself. Otherwise, how will she learn anything? "I already did second grade," I told her—although I never had assignments this advanced. "This year, it's your turn."

So, she's built a low wall out of strips of cardboard, collected and hoarded for arts and crafts projects from the starched collars of the shirts Scott used to send to the Chinese laundry. She's covered the cardboard with aluminum foil to represent "real metal."

"I want it to be made out of shiny metal so when it's rainy the flame will always make it bright and when it's sunny out, it will be *really* bright!" She's fashioned flames from colored construction paper and cellophane, gathering them into a sort of cheerleader's pompom. A twisty tie of paper and wire holds the cluster of flames together and we've punched a hole through the cardboard base so the "stem" can be secured to its underside. It looks pretty good. The concept was essentially Zoë's and the choice of materials was entirely her own.

I tell her she should be very proud of her creation, but she's too tired to appreciate the praise. I bathe her, put her to bed, and tuck her in. She'll have to be bright-eyed and bushy-tailed in a mere handful of hours.

If I return to my own sightseeing research, *I'll* be pulling an all-nighter. I take *Time Out* into the bedroom with me, thinking I'll finish my reading, but I fall asleep with the light on. When I step out of bed the next morning, I practically trip on the magazine, unfurled in a slippery tent-shape on the floor.

Chapter 6

"Don't kill me, Claire. I can't do it." This afternoon was Claire's first Saturday tour group and I'd promised to pick up Zoë from Xander Osborne's birthday party while Claire worked.

"I'm kind of in the lurch, here," she whispered into her cell. "I've already got one strike against me with Go Native! for leaving those old ladies on the Lower East Side. They put an official reprimand in my file."

I felt like shit. "Clairey, I must have been nuts when I told you I could get Zoë. What was I thinking? *Nina* is at the party. She's the fucking hostess. And I'm Public Enemy Number One!"

"I thought she didn't know about you," Claire said.

"She knows now. And she also knows who I'm related to. Little kids have big mouths." I didn't want to let my sister down, but showing up at Chelsea Piers at four o'clock was a bad idea. I could just see the designer-clad Nina Osborne in custom-made Manolo Blahnik skates chasing me around the rink with a Polo Ralph Lauren hockey stick. "Can't you get the mother of one of Zoë's friends to bring her back with them until you get home?"

Claire's voice was small and tense. "I tried them first. They've all got other plans. You were my court of last resort. What am I supposed to do, Mia? I can't leave work. And this would make the second time in two weeks. I really need this job."

"What? I can't hear you. You're breaking up." There was tons of static on the line.

"We must have just gone through a dead zone. I said I really need this job!" Claire shouted into her phone. "Oh, hell. Now I've got fifty-two kids and twelve chaperones from the Willahatchee High School Marching Band looking daggers at me."

"Look, I'm sorry, Claire. My bad, okay? I'll owe you one."

"You're gonna owe me big-time. Goddamn it, Mia! Look, I've gotta run. My Go Natives are getting so restless I think one of them may stuff me into a tuba."

Claire ended the call and I felt even shittier. What I couldn't tell her is that things suck between Robert Osborne and me. We met cute, but things went south fast. I'm thinking of ending it. It was swell for a while, but there's not much spark anymore. This is not a long-run kind of thing. I like that he dresses well, but I can't keep pretending that I give a shit that the American Kennel Club renamed his breed of dog. Too bad, though. See, I love to screw but I'm not trying to screw up. I want "forever," too, just like most other chicks.

I fired up my computer and went back to tackling Excel. If I was ever going to learn this on my own, I needed to make a sample chart. Something to practice with so I could get the hang of it.

Ugh. My mind was too preoccupied. Men.

Wait. *Yeah. Men.* That's it. If I generated a chart of all the men I've dated, broken down by certain key characteristics, maybe I can see where I've been going wrong. What mistakes I keep making.

I opened my address book and started to input the names of my flops. In recent history alone, there was Hal, of course, then Luca, and before Hal there was a guy I picked up in Coyote Ugly named Skeet who wanted to be called "Cowboy" and who thought Alcohol, Tobacco, and Firearms was a shopping list. I didn't think I needed to learn a computer software program to tell me where I went wrong with those three. None of these men spelled stability. I thought Robert Osborne might, but the price tag was too high. He was still his own favorite subject. Even in bed.

....

The Upper West Side is a Mecca for filmmakers. I was telling my tour that some of *Spiderman II* was shot in the Museum of Natural History and they seemed kind of excited about that, even though we didn't set foot inside. I don't know what it is about tourists and film geeks, but pointing out a building inside of which Tobey Maguire spent a few choice hours really gets their motors going. I guess that's one reason why Letterman's "brush with greatness" segments were such a hit. The chaperones want to see stuff from their generation, including the Dakota (*Rosemary's Baby*) and the phone booth where Richard Dreyfuss called Marsha Mason in the pouring rain in *The Goodbye Girl*.

"The Richard Dreyfuss phone booth isn't there anymore," I say. Another slice of New York history that has gone the way of the subway token.

"What happened to it?" the Willahatchee music teacher wants to know. He's already told me that he admires Dreyfuss's musicianship, not only his guitar-playing hobby in *The Goodbye Girl*, but as the title character in *Mr. Holland's Opus*.

"No more phone booths. We got rid of them years ago. Too many drug deals, muggings, and public urinations. Sorry, folks, but it's true." I realize that this doesn't paint the prettiest picture of my city, so I add, "But now New York is so much safer thanks to a kick-ass former mayor and a couple of kick-ass former police chiefs." I conveniently omit the obvious, the breach of security that will occupy a corner of our minds for the rest of our lives.

I'd gotten advance permission from Go Native! to take my band on the Roosevelt Island tramway, site of *Spiderman*'s climactic scene between our homespun hero and Willem Dafoe. This is where my tour will culminate as well. We'll cross over to Roosevelt Island and back and then Frank will return the good citizens of Willahatchee to the Trina's Tours office.

Unfortunately, there appears to be some sort of a backlog of cross-river travelers at the Manhattan side of the tram. I try to ascertain what's up and hear only a couple of speculative comments that the tram was "broken for a while," but now it's up and running again. All the folks in front of us actually live on Roosevelt Island and need to get home. Besides, they were here first. I ask my tour if it's okay with them that we wait a bit. They're fine with that, understanding the situation.

A half hour later, we're all still on line. The tram buckets are larger than the little four-seaters in Disneyland, but compared to a subway car, for example, they don't carry too many passengers. "Does anyone need to be anywhere soon?" I ask my tour. Sixty-four heads respond in the negative. After another twenty minutes or so, I've sent the first group over to Roosevelt Island and am lining up the balance of my guests for the next Manhattan-side tram. I load them in, then glance at my watch. Uh-oh.

Even if I can catch a cab right this minute, and even if the traffic is moving, it's a long ride from 59th Street and Second Avenue to 23rd and Twelfth. We would have been fine, had it not been for the tram backup. I would have made it to Chelsea Piers just a few minutes late. I feel desperation coursing through my veins. I can't afford to be any later to pick up Zoë, or the poor child might be sitting there all alone—in a *best*-case scenario. All my options suck. I'm a victim of Murphy's Law this afternoon, stuck between risking child endangerment and risking my employment.

"Folks!" I shout, getting my tour group's attention. Well, half of them. The other half just landed on Roosevelt Island and are supposed to return with the next Manhattan-bound bucket. "Look, I'm really sorry about this, but I have a bit of bad news. I'm going to have to play the Goodbye Girl myself." I make a plea for sympathy to the mothers in my audience, and, surprisingly, I get it. The Willahatchee chaperones are soccer moms and they show solidarity.

"You go get your daughter, sweetie."

"We'll be all right. It's not your fault."

"We'll tell the others for you, so don't you worry."

"It's the curse of the working mother," they commiserate.

I'm so grateful, especially after the orgasm grannies' outright hostility, that I burst into tears. I thank them profusely and assure them that I'll be watching from my window on Thanksgiving morning, cheering like crazy for the band as they march loudly and proudly down Central Park West with the rest of the Macy's parade participants.

I arrive at Chelsea Piers to find Zoë hunched over on a bench outside the skating rink, looking like Charlie Brown after a particularly resounding defeat. Behind her, Nina, a man I assume is Robert—neither of them speaking to the other, but exchanging glares of death—and a homely young woman who I guess is the new *au pair*, are packing up Xander's gifts. They are loading up an industrial dolly. I've attended weddings that have brought in less of a haul. And this kid got all this loot just for turning seven. His own wedding, should any young lady be masochistic enough to marry him, can't help but be anti-climactic. The chill in the air isn't just coming off the rink. I absorb Nina's icy stare and it's immediately evident why Mia didn't want to set foot in the place.

"Hey, kiddo," I say, kicking Zoë's bench. Behind me, the Osbornes are trying to figure out what to do with the leftover cake, a confectionery replica of Madison Square Garden.

"Hey." She's almost inaudible. "I thought MiMi was coming to get me."

"MiMi couldn't make it sweetie. Something came up."

"Well, you're late. The party ended at four o'clock."

I kneel beside the bench so we're at eye level. "I had to work. You know that. I got here as fast as I could. So, did you have fun?" She nods. "Did you decide to play hockey after all?" Another nod. A glum face.

"You missed it," she says, a perfect tear rolling down the side of her nose. "All the moms and dads were here and they were cheering and first they taught us how to play and then we even played a real hockey game and I scored a goal. You missed it."

Every day, no matter how much I do, I feel in some way like I'm failing this child. The only reason she'd wanted to go to the party was because she has a crush on Xander; she was terrified of the ice hockey theme, but she suited up with the other kids, faced her fears, got on the ice, learned the game, and even scored a goal. And her mommy wasn't there to see her do it. "I'm so proud of you, sweetheart," I tell her, kissing away the tear that by now has reached her chin. "I'm very, very sorry that I didn't see you play hockey and score that goal."

"And Xander was the goalie, too!" she says, breaking into a smile. "I got him good! Oh." She holds up a slightly smushed paper bag.

"Whatcha got there, Z?"

"A goody bag." She thrusts it into my hands. I open the sack to discover what the Osbornes consider "goodies" for second graders. In addition to a Knicks key chain and a Toblerone bar, there's a Yankees cap (just for the record, we Marshes are Mets fans), a parent/child guest pass good for one month's activities at Chelsea Piers, and a pair of Rangers tickets. Rinkside, or whatever they call them. *The only thing missing is a coupon for a year's tuition at Thackeray*. Total value of the goody bag: a few hundred dollars. And the Osbornes did this for over three dozen kids. Plus the cost of the two-hour bash. Welcome to the world of birthday parties given by wealthy, competitive parents for their overachieving offspring.

I slip the goody bag into my purse and extend my hand to Zoë. "Ready to go?"

She hops off the bench. "I think I like hockey," she says as we walk toward the bus stop. "You get to beat people up and don't get in trouble for it."

Two days later, at 3 P.M., Zoë comes barreling down the stone steps of the Thackeray Academy, carrying her dented Veterans Memorial. Her eyes are puffy and red. Without greeting me first, she grabs my hand and drags me to the nearest trash basket, where she unceremoniously dumps her project. Then she literally kicks the can.

"Zoë, what happened? We worked so hard on that and you did such a good job all by yourself!"

"I got a U," she replies, all her tears evidently spent.

"Wait a sec. You did the assignment. You handed it in on time. Why did Mrs. Hennepin say it was Unsatisfactory?"

Her face looks stricken. "I don't know."

"Let's go." I retrieve Zoë's project from the garbage can and march her back into the school and straight down the hall to the headmaster's office.

As I'm about to enter Mr. Kiplinger's sanctum sanctorum, his secretary, Mrs. Tejada, tells me I can't get in without an appointment. "Yes, he's a very busy man, I know," I say sarcastically.

Mr. Kiplinger is on the phone when Zoë and I step inside his office. He waves us away but I ignore his waggling hand. His cuffs are monogrammed with thread the color of burnt umber. When he sees that my daughter and I aren't going anywhere, he motions for us to sit. I wait for him to conclude his call, then skip the pleasantries. I place the memorial on the desk in front of him.

"Please tell me why Zoë's special project was given a U," I calmly demand.

"You know perfectly well that the issue of grades is not my purview, Ms. Marsh. You should be addressing this with her teacher."

"Fine. Then we'll get Mrs. Hennepin down here."

It's clear that Zoë and I are going to wait until this situation is resolved, so Mr. Kiplinger buzzes Mrs. Tejada and asks her to summon both Mrs. Hennepin and Mr. Mendel. As we wait, I whisper to Zoë that it's not nice to kick Mr. Kiplinger's desk, although *I'd* like to kick *Mr. Kiplinger*.

"Well . . . Ms. Marsh. I didn't think we'd be seeing you again so soon." Mr. Mendel gives me an insipid handshake. "Hello, Zoë."

"Hello," she parrots sullenly.

"We don't seem too cheery this afternoon."

"You wouldn't be if you worked your tail off on your homework, delivered it in a timely fashion, and then got a 'U' on it. Mrs. Hennepin, would you kindly tell me why you judged Zoë's Veterans Day memorial 'Unsatisfactory'?"

She fixes me with steely eyes beneath the white elastic hairband. "Ms. Marsh, did you supervise Zoë on this project?"

"Of course I did."

"Frankly, I'm surprised," she says.

"And why is that?"

"Well . . . it's not up to Thackeray standards. It looks like a child did it."

"A child *did* do it. And she's in second grade. She's not a design major at Pratt."

"There's no need to become sarcastic. It's unhelpful," Mr. Mendel volunteers helpfully.

"Zoë doesn't need to be an art college student to deliver a satisfactory project. Lily Pei turned in a plaza with a fully functioning waterfall," argues Mrs. Hennepin.

"Lily Pei. *Pei.* As in *I. M.* Pei, perhaps? Don't tell me there's a professional architect somewhere in her family who more than supervised her homework?"

"The parents are demanding much higher standards nowadays," Mr. Kiplinger says. "We've had to change with the times since you were a student, Ms. Marsh; and we expect our parents to help their children with their homework in a hands-on way."

"Hands-on, huh?" I can imagine Lily Pei's entry in the Regina Hennepin Veterans Memorial Sweepstakes. It's probably on foam core board with 3-D buildings and little passersby, all done to perfect scale.

"Mentoring, especially for children Zoë's age, is of vital importance to their development."

"Mr. Mendel, if my parents helped me as much as Lily Pei's great-grandfather has, to use your own example, it wouldn't be considered 'mentoring.' It would be called 'cheating,' and we'd all be sitting in this office just the same, to discuss the dangers of *that.* I think your judging my daughter's own handiwork and creativity as 'Unsatisfactory' is what's damaging here. It's not the grade itself that concerns me—that a U on her second-grade transcript will irrevocably screw up her chances of getting into the Ivy league. What troubles me is, how can a six-year-old little girl possibly live up to the standards you're now imposing on her?"

"I think you're mischaracterizing things, Ms. Marsh."

"I'm inclined to agree with the school psychologist," Mr. Kiplinger says, deliberately invoking Mr. Mendel's credentials.

"Thackeray always prided itself on playing to a child's strengths, on encouraging their individualism and creativity, as long as they learned the concepts of responsibility, diligence, and attention to detail. What kind of harm does it do to a child's self-worth to make it quite clear—by giving her a *failing* grade— that homework fashioned by her own hands is inadequate?

How are children expected to learn about anything other than cheating and laziness, when their parents are the ones who are doing the homework?"

"You're very angry, Ms. Marsh. That's hardly a positive environment in which to raise—"

I slide my chair away from the desk and address Mr. Mendel. "You let me finish! Mrs. Hennepin, I told Zoë when we worked on her veterans memorial that I've already been in second grade. I have an art background. Of course *I* can put together a project that can be compared with Lily Pei's. But how are Zoë and Lily supposed to learn how to do it themselves? Even though the result might be imperfect in your eyes?"

I feel like a crusader of sorts. Joan of Arc or Susan B. Anthony. "How can these children grow as students and as human beings when the school's policy stomps on their vast imaginations and fragile self-esteem?"

"And what kind of example are *you* setting for Zoë?" Mrs. Hennepin demands. "You're very headstrong. You Marsh girls have always tried to buck the rules and mock authority. If you want Zoë to have a positive and fulfilling experience at Thackeray—"

"You know something? We're going in circles again, here. That's all I ever seem to get from you folks. The runaround. You're making me dizzy. I fully understand that parents and teachers are expected to be partners in their children's educations. But I won't have Zoë raised by committee."

I offer Zoë my hand. She's been silent and extremely well behaved during the entirety of this impromptu meeting. After she stopped kicking Kiplinger's desk, she took her social studies reader out of her knapsack and immersed herself in its pages.

She hops off her chair and stuffs the book back into her bag. Then she turns to Mrs. Hennepin with narrowed eyes.

"Buck *you!*" she says to her teacher, before bolting from the room.

I leave before they can schedule another conference.

· · · · · · · · · · · ·

Dear Diary:

Because I had to wake up so early today, Mommy wanted me to take a nap before we go to Sag Harbor to have dinner with Granny Tulia and Grandpa Brendan. But I had to write in my diary because I don't want to forget and I want to tell all about the Macy's Thanksgiving Day Parade and the Powerpuff Girls and MiMi and me.

MiMi was right. We really did have to get up when it was still dark out. It was cold but it wasn't raining. Mommy made me put on two pairs of tights. I put on a long underwear shirt too, because I just wanted to wear my special outfit and not have to put on a coat. I wore one of my white school blouses and I have a light blue jumper and Mommy put my hair in two ponytails so I looked like Bubbles. MiMi told Mommy that each of the little girls on the float had to dress like one of the Powerpuff Girls. So the girls with red hair had to dress like Blossom and the girls with brown hair had to dress like Buttercup. We didn't have to buy anything new, but in case some people did, Macy's has a Power- puff Girls section in the kids department.

MiMi came to get me. Mommy was still wearing her bathrobe and she said goodbye to us and she wished she was allowed to come on the float with us. I felt very grown up doing something special with MiMi. She's my favorite person because we always do something really fun that none of my friends get to do.

When we got to where the parade was going to start it was still dark out and all the balloons were lying on their sides on the street with big nets over them. When my Daddy lived with us we used to go watch them blowing up the balloons on the night before Thanksgiving. Then we would have hot chocolate at E.J.'s which is a restaurant that Daddy says looks like a restaurant Grandpa Brendan might have gone to when he was a teenager and it gives very big portions.

This year Daddy didn't take me to the balloons or for hot chocolate. I wished he would have, but he told Mommy and me that he was busy at Serena's restaurant.

The TV star on the Powerpuff Girls float was really pretty and MiMi made her look even prettier with her makeup. Her name was Janyce. She had beautiful long black hair and a white fur coat and she looked really warm. She was young like Mommy and MiMi and when one of the other little girls asked her if she was rich because she had a fur coat she laughed. She told all the little girls that we were supposed to smile and wave at everybody and to go from one side of the float to the other so that we didn't play favorites with people on only one side of the street.

But something made me disappointed. The real Powerpuff Girls weren't there. I know they are just cartoons on TV but for the parade they had ladies dressed up like Buttercup and Blossom and Bubbles with big heads on them like big puppet heads, like the seven dwarves wear in Disney World, and I thought they looked silly, because the heads were so heavy that they wouldn't be able to fly. I asked MiMi how we were supposed to jump up and down and cheer for the Powerpuff Girls when it was just regular people inside costumes like Halloween. MiMi said we should use our imaginations and pretend they have super powers.

That was okay. By the time the parade started I was having so much fun that it didn't matter that they weren't the real Powerpuff girls on the float. It was so special being in the parade and being right near the bands and the balloons and the other floats and the clowns. The clowns didn't scare me this time. MiMi said they were just people who work at Macy's and being a clown in the parade was a big treat. MiMi even helped some of them with *their makeup. I got to see the Jimmy Neutron balloon close up and the Captain Nemo balloon, too. The people holding the strings were all dressed in costumes. The people with the Big Bird balloon were all dressed like Big Bird with yellow tops and yellow pants and yellow hats that looked like rooster hats. It was very exciting and like being at a great big party. I didn't even think about being cold.*

I was waving at all the people and we passed my house and I waved up at our window and I think I saw Mommy up there waving back. We stopped a few times along the way for Janyce to sing her song. She didn't really sing, though. Someone pressed a button and it was her singing on a CD, but she opened her mouth and was pretending to be singing the song. There was a lot of pretending today. I asked her why she wasn't singing for real and she said that even with a microphone, not a lot of people would hear her and it was so early in the morning and it was cold and those things were not good for singers. And the float went fast enough that people couldn't tell if she was singing for real or on tape. It was still her voice, she said, so she wasn't really cheating. At the end of the parade she gave each of the little girls a copy of her CD with her autograph on it. She was wearing a beautiful blue sparkly gown on it and she looked like a Barbie but with dark hair.

MiMi rode on the float, even though she was too big to be a Buttercup, but she dressed up, too. She took pictures of me with the ladies dressed as the Powerpuff Girls with the big heads and with the beautiful singer Janyce and I'm going to bring them to school for show and tell next week. It was the best morning. I hope I get to do it again next year. I love my Aunt MiMi soooooo much.

·············

If the Pilgrims had been forced to brave the rigors of the Long Island Expressway, they would never have left England. I thought about taking Zoë to my parents on the train, but that's a three-hour trip and the closest stop to Sag Harbor is Bridge-hampton, which means a cab ride to my parents that costs half the price of the train fare, or else disturbing their dinner preparations by asking them to come fetch us. So I rent a car, which costs a fortune in New York City, but MiMi and I, plus her date, are splitting the expense and it probably isn't much more than the sum total of four round-trip fares on the Long Island Railroad. And at least this way, our time is our own and we're not dependent on the train schedule.

Second Avenue is a parking lot until we get south of 59th Street and the bridge, then it becomes a snarl again as we approach the Queens-Midtown Tunnel. Zoë must be really exhausted from the parade this morning, because she and Baa are zonked out in the booster seat. I pull up to Mia's building in the East Village and honk the horn. Our special Marsh signal. She comes down the stoop in an oversized trench coat, wet hair tucked into a bun, followed by Happy Chef (I guess Robert Osborne is history; I'll ask her about it tomorrow), gingerly negotiating the steps while balancing a decorated sheet cake. I scoot over to open the front door.

"Happy early birthday, sweet thing," Happy Chef says, leaning in down to give me a peck on the cheek. "I'm singing for my supper tonight," he adds, indicating the cake. "Maybe I should sit up front with it."

Thanking him profusely for such a generous treat, I agree, consigning Mia to the back where my Powerpuff Girl is still sleeping. Ordinarily, she wakes up as soon as I stop the car. Apart from the appalling traffic, it's an uneventful journey to the East End. Zoë awakens about two thirds of the way there and asks to sing, which means an invitation to all of us. She likes it when Mia and I run through the shows we did in after-school and camp programs when we were kids: *Oliver! Annie, Bye, Bye Birdie, Grease, Peter Pan*, and *You're a Good Man, Charlie Brown*.

Mia was one of the best Lucys on the planet. Of course that review has to be filtered through the eyes of her then eight-year-old kid sister, but she really did internalize the role and I think she's always seen being the queen of crabbiness as a sort of badge of honor. Zoë loves it when Charles and Mia rock the car with their rendition of "Summer Nights" from *Grease*, reprising the roles they played when they met at the Cultural Arts summer camp up in Pearl River sixteen years ago. She and I chime in on the doo-woppy choruses. I bite my tongue, resisting teasing Mia about that being the last time she ever played the "good girl."

As we roll into Sag Harbor and pass the Whaling Museum, Zoë starts bouncing up and down—as much as the booster seat will let her. "We're almost there!" she announces, clapping her hands, then turns the almost-there-ness into a chant that lasts for the next few minutes. I finally allow myself a moment to enjoy the surroundings. There's a surprising amount of foliage for late November, though the leaves on the trees have lost their burnished luster. I turn off the main drag and pull into my parents' driveway, giving the Marsh honk of the horn, then shut off the engine and catch my breath. I think I've been holding it ever since we left the Upper West Side.

My parents emerge, my mother wiping her hands on a hot pink dishcloth and my father carrying a small, yellow-ruled notepad and pen, to which I believe he must be surgically attached, as he never seems to be without them.

"I love it when the babies come back to the nest," Tulia says to no one in particular as she takes the cake from Charles. "Why, thank you. This looks stunning as usual. Another masterpiece." The master baker blushes a bit and says something modest and self-deprecating, to which my mother responds in kind and their exchange threatens to become an Alphonse-Gaston "after you" routine.

Charles finally gets out of the car and stretches. I don't think he's moved a leg muscle in three and a half hours, for fear he'd ruin my birthday cake. Yet another thing over which I can self-impose a little guilt. "Now I'm nervous," Tulia teases, properly greeting him, "with a real chef at the table tonight."

Zoë, released from her booster seat by Mia, has launched herself full throttle into my father. She's got her arms around his waist and is blowing raspberries against his tummy, just the way *he* always did to *us* when we were little. She's laughing her head off, thinking this behavioral reversal is a hoot.

"Hey Dad, hey Mom," Mia says, giving each of them a peck on the cheek. "What can I do to help?" She follows our mother into the house.

"How's the celebrant?" my father asks me.

I stand in their front yard, inhaling the aromas of autumn . . . the decaying leaves, wood-burning fireplaces—one of my favorite scents ever—fresh, crisp air, and the mélange of fragrances emanating from my mother's kitchen. "Better, now, Daddy," I reply. "Sometimes . . . sometimes, you know, everything's moving so fast that you forget . . ." I inhale again. "You just . . . it's that . . ."

"I know," my father says softly. He gives my shoulder a little squeeze. "Come inside when you're ready."

He's always been able to decipher my shorthand.

There's a log or two blazing and crackling away in the fireplace in the living room. The rooms are numerous but small given the cost and difficulty of heating large spaces back when the house was built. My mother takes its landmark status very seriously and has been quite keen on keeping the interior design as period-accurate as possible. If you're not prepared for it, you think you've been thrust into a time warp. Don't enter the parlor and living room expecting to see a wide-screen TV blaring one of the Thanksgiving football games at no one in particular. You have to know where to find it—upstairs, tucked into an 1830s armoire, along with the DVD player and my Dad's state-of-the-art stereo system.

Zoë is now out in the yard, playing croquet with her imaginary friend Wendy and with my parents' Irish Setter Ulysses, perfectly safe, taking out her second-grade frustrations on the wooden ball, fighting with Wendy over whose turn it is. I walk into the kitchen to see how I can help my mother. Mia is garnishing something. Happy Chef has been put to good use adding the finishing touches to a ginger-carrot soup. Orange for Zoë. I give my mother a kiss.

"Well, we can't have the child starving, can we?" she says. "Everyone should enjoy the Thanksgiving bounty." Charles holds out a wooden spoon for her to taste the soup. "What is that?" She makes little tasting-smacking sounds. "Did I put that in there?"

"Nutmeg. No, I did," Charles says.

"I like it! I'll have to remember that for next time. You girls were terrible eaters," Mommy reminds us. "Clairey, you still won't eat anything if you think it smells bad."

This is true. Bologna and peanut butter were crossed off my dietary list decades ago. Ditto for most cheeses, with the exception of cream, cheddar, smoked gouda, American, ricotta, mozzarella—and mascarpone, since no one in her right mind could give up tiramisu.

"Where's the bird?" Mia asks.

"Oh, yes, the turkey!" My mother opens the oven and peers in to check on it. "Meet Hedda," she says proudly. Yes, we have a Marsh family tradition of naming the turkey every year.

"What?" Mia says.

"Hedda Gobbler!" my mother crows. She thinks this is hysterical. "Don't you get it? It's—"

"We get it, Ma," Mia says, shaking her head.

I chuckle. Leave it to a Marsh to invoke Ibsen.

"What are you wearing, sweetheart? I love it. Let me look at you." My mother wipes her hands on the fuchsia cloth and goes over to explore Mia's outfit, fingering the drapery as Mia poses and twirls.

It's only then that I actually take a good look at my sister's regalia. It just shows how preoccupied my mind has been, with all the stresses of getting out here. She's wearing a sari. Her dark hair has been smoothed into a bun with a henna'd center part. She's replaced her gold nose stud with a tiny, ruby ladybug and her arms are laden with narrow golden bangles.

"Thanksgiving commemorates the meal shared between the Pilgrims and the Indians, right?" Mia says. "So I thought it would be fun to dress as an Indian. The *other* Indians. I mean, why do the expected? The predictable? Besides, since when has this family ever had a totally traditional Thanksgiving?"

"I think you look beautiful," our mother says. "It suits you."

"You don't think it's a little . . . I don't know . . . offensive?" I suggest.

"To whom? Unless Mia's intention is to mock another culture— which it isn't, sweetheart—?" she says, looking to her older daughter. Mia shakes her head. "—then I think it's lovely. After all, people from Eastern nations sometimes wear Western dress, and they're not poking fun of us. At least I don't think they are. This is how designers get their brainstorms, Clairey. By the way, your earrings are lovely." She comes over to more closely admire my lacquered autumn leaves flecked with gold dust.

"Thanks. I made them. A couple of years ago. I thought you'd seen them before."

Tulia shakes her head. "I'd remember. Sweetheart, they're wonderful. You were always so clever with jewelry design."

"I guess it's in the genes," I say, giving her a hug. She smells like patchouli and allspice. I poke my head out the back door of the kitchen. "Zoë? Wendy? Time to come inside. Granny Tulia has some snacks for you." I pour some cheddar-flavored Gold-fish into a bowl and hand it off to her as she scampers past me. "So, who won?" I ask, referring to the haphazard croquet game.

"Ulysses. But he cheated. He kept pushing the balls through

the wickets with his nose." She skips off toward the parlor to find her grandfather.

"Claire, would you finish setting the table, please?" Tulia asks. "Everything is right where it usually is."

"Of course." I peek into the dining room to see what still needs to be done. My mother has covered the table with linen cloths of cranberry and burnt orange. Handmade bayberry candles in sterling holders flank the centerpiece, an abundant cornucopia of seasonal fruits and vegetables, including some funky-shaped little squashes, russet-colored Indian corn, and a pineapple—a symbol of hospitality. I start counting place settings. Tulia has already distributed the napkins and the goblets for wine and water. I need to add the flatware for . . . wait . . . Tulia and Brendan are two. Mia and Happy Chef make four. Zoë and I are six. The table has been laid out for seven. Although my parents are extremely permissive, I highly doubt that the imaginary Wendy or the four-legged Ulysses are being asked to dine with us.

"Mommy," I call to the kitchen. "You've got this set for seven."

She comes into the dining room and surveys the table. Then her mouth falls open and her eyes register horror, a living facsimile of the ancient Greek mask of tragedy. "Oh, God, Clairey. I must have forgotten to tell you! I thought it would be nice for Zoë to have her daddy at Thanksgiving Dinner, so I invited Scott to join us."

Chapter 7

My mother doesn't have a malicious fiber in her body. So I know, to her own way of thinking, her intentions must have been kindly at some point. "You . . . invited my ex-husband?" I stammer, barely able to form the words.

"It's a holiday. Two special occasions, in fact," she adds, referring to my birthday celebration. "I really did think it would be a treat for Zoë to see her father on Thanksgiving. You can't stop her from adoring Scott. I thought you and he were . . . all right with each other; that you were amicable. Aren't you?"

"A treat for Zoë is a trick on me. Wrong holiday, Tulia." Suddenly, I'm a child again, life isn't fair, and I stomp off angrily into the living room.

"What's the matter, pumpkin?" my father asks, glancing up from his writing tablet.

"Scott is."

"She didn't tell you?"

"She *just* did. Does that count?"

Daddy shakes his head. "You know it's not like your mother to be manipulative. She probably really believes she mentioned it. She invited him a few weeks ago. She thought it would be lovely for Zoë."

"So she says," I reply glumly. "Some happy birthday." I look over at him. His mind is only half on me. Typical, but that's who my dad is and I've grown used to it over the years. It doesn't mean he wasn't listening. "What are you doing?"

"Putting the finishing touches on your poem. You Marsh women always make fun of my indifference to tradition, so I thought I would use a classic form this year. You're getting a sonnet."

"Cool," I say, still working on the fact that my mother has invited my ex-husband to celebrate Thanksgiving—and my birthday—with our immediate family. If Tulia's hair weren't its completely natural shade, I could swear her brain had been addled by the chemicals in her hair color.

There's a knock at the door. "I want to get it," Zoë shouts, and comes barreling through the living room from somewhere, Ulysses right on her heels.

I realize that she hasn't been prepped to see her father, so I try to avoid the potential catastrophe that this surprise might cause. "Sweetie, maybe I should—" But the door is open and it's too late. Zoë releases a yowl, like a cat whose tail has just been trampled by a Doc Martens, and runs screaming from the room. I had a feeling it would be bad, but I had no idea it would be *this* bad. Then I see why. Oh, God. Zoë was right. Can I run screaming from the room, too? Scott has brought his girlfriend, Serena Eden.

"M-o-o-o-o-o-o-o-o-o-o-m!" I yell, a primal scream. My father plays the ultimate spectator as my mother enters the room. Her face falls and I quickly do the math. Scrawny, raw-food-vegan-nuts-and-berries-eating restaurateur makes eight. Clearly Serena was *not* on the guest list.

"Excuse us, please," Tulia says to the new arrivals. She takes my elbow and pilots me into the kitchen, leaving them on the doorstep, unsure whether or not it's okay to cross the threshold.

"I'm going home. I'm taking Zoë and we are going home. What were you thinking?" I whisper.

"What was *he* thinking, is what I'd like to know," my mother hisses. She looks completely defeated. My mother isn't good at coping when things don't run according to plan. She lives in her own world—that, granted, is shocking pink—and deviation discombobulates her (ironically, since this family does nothing *but* stray from the straight and narrow). "Besides, what's she going to eat?"

"I'll go pick some grass for her," Mia says, joining the discussion. She'd gone to placate Zoë, who now refuses to come out of one of the upstairs bedrooms.

"Are they still standing in the doorway?" I ask.

Mia checks and nods in the affirmative. "They don't look like they want to be here any more than we want them. Does that bitch always look green, by the way? She might want to eat something—I don't know—*brown*. At least she'll look healthier."

This reminds me that my daughter is still eating only orange food. Did June Cleaver ever have these problems? Or Bonnie Franklin on *One Day at a Time*? And I don't recall Bonnie's ex-husband darkening her doorstep with his skinny new fling. Schneider, the ubiquitous super, would have cold-cocked him with a ball-peen hammer.

"Well, what's done is done, so let's make the best of it," my mother sighs. "Mia, would you add another place setting, please? As far away from your sister as possible. Claire is sitting to Daddy's right."

"How 'bout the dog house?" Mia mutters and exits into the kitchen.

I pour myself a double sherry and contort my face into a mask of cordiality, welcoming Scott and Serena inside. Boy, I can't wait for this wine to kick in. I foist Serena on my father, who is better than any of us at concealing his displeasure over something, and escort Scott into the backyard.

I hate him because I still get a rush of adrenaline whenever I see him. I hate him because I wanted things to work out. I hate him for so swiftly moving on. I hate him because I'm turning twenty-six this weekend and I have to start my life all over again with a daughter who is halfway to puberty. Did Zoë and I count for nothing? I feel compelled to reiterate all of this to him. So I seize my opportunity and I do. Right after I slip inside to the bar cart and grab the sherry bottle.

"We're both impetuous people, Claire. We married practically on a whim and we—"

"I'm not exactly as impetuous as you seem to think I am," I interrupt. "I . . . Yes, I know our *courtship* was kind of a whirlwind . . . but even so, I knew I wanted to be with you forever. You . . . you get obsessions about things. Math, technology, me. I was dazzled by the passion. We all were. Your passion made you so fucking sexy." I rarely curse, but right now I'm riding on a wave of pure emotion. "You've got to know that every girl in Thackeray had a raging crush on you, don't you? You think it was a coincidence that there was such a sudden rush to learn computer skills when you got hired?" I sit on one of the swings and dig a line in the dirt with my toe. "You know, Zoë was a toddler by the time I realized that I was just another obsession."

"I think you're viewing things through hindsight." Scott runs a hand through his thick, glossy hair and even though, at this moment, I hate him with an intensity akin to love, I find myself wanting to do the same. Our divorce is so recent it still doesn't feel real, although the ninety-eight-pound girlfriend sitting uncomfortably in the living room should be *proof* enough, if I'm still demanding it.

"Maybe I am. Maybe not. I don't know. It's too bad you weren't a history teacher," I say ruefully.

He chuckles. "Why?"

"Because you'd recognize its repetition. You got a Vegas divorce from your first wife because you fell in love with me. You dumped me when you became obsessed with Serena. And please don't try to tell me that woman is a meal ticket, because if you really believe that, you'll starve."

He fixes me with those blazingly intelligent gray-green eyes. "I suppose if it's a numerical sequence, you can tell me what happens next," he says with a tinge of autumnal melancholy.

I nodded. "You move on from Serena, too. Eventually. Scott, Zoë needs a father. You have no idea how hard it is to do this alone. Please don't leave her out of the equation."

"You've got a lot to offer the world, Claire," he says, sort of changing the subject. "Don't neglect your artwork. Don't neglect yourself."

"And when, do you suggest, am I supposed to focus on it? On me? Since you left us, I have no life—but you haven't come around long enough to notice. My social life has become entirely subsumed into our daughter's. Zoë has a busier schedule than the mayor. Except maybe that her bedtime is a bit earlier. I don't see you offering to help out much. Scott, you're supposed to show up every other weekend to be her white knight and take her on an adventure. Lately, you haven't even done tha. You say *you're* too busy. And Zoë doesn't even stay overnight at your place since you're living with Serena. For the other twenty-something days of the month, it's just me. While Zoë makes the rounds of parties and after-school programs, I'm the mommy, the daddy, the chaperone, the chauffeur, the nurse, the teacher, the baby-sitter, the bad cop, the Wicked Witch of the West. And . . ." I feel hot tears welling up behind my eyes. ". . . it's . . . overwhelming. I'm not a selfish person, but there are times when I do wish I had a minute or two to myself. Or a chance to see my own friends—if they even remember who I am by now. I need your help here."

"I'm afraid I'm more of a disruption," my ex says apologetically.

"You are when you bring your girlfriend to family occasions," I mumble, wiping away a tear. I wish I had it in me just to lash out at him, but I've always had problems expressing anger. Although I've been known to lose my temper—as the Thackeray educators would attest—I become horribly uncomfortable and embarrassed by yelling and screaming. Anyone's. "Zoë blames me for the divorce, you know. She adores you. As long as you're her hero, you could at least play the part."

Scott nods toward the house where Serena is sitting, making small talk with Brendan. "Well, the damage is done for the day. I'm sorry about this. I didn't think, after almost half a year, that her presence would have such a negative effect. I'll make it up to you, I give you my promise."

"It amazes me how such a brilliant man can be so clueless about some things. Like human nature. Your promises to me mean nothing, Scott. Make it up to Zoë."

My mother pokes her head out the kitchen door and beckons us inside. "We're just about ready to sit down," she tells us. Scott and I agree to an amicable détente for the remainder of the evening. We go into the house and I send him to speak with Zoë. A few minutes later, they come tromping down the staircase, Zoë riding piggyback.

"Soup's on!" Mommy announces, and we gather in the dining room. "I made little place cards, so everyone can find their own seat. You're over there, Claire," she says, "and Serena, we've added a chair down by my end of the table. I'm sorry you won't be sitting with Scott tonight, but I thought he should be next to his daughter." She smiles at me. "First, we'll say grace and then I'll get the first course and the bread."

We sit, join hands, and bow our heads. "There is a force beyond us, the power of which can never fully be comprehended by humanity," my father says in his rich baritone. "Let us thank this power for its inscrutability. And be thankful, too, that, somewhere between free will and the concept that everything happens for a reason, we are all able to join together at this table together to healthily—and happily—celebrate another Thanksgiving and another natal anniversary for Claire." Daddy raises his eyes and winks at me. "Okay, folks, now we can dig in!"

My mother, Mia, and I jump up from the table to get the soup. "Carrot-ginger, so Zoë will eat it," Tulia tells everyone. "And I made cheddar brioches. Zoë, would you like to get the basket?" My daughter hops off her chair, eager to participate. "Now that's what I like, all my girls helping!" Mia places a bowl of soup in front of Serena and stands back, waiting.

"This is cooked, isn't it?" Serena asks.

Mia gives a little snort. "Can't you see the steam?"

"Then, I'm so sorry, but I can't eat it." She waves away the warm bread, too.

"You're *crazy*!" Zoë says to her, her mouth full of fresh brioche. She tastes her soup, which is pretty sophisticated stuff for a second-grade palate. Still, it's orange, and so are the rolls.

"Z, that's not very nice," I say, trying to keep the peace while suppressing a smile.

"She eats even more weird than *I* do!"

"For your information, my dietary choices are healthy ones and it would benefit mankind and the environment if we all thought about the beasts of the field and the birds of the air when we sat down to a meal."

The conversation picks up speed. "—And speaking of birds of the air," my father says, elegantly gesturing to Serena to zip it, "where's the turkey?"

"You're silly, Grandpa Brendan. Turkeys don't fly!"

"Zoë, don't call your grandfather 'silly,' it's not nice."

"It's fine, Claire. I was doing what's called a segue."

"Oooh, can I have a Segway for my birthday?" Zoë asks me. "Absolutely not."

"Just for kicks and giggles and old times' sake, why don't we go around the table and share what we did today," my father suggests. Mia glares. She's never liked this manifestation of familial bonding. My father acknowledges her look, but says nothing. "Zoë?"

"I went to the parade with MiMi today and I rode on the float with the Powerpuff Girls and I had the best time," she beams.

"That sounds very exciting!"

"It was," she nods.

My father turns to me. "Claire?"

So we *are* going in reverse birth order, according to Marsh tradition and custom. "I had a lovely day until . . ." No, I won't spoil this dinner for the others. Not after my parents have worked so hard. "I waved to Zoë from the living-room window this morning and spent half the afternoon on the Long Island Expressway singing show tunes. But I'm glad to be here sharing the holiday with people I love," I say, ruffling Zoë's hair.

My father smiles. "Your turn, Mia."

"Pass."

Brendan is about to say something when Charles jumps in, leaping to Mia's rescue. "I'll take Mia's turn. I spent the day slaving over a hot stove and a pastry bag, because there's nothing I wouldn't do for my best friend's ageless baby sister, the best tour guide in New York."

I blow him a kiss. "Second best. On a good day."

Scott and Serena exchange glances. "Well, after a successful meal last night at Eden's Garden, where we served a full Thanksgiving dinner with a turkey made out of chopped walnuts and pecans, I closed the restaurant so I could spend the day with my . . . with Scott."

Now it's the Marshes' turn to exchange looks. "Should we kill her now?" Mia mutters. She may sound like she's got a chip on her shoulder, but that's just my sister being loyal, which is one of her loveliest qualities.

"And I thought it would be delightful to see my daughter on Thanksgiving," Scott says.

My mother gestures toward the kitchen. "Well, you all know

what I've been doing today," she says, her voice gay, trying to lighten the mood.

"And the fruits of my labor today will be shared after dinner," my father says, referring to the birthday poem, I assume. "See, Mia, that wasn't so bad."

"On that note, I think I'll get the turkey right now," my mom says, our cue to clear the soup plates. "Mia, Claire, you get the potatoes and the veggies!" Well, at least we're working off the calories by running back and forth from the dining table to the kitchen. Mia ladles the carrots into a bowl and I don the oven mitts and dive for the yam casserole, Tulia's secret recipe, made with Marsh-mallows, as Zoë calls them. For years she thought the candy was named for our family.

Mommy wheels out the turkey on an antique wicker bar. "Ladies and gentlemen . . . meet Hedda Gobbler and her very special dressing, just for my granddaughter!" Yes, *dressing*, as opposed to stuffing. The turkey is wearing an orange paper dress that resembles a frilly Victorian apron. My mother is a highly creative fashion designer, but I'll bet this is the first time her client was a fowl. Leg of lamb paper booties have nothing on Tulia's couture'd bird.

Zoë bursts out laughing. "It's a girl!"

"And it's orange. So, you'll have some, right?" Tulia says playfully.

"I want a wing!"

My father grips his favorite carving knife as if it's Excalibur; and, as he does every year, proclaims, "At last my arm is complete again!" Those of us who have seen *Sweeney Todd* shudder and laugh, also an annual ritual. Brendan carves and Zoë gets her wish, waving the wing in lazy circles above her dinner plate, until I suggest that she might try eating it. She's having such a good time that she forgets to mention that the meat isn't orange anymore, now that its paper apron has been removed.

Basically, we've got an all-orange meal and we're doing just fine until . . .

"Zoë, did you know that carrots have feelings?"

She looks at Serena, mid-forkful, wide-eyed. "Really?"

"Really. And when you pull a carrot from the ground to eat it, it's just like killing an animal for the same purpose. It has feelings. And it feels pain."

Zoë pushes her plate away, leaving most of her food untouched. "You mean it cries?"

"More or less, yes."

"And do its friends cry because it died?"

"Yes, I imagine they do." Six pairs of eyes, including Scott's, turn to glare at Serena.

"Zoë's right about your being crazy. You're a *fucking nut*, you know that?" Mia says, throwing her napkin on the table.

"Mia, language!" my mother cautions.

"Yes, Mia, think of something more creative than 'fucking,' " my father says, abetting her cause.

"Fucking can be *really* creative, Dad," Mia mutters under her breath.

"Sweetheart, eat your dinner," I say, gently nudging Zoë.

"I can't. All my vegetables are crying. And Hedda, too." Now *she's* crying. As if Serena isn't doing enough damage, this is what we get for anthropomorphizing the turkey.

The words start flying across the table again. "Don't listen to her, Zoë, Serena's full of shit!"

"Mia!"

"Yeah I know, Dad, 'shit' isn't creative enough. Do you really want me to run through a bunch of synonyms right now?"

I try to play peacemaker. "Serena, you've upset my daughter. Please tell her that you have a silly sense of humor and that you were making it up."

"She'll have to learn *sometime* that an unenlightened diet makes mankind an accessory to murder."

"Honey, you don't need to be the prosecutor for vegetabular homicide," Scott jests, placing his hand on Serena's forearm.

"Don't patronize me, Scott!" she snaps.

"Don't raw things feel pain?" Mia challenges. "Don't they feel *more* pain when you bite into them, because they're still alive?" I bet if *I* bit Ulysses right now, he'd get real vicious. "While Hedda, here," she says, spearing a slice of tender breast meat, "is long past caring."

"It's different," Serena says defensively. She shifts into the touchy-feely good karma voice that makes me gag. "You see, when you ingest *raw* food, you're absorbing all its nutrients while becoming one with it."

"What?" This is insane.

"Your body absorbs its good energy, Claire. You take on the living spirit of the carrot or the squash or the walnut. When the food is cooked, its karma or spirit dies with it. But when you eat it in its raw state, it understands that by your doing so, you are celebrating its existence and accepting the power of its gift to you—the painful sacrifice of its life—you're accepting the power of its body and soul. It's much the same idea as those practiced by the tribal cultures who believe that when a young man kills a certain animal—a bear, for instance—in a hunt or ritual, he assumes that animal's spirit. Tomato plants are re-markably smart. When we eat the raw tomato instead of a cooked one, we take on its native intelligence—to repel pests, for example."

I find myself wishing tomatoes were more orange so they could have been on the menu. "I'm getting a splitting headache," I announce, but no one is listening. "Isn't it enough that you're ruining my family's Thanksgiving and my birthday celebration by showing up uninvited and then refusing to eat my mother's cooking? Isn't that enough?" I glare at Serena. "No, I guess it's not, because you've decided to take up a crusade to embarrass the lot of us and terrorize my daughter!"

Zoë switches allegiances with alarming alacrity, from believing Serena's malarkey about vegetables in mourning and smart fruit to acting as my champion. "You're a mean lady and I hate you," she yells, lobbing a brioche at Serena. The roll doesn't make it as far as the intended target, but knocks over Serena's water glass instead.

"What have I told you about throwing food?" I say, reaching across her body to grab her wrist just as she's about to toss another missile. "You're making Granny Tulia very unhappy. She worked so hard to make this meal extra special for you." In attempting to intercept the second flying roll, I succeed only in knocking over my own wineglass. A deep claret-colored stain spreads across the linen tablecloth. "Mommy, I'm sorry," I sigh, knowing it needs to be dry-cleaned. "Send me the bill." It's the last thing my budget needs, but it's the least I can do.

Zoë becomes immediately chastened. "I'm sorry, Granny Tulia. Everything was delicious."

"Maybe you should go out and sit in the car," Mia tells Serena.

"You're welcome, sweetheart," my mother says to Zoë, evincing no anger whatever. The Marsh volatility has never fazed her in the least. "We even have a special orange dessert."

Serena glances across the table at Scott, but doesn't budge.

Zoë looks confused. "But Happy Chef made Mommy a birthday cake. With real buttercream. And flowers."

"Oh, dear, and I thought you might not want any birthday cake because it doesn't have orange frosting, so I went and made a pumpkin pie." My mother's poker face is masterful. So much so that Mia hasn't even caught on.

"From scratch?" Mia asks. Tulia nods.

"But . . . but . . . but . . . I want *birthday cake*," Zoë says. Whenever she's working out a difficult situation in her head, she has a tendency to repeat the first word of a sentence until she's got her thought organized.

"Even though it's not orange?"

Zoë takes a dramatic pause, first realizing, then acknowledging and accepting the consequences of her response. "Uh-huh. I want pumpkin pie, too, but it's bad luck not to have birthday cake."

My mother rises and Mia and I begin to clear the dinner things and get ready for dessert. Happy Chef joins us in the kitchen so he can set up the candles in my cake.

"Just be symbolic, okay? Don't go sticking twenty-six candles in that or you'll burn down the house," I tease.

"I wouldn't dream of it." He grins. "Twenty-*seven*. One to grow on, remember?"

"You're evil, you know that?"

"Shut up. You're a kid," Mia says. "You've got another four years before you hit the big three-oh. Now *that's* depressing!"

My mother laughs. "Yes, Mia, you're *sooooo* old. I'm surprised your bones don't creak when you sit. Get over it, both of you!"

"Ladies—and Charles—aren't you forgetting something?" my father calls in from the dining room.

My mother's hand flies to her mouth. "Oh, God, his big moment. Wait, we'll bring the desserts inside, but we can't light Clairey's candles until the end of her poem."

I look at Happy Chef, artfully arranging the candles so as not to spoil the lettering or the roses. "That's the tradition." I shrug. "We've been doing it since forever."

Mia and I bring out the plates and forks, Tulia's got the pumpkin pie, and Charles carries the cake, resting it in front of my place setting.

My father shuffles to his feet, rising as though the birthday poem isn't a big deal at all. I feel a shudder of excitement as my mother rushes back to the kitchen to turn off the light, leaving us illumined only by candleglow. The shadows flicker on the wall and the bayberry scent seems even more intense when the tapers themselves become the stars of the show.

"I've been doing this since Tulia first consented to make me the happiest man alive—for *her* birthdays, and then, when the girls came along, for theirs—and now, for Zoë, too. You all know that I tend to play fast and loose with the classical forms when I write, but I thought, for Claire this year, that I would revisit the sonnet—the Shakespearean, not the Italian—for those of you keeping score. So, be kind, as it isn't my usual thing—"

"Disclaimer, disclaimer, disclaimer," I tease, knowing that whatever he's chosen to write, to say, is quite a gift.

"Well, then, the birthday girl has spoken. So without further ado, 'A Sonnet for Claire on the Occasion of Her Twenty-sixth Birthday.' " Brendan clears his throat and lets the words flow, his voice like velvet in the near darkness.

" *'Mid Hunters' Moon and russet-colored corn*
And autumn days that wax too short for mirth,
A fair-haired child, a pilgrim soul, was born.
We called you Claire, for 'lighting' up the Earth.

You worshipped wonder in your golden youth,
Chased shooting stars and mourned them when they fell.
Along the yellow highway you met truth
With dauntless courage, heart, and brains as well.

Your path is arduous, but with your strength
And dint of will, you surely will prevail.
To reach the pot of gold at rainbow's length
You'll try again, if ever you should fail.

With child in hand, surmounting double strife
You'll beat the odds—and win the game of life."

"That's really beautiful, Daddy. Thank you." My eyes are wet, my vision blurred by tears. Tulia and Mia murmur their compliments. Scott looks uncomfortable, Serena more so.

"I could really use a cigarette," she says, getting up from the table. She glides out of the room and leaves the house.

"She doesn't *smoke*, does she?" I ask Scott, thinking how hypocritical it would be for Miss Raw Food to be having a nic-fit.

"No, Claire, she doesn't. She just said she could really *use* a butt right now. She's under a lot of pressure this evening."

"And I'm not? Thanks to you?"

"I liked Mommy's poem a lot, too," Zoë says.

"Well, fire her up, Charles," my mother instructs Happy Chef. He strikes a match and lights the candles while everyone, minus the missing Serena, sings Happy Birthday. Zoë, the little wench, insists on taking a solo, singing the "how old are you now?" verse, thereby compelling me to reply. I wish I could lie about my age, but the cat's already out of the bag, and besides, it would be teaching my daughter a bad lesson, so I'm screwed, and warble the truth.

"Make a wish, Mommy! And don't forget to close your eyes. And don't say it out loud or it won't come true."

Once, it would have been for a great pair of shoes or a bracelet, or a fabulous vacation. World peace is out of my control. Come to think of it, I could still use that vacation. I shut my eyes and send my little prayer to the birthday gods, then take a deep breath. Everyone knows that if you don't blow out all your candles in one shot, your wish won't come true. Why do you think I didn't want twenty-seven candles? But I wish and I whoosh and I get 'em all.

I start to cut the cake, and Zoë reminds me that the birthday girl gets the first slice, so I set mine aside and start serving the rest of the family. Serena returns to the table and waves her hand to decline dessert. Not even the pumpkin pie, because it, too, is dead. Zoë and Mia start to attack Serena again, but I shush them. One food fight per meal is more than enough.

My mother, who has been passing around plates of pumpkin pie, sends down a plate for Zoë and winks at me. I take the hint and stop slicing my birthday cake at six pieces, then sit down to dig into my own.

Zoë looks at her plate. "But . . . but . . . but . . . I said I wanted birthday cake, too." Her eyes tear up as though she's turned on a faucet behind them.

"I was just double-checking. I didn't want to ruin your special diet by serving you food that wasn't orange," I say evenly.

"I told you, Mommy, it's *bad luck* not to."

"Okay," I sigh, catching my mother's eye. She grins. "It's your rule."

Zoë tucks into the birthday cake with the fervor of someone whose jaw has just been unwired. She puts down her fork and looks up. "The rule is . . . the *rule* is . . . the rule *is* . . ." She says, waggling her hands, as though that will help her to better organize her thought. "The rule *is* that once you have one thing that isn't orange, you don't have to have everything orange anymore."

My mother, part psychologist, part partner in crime, sucks in her cheeks, trying to hide our giddy victory from her granddaughter. The spell is broken. I sigh, exhaling enough air to extinguish another twenty-seven birthday candles and blow Tulia a grateful kiss.

Chapter 8

 Dear Diary:

Mommy and I are fighting. After Thanksgiving and her birthday, she asked me to think about what kind of birthday party I want to have. Ashley's mommy and daddy gave her a Barbie party at a really fancy toy store when she had her birthday. All the girls in our class were there. We got to dress up in our pajamas and sleep in the store. It was so fun. I asked if we could do that, but I want a Powerpuff Girls party instead of Barbie. Mommy said we couldn't do that this year. I asked her why and she said because it costs a lot of money to have all those little girls at a party at the store. So I said maybe I could only invite a few people, like the girls who are really my best friends instead of the whole class. Except at my school we are supposed to invite the whole class when we have birthday parties so nobody feels left out. I want to invite Xander Osborne, so maybe I shouldn't have a Powerpuff Girls party because boys don't care about the Powerpuff Girls.

Mommy told me if I wanted I could have a Powerpuff Girls party at home with a PPG tablecloth and napkins and party favors. But that's not fun. That's for babies and all my friends do stuff that's really special and grown-up for their birthdays.

My friend Ben from yoga class had his birthday party at the planetarium. We all watched the movie about how the Earth was created and the big bang. I don't think Ben's dad liked it very much. He's a rabbi. He walked out of the movie and almost tripped on the stairs because it was so dark. He stepped on Mommy's foot because he couldn't see where he was going. Afterwards we had cake and ice cream and pizza and we had a quiz on all the planets and the kids who got the answers right got prizes. I got a glow-in-the-dark mobile of the planets and it's hanging in my room over my bed.

Everything I asked Mommy if we could do for my birthday, she said no. She kept saying I should think of something else and when I did, then she told me we couldn't do it. It's not fair. She made me cry and then I made her cry. And then I went into my room and closed the door hard and cried on my bed. Only Baa understands what kind of party I want.

Mommy came into my room and said we have to talk like big girls. That if I don't want a party for babies, then I shouldn't act like one. So I asked if we could all go to a play like we did for April and May's party last spring. That's for big girls. Because my birthday is the same day as Christmas Eve, maybe we could go see the Rockettes, like Mommy and I do together every Christmas. I want to be a Rockette when I grow up. They get to wear lots of different outfits in their show. My favorite one is the purple velvet one with the white trim. It looks like an ice-skating dress. Maybe next year I can take tap-dancing instead of ballet. If I don't become a Rockette I might be an astronaut when I grow up because I really like the planets and the stars. Or I could be a Rockette at Christmas when they have their show and then the rest of the year I could be an astronaut.

Mommy said no to the Rockette show and no Powerpuff Girls sleepover party at the really fancy toy store.

Ashley's big sister Tennyson had a party at their summer house, which is near where Granny Tulia and Grandpa Brendan live. They have little ponies that are as big as really big dogs and we got rides on them. I got to go to the party because I'm Ashley's best friend and Mommy and I went out there on the train and we stayed overnight at Grandpa Brendan and Granny Tulia's. Ashley and Tennyson's mom and dad have a big room where they can show movies. It looks just like a real movie theater, only smaller. So after the pony rides and swimming in their pool, we saw the new Disney movie that isn't even in the real movie theaters yet. We had popcorn from a popcorn making cart they have that looks like the one at the circus. I know we don't have ponies but maybe we could have something like that. Mommy said she would think about it but she didn't look like she was thinking very hard.

Mommy always has to work now. Her job gave her more tours so sometimes she can't pick me up from school. When she has to work, I go home with Ashley or I go to April and May's house for a play date. Sometimes MiMi comes to get me, when she doesn't have to work. Last week after school MiMi came to get me and we took a taxi down to the Lord and Taylor store to see the Christmas windows. They were all from Peter Pan and they had puppets that flew inside the windows. Michael had his teddy bear and John had his umbrella and his black hat and Wendy was blonde and wore her hair pulled up at the sides and in a little bun just like my imaginary friend Wendy.

We walked up Fifth Avenue and we stopped to look at the big Christmas tree and the people skating and we saw the Christmas windows at the fancy store near there, too. That store had an old-fashioned Christmas in the windows and it looked like the house that Granny Tulia and Grandpa Brendan have in Sag Harbor. The windows had Christmas trees decorated with candles on them and fireplaces and ladies in beautiful long dresses and kids playing with old toys. My feet ~~hurted~~ started to hurt so we got in *another taxi and we went to the Plaza Hotel and we had hot chocolate with Marsh-mallows and looked at the painting of Eloise. I bet Eloise could have had any kind of birthday party she wanted. She would have just had to say it, and Nanny would have said it was okay.*

MiMi took me home after that and then after I said hi to my Mommy, I went into my room to read Harriet the Spy *and I heard Mommy and MiMi get in a fight. Mommy said to MiMi that SHE had wanted to take me to see the windows and the Christmas tree because we do that together every year at this time. And SHE wanted to take me to see Eloise, too, as her special treat to me for getting 100s on all my spelling and writing tests. Mommy told MiMi that she was spoiling me. I don't know what that means, but spoiled things like milk and meat aren't good things and you have to throw them away.*

When I heard Mommy say that, I came into the kitchen where she and MiMi were talking because I didn't want her to throw me away. I was crying and she told me not to cry. She said she would never throw me away in a million thousand years and that "spoiled" is an expression. She said it means that MiMi was giving me so many special treats that I would get used to having treats all the time and not like to do normal stuff anymore.

MiMi said she likes to take me places and it makes her happy to do it. It makes me happy too and I told them. I told Mommy that I love doing nice stuff with her, too, but that we hardly ever get to do that anymore. They told me to go play in my room, but I didn't want to do that. I wanted to be with them in the kitchen, so I had a glass of milk and I stayed.

MiMi told Mommy it wasn't HER fault that Mommy is so busy. She said that just because things are hard for Claire, it doesn't mean that she (MiMi) should be stopped from taking me fun places and getting me treats. MiMi said to Mommy that she makes "good money" (what is bad money?) and Mommy has no right to tell her how to spend it. Mommy said she didn't like it that MiMi was acting like the mommy. She said MiMi was "playing house" with me and that having a child is more than going to fun places together. She said MiMi doesn't see me when I'm sick or in a bad mood. And she said that if MiMi had a child of her own, she'd see how hard it is to raise her.

Then they were really shouting at each other and it made me so sad because I hate it when people are mad at each other and I hate shouting. I went away when they started shouting again and I crawled under the piano, which is where I like to hide when people fight. That's where I went to hide when Mommy and Daddy started fighting. There is a big red pillow and a big orange pillow under the piano and I would crawl in between them and make a Zoë sandwich until they stopped being mad at each other.

MiMi is the best aunt in the whole world! I love her so much. Sometimes I wish I lived with her instead of with Mommy. Mommy is always saying what I'm not allowed to do. And sometimes she even yells at me, even though she always says how much she hates yelling. I don't like it when she yells so I yell back. MiMi doesn't make me do my homework. And one time she took me to a makeup store for grown-ups called Sephora and she let me pick out a nail polish. I couldn't decide what color I wanted and they had all the colors in the rainbow. I thought yellow or orange or blue or green would have looked yucky and I don't like red polish and I wanted something special so I picked purple. We went back to MiMi's house and she painted my nails for me. Mommy never did that. She doesn't let me wear nail polish. She says it doesn't look nice on little girls and I can have it when I grow up, but that's a billion years from now and I don't want to wait that long.

I have another problem. Miss Gloo, my ballet teacher, says we have to be at her studio right after school for final practice for our recital, but final ballet practice is the same time as the whole school's Christmas pageant and Mrs. Hennepin and the headmaster, Mr. Kiplinger, said that nobody is allowed to miss the pag-

eant. I'm supposed to sing in it, too. My class is doing "The Little Drummer Boy" and I have a solo line and everybody else in the class sings the "pa-rum-pum-pum-pum" part. In art class we made torches with flashlights and red and yellow and orange tissue paper and we're going to walk down the risers in the gym down to the floor where we will sing, but we start the song at the top of the risers. It will be all dark in the gym except for our torches.

I really want to sing at school. I like singing and I don't get scared to do it in front of other people. But Miss Gloo says if we miss the last recital practice or we're late, then we can't be in it. And I really like ballet, too. We're doing "The Waltz of the Flowers" from The Nutcracker *with real costumes and everything. The costumes are so pretty. We're all going to be wearing different flower colors. Ashley's is blue and my friend Chauncey's is pink. My tutu is yellow. My favorite color. I asked for yellow and Miss Gloo said yes. And we get to wear ribbons and flowers made of silk in our hair.*

MiMi is taking me to the real Nutcracker *at Lincoln Center for my Christmas present. This is another thing that Mommy and MiMi got mad at each other about. Mommy said that SHE wanted to take me to* The Nutcracker *as a present for being in my ballet recital. And MiMi said she wanted it to be HER birthday present to me. Mommy told MiMi that MiMi is taking away all the things that SHE wants to do with me as a Mommy.*

· · · · · · · · · · · ·

There was a "police emergency" in the subway—which usually means a body on the tracks—so I barely made it on time to Zoë's ballet class this afternoon.

As I sit in the waiting area, I suddenly remember that it's my turn to bring snack this week. Fortunately, there's a Korean grocer on the corner, so I rush back to grab some grapes and a bunch of juice boxes. The Atkins devotees will just have to suck it up. Or not, actually. At the last minute, I pick up some peanuts and trail mix, too. Unimaginative, I know, but I don't have all day to play dietitian and food stylist. This is the kind of snack that dads can get away with. Everyone finds it charming when a father shows up with nothing but a brick of Cracker Barrel and a box of Triscuits. That doesn't cut it for the moms, however. We're expected to Martha Stewart it.

The little girls are adorable, practicing their dance for the end of season recital. Some of them, my daughter among them— ham that she is—really glow when they know they have an audience.

After class, Miss Gloo, the ballet mistress, gracefully crooks a slender finger and invites me to listen to whatever it is she has to say. "I hope you've taken care of Zoë's scheduling conflict," she begins. "She's such a bright light up there. I'd hate to lose her for the performance."

Zoë is double-booked. Her Thackeray holiday pageant coincides directly with Miss Gloo's recital. "I'm working on it," I assure her, omitting the fact that I don't exactly have Favored Nation status at Zoë's school these days.

"Oh . . . and one other thing," Miss Gloo says, her face coloring ever so slightly. She lowers her voice. "I still haven't gotten your check yet."

"My check?"

"For Zoë's recital costume. We rent them from a professional costume house. The seventy-five dollars covers the cost of the rental, plus the fee for shipping and for dry-cleaning the costume after the performance."

I will my eyes not to pop. "And she's going to wear this costume for . . . ?"

"Her class's dance runs about ten minutes. And of course, there's the final dress rehearsal and run-though the same afternoon."

"I'm sorry—I must have . . . Zoë must have forgotten to give

me the permission form. This is the first I've heard of it." I open
my purse to look for my checkbook.

"You . . . you can charge it instead, if you prefer," Miss Gloo
says. I think she's figured out my situation and is trying to help
me handle it gracefully. I do appreciate her compassion.

"Thanks very much. I'll do that, then." At the front desk I fork
over my credit card. It buys me another month to worry about
paying for a little yellow tutu that will be worn for all of twenty
minutes.

•••••••••••

Whatever I do turns out wrong these days. I love taking Zoë
out—I feel like a modern-day Auntie Mame—but it's pissing off
Claire. We had a huge blowup over it last week. For months,
she's done nothing but schlep Zoë from place to place and I
know she's burned out. So, I figured I would step in and help her.
But she's not making it easy; I say I want to take my niece somewhere, Claire says *she* wanted to do that. But she *didn't* do it.
And now that she's working so hard, when was she going to get
to it? She's running herself ragged just to be sure she's got the
money for her co-op's monthly maintenance payments. Mommy
and Daddy offered to help her out but they already pitch in a lot.
They pay for most of Zoë's education. And Claire hates hand-
outs. It's a lose-lose deal. So what's the trade-off? Do I say,
"Okay, I won't bring Zoë to the places *you* want to take her to?"
Great. I can live with that. But then the kid doesn't get to go at
all, because Claire can't swing it.

I love my time with Zoë. And I have a great job, really feel
blessed to be making a living doing what I love. Each job is an adventure. But the more I get to know Zoë, the more I see what I
lack. A piece of me is missing. Maybe I'm beginning to acknowledge that I want to be a mom. I *do* want it all. Three decades of
feminist history tell me it's possible. Do-able. To at least want it.

Although right now I want to wring Claire's neck. I don't know how she does it as well as she does. I know this: I could not be a single mom. I'm hitting a crossroads in February—the big three-oh—so I've been searching my soul a lot. And I can count up what I still want on one hand. Two fingers, in fact. Husband. Child.

I think it's time for a trip to my astrologer. Celestia Schwartz lives near St. Mark's Place, and like a good table at Balthazar, it takes weeks to get an appointment. But you can't be allergic to cats, if you plan to go there. They'll climb all over you during your session. She gave me a kitten once as a gift, many years ago, and the poor thing turned out to be incontinent. It also clawed its way through a one-of-a-kind design by my mom. Tulia was not too cool about that and it takes a lot to knock her off-balance. The kitten went back to Celestia. She told me it had been home-sick and its karma had gotten messed up by leaving her, and she should have foreknown that might happen. She gave me a free session to make up for it. *That* was a gift, too; she charges two hundred and twenty-five bucks for a reading. It might be a fun birthday present for Zoë, too. My niece is a Capricorn. An old soul in a little body. Sometimes I'm amazed by what the kid is thinking. She's way ahead of me in some ways. Like with men, for instance. I bounce from guy to guy, hoping each will turn out to be The One. She's got her One all picked out. Xander Os-borne, holy terror of Thackeray's second-grade classes. He may yet beat the Marsh sisters' record in the hell-raising department. With Christmas around the bend, Zoë's already learned about mistletoe. Now, *that's* a Marsh woman!

••••••••••••

"What about 'July in Christmas'?" I ask Zoë. She makes a funny face. This is, at a conservative estimate, probably our thirty-ninth conversation regarding a theme for her upcom-ing birthday party. "There's an expression—'Christmas in

July,' " I explain, telling her what it means. "So, what if we do the opposite?"

"The opposite?" She's still looking at me as though I'm six letters shy of the full alphabet.

"Yeah!" From concept to realization, my brain is working at a furious pace. I share my epiphanies as fast as they come. "It's really cold and yucky out in December, right?" Zoë nods. Duh. She's with me so far. "Remember when we talked about Tennyson Silver-Katz's birthday with the barbecue?"

"And with the ponies?" she asks, wide-eyed. This is too good to be true.

"No ponies, sorry. But what if we had a real picnic? Underneath their winter coats, everyone could dress in shorts and dresses like it's summertime. And we could have checkerboard tablecloths on the floor and pink lemonade and hot dogs and hamburgers and macaroni salad—"

"Granny Tulia's recipe?" she asks, sensing that maybe Mommy isn't such a dullard after all.

"Absolutely! And since we'll invite her and Grandpa Brendan to come in from Sag Harbor, maybe she'll make it for us herself."

"Yum!"

"It's even orange!" My mother adds Kraft Catalina dressing to the recipe. Her now not-so-secret ingredient.

Zoë rolls her eyes. "I'm over that. I don't *have* to eat just orange food anymore. Remember?" She gets another idea and starts bouncing up and down on the dinette chair. "Oh, oh, oh, can . . . can . . . can Happy Chef make me a special birthday cake? Something July in Christmasish."

"I bet he will, if we ask him nicely."

"I want a mermaid. Who looks like me. With blonde hair. But she has to be birthdayish and Christmasish too."

"I'm sure Happy Chef will think of something super-special that fits all your requirements." I feel like a huge weight has been lifted from my chest. We can have the party at home and a little creative thinking can transform the place from an Upper West Side apartment into a Fourth of July picnic. Under a tinseled tree.

"I know something else Julyish. Fireworks!" Zoë chirps.

The oppressive weight rolls back into place. "I don't think so, sweetie. But . . ." *Let's go, right brain, kick it up another notch or two* . . . "What if . . . what if we made decorations that look like exploding fireworks with colored streamers? We can make it an arts and crafts project we do together. How does that sound?"

My daughter is not taken in by my extra-wide smile. "Why can't we have real fireworks?"

"How 'bout you answer that one yourself? Look up. What do you see?"

"The ceiling."

"So?"

She laughs. "They'll have no place to go and we could have a fire. But . . . but . . . but . . . but . . . we could have them outside!"

"Where? We don't have a terrace."

"No, silly! In the park!"

"Fireworks in Central Park?"

I'm getting the Mommy-is-an-idiot look again. "They do it all the time, remember? We look out the window and see them in the summertime with the concerts at night and when it's the New Year."

"You're right. You're absolutely right. But you need to get a special permit from the police department to set off fireworks in Central Park."

"So, get a permit," she says, as if I'm still missing something.

"Zoë, your party's going to be in the daytime, anyway. You wouldn't even be able to see the fireworks." I watch her working on another counterattack. This is not going to be as easy a sell as I had hoped. "Why don't we talk about the guest list," I suggest, trying to make a clean segue.

"Everybody. But not Mrs. Heinie-face. I have to invite every-one from my classes and some of their moms and dads and I want my daddy and MiMi and Happy Chef because he's mak-ing my cake and Granny Tulia and Grandpa Brendan." Her eyes are shining. "At least if we have the party here we won't have to worry about how to get all the presents home."

Though I'm pleased that she's become excited about this home-made July-in-Christmas party idea, I frown. "You know it's not all about the presents. Birthdays are supposed to be your chance to share your own special day with all the people who are important to you." What am I blathering? The kid has to invite all her class-mates, including those she rarely speaks to, has never gone on a play date with, and would not ordinarily see outside of school, were it not for Thackeray's attempt to level the playing field. The inclusive exclusive-private-school version of No Child Left Behind. How-ever, given the kinds of lavish affairs hosted for grammar schoolers by their moneyed parents, the parties themselves have become a competition, not between the kids, but among the adults. *You're right, Zoë*, I'm thinking. *It is about the presents. Damn it.*

We make a list of all the children's names so I can get an idea of exactly how many invitations we'll need and the proper way to address them.

"Don't forget Xander," Zoë says, panicked that I might. She watches over my shoulder, just to be sure.

"Alexander Osborne," I write.

"Not Alexander. *Xander*."

"Xander's a nickname for Alexander, sweetie. Like Al or Alex or Alec."

"His real name's Xander," she insists. "Xander Pope Osborne. His mom didn't want anyone to ever call him Al."

The names these days! From the loopy to the pretentious. J.D. Tift. Tennyson. Shelton. All of those are girls, by the way. And there's actually a little girl in her yoga class named Junior. A year and a half ago I wouldn't have guessed that her good friend Chauncey was a girl if I didn't know her from ballet class. I think parents are doing their kids a disservice by foisting gender-neutral monikers on them. Chances are, the outside world isn't going to figure it out the first time around.

I despair of the sort of goody bags I'll have to coordinate in order to keep up with the Osbornes and their ilk. God, I used to live in that world back when Scott was earning money hand over fist. It disgusted me then, but I fell into lock-step with the rest of them because we could afford to and because I didn't want to embarrass Zoë. Now I have no other option but to give her a birthday party as close to what I really feel is appropriate for a second grader and her friends. And there's a part of me that feels very good about that. Relieved, somehow.

Claire Marsh is going to buck convention by throwing her daughter a conventional birthday party. The kind she had when *she* was growing up. I can hear Nina Osborne now. *How . . . retro.*

I just hope Zoë survives it.

∙∙∙∙∙∙∙∙∙∙∙∙

Dear Diary:

It's snowing! MiMi took me to see The Nutcracker *this afternoon and when we came outdoors it was snowing. All the buildings in Lincoln Center where they have the ballet are white, and they were covered with white and the ground was white and it was so beautiful. I didn't have a hat on because we didn't know it was going to snow and I hate wearing a hat in the winter. I only do it if it's snowing and Mommy makes me wear one. So the snowflakes landed on my head and it was like I was a fairy princess with sparkly jewels in my hair. MiMi said, "Follow me!" and we danced in a circle around the fountain in the middle of all the buildings. There's no water in it now because it's almost wintertime and they only have water in it in the summer, but we danced anyway. MiMi said I should do exactly what she did, and she kept doing all sorts of silly steps and I did them too. People stopped and were looking at us and some of them did a few silly dance steps for a couple of seconds but then they stopped. MiMi doesn't care if people are looking at her and she told me if I was having fun, I shouldn't care either.*

Then she stuck her tongue out and was trying to catch snowflakes on the tip of it, so I did the same thing, and then she tasted one and she said "umm, butterscotch." So I caught a snowflake and pretended to taste it and said "yum, blueberry," which is one of my favorite flavors. That and raspberry. Then MiMi caught one and said "piña colada," and she made me laugh because I know that's a summertime flavor. I caught another snowflake and said "Grandpa Brendan's spareribs." He's going to bring them for my birthday party. We're going to have all my favorite foods from when I go to Granny Tulia and Grandpa Brendan's house in the summer. And my birthday cake from Happy Chef is going to have real blueberries and raspberries on it and it will be red, white, and blue for July and red and green for Christmas. My mermaid is going to have holly berries in her hair and she's going to be riding on Rudolph instead of on a seahorse.

I loved The Nutcracker. One of my favorite parts was where the Christmas tree kept getting bigger and bigger from magic and it got so big that it was bigger than Clara's house. The fight with all the giant mice and the Mouse King scared me a little but I knew that the Nutcracker was going to win. MiMi whispered to me something about the big mice and the subway but I didn't think it was funny. Now I'm scared to go in the subway. The Sugar Plum Fairy was the most beautiful lady I have ever seen. She was even more pretty than Janyce from the Powerpuff Girls float on Thanksgiving. I loved it the best when she danced on her toes.

Mommy is giving a tour this afternoon. I can't wait to get home and tell her all about how beautiful the ballet was and about how MiMi and me had fun after it.

Chapter 9

I feel like I've done nothing but shop. And I haven't really bought anything. I haven't even started on yuletide gifts for my family or birthday and holiday presents for Zoë. At least I've begun to work on the items for the goody bags and have selected the paper goods for her July in Christmas party—which isn't easy, given the fact that such things are seasonal and the local party goods suppliers have been looking at me like I'm nuts when I ask for red, white, and blue stuff. They retreat to the stock room, grumbling all the way, and return with some dusty shrink-wrapped tablecloths and napkins that for some reason they never returned to the manufacturer as soon as Labor Day rolled around. Then they have the nerve to want to charge me a premium because the items are out of season.

Thinking out of the box is, at the very least, much more creative than just cutting a check and letting a professional party planner, or the venue, work their magic. I found someone in the press office of the Brooklyn Cyclones, the Mets' local minor league farm team, who will provide me with some kid-size premium items. Their season's long over and they'll have new tee-shirts made up next spring. That ought to delight the boys, anyway. A little additional persuasion and the marquee-name former Mets who now coach and manage the team, agreed to sign a few things that I can give away as prizes for games like Pin the Tail on the Donkey and Musical Chairs—which I'll have to organize as heats, since I have neither the space nor the chairs for forty-plus kids to sit on at once. I wonder if they even know how to play these old-fashioned birthday party games.

For the girls and whatever moms decide to tag along, I'm making jewelry items out of summery-looking "findings": brightly colored beads and little plastic cherries, strawberries, fish, and butterflies, mixed in with wintry symbols like holly and ivy. It may sound like a bit of a fashion risk, but the concept does seem to work, and it's the most creative thing I've done in weeks. No two designs are identical, though the earrings are matched pairs. I have everything stored in tackle boxes and at night after Zoë goes to sleep, I sit in front of the TV and bead, bead, bead. It's very relaxing, actually.

This afternoon, I've got a bunch of Parisians on my sightseeing tour. Zoë and Mia are off at *The Nutcracker*. I had to relent, much as it pained me, and allow Mia to treat Zoë to the ballet. Between my tour schedule and organizing the birthday party, I admit I am significantly swamped.

The French do love their cinema, so the "Location! Location! Location!" tour tends to be a hit with them. This month I've added sites where holiday classics like *Miracle on 34th Street* (all three versions—I sound like the old ladies from the *Harry/Sally* orgasm tour)—were shot. Or would have been, had not Hollywood back lots and soundstages been the sometime stand-ins for New York City. I wish I could think of a Jerry Lewis movie to include. I pride myself on customization.

However, I quickly ascertain that my Parisians have little interest in how Hollywood celebrates Noël in New York. So I opt to show them some Upper West Side standbys, starting with the über-deli Zabar's, a frequent co-star in local films. The corner of

83rd and Amsterdam is also a good place to land, since some of *Hi Life* was filmed on that corner at the funky, deco-decorated bar of the same name; and Café Lalo, a particularly charming old-world patisserie, was where Meg Ryan awaited her mystery date in *You've Got Mail*. It's another one of the food stops on my movie location tours, so this should work out well.

Sacre bleu! Quelle mistake!

I've always thought that Lalo served up some of the best desserts I've ever tasted. In fact, I've blown many a diet just because the pastries looked and smelled so good I just had to sample them. Ah, but not for *mes très* discerning *amis*. We commandeer the entire restaurant—and it's small—while my Parisians sit down for cappuccino and cakes.

Mais non, they sneer at the filling in the éclairs. The *millefeuille* dough in the napoleons isn't crisp enough to suit their finely honed Gallic palates. This could be my Waterloo. They insist on smoking inside the eatery, decrying our city ordinance that prohibits lighting up in restaurants and bars as the most ridiculous act of American jurisprudence since innocent-before-proven-guilty. I am mortified by the way they treat the staff and find myself near tears, apologizing profusely to the management. At least there are no other customers in the café to be tainted by my tourists' appalling snobbishness. And people think *New Yorkers* are rude!

L'addition s'il vous plait! I collect their money, reminding them that the tip is *not* included west of the Champs-Elysées, pay the bill as fast as I can, and usher them back onto the bus.

Fine. We'll do something more French. I ask Frank to drive down Columbus Avenue, and stop at 76th Street so we can get out and admire the façade of Andie MacDowell's apartment building in *Green Card*. Not a good movie, even by B-picture standards—I fell asleep watching it on an airplane—but it's all about Franco-American relations, so to speak; and after all, Gérard Depardieu is one of their national treasures, and an international hunk—or used to be—at least in my humble opinion, weight problem or not. I've never minded a bit of extra *avoir du poids*.

There are many aspects of the French that I highly admire: their culture, couture, and cuisine. Their art and architecture. The fact that they all take off for the entire month of August. And I studied their language in high school and in college. That said, these particular natives are making me ashamed of my Francophilia. In fact, they are setting my New York teeth on edge. Couldn't they at least *pretend* they're having fun? Was Lafayette the last Frenchman to enjoy America?

We hop off the bus and walk a few yards along 76th Street. "*Mesdames et messieurs*, if you look over here—*cette maison meublée*—you will see the apartment building where the American woman Bronte (now *there's* a name!)—Andie (another one!) MacDowell—and the Frenchman—Gérard Depardieu—shared the garden apartment when she bailed him out of his immigration predicament and married him so he could get his Green Card, in the movie of the same name. This kind of building is very typical—*très typique* of the neighborhood—*dans notre quartier*."

They begin to mutter among themselves. I hear one ask another what I had said. *Now* they're deciding to pretend they understand no English? I thought they only do that over there. *En français*, the word for "snob" is exactly the same.

" 'Bail out?' 'Bail-out?' *Qu'est-ce-que c'est* 'bail out'?" They are frowning, grumbling.

"Bail out? It means to rescue . . . save—*sauver—secouvrir, délivrer*," I say, trying on a bunch of synonyms, hoping one will fit. "We Americans have been bailing out your Gallic butts for centuries." It was intended to be a lighthearted joke, although all jokes have their roots in reality, and my guests are now grating on my second-to-last nerve.

"I have understood that Americans are not students of history, but you have education, evidently. You speak French *pas mal* . . . not badly . . . for an American. You have studied the Revolution, yes?" a wiry man asks me. For most of the afternoon, he has been scratching at his mustache, as though it's pasted to his upper lip with spirit gum.

"Which revolution? Yours or ours?"

"I was speaking of yours. The American Revolution. When I believe it was the French who helped to save *your* uncivilized *butts*, as you say."

I wonder if the word "gall"—as in insolence, impertinence, rudeness, audacity, effrontery, or chutzpah—comes from "Gallic," somehow. "And I believe the last time Franco-American relations were truly amicable, apart from World Wars I and II, when we saved your collective *derrières* again—was during the War of 1812," I smile. "And if I recall my history lessons correctly, the reason it was harder for our 'uncivilized' G.I.s to push those pesky Nazis out of your sidewalk cafés, was . . . oh, wait, it's on the tip of my tongue—it sounds like a lovely soup: *Vichy.*"

Mon ami is not amused. His face turns an apoplectic shade of *rouge*. Swept away by jingoism, he utters a rather unfortunate epithet. I say unfortunate because I happen to understand it. And I don't appreciate the sum total of my being referred to, or reduced to, a single below-the-belt body part.

Better judgment evanesces. I retaliate, calling him a bastard and a pig in his native tongue, which isn't nearly as nasty as what he'd just said to me.

It could get uglier in a minute or two. And it's starting to snow.

I herd my group back onto the bus, trying to do enough damage control to stave off a true battle royal. But, as we motor to the next sight, Tavern on the Green, my nemesis continues to push, prod, and provoke, until the words just come tumbling out of my mouth. "Yes, your country is gorgeous and your food is superb, but what about that fly-space issue during the Gulf

War? And your government's inflexible position on the invasion of Iraq—which, no doubt, was at least partially predicated on the extent to which France and Saddam had been cuddling up to one another economically. And there were the centuries of anti-Semitism." I've never been political in my life, and suddenly opinions are pouring out of me like water over an unchecked dam. I have violated one of the cardinal rules of international camaraderie: *Never discuss sex, religion, or politics.*

By the time we return to the Go Native! tour office, it would have taken the entire General Council of the U.N. Assembly to reestablish détente.

Monsieur Fouché—the same name as Napoleon's infamous Minister of Police, oh, this does not bode well—marches himself into the tiny room and immediately launches into an emotional tirade. He is the group's organizer, and on behalf of his countrymen he demands a full refund. My boss asks for my side of the story and I explain that it began as a linguistic misunderstanding that quickly got out of hand, degenerating into childish name-calling, which I admit was less than professional on my part, but (putting aside my earlier remarks as hyperbole), I doubted that the unfortunate skirmish of words heralded the end of official diplomatic relations between our two nations. My boss rolls his eyes at me and without another word, proceeds to quiescently refund the Parisians' money. This seems to satisfy Monsieur Fouché, leading me to wonder whether his group tries this everywhere they go, provoking their guides into fits of pique, then insisting on reparations.

They depart the Go Native! office for their next tour: the Statue of Liberty, where I suppose they will congratulate themselves on their country's generosity to this city of non-smoking ingrates. If they could, they would probably rewrite the final line of Emma Lazarus's ode to immigration so it snidely reads, "I lift my lamp beside your golden arches."

"I'm sorry about what happened this afternoon," I tell my

boss. I am genuinely contrite. "At least I'm willing to admit my mistakes," I add, with a nervous half laugh. I cross my fingers behind my back the way I used to when I was a little girl.

My boss motions to the chair opposite his desk, a gunmetal gray monstrosity that might have looked modern during the dawn of the Cold War. "Have a seat, Claire." I do. This doesn't feel good. "Claire, you're a very intelligent woman."

"Thank you, sir."

"And when you're on the ball, you're really on it. You're bright, articulate, personable . . . in essence, everything we look for at Go Native!"

"Thank you, sir."

"But . . . we have some judgment issues to discuss. I know you have a young child at home or in school, but you can't just up and leave a tour to fetch her."

"That was an extenuating circumstance. I got a call from the school nurse. My daughter was ill and I had to take her home. I don't have child care anymore, now that I'm divorced—" This is far more information than this man needs to know. So I bite my tongue and leave it at that.

"Once, I can understand. And, although we placed a reprimand in your file, had nothing else occurred, I could overlook it. But you abandoned an entire marching band in the middle of the Roosevelt Island tramway, Claire!"

"Almost, but not quite," I admit sheepishly.

"Another 'extenuating circumstance,' I suppose."

"Well . . . yes, actually . . . and the chaperones said they were fine with my needing to leave. The tour was running over schedule, and I had to pick up my daughter at four P.M. on the other end of town."

"Not everyone was 'fine,' Claire. And even if they had been, this is your job and your responsibility is to finish what you start. I have a business to run and much of my success depends on good word of mouth. Now, I'm aware that this is your first job. And I don't think you take the concept of employment very seriously."

I assure him that I do and that this job is very important to me and that I can't afford to lose it. What can I do to atone for my transgressions?

My boss shakes his head. "I'm afraid that today was the third strike. I can't have you insulting our clients, no matter how obnoxiously they may behave. You've got to be the grown-up and pretend to be deaf, or turn the other cheek."

I'm being told to act either retarded or Christ-like. And I feel like I'm seven years old. *I will not cry. I will not cry. I will not cry.* And I wish I didn't always have to be the grown-up. It's exhausting.

He opens a file drawer and removes a large check ledger. "I'm afraid I'm going to have to let you go."

"But . . . but . . . but . . ." I sound like Zoë. "But Christmas is just around the corner. I won't be able to buy my daughter presents." I may sound like the beleaguered Bob Cratchit, but it's true. "And her birthday is coming up. It's on Christmas Eve, and I haven't shopped for that yet, either."

"You know I'm not a hardass," my boss says. "But I can't do it, Claire. I run a competitive business and three complaints about a single employee within just a couple of months' time . . . ?" He leans back in his chair and folds his hands across his ample belly. I notice a gravy stain on the front of his navy double-knit shirt. "If you were in my position, what would you do?"

"*Four* strikes?" I ask meekly, hoping for a smile, at least.

He shakes his head and writes a check. "This is for this week's pay plus two weeks' severance. I can't give you another chance; I'm no patsy. But I'm no Grinch either. I hope this will help you pick up a couple of things for your kid." He hands me the check and feels the ridiculous need to shake my hand and wish me luck.

The world of the suddenly unemployed would like to welcome Claire Marsh to its ranks.

*   *   *

Zoë and Mia, who has a set of keys to my apartment, are already there when I arrive home. Zoë is in full dance regalia, wearing one of her ballet class outfits, complete with pink slippers and floral headdress. She's prancing around the room to *Peter and the Wolf*, humming along with the music. Mid-pirouette, she stops to glance at me and her little face pales.

"Are you sick, Mommy?" She runs over to give me a hug.

I can't decide whether to talk to Mia and our parents before sharing my bad news with Zoë, or to not bottle it in and let her and my sister hear it all right now. But I don't want to burst Zoë's happy bubble. There's something about a state of innocence, almost like a state of grace, that's as beautiful and fragile as a Fabergé egg. "How was the ballet? Did you enjoy it?"

"Uh-huh!" She launches into a play-by-play, dancing around the living room to recapture some of the scenes. Watching her, I begin to wonder if *The Nutcracker* might have been performed just as effectively to Prokofiev.

"Hey, Mom, can I watch a video?"

"Sure."

Zoë removes a package from a shopping bag and hands it to me. "MiMi bought it for me, for an extra early Christmas present. It's the video of *The Nutcracker*."

"Well, that was mighty generous of MiMi." I smile at Mia. "Did you thank her properly?" My daughter nods, then gives her aunt a huge hug. "I like their dancing in 'The Waltz of the Flowers' better than what we're doing in Miss Gloo's class. But I know it's only because we're just kids and we don't know so many steps yet." She hands me the box to open for her and I get her set up in front of the TV in the den with a glass of juice and a few cookies. Then I lead Mia into the kitchen, where it always seems that life's most meaningful conversations—from family conferences to drunken party confessions—take place.

Mia removes an opened bottle of Chardonnay from my refrigerator and pours a goblet for each of us. "What's up, kid? You look like shit."

There's no easy way to do this. "I just got fired."

"You *what*?" As Mia's hand flies to her mouth I encourage her to use it for volume control. "What happened? I thought they loved you at Go Native!"

"Three strikes," I say glumly. "Two involving needing to leave a tour to pick up Zoë."

"And the second one was my fault, wasn't it? Oh, shit, Clairey. I should have just stuffed it and gone to get her from that birthday party. This is at least one-third my fault. Fuck." She buries her head in her hands. At this moment, I don't know which of us feels worse. I come over and put my arms around her and when she hugs back, we both start to cry.

"I don't know what to do," I sob. "I thought I had something perfect. I really did enjoy being a guide. How often do you get 'fun with fairly flexible' when it comes to jobs? How often do you get even *one* of those things? I've got a check that will barely cover us for a few weeks . . . in a slow month. But this couldn't have come at a worse time of year. How do I tell Zoë I need to cancel Christmas? And her birthday?"

Still holding me, Mia reaches for my wineglass. "Here. You'll think better." At least she cadges a laugh out of me. "First of all, we're not canceling Zoë's party. You've already gotten the favors, the paper goods, and the decorations. We—me and Mommy and Daddy and Charles—have planned all along to help out with the food."

"Presents. I haven't even shopped for her yet. And what about the rest of you?"

Mia swats my head in a playful love tap. "You don't think we love you just 'cause you give us stuff, you nut job? We've all got everything we need, and some of us have more than we can handle or deserve. You owe me squat. I bailed on you and got you up shit's creek with your job. I'm going to Sibling Hell for this."

I chuckle. "Oh, that might have been the final straw, but your transgressions are far worse than that. You're going to Sibling Hell for giving all my dolls haircuts while I was at Amy Reisman's for a sleepover."

"I made them look *stylish*. And that was almost twenty years ago!"

"You think there's a statute of limitations on Sibling Hell? And you promised me that their hair would grow back! I had to use all my saved-up allowance to go to the doll hospital on Lexington Avenue and get a wig for Baby Dear. And if you hadn't given her a mullet, my Ginny would have been a collector's item by now."

"No way. She was not in mint condition. You'd spilled ink on her arm."

"That was *so* not me," I insist, regressing further. "That was you. You were trying to give her a tattoo." Mia blushes, a clear acknowledgment of guilt. "And then there was the time that you thought my birthday poem from Daddy was better than your poem, so you stole mine out of my scrapbook, and scribbled your own name on it."

"I did that?" she asks, evidently not recalling such a seminal incident from our childhood.

I nod. "You said the older sister should get the better poems. You turned it into a form of literary primogeniture."

"I don't remember that at all. What happened to the poem?"

I grin. "I stole it back, brought it to Daddy, and he typed up a replacement for me."

She tops off our wine and changes the subject. "What was the third strike with Go Native! by the way?"

"I nearly destroyed diplomatic relations between us and the French."

"Oh, I wouldn't blame yourself. That's been going on for centuries. Didn't Mark Twain say something bitchy about them around a hundred and fifty years ago?"

"Not in front of a busload of them." I look down into my wine and begin to cry again.

"You'll be fine, kid," she says, stroking my hair. "You'll get through this. You've braved worse."

"Nice platitudes, Mia, but this isn't a goddamn after-school special. I'm totally broke and now I need to look for a new job at the worst time of year. I can't ask Go Native! for a reference— I got fired for cause—and that's the sum total of my work experience. I probably can't even go to a rival tour company because I'll still have to finesse my way around how I left my last job, and all they'd need to do is call my boss and the whole truth will come out."

I polish off my wine and Mia empties the bottle into our glasses. "I hate the way my life is impacting Zoë. You know some of her classmates' mothers have called me to 'make sure' I'm really having the birthday party *here*, because it's so out of their realm of comprehension. I can hear the disapproval in their voices, hear them mentally tallying up what I'm most likely spending on Zoë's party and the kind of party it is versus what they all do these days—you know, renting Shea Stadium or taking forty kids and their mothers to a Broadway matinee. It's that horrible 'store-bought versus home-made' snobbery. It's between their words. In their silences. I feel it, like a damp, cold chill. At best, they think poor Zoë's mom is doing something 'quaint.' They make me feel church-mousy. And if that's the way a bunch of grown women are acting, imagine how their kids are treating Zoë. Seven-year-olds have a remarkable capacity for cruelty. She was really into the July-in-December theme until a couple of the girls teased her about having a party at home, which they think is for little kids who are too young to appreciate the finer points of the planetarium. When I picked her up at ballet class this week, she was in tears because her supposed friends Chauncey and Bathsheba Marie had been calling her a baby."

"Kids have always been cruel," Mia commiserates. "Particularly the Thackeray crowd. You and I didn't escape unscathed, you know. What about our clothes?"

Eek. We wore Tulia's custom one-offs, which would now be considered funky and trendy. To have a mom that was a fashion designer? *Now* it might be the height of super-coolness, but back then, we were just considered weird. I guess we were, sort of. We were Mommy's pint-sized guinea pigs—and she didn't design children's garments, so there we were, tricked out in ultra-sophisticated, offbeat clothes. Jump back several years and imagine Roberto Cavalli couture, worn by a couple of preteens. Come to think of it, that's how they dress these days!

I take a deep breath. "I'm going in to speak with Zoë before I lose my nerve. Don't go anywhere yet. I may need you for moral support."

My daughter is still in the den, mesmerized by the same ballet she saw just a couple of hours ago. The sound is up so loud, the orchestra might as well be sitting in the living room. I grab the remote and mute the volume, then kick off my shoes and curl up beside her on the sofa, putting my arm around her shoulder.

"Hey! Mom! I was watching that!"

"I'd like to talk to you for a few minutes."

"Can we do it later?" she whines.

"No, young lady, we can't. As long as I pay the maintenance, I make the rules around here." She wrenches away from me and pulls her knees into her chest, showing baggy little elephant wrinkles in her white tights, just around the ankles. I reach out for her again, but she shrugs away. She's probably a bit overtired.

"Well, it looks like I'll be spending more time around here from now on." Zoë's face lights up and she launches herself into my arms, but when I tell her the reason and what it's going to mean in the belt-tightening department, she doesn't take it as well as I'd hoped. In fact she bawls as though a dam had burst behind her eyelids.

"Christmas won't be Christmas without any presents!" she laments and a smile flits across my lips for barely an instant. In a few years, when she reads *Little Women*, she'll know the reason.

"I didn't say there weren't going to be *any* presents, Z," I reply, searching for words of mollification. "We'll have a few really special ones, instead of—"

She vaults from the couch with the same intensity she'd used only a minute ago to hug me, nearly landing on her tush as she skids in her stocking feet across the slippery hardwood floors. "It's not fair!" she wails as she heads for the kitchen. "What are you trying to do to me?"

This is a phrase she heard me say all too often to her father when our marriage was in tatters, specifically after he'd confessed that he had fallen in love with someone else. She has mimicked perfectly the same moaning tone, with the emphasis and rising inflection on the word *do*. "Zoë . . ." I say, trailing her. She's not listening. "Zoë, honey, I'm not trying to do anything to you. Believe me, I'm not doing anything on purpose. I'm not trying to hurt you or punish you. Zoë, look at me. *Look* at me." She refuses. I try again, my frustration increasing. "Z, *look at me*. We'll get through this together. There *will* be Christmas. I promise."

My daughter can go from adorable and docile to full-fledged temper tantrum faster than a Ferrari can reach its maximum mph. In this case she'd already been working up a head of steam. "I don't want to live here anymore!" she sobs, throwing her arms around Mia's waist. "I want to live with MiMi!"

Stricken, and feeling as though I've just been stabbed in the heart, thinking it would be better just to die quickly rather than know I'll live forever with the pain, I look at my sister. We converse above Zoë's head, through intense eye contact and by reading each other's lips. "I can solve this," I insist.

"Take a day or so of quiet time," Mia says. "You need it."

We spar for a couple of minutes. Mia thinks she's helping. My head is spinning. Zoë continues to cling to her aunt, tossing in the occasional insult at me, who is, in her eyes, always taking things away from her, or a compliment, for Mia, who always gives her things, takes her great places, does "fun stuff," and gives her treats "just *because*."

And so . . . a half hour later, I am watching my only child and sole proprietor of my heart, Baa tucked under her arm, march out the door with her savior: my older sister. I wait until the yellow knapsack and wobbly Powerpuff Girls suitcase disappear into the elevator, listen as the car descends, then return to my empty apartment, locking the door and sliding to the floor, too blinded by tears to move.

I don't know how long I stay there, my back against the door, hugging my knees to my chest, Zoë-style. It doesn't matter.

Chapter 10

It's been a great few days. I love having a kid around. It's so cool to see the world through Zoë's eyes. Though I don't know how Claire does it. I've been working at Bendel's helping to launch Lucky Sixpence's makeup line, taking my lunch break later in the day so I can pick up Zoë from school. If she's got an after-school activity, she heads over there with another kid and its nanny and then goes home with them until I can get her. It's a quick cab ride from the store, but it's a bit of a haul from the Upper West Side, where all of her activities are, to the Lower East, where I live. There are times when I think I spend half the day in transit.

If Zoë's stay lasts into next week, I don't know how I'll swing it. I'm doing the makeup for the popular, wildly un-PC, reality TV series called *Hissy Fit*, where Southern belles, Jewish-American princesses, and gays compete to see who can be more demanding—and get away with it. I'll be at the studio day and night when I'm not following one of the contestants around trying to make them appear as natural as possible. Zoë can't tag along. And she won't go home yet. True, we're both having a blast. She has no bedtime and we make PB & J sandwiches at midnight if the kid is up that late. Claire gags at the smell of peanut butter so they don't keep it in the house. We go out for pizza—I hate to cook—and ice cream cones. My niece was fascinated by all the tattoo parlors along St. Mark's Place and asked for one. We picked out a design together, then I went home and painted it on her arm. She tapes a baggie over it when she bathes so it won't wash away too soon.

I haven't talked to Claire since Saturday afternoon. She won't call me. She could be pissed or she could be totally restructuring her life. Either one is in character for her.

In a way, I feel bad—a bit guilty—that Zoë isn't homesick. Yesterday I asked if she wanted to call her mom and she got moody and pouty and said no, adding, "I'm still mad at her." Stubborn kid. A true Marsh chick. The only time my niece mentioned anything having to do with home was when I took down my old Twister game from the closet and taught her how to play. She loved it and suggested it might be fun to play at her birthday party. I agreed and said I'd bring it.

This evening we had an appointment with Celestia for a reading; one for Zoë and one for me. We walked along 10th Street, holding hands. It was a scarf-and-mittens kind of night. I hate it when it gets dark so early. It makes me feel like, as the days grow shorter, I'm getting older. Which I am, I know, but the long nights emphasize the obvious and depress me. Maybe because I've had no one to share them with for a while—a guy, I mean. I'm doing this backwards. I should find the guy, *then* get the kid. I'm even surer now—from observing Claire and from six straight days with Zoë—I do not want to do this alone.

Zoë was wearing one of my floppy velvet hats, which is about ten sizes too big for her. But she told me that she's supposed to wear a hat when it gets this cold, so we scrounged through my stuff 'til we found one she liked.

When we got to First Avenue and turned south, she suddenly broke stride and applied the brakes. "This is where my Daddy works," she announced, as if I didn't know it.

Eden's Garden was pretty empty. Scott's usually at the restaurant in the evenings to handle whatever Serena wants him to. Most often, he's at the cash register, which is tucked away in the back, since Serena learned it was bad feng shui to have the money near the front door, where it can spiritually fly out. "Do you want to go in?" I asked Zoë. She nodded. So we did. A rail-thin waitress, probably an NYU drama student, greeted us at the door, asking if she could help us. "Yeah, drink a shake," I muttered. Her skin was so pale, I would have used up half my box of cosmetics just to make her look alive. "Do you eat here?" I asked her.

"All the time," she assured me.

"That's what I thought," I said. She took it as a compliment.

"Is Scott here?"

The girl looked a bit stunned, as though this was a strange question. "Yes . . . he's here." She seemed unsure why anyone would come to Eden's Garden to see *him*.

"Tell him his kid is here to say hi," I said.

She brightened up. "Oh, I'll go get him. Hi, there," she said to Zoë in the kind of singsong voice kids hate. "What's your name?"

"Zoë."

"That's very pretty," the chick said, now out of conversation. "I'll go get your dad, okay?"

"Okay."

I glanced down at Zoë, who was swinging back and forth from my arm. Her face looked anxious.

The restaurant is pretty small, so it was a minute or less before Scott came out to greet his daughter. "Hey, kiddo! How's my girl?" Zoë gave him a huge hug.

"Are you growing a beard?" she asked, tickling the graying stubble on his cheek.

"Maybe. But only if my best girl likes it. Do you like it?"

She thought about it. "I don't know yet. It isn't a real beard yet."

"So, whatcha doing down in this neck of the woods?"

Zoë giggled. "Woods don't have necks!"

Scott pretended to think about it. "You're right, they don't. It's a silly saying. Made up by a grownup. So what are you doing in . . . Eden's Garden?" He looked at me. I figured I'd let Zoë say whatever she wanted to. "Hey, Mia." He gave my cheek a quick peck. "I haven't seen you in . . . about two or three weeks!"

"You'll see me in another two or three, if you're not going to fink out on her," I said, my voice a low threat, my face a smile.

"We're . . . We're . . . We're going to see MiMi's astrologer," Zoë told her dad. "It's for my birthday."

"What's she gonna do? Tell you you're going to be a year older?" he teased.

"I don't know. I *will* be another year older."

"Do you two want something to eat?" he asked, gesturing to an empty table.

Zoë made a face. "No. I don't like the food here. It tastes funny."

"That's 'cause it's good for you."

She stuck out her tongue like she'd tasted something foul. "No, it's not. *Roast beef* is good for you." It's one of her favorite foods. "And cherry vanilla ice cream 'cause it has fruit in it."

"Would you like to say hi to Serena?"

What a jerk.

"No! I hate her. I want to say hi to *you*. Will you . . . will you . . ." She fought for the words, looking like she was afraid to learn the answer. "Will you come to my birthday party? *Pleeaaaaaase*."

"Of course I will, pumpkin."

"And don't bring *her*."

"Yes, please don't," I added. It was worth saying twice.

"Daddy?"

"What is it, sweetheart?"

"I miss you." She looked back at me, over her shoulder. "And Mommy misses you, too." I wondered if she would tell him where she'd been for the past few days . . . and why. "Why did you and Mommy have to get divorced?"

I was waiting to hear it from his lips, too. *Yeah, tell her. Tell your kid you fell in love with someone else—who, by the way, couldn't hold a candle to my sister if it were hot-glued to her palm—and ran away from home.*

"Was it because I was bad sometimes?" she asked, tears rolling down her cheeks. "And if I'm never bad again, will you come back and live with us?"

"You weren't a bad girl, Zo," he said, using the single-syllable nickname he came up with for her when she was an infant. Claire calls her "Z." Funny, how they couldn't agree on a pet name for their only child.

"And, even when you misbehaved from time to time, I didn't move away because of that. I promise you."

"Then what was it?" she asked, looking at him with the saddest Bambi eyes I've ever seen. She was breaking *my* heart.

Scott took her hands in his and smoothed them over with his fingers. "It's a long story, pumpkin."

"I have time," said the wise-assed little pragmatist.

I watched Scott to see how he'd dance out of this one, thinking how much scorn I felt for a man I once admired, the guy who'd rocked Claire's world—and "Zo's."

"You know something?" he said, looking into her huge eyes, "I don't even know *how* to tell it. And that's the truth. But can I have some time to think about how to do it? I mean a lot more time than five minutes," he added, guessing where his own kid would be going. He's not dumb. In fact he's brilliant. Frequently clueless, often insensitive, but never dumb.

"I guess so," Zoë sighed. "We have to see Celestia anyway. You *are* going to come to my party, *aren't you?*" she said, just to be sure he remembered. "You. Not *her.*"

"I wouldn't miss it!" he grinned. "Just me. Promise." He hugged her and bid us both goodbye.

"He *better* come. And he *better not bring her*," she said as we crossed the street.

"You can say that again!"

"He *better* come. And he *better not bring her*."

I laughed. "That's just an expression."

"What's an 'expression'?"

"It's like . . . a . . . saying." She gave me a confused look. "An 'expression' is a figure of speech." I'd made it worse. Claire is better at explaining these things. "An 'expression' is a silly thing that isn't meant to be taken totally for real, but it sort of sums up a little part of life. Like when I said 'you can say that again!,' what I was saying, but as an 'expression,' was 'you're so right! I totally agree with you!' "

She nodded. "Oh. Okay. Like . . . like . . . like when you say it's raining cats and dogs, it isn't *really* raining cats and dogs but it's raining so hard that the raindrops are *as big as* cats and dogs."

"You're better at this than I am, kid."

Celestia lives on the top floor of a walkup on East Eighth Street, on the stretch better known as St. Mark's Place. With what she charges for a reading she could live on Park Avenue, but Celestia expanded differently. She now owns the building, which is prime real estate, and enjoys her eight-hundred-square-foot roof garden and patio. Try getting a patch of green like that uptown.

"Hey, there, little fish," she said, greeting me. I'm a Pisces, so she came up with that name the first time we met.

"It smells good in here. Like grapefruits and oranges," Zoë observed.

"Thank you. It's called incense. And I'm very glad you like how it smells. I think the smell puts me in a good mood."

"Me, too. But I'm tired," Zoë said, slumping against the wall. She's not used to climbing five flights of stairs and her legs are a lot shorter than mine.

"Well, 'tired,' can I get you some pink lemonade? I made it fresh. From pink lemons."

Zoë laughed. "I want to see the pink lemons!"

"Nuh-uh. They're my special secret."

"Where do you get them?" nearly-seven-year-old inquiring minds want to know.

"I grow them right here in my garden. And I'm the only one in New York who has them."

"Watch it. Next thing, she'll be believing you raise brown cows that only give chocolate milk."

"They don't?" Celestia said airily. "Listen, most of life's fundamentals revolve around people believing what they want to about something. It's all a romantic equation. Belief equals faith plus an inexact science. Look at marriage. Organized religion. Astrology—which is actually more exact and explainable than the workings of the other two. 'God is everywhere' is, you'll admit, a bit more ephemeral than my saying that Mercury is in retrograde until the twenty-third of the month and—"

"And my Saturn is in the garage."

"Don't mock me, Mia."

"I'm not. Or I wouldn't be forking over a sizeable percentage of my salary." I formally introduced her to Zoë and Celestia asked who wanted to go first.

"You," Zoë said to me. Celestia brought Zoë her lemonade and explained that what she tells people is a secret, so would she mind waiting in the other room until it's her turn.

Zoë was cool with that. She likes secrets. "Can I make a picture?" she asked, seeing an easel set up with a box of colored chalk beside it.

"Sure, go for it. That's what it's here for." Celestia flipped the pad to a clean sheet. "This is to wipe your hands when you're through," she said, pointing to a Mason jar of water and a roll of paper towels. My niece made herself right at home. When one of Celestia's cats slinked by and brushed her leg, Zoë exclaimed, "Oooh, can I play with him?" She reached down to pet the pewter gray longhair.

"It's a 'she,' and yes, you can play with her. She's very friendly for a cat. Her name's Diana."

"Like the princess?" Zoë asked Celestia.

The astrologer shook her head. "Like the goddess. Diana was a moon goddess and the goddess of the hunt. She likes *mice*," Celestia whispered.

Zoë jumped back like she'd received an electric shock. "No! I'm scared of mice." Her lip began to tremble.

"Don't worry," Celestia soothed. "There aren't any mice indoors. And she never goes hunting when I have houseguests."

My niece brightened. She didn't look totally convinced, but, as Celestia might say, she wanted to believe that was the truth. I went into Celestia's reading room. The walls are deep lapis blue. Her furniture—huge silk pillows and overstuffed couches—are upholstered in shades of blue and indigo. You feel like you're sitting in first class on an astral plane.

"Your chart indicates some big changes coming up for you," she said, going over the printout she'd made in advance. "In the next few months, Jupiter will be moving into your tenth house, the house of social identity and career. Now that you're aware of that, you can harness his wattage to really take some strides. Your aspects for creating business partnerships are sensational."

We spoke some more about what that meant. Maybe *Mi♥amore Makeup* might become more than a pipe dream. Celestia said I should be alert for opportunities that would be placed directly in my path and that I shouldn't pre-judge things because I might miss out. The universe helps those who help themselves, she reminded me. "However . . . this is not an auspicious time for romance," she added.

"For this I needed to pay you over two hundred bucks?"

Celestia laughed. "Well, you'll want to know that your outlook is much brighter come spring. And again, as with the career breaks, don't make immediate assumptions about men, for better or for worse."

"Oh, I think I can make *some* assumptions. Like my best friend

Charles is not going to suddenly switch teams." He wouldn't be my type even if he did, but I wanted to make my point.

Celestia rolled her eyes skyward. "You know what I mean. Now, later next year you're going to have some powerful planets conjoining in both the career and romance sectors of your chart, which hasn't happened for you in a while."

"Try *ever*."

"So be prepared for the unexpected."

"How the fuck do I do that?" It sounded like a total oxymoron.

"You'll know it when it happens." She smiled.

"So if something *never* happens to *me*, and then suddenly it does happen, that'll probably be 'it,' huh?"

"Something like that."

I was giving her shit because it's fun, but actually, she was very helpful. If something's coming—whether it's a bouquet of two dozen long-stems or a Mack truck at sixty miles per hour—I like to know about it beforehand.

I left Celestia's inner sanctum and she called in Zoë. The kid took the "secrets" part of her session very seriously and refused to tell me what Celestia had said to her. She showed me the chalk drawing she had made while I was inside, though. It was a picture of her giving her mom a kiss.

"I think I want to go home now," she said.

I brought her back to my place, we packed up her stuff, then called Claire. Zoë had added an inscription ("I love you Mommy") to her picture. We rolled it up and secured it with a rubber band. She clutched it tightly during the entire bus ride uptown.

"I see a penis!"

"What?" I turned to see what she was talking about. So did all the other passengers on the number 15 bus.

She pointed out the window. "Look! A penis!"

"Shhh!" I craned my neck and realized she was talking about one of the towers atop Tudor City, an apartment complex with faux-Elizabethan architecture, located across from the United Nations. I had to laugh. The towers do look a bit like circumcised granite. I scoped out the other riders. A couple of them were blushing. I guess they saw what I did. What Zoë did.

"Just out of curiosity, where have you seen a penis?" At least she'd used an acceptable word, as opposed to one of the seven George Carlin joked that you couldn't say on TV. It could have been a lot worse.

"I saw Daddy *and* Mommy naked when we went camping once. We had to take a bath in the lake because there was nowhere else to do it. And I saw Xander."

"You—you what? This wasn't when you asked him to elope, was it?"

She cocked her head and looked at me like I'm a goofball. "Noooo." She leaned over to whisper in my ear. "He took a pee-pee in the sandbox at recess."

Great. I hope he doesn't feel the urge to take a leak in one of Claire's planters during Zoë's party.

At 79th Street we boarded the crosstown; and after disembarking on the West Side, Zoë started to do her "we're-almost-there" skip in front of the natural history museum. The elevator man greeted her as though she were Elizabeth the First returning from one of her Progresses. I had a lump in my throat and mixed feelings. A kid's perspective on life is a great ass-kicker when you've become a little jaded or so busy being an adult that you've forgotten what it's all about in the long run. I'd really miss having her around, and at the same time I was glad to bring her home to Claire. Maybe even a bit relieved. I could go back to my life, child-free. Some of what I felt was guilt. That I could have what Claire could not. But maybe she wouldn't have switched with me for the world.

Claire had scarcely opened the door when Zoë threw herself into her mom's arms. They held each other for a while, as I watched, a third wheel on a bicycle, Zoë's chalk sketch crushed between them. "You know what?" I said to Claire, "I think the kid missed you."

Zoë lit up like a bonfire. "You can say that again!"

•••••••••••

Dear Diary:

I had the best time with MiMi. It's like having a Mommy and a big sister at the same time. She didn't yell at me even one time, even when I spilled chocolate milk on a scarf of hers that is old and made of silk. I was using it for dress-up to play a lady from Spain with a big comb in my hair and a piece of lace. The scarf is shaped like a triangle and it's black and it has fringes on the edges and flowers sewn onto it. She said it was called a piano shawl but I never saw a piano that was wearing one. Why does a piano need a shawl?

I didn't have to eat vegetables when I was with MiMi. She doesn't like vegetables so she didn't make me eat them.

We went to see Celestia, who is MiMi's astrologer. She told me where all the planets were in the sky when I was born. She showed me a picture she made and it had all kinds of squiggly little lines on it like the picture-writing I saw in the museum when we took a class trip and saw the mummies. She said because of where the planets were on the exact minute when I was born that I act more grown-up for my age than a lot of other kids. And she said that I get mad when I don't get what I want. I thought that was funny because I could have told her that without her making a picture of the sky. She said a lot of things that are the truth about me. It was like magic. She also told me that things would get better at school for me by the end of the year. It's sort of like a birthday wish and I really, really, really hope it comes true. MiMi wanted me to tell her what Celestia said, but Celestia said it was a secret between us and I didn't have to tell anyone else what she told me if I didn't want to. I loved her house. She has a garden on her roof, but I couldn't really see it because it was night-time. And the room where she told me all about the planets was dark blue and it was so beautiful. I sat on the floor on a big pillow like Mommy has under the piano, except Celestia's pillow was purple. Inside the room was like night-time when you look up at the stars, like when we went camping in Lake George. I want to paint my room blue so it looks like that. And maybe we could paint the planets and the stars on the ceiling. Mommy is very good at art. I know she could paint it. When I was little, my room had paint-ings on it that she made. There was a line of pink elephants and their trunks were holding onto the tails of the ones in front of them. And there was a purple cow that jumped over the moon.

We saw my daddy last night before we went to see Celestia. He looked more older than he did when we all lived together. I wish I could see him more. He's busy a lot and he's busy with HER. I know what my birthday wish will be when I blow out my can-dles. I can tell it here because this is my diary and I'm not saying it out loud. It will be that Daddy will come home forever and we can all live happily ever after. And Mommy won't be sad any-more and she won't get angry at Daddy or at me and on Sundays I can jump on their bed and we can have Daddy and Mommy cuddles like we used to. And then Mommy will make bacon and pancakes and we will play in Central Park and go on the carousel and I would get on the biggest horse, the one that looks like it has armor. When Daddy was here, I was scared to get on it. But Celestia said I was grown-up for my age so now that I will be seven I'm not afraid anymore.

Daddy said I was his "best girl." I wish I had a second birth-day wish that Mommy would be his best girl, too.

Chapter 11

There's snow on the sidewalk and checkered table-cloths on the living-room floor. T minus three hours and counting, as they say in Houston. We're not having the party on Zoë's actual birthday since most people spend Christmas Eve with their families, so we chose to hold it on the last Saturday afternoon before the kids get out of school for Christmas vacation and jet off to St. Bart's, Aspen, or Gstaad. A party on the weekend means some of the dads will come, too, but that also means I need to have some alcohol on hand. It's an additional expense, since the moms never expect liquor, although with Nina Osborne in the house, I may require a little nip or two myself. Zoë has been fully awake since 6 A.M., has changed her outfit at least three times, and has been bouncing off the walls to such an extent that I sat her in front of the TV for non-stop Powerpuff. I've never cared much for cartoons. I dislike the violence and the cavalier attitude toward using it. Whenever I voice my opinion, Zoë insists that she knows it's "all just pretend" and that it's not nice to hit people, throw acid at them, push them through plate-glass windows, down manholes, and off cliffs.

However, from watching them with Zoë, I've learned that

the Powerpuff Girls, like most cartoons geared for kids, does contain a few inside jokes to delight the adults, with the Girls tossing off words like "angst" and phrases like "witty retort." And, given our current household demographic, promoting Girl Power probably isn't such a bad idea. The counselor I visited during and after my divorce suggested that I "journal," (it makes me cringe when people turn nouns into verbs), but I think the Powerpuff Girls might have been more therapeutic.

Methodically, I run through my party checklist. Furniture moved aside and shoved against the walls (thereby exposing dust bunnies there hasn't been the time to vacuum up since my former housekeeper Hilda manned the Electrolux): check. Extermination of previously mentioned neglected dust bunnies: check. Small throw rugs rolled up so they will not become anointed with mustard, ketchup, and lemonade: check. Gallons of same lemonade chilled: check. And on it goes with the paper goods, the cocktail franks, the goody bags (Zoë and I filled them last night), and pinning the tail-less donkey to the front door.

T minus two and the clock is ticking.

I'm on my hands and knees on the kitchen floor trying to corral the contents of a bowlful of Jelly Bellies that took a tumble off the counter in my haste to create order out of the chaos. It's a commodious room as far as New York apartments go, but I've never tried to throw a party for sixty. Even at our most socially ambitious, Scott and I never came nearly that close. And I'm a bundle of nerves, as anxious as a Miss America contestant who discovers she has cellulite just as she's about to strut the runway in her swimsuit.

Zoë skids in, panic stricken. She's wearing her Dorothy outfit: white blouse, gingham pinafore, ruby slippers. "You have to make ponytail braids!" she insists. "I can't do it!" Her little hands splay in frustration. Her hair is a knotted mess.

I look up from the terra-cotta tile. "I thought you were wearing that pretty red shorts outfit that Granny Tulia gave you."

She shrugs. "No. I want to wear this. Braid me!"

"It's not nice to demand. What happened to 'please'?"

"Braid me, *please*."

"As soon as I finish picking up the candy, I'll take a look at your hair."

"No, *now*!" she says obstinately. "I need it right for the party."

"Zoë, the party is two hours away from now. I'm in the middle of something. You can see that. Now, it'll go faster if you come down here and help me."

Her eyes narrow. "No. I'm the birthday girl and the birthday girl doesn't have to help with her own party."

"You think so, huh?" I wipe my forehead and toss a dustpan full of jelly beans into the trash can. My knees hurt. I just turned twenty-six and my knees hurt. "Well, the birthday girl isn't going to *have* a party if she behaves like a little selfish brat." It's an empty threat and I know it. I thought we both knew it, but I was evidently mistaken.

Instant tears. Bawling. Wailing. Keening. You would think someone had been murdered in front of her. "It's not faaaair."

I'm in no mood for melodrama. "You know what's not fair?" I snap. "What's not fair is Mommy doing all of this by herself." I'm fully aware that I'm referring to more than this afternoon's gala event. "And you know something else? I'm learning that sometimes life just *isn't* fair and there's not much we can do about it. But you know what helps a lot when it comes to getting over the 'unfairness' part of it?" She looks at me, surprised and inquisitive. "Teamwork," I tell her. "Teamwork makes things go faster, it makes them more fun, and you don't feel like you're the only one in the whole world who thinks things are unfair." I watch her mulling over this notion for a few moments, tugging on her hair. "So, how about you help me pick these up. And as soon as we're done, we'll wash our hands and I'll fix your hair."

After a few seconds, she descends, although her method of

eliminating the jelly beans from the floor involves putting them
in her mouth. "Zoë, those are dirty. Throw them away, please."

"I'm only eating the Marshmallow-flavored ones," she lies.
"And the buttered popcorn-tasting ones because they have spots
on them so I can't see the dirt."

"Well, stop it," I say, tugging her fingers from her mouth. She
exhales in a dramatic show of dissatisfaction and flounces off.
"You're not poking through the loot bags, are you?" I add, hearing the crinkling of paper.

The rustling stops. "No." Her voice is sheepish, as though she
believes for an instant that maybe I *do* have eyes in the back of
my head.

I locate the last jelly bean, scrub the surrounding area, and
wash up. "Okay, Z! Hair time. Let's go, because Mommy still
needs to take a shower."

She comes back into the kitchen wearing a beguiling smile.
"Can I have this?" On her wrist is one of the pieces of jewelry I
made, pilfered from a goody bag.

"No, I'm sorry sweetheart, I made that for one of your
guests." Her lower lip begins to tremble. If she weren't about to
turn only seven, I'd swear she was premenstrual. "Tell you what.
I'll make you another one just like it tomorrow."

"But . . . but . . . I want *this* one. Make another one for the
guest."

"Zoë, you know I don't have time to do that right now." Her
tears flow, but I've just about had it. "You're being very unrea-
sonable," I tell her, as though this will actually have an effect. "If
you want a bracelet like that one, I'll make it when the party's
over. Now tell me which bag it came from, and we'll put it
back."

"No!" I try to remove it from her wrist. She tugs back and the
bracelet breaks. Now I've got a new mess to attend to. She becomes hysterical, I become livid.

"All right, Zoë, go to your room. Now. *Now!*" My out-of-character explosion startles her. She flinches as though she's afraid I might smack her, which I wouldn't ever do, but am sorely tempted to at the moment. "I am *this* close to calling off your birthday party," I shout, bluffing, and not indicating with my body language exactly how close "this" is. "Now I mean it. Go to your room."

"I still need my hair in ponytail braids," she insists.

"Yes, I see that. Your room, Zoë. *Now*."

"I'll do it, but it won't change anything!" She stomps off, rattling some of the china in the breakfront with her angry footsteps.

Once she's gone I replace the broken bracelet from my secret stash of spares that I made, anticipating the possibility of a last-minute emergency.

The doorbell rings and I admit my parents, laden with food and gifts. My mother kisses me on both cheeks because she admires continental affectations like that, then immediately bustles off to the kitchen to refrigerate the perishables. My father busies himself with what he always does when they come to visit. He scans my bookshelves for new acquisitions. He always wants to know what I'm reading, as though it's a window into the current status of my soul. I'm waiting for him to spot the well-worn volume of *Overwhelmed and Abandoned: Divorced Mothers with Kids Vent Their Spleens*. Not quite the page-turner one might be led to believe.

I ask my mother if she wouldn't mind keeping an eye on Zoë while I take a much-needed shower, and if she would please do her granddaughter's ponytail-braids. Mission accomplished, I head off for the bathroom and a few minutes of blessed solitude and self-prescribed aromatherapy. To dispel some of the steam, I keep the door open a crack, and while I'm in the shower, I hear the doorbell again. We've still got an hour to go before lift-off; who else could be arriving this early? I told Mia that showing up fifteen minutes ahead of time would be fine, and she tends to run late, not the other way around. I holler for one of my parents to please get the door, since I'm dripping wet and naked, except for a towel wrapped unattractively around my head. But the ringing persists, as do my repeated requests. Do I have to do everything myself? I don my terrycloth bathrobe and create a path of wet footprints toward the front of the apartment.

"Anybody home? It's me. Open up!" The familiar voice on the other side of the door is not one I care to greet in my present state. I peer through the peephole to make sure he's alone, at least, then open the door.

"You're early, Scott." It's an observation, not a critique. He leans over and gives me a cordial peck on the cheek. "Are you growing a beard?"

He hands me a bouquet of Korean deli roses and strokes both sides of his face. "Why? Do you like it?"

"I don't know yet. It isn't a real beard yet." Not that it's any of my business either way anymore. I pull the robe more tightly around me, ashamed of my *dishabille*. Amazing . . . I used to walk around this apartment mostly naked, in front of this man, and now my state of mid-toilette undress feels wildly inappropriate. And I'm mortified that the former love of my life is seeing me without makeup. "I asked my parents to answer the door," I continue, stammering a bit. "They were here before I went in to take my shower."

"The birthday girl is freshly coiffed," my mother says gaily, emerging from Zoë's room. "Oh, Scott, I didn't know you were here."

"Evidently," I reply.

She gives me a funny look, as though there's some post-marital reason I am romping in my robe in front of my ex-husband.

So, she'd been at the other end of the house, in Zoë's room, probably with the door closed, doing my daughter's hair and dispensing some grandmotherly advice, which is why she didn't hear, or was disinclined to answer, the door. "Where's Daddy?"

"You don't have enough ice," Tulia says. "So I sent him on a quest. He was all curled up with a volume of e.e. cummings. It's good for him to be useful. From the sound of things, I'm guessing he's not back yet." She retreats to the kitchen, her heels, (having swapped her snow boots for a pair of hot pink mules), clicking across the parquet.

Uneasy, I shift my weight. "How's . . ."

Scott reads my mind. It's remarkable that after several months of being divorced from me, he still can do it. "She's fasting. One of those ritual fasts. She does it four times a year. Every solstice and every equinox. Her whole staff fasts with her, so she closes up the restaurant for a week each time."

"Doesn't sound very good for business. Are you . . . ?"

Scott shook his head. "You know I'm not a fanatic. Oh!" He reaches into his breast pocket to retrieve a red envelope. "This is for Zoë. It's a check. Buy her whatever she wants." He studies my expression, then adds, "It's for her birthday and for Christmas."

I nod. I thought as much. Hopefully, it's enough to get her something meaningful for each occasion that's bigger than a set of pierced earrings (not permitted for *my* seven-year-old) and smaller than a pony. For a moment, I look at my former husband and think back to exactly a year ago. There was no Serena Eden. We Marsh Franklins were one happy family. Three peas in a fixed mortgage, low-maintenance pod. Wait, who am I kidding? If familiarity is said to breed contempt, then nostalgia must beget insanity. A year ago, we had a bank account lower than Death Valley and were continually fussing and fuming at one another. A little rhyme pops into my head and I end up smiling at the sardonic catechism that sums up my adult life: Matrimony, Acrimony, Alimony.

The iceman cometh, shoves his bounty into the freezer, and I foist Scott upon him and my mother so I can go get dressed. I suggest to Scott that he take advantage of the last few minutes of calm before the storm to visit with his daughter. As I pass Zoë's bedroom on the way to mine, I knock to let her know that her dad's here. She bursts through the door and races down the hall to the living room.

Mia and Charles arrive, we set the cake aside, and I get them started on blowing up balloons. Soon, with the Christmas tree in the corner, the mistletoe hung in the foyer, the red, white, and blue streamers and the tri-colored foil pom-poms that are meant to resemble fireworks, plus the balloons that Mia is af-fixing by static electricity to the walls of the living room, dining area, and den, it looks fantastically festive. My mother is in the kitchen popping corn and the apartment smells like a carnival midway. My father, true to form, is checking over Zoë's birth-day poem to see if he needs to add any further ruffles, flour-ishes, and syllables.

Like a stage manager, at five minutes to showtime I let every-one know that the guests are about to arrive. Zoë is so pumped, she's behaving as though she's on an invisible pogo stick.

Now comes the deluge of second graders bearing gifts. I set aside a corner of the den where they can be deposited and di-rect everyone to Zoë's bedroom where they can shed their coats. I'm delighted that the guests took seriously the directive we printed on the invitations: to dress for a picnic in July. Out-side the window snow is falling, blanketing Central Park West with a blissful quiet, while up in toasty-warm apartment 7D, the guests, attired in shorts, tank tops, and sundresses, are en-joying tall glasses of lemonade or short ones of eggnog. The living-room fireplace is the apartment's most wonderful feature and we actually *do* have chestnuts—and weenies—roasting over an open fire. The spareribs are being reheated as well. Happy Chef and my father are taking turns playing King of the Grill.

"This is so adorable, Claire!" June Miller, the mother of Zoë's friends April and May, is one of the nicer moms. At least she's pretty normal. I suppose what I mean by that is that she hasn't treated me any differently from the time when Scott and I were married and financially comfortable, to nowadays. "I love what you've done with the decorations. I wish I had the nerve," she whispers, topping off her eggnog with a generous shot of brandy.

"This isn't about nerve," I assure her.

"Oh, you know, everyone spends *so* much money these days on birthday parties, I always feel I need to do the same, just to compete." Of course, those had been my own sentiments until recently. June looks up when she hears my door open again. I've rigged a string of jingle bells from the peephole latch, so each guest's entrance is announced like the coming of Santa. "And speaking of everyone . . ." She raises her glass toward the doorway. Nina Osborne and Jennifer Silver-Katz have arrived more or less in tandem with their respective progeny in tow. Jennifer gives me an air kiss and in hushed tones assures her older daughter Tennyson (whom we invited because Zoë went to Tennyson's party last summer—who could forget the Shetland ponies and the screening room?) that this isn't "weird," and she should just stuff her ten-year-old opinions and "pretend to have a good time." When Tennyson balks, Jennifer tells her, "Then think of it this way: You'll have something to discuss with your therapist on Thursday."

Ouch. I dread the day when Jennifer decides it's time to sit the girl down for the serious sex talk.

"I really wondered if you were going to pull it off," Jennifer says, bypassing the eggnog and going directly for the hard stuff, applying to Scott, who is tending bar.

"I had my doubts, too." Nina chimes in. She's a nearly unnatural shade of bronze. It's the kind of color one acquires through genuine exposure to sunlight at someplace very expensive like St. Tropez or Cabo San Lucas, and then touches up at Completely Bare. "You have a lot of empty space, though, so you can manage the crowd. I'd have my heart in my mouth if it were me. I can't imagine fifty or sixty people traipsing all over the place, scuffing up my hardwood and soiling my upholstery. But

I guess you don't really have to worry about things getting ruined. How lucky! I don't see much that anyone could damage."

I smile malevolently. "Oh, I'm sure your son will find a way to make his mark. He's so resourceful."

"He gets that from me," Nina replies with just as much venom. She looks around the living room and peers into the dining gallery where the floor is all set for a picnic, but with paper cloths, pointed hats, loot bags, and colorful, curlicued blowers. "It certainly is quite . . . *retro*," she says.

"Oh, look!" A mother I have never met, a blonde woman who points to an adorable Asian girl and introduces herself as "Mei-Li's mom," is fascinated by one of the party games. "A pin-the-tail-on-the-donkey! I didn't know they still made those. The last time I saw anything like this was at a house party in the Hamptons where we played a sort of . . . adult . . . version. It was called 'put the you-know-what in the you-know-where.' Well, that wasn't the real name, but we *are* in mixed company. And," she giggles, "there was no single right answer! Almost everybody went home a winner." She winks and I feel like I need another shower.

I thought I knew all of Zoë's friends' parents. I'm beginning to wonder, *who* are *these people*?

My daughter seems to be having the time of her life. I'm tremendously relieved, and glad that the party is coming off so well. Her classmates were pretty hard on her when they found out her birthday would be celebrated at home and not somewhere more customary—like Disney World. But the kids themselves do appreciate the simpler things when they're presented to them, and they're all having fun. Even Scott is behaving in an exemplary fashion. At the moment, he's got twenty-five of the pint-sized guests playing duck, duck, goose.

I notice a serious-looking little child leaning against my father, who is now seated in an armchair reading a book while all around him, chaos reigns. I go over to speak with the boy in an effort to draw him into the game, but he's not interested. His name is Bram and he's got an awkward, owlish quality that makes him seem two decades older. I hear him tell my father that he wrote a poem for Zoë for her birthday too, but he would never want to read it out loud. "You could put *snakes* in my bed and I wouldn't do it!" he insists. I'm charmed that there's a little boy who has a crush on her and who apparently feels so deeply that he's poured his heart out in, I assume, rhyme. Yet, I've never met this child before today. He's here because she had to invite the entire class. For all his seven-year-old angst, Bram evidently isn't on my daughter's radar screen. Not like—

"Zoë!" The girl of the hour has dragged Xander Osborne under the mistletoe and is kissing him fully on the lips. Surprisingly, he's not objecting; not tossing something in her face, not climbing a tree to get away from her. This does not bode well. But . . . can I admonish her? Them? I was the one who hung the mistletoe and I know perfectly well what the customs are.

"You know what?" Mia says, suddenly sailing over. "Mistletoe gets attached to tree branches by bird poop. It's a *parasite*, which is as bad as a weed. So, you sure you still want to keep that up?" she adds, referring to the lip lock.

"No way!" Xander says, jumping backwards. He's wearing a Jeremy Shockey football Giants jersey. If I recall correctly, this is a player who gets his name in the news through his much-publicized altercations, both verbal and physical, with colleagues and coaches.

"Way," says Mia.

Zoë makes a face. "Yuck!" she exclaims.

Xander wipes his mouth with the back of his hand. I'm not sure what that has to do with Mia's need to share a stunning tidbit of scientific knowledge, but I know I'll never look at mistletoe the same way again.

"I'm very surprised at his behavior," Nina says, and for once I concur. "He hates girls these days. He was on a play date recently with Drew Rockefeller and he snapped off the heads of her Barbies. Only the blonde ones, actually." I rake my hand through my own golden hair, remember Nina's story about the fate of her former *au pair*, and look at my dark-haired sister, who has been eavesdropping. Mia exhales, relieved. She's long over Robert Osborne, anyway. At least she certainly acts like it. This afternoon, she's been flirting up a storm with Gideon Rathbone, the "veddy British" daddy of Zoë's ballet classmate, pudgy little rosy-cheeked Chauncey. I'm so busy playing hostess and cruise director that I haven't had too much of a chance to watch them, so I can't tell whether he's suffering her attentions with the utmost politeness, being English, or whether he fancies her.

Suddenly, there's a shriek from the living room. Ashley runs over to her mother, who is busy self-medicating near the bar cart. "He pulled my hair!" she yowls, pointing to Xander. Duck, duck, goose has become something of a melee. I think that's my cue to serve lunch.

The parents wrangle their respective kids and soon they are sitting on the floor at the designated place settings with a minimum of territorial squirming and fighting over preferred seating assignments. Xander is to Zoë's right. Ashley is to her left. At the other end of the room, little Bram, who is so far away because I'd never really heard of him, looks forlornly northward toward the guest of honor. Something in me wants to warn the poor bespectacled boy that it never gets any better, no matter how old you are.

Tulia's macaroni salad is pronounced "weird" by a few of the kids, but essentially it's a hit. Apart from Xander acting like a hellion, which I expect he does no matter where or when, the children have really embraced the July-in-Christmas concept and are having a good time. I feel very relieved for Zoë. However, I can sense, as well as see, some of the parents—only the moms, really—wearing their disapproval like a pashmina. I wish

I could just walk up to a couple of them and tell them to go screw themselves, but I hate ugly scenes, even though I've been caught up in more than a few of them in my lifetime.

Just before it's time for cake, my father commands center stage. He tells the guests that this is a tradition in our family and there are a couple of exclamations, like, "Oh, yeah, he did that last year, too." The kids aren't as impressed. Poem-shmoem. Some of *them* probably get a birthday pony.

My father clears his throat and holds up his hands for silence, a gesture that may be effective among the literary set, but not with this crowd, particularly since they are embarking on a major sugar high. Finally, we get the room quiet enough to hear one's thoughts above the din, and Brendan begins.

For My Only Grandchild On Her Seventh Birthday

Now that you are turning seven,
And the world has more to offer,
Treat each yummy bite of heaven
Like a treasure for your coffer.

Let each day be an extra present,
Think of it a brand new toy,
You'll find each fresh adventure pleasant
Brimming with untrammeled joy.

"Happy birthday, sweetheart," he says, kissing Zoë on the top of her head. She says thank you and applauds him, which gets the other kids, and then their parents, clapping, too. Later, Zoë will be asking us what some of the words mean, and being a poet's granddaughter, she'll regard each definition as a gift. Words, to Zoë, are like Jelly Bellies. You can never have too many.

Finally, it's time for cake and watermelon. There are gasps of delight from more than two dozen jaded second graders when they see the masterpiece that Happy Chef has created. Zoë's mermaid—like a fishtailed Godiva riding a red-nosed reindeer, is quite a cake. It must have taken Charles several hours to put the whole thing together and decorate it and it's his gift to us. I turn out the lights, everybody sings, mostly on key, and Zoë closes her eyes for a wish. I find myself tearing up and I clutch my mother's hand. Zoë extinguishes all seven candles plus one to grow on in a single breath, then opens her eyes and surveys the results. She beams, utterly satisfied, as we cut the cake and enlist the parents to pass out the slices.

The rest of the afternoon goes by in a blur. Mia's Twister game results in much giggling, although there are a few smushed fingers and toes. Pin the Tail on the Donkey is received as a tremendous novelty; and I derive great satisfaction out of hearing the overindulged sons and daughters of the privileged, pushy, and powerful beg their mothers and fathers to have the game at *their* next birthday party. Bewildered little Bram ends up winning that one, garnering a Brooklyn Cyclones baseball autographed by manager Tim Teufel, a former Met who played second base for the World Series Championship team in 1986. I can tell that the other boys—and all the dads in the room, except for mine—are jealous. Secretly I'm pleased that the lovestruck little bookworm got the biggest treat of the day.

June Miller sidles over to me, a smidge tipsy. "Zoë's party is delightful," she whispers, "but—and I'm speaking as a friend—you really shouldn't award prizes when the kids win a party game. It's not nice. See?" She points discreetly to a sore loser named Sheraton Sheridan, a little girl who is none-too-discreetly bawling her head off, having just learned the hard lesson that some things in life aren't fair.

At least my homespun goody bags are well received. Despite Sheraton's tearful tantrum, neither she, nor anyone else, is going home empty-handed. The females of all ages pronounce my jewelry designs "fun." They immediately don their bangles and show off for one another, indulging in the occasional trade. I don't mind as long as everyone is happy.

At long last, the madding crowd disperses, my family helps with the cleanup, Zoë falls asleep on the couch, and I would give my last nickel for a foot massage.

And then there were two.

"Well, happy birthday, Z."

"Thank you, Mommy." Zoë's got her head in my lap. I'm stroking her hair, which feels soft as cornsilk.

"You liked your party?"

"Uh-huh," she says, her voice sleepy. "At first I was afraid it wasn't going to be fun, but it was. It was *really* fun. I know that Xander was bad, but I still like him."

"Obviously." I expect her to respond, but she doesn't. "I mean, you kissed him under the mistletoe. You didn't kiss anyone else under the mistletoe."

"I know. He's the only one I wanted to give a kiss to."

"You don't like Bram? He seems very nice."

Zoë scrunches up her face. "Yuck!"

Poor Bram.

Chapter 12

 Dear Diary:

My hand hurts a little bit, but it's okay because I had a play date with Xander today. His nanny came to meet him and me at school and we went back to his house. His nanny is very nice but she is very funny-looking, too. She has black hair and when she took her coat off she was wearing a short-sleeved shirt so I saw that her arms were really hairy and she has hair over her lips like a chocolate milk mustache and on the sides of her cheeks near her ears. It was hard not to look at her a lot. Xander calls her fuzzy face but her real name is Frida. I told him I thought he was being mean to her.

Frida gave us sushi for a snack. I think the seaweed is icky so I just ate the rice off of it with my fingers. Then we went to play with Xander's Legos. He has more Legos than I have ever seen. I said I wanted to build a castle so we made the biggest one we could but then Xander put his little army men on the top of it and they have guns and he said they were going to shoot anybody who tried to come into the castle and if anybody tried to go outside except the king, the army men would shoot them, too.

Xander was mad at me because he didn't win Pin the Tail on
the Donkey but I told him he couldn't win because he cheated. He
smushed the blindfold up over his eyes and peeked out from it
and MiMi caught him cheating so she DISQUALIFIED him.
That means she kicked him out because he didn't play fair. He
wanted to win the baseball. But he said if he kept asking his
mom, she would buy him a baseball and she would get people
who were even more famous to sign it. Xander said his mom says
that if you have enough money you can get anything.

Xander pulled Ashley's hair during duck, duck, goose and
made her cry and Daddy ended the game. And MiMi disqualified
Xander from musical chairs, too. He pushed my friend Ben from
yoga class off his chair so hard that Ben broke his glasses and got
a cut on his face. MiMi was funny. She said it was good that Ben
knows how to do yoga so he didn't break himself. Xander's mom
thought that MiMi was not being fair but MiMi said that it was
Xander who didn't play fair. It was a surprise that Mommy let
me have a play date with Xander because Xander's mom doesn't
like her. But Mommy told me that was exactly the reason that she
said I could go over to his house. She was smiling a lot when she
said it.

While we were playing castle Xander's mom came home
with a present for him. She bought him a puppy. I wish I could
get a puppy. My daddy said that dog hair made him sneeze so
we couldn't get one. He didn't like it when we went to visit
Granny Tulia and Grandpa Brendan because Ulysses would
jump on him and give him doggy kisses. Xander's puppy
doesn't look anything like Ulysses. It's brown and sort of ugly.
His mom said it was a "rotten" dog. It's a boy dog and Xander
named him Draco.

Draco was barking a lot. I think it's because he wasn't used to
Xander's house. His house looks like a museum with beautiful
paintings on the walls. There is a painting of his mom that is as
big as she is. She's wearing a beautiful black dress and she looks

*like a princess. We were only allowed to play in some of the
rooms. Xander's room is much neater than my room. He said that
Frida puts all his things away for him every day. Hilda always
wanted me to put my own things away when I was finished playing with them. I didn't like that but mommy said if I took something out to play with it I should be the person to put it away
again when I was finished playing.*

*I wanted to play with Draco because a puppy is much more
fun than Legos. I wanted to pet him the way I pet Ulysses.*

•••••••••••

"It's always something with you Marsh girls, isn't it?" This afternoon Mrs. Hennepin is wearing her reading glasses, little rec-
tangles that make her resemble the unfortunate, though
mercifully hypothetical, progeny of Ben Franklin and the
Peanuts character Sally Brown. We're in the parent-teacher conference room, which is tastefully decorated for the holidays with
a poinsettia plant and a menorah (at least it's not one of the electric ones), resting on top of a runner made of kente cloth.

In my corner of the couch I tuck my legs underneath me, re-
verting to curled-up, childlike body language. I'm about to pull
a lock of hair in front of my face when I remember Mrs. Hennepin's previous comment about my hair-chewing habit. "You
talk as if there's a whole raft of us," I say. "Actually, eighteen
years has passed since I had you, and Mia was never in your
class."

Like a campaigning politician caught in the glare of the
media headlights, Mrs. Hennepin chooses to ignore the facts,
preferring to maintain her revisionist version of events. "You and
your sister always expected special treatment, which your parents not only encouraged, but championed. And if I make an exception for Zoë, then I have to make exceptions for other
students and then exceptions become the rule."

"Zoë's a special kid," I argue. "And she happens to have a scheduling conflict with the Thackeray pageant and the final dress rehearsal for her ballet class recital. She's been practicing for weeks."

"Then she shouldn't need to attend the rehearsal," Mrs. Hennepin counters, using teacher logic.

"If she doesn't go to the rehearsal, she's pre-empted from performing in the recital," I explain. I feel like Sisyphus pushing that huge boulder up the side of the mountain, ready to rejoice when he nears the plateau, only to slip even further backward down the slope, forcing him to begin anew the arduous labor.

When someone has spent the better part of the past half century in a room full of seven-year-olds, it can't help but severely limit their ability to speak to adults without the cadences of condescension creeping into their voice. "Claire, in the eyes of the Thackeray faculty—and most assuredly in the eyes of every parent who has a child enrolled here—each one of them is special. Exceptional."

"Then if it's widely accepted that every kid in this school is exceptional, then the exceptions *have* become the rule, haven't they?" This is Marsh logic. If my father could see me now! Brendan would be so proud.

"I didn't agree to this conference in order to argue semantics with you, Claire."

"Too bad," I mutter.

"My point is, that if I give Zoë permission to leave the assembly early—after the second-grade presentation—I'll have to acquiesce to every other parent who wants to color outside the lines."

"You never did like it when we did that, did you?" I ask her. "Color outside the lines, I mean. It made you very anxious, didn't it?"

Mrs. Hennepin steeples her fingers and leans forward, resting her elbows on her knees. "What I am about to say to you does not leave this room. Do you understand?" She doesn't wait for an answer. "I don't like you, Claire."

Considering I can recall in glorious Technicolor every graphic detail of my own miserable year of second grade, this news does not come as a revelation. Nevertheless, it stings like a slap on sunburned skin. "I don't mind telling you the feeling is more than mutual," I reply. It wasn't a diplomatic thing to say, I know, and it probably sunk Zoë even lower into her predicament. Give me a demerit for a lapse in judgment. If circumstances were different and I wasn't going to bat for my daughter, I would have savored the moment, having waited nearly two decades to tell this paragon (not!) of pedagogy what I think of her.

Mrs. Hennepin removes her eyeglasses and blinks a few times. Then she leans back in her chair. "Well, I commend you on your candor, if nothing else." She still sounds like she's talking to a schoolchild, only using bigger words.

"Tell you what," I say, "I never made you the promise you requested a few minutes ago. But I'll make sure the unprofessional behavior exhibited in your explicitly stated opinion of me does not leave this room if you can see your way toward accommodating Zoë's heavy schedule on the twenty-third." I wait for Mrs. Hennepin's reply, unable to recall the last time *I* had competing social engagements on the same afternoon.

She stands up and looks like she is about to extend her hand to me when she notices a blinking light on the conference-room phone. At Thackeray, parent-teacher confabs are considered consecrated time, so the phone doesn't ring obtrusively. It sparkles tastefully. Mrs. Hennepin punches the lit button and picks up the receiver. She listens for a few moments, then covers the phone with a liver-spotted hand. "Claire, do you know a Frida Nomar?"

The name rings a bell, so to speak, but I can't quite place it.

Yet, if someone knows enough to reach me here, it must be important. "What is this in reference to?" Mrs. Hennepin asks the caller. She listens for the response. "I think you'll want to take this," she says, handing me the phone, her face paler and more agitated than I've ever seen her. "It's Xander Osborne's nanny. Zoë's been bitten by a dog."

Zoë is a brave little girl. And a resourceful one, too, since she figured out fast how to do things with her left hand until the wound on her right one healed. And at least Nina had purchased a puppy that had had all its shots. Zoë was hysterical when I rushed her to the pediatric emergency room. Xander wanted to come along and refused to take no for an answer, and the last place Nina wanted to visit was a hospital. She actually had a few choice words for *my* mothering skills because my daughter had tried to do what dog-loving little girls do, and pet a puppy. Of course the baby Rottweiler did what it does, too. They'd each obeyed their natural instincts, but Draco, like his boy-owner, wasn't one of the more socialized creatures on the planet; and perhaps, like his Harry Potter namesake, was just hell-bent on malevolence.

So Xander and Frida tagged along.

The emergency-room doctor was a young, blonde woman who put both Zoë and me at ease. Until she took out the big needle. She said she had to give Zoë a Tetanus shot as a precautionary measure, and my poor little girl howled herself hoarse. It was breaking my heart. Even Xander, who at first thought the needle was "really cool," freaked out when Dr. Greenzeig began to administer the injection. This, of course further traumatized Zoë, so Frida had to remove her charge from the room and bring him back home.

It only took four stitches to close the wound, but Dr. Greenzeig bandaged Zoë's entire hand so she couldn't get at the sutures. The poor kid had to go through her last day of classes before Christmas vacation writing as a lefty. She was the only second-grader to hold her flashlight torch aloft with the opposite hand during their performance of "The Little Drummer Boy" in the holiday pageant—from which Mrs. Hennepin excused her, following the second-grade presentation. Maybe the teacher really was concerned that I'd rat out her indiscreet insult. Or maybe she just admired Zoë's post-dog-bite attitude and decided to cut us a break. When it came to the recital and "The Waltz of the Flowers," Zoë said something so clever that I can't remember when I've been prouder of her pluck. Of course all the little girls wanted to know why her hand was covered with gauze, and she told them, with the most charming air of authority, "I'm a flower. And a bee tried to pollinate me. But he stung me by mistake."

Her indomitability made Zoë even more popular. She was a walking, talking show-and-tell. But she turned down two invitations to New Year's Eve parties—yes, her set hosts kid-friendly extravaganzas, even though the ball drops in Times Square well past a second grader's normal bedtime. My only "friends" these days are the mothers of Zoë's friends, and I'm not very close with any of them. So, Zoë declined the invites because she wanted to usher in the New Year at home with her mommy (who had been feeling a little sorry for herself that Zoë had twice as many invitations as she did and that carefree Mia was heading off to Lucky Sixpence's glitzy soirée). My daughter's move wasn't entirely altruistic: from our living-room window we have a fantastic view of the midnight fireworks over Central Park.

We now have our silly hats and our noisemakers and, having ordered Chinese food from Zoë's favorite restaurant, have finished our celebratory meal with homemade hot fudge sundaes (I know, I know). Zoë starts to get sleepy at around nine-thirty, even though she enjoyed an extra-long afternoon nap, but she soldiers on, insisting on staying awake long enough to see the fireworks. I'd splurged on a split of good champagne, and just before midnight, I pour Zoë a flute of ginger ale and pop the cork on my Piper-Heidsieck. We turn to face the TV set as if to toast it, while we count down with viewers everywhere, with millions of New Yorkers crushed against one another in the midtown streets, and with a man who was a legend in the music industry back when my parents were young. Dick Clark shouts into his microphone "ten . . . nine . . . eight . . ." and we yell right along with him. My right arm is around Zoë's shoulder; her left grazes my waist. There are tears in my eyes. I become more sentimental than usual on New Year's Eves.

"Three . . . two . . . one . . . HAPPY NEW YEAR!" Elsewhere, lovers and strangers are kissing one another, corks are popping, streamers and balloons are cascading toward crowded dance floors.

Zoë and I clink glasses and take our first sips, while outside we hear a *boom*, signaling the start of the annual Central Park footrace and the fireworks display. We rush to the window to enjoy the glorious free show. I look down at my daughter, the flower of my heart, fruit of my loins, and, occasionally, the bane of my existence. "You know, the very first person you kiss in the new year is supposed to bring good luck for both of you." She outstretches her arms and I kneel so that we're about the same height. Zoë kisses me softly on the mouth and throws her arms around my neck. I realize I am crying. I start to wipe away my tears with the back of my hand and Zoë runs off to get me a tissue.

"Why are you crying, Mommy?" she asks, her little face a picture of confusion and concern. "Are you sad?"

I am sad, actually. But it's different from an ordinary sadness. It's not the kind that's easily pinpointed or explained to a seven-year-old. "I'm just thinking how lucky we are already," I tell her.

"You know what they say on New Year's Day?" She shakes her head. "Out with the old and in with the new." I grab my champagne glass and raise it in a toast.

"Out with the old and in with the new!" Zoë echoes. "Happy New Year, Mommy," she adds with shiny eyes.

I give her a hug and our glasses meet behind her back. "Happy new year, kiddo."

Chapter 13

 Dear Diary:

I hate school. I hate gym most. Now that it's wintertime, we don't play outside anymore for recess and gym. We play poison ball and kickball in the gym and we have tumbling and swimming. Tumbling is the only one I like. I'm not good at playing ball. Some of the kids are really fast and some of them play like it's hockey like we played at Xander's birthday party and they bump into you and knock you down. Xander and his friend Asha knocked into me when we were playing poison ball and I fell down and got a big bump on my leg. They didn't even say they were sorry.

It's so noisy in the gym, too. Everyone is yelling and it makes an echo and it gives me a headache. The gym teacher, Mr. Sparks, said he didn't believe me and he was going to call Mommy and ask her if I really get headaches from loud noises. He did call Mommy and Mommy told him that I got headaches so now I don't have to play ball in the gym anymore.

They put me in swimming instead. All the girls in my class made fun of me because of my bathing suit. It used to be my fa-

vorite bathing suit but not anymore. My friends have really grown-up bathing suits and I still have an Ariel bathing suit. This girl from the other second-grade class, Gelsey, said that nobody wears Disney bathing suits after first grade. I told Mommy what Gelsey said and Mommy said that my Ariel suit still fits me. She said that we only have swimming in school for a couple of months until springtime and she will buy me a new bathing suit in the summer. I was really angry and I was crying and I told Mommy she didn't understand. Mommy said I didn't understand and that if Gelsey thought I should have a different bathing suit, then Gelsey could buy me one. But Gelsey doesn't have her own money.

I don't like swimming in school either. The pool smells yucky and we have to take a shower before and after swimming and the floor in the showers feels icky.

Mommy got a new job. She is working at the big museum with the steps selling things in the gift shop. When she comes home she says her feet hurt a lot from having to stand up all day. She said she has to work really hard because people are bringing back presents they got for Christmas that they didn't like. She even saw some of my friends' moms. She saw Mei-Li's mom and she saw April and May's mom, June. June is the only mom who lets the other kids call her by her first name instead of Mrs. Miller. I wish Mommy didn't have to work because then we would get to be together more. June told Mommy that she misses her when I go to their house to play with April and May, because a lot of times Mommy used to go with me and they would talk in the kitchen while we played. Moms don't always go on play dates but Mommy and June are friends so it was like they had a play date, too. When I was little Mommy went with me all the time on play dates. After first grade started she didn't go so much and since Daddy left she hardly ever goes at all.

April bragged that she has a boyfriend that goes to another school. His name is Grayer. What kind of name is that? I think

April made him up because no one has a name that silly. If I were going to make up a boyfriend he would have a real name like Michael.

....

My feet are killing me. I'm walking in the door from a very long day at the Metropolitan Museum of Art's gift shop, and now it's time to get dinner on the table. For the past week and a half, since I started at the Met, post-job anything has been an effort. Like the sightseeing guide gig, I have to be "on" all day. At least I'm surrounded by pretty things, but fielding questions from uncomprehending, curious, and disgruntled customers is giving my nerves quite a workout.

I've been so caught up with the new job that it's all I can do to find some quality time to spend with Zoë, which, lately, has been manifesting itself solely in doing her homework with her before putting her to bed. In fact, *I* was the one who was up last week until two-thirty in the morning building an igloo out of Styrofoam. As much as it galls me, I think I've finally caved in and adopted the "if you can't beat 'em, join 'em" philosophy when it comes to Thackeray's view on parental "supervision" of their children's homework.

I feel like I'm walking through the world wearing blinders. I drop Zoë at school, head across town to the museum, spend eight hours behind one of the jewelry counters, then pick up Zoë from a friend's house, where she spends her after-school and after-after-school program hours until I'm able to re-trieve her. I haven't even taken the time to look at a news-paper or catch up on housekeeping. For all I know, Armageddon may be imminent and all I'm aware of is an in-vasion of dust bunnies.

I'm reheating some leftover beef barley soup for Zoë and me when the phone rings. "Have you spoken to your sister recently?" my mother wants to know. I admit that I haven't and fill Tulia in on my crazy new schedule.

"Mia's been very upset lately. Did you know that?" I confess that I don't. And I feel guilty about that, because I *should* know these things about my sister. We live only a few miles from each other and sometimes it seems like we're several time zones apart. "She's looking at turning thirty next month as an event worthy of a Willard Scott announcement." My mother manages a laugh. "Of course, when you get to be nearly twice Mia's age, you realize how insignificant the three-oh, and even the four-oh, are in the grand scheme of things. Besides, there's a lot of truth to being as old as you feel." Following that formula, I feel about a hundred and ten. Tulia, however, is in a state of perennial bloom. I think her whimsy keeps her outlook youthful. It's a good object lesson. Tulia's the kind of woman I wouldn't mind turning into in my old age.

Zoë wanders into the kitchen and wants to know who I'm talking with. I let her know it's Granny Tulia, then tell my mother I'll speak to her soon and hand the phone to Zoë to say hello to her grandmother.

The clever little devil launches into her litany about how unfashionable her Ariel bathing suit is (yet she dressed as a mermaid for her school Halloween party, and had a mermaid birthday cake), adding that she has to take more swimming classes this winter because she's been excused from the activities that take place in the noisy gym. By the end of five minutes, she has extracted a promise for a new swimsuit, courtesy of Granny and Grandpa.

Zoë hands back the phone. "Granny Tulia wants to talk to you." She grabs a brownie—at least we took time this past weekend to do a little mommy-daughter baking—and skips out of the room, wearing a smug expression thinly disguised as a triumphant smile.

"You shouldn't do that. You're spoiling her," I tell my mother.

"You know it's our pleasure. And a grandparent's prerogative."

"It undermines my authority. We've been through this before. I told her that she'll have to wait until the summer to get a new suit. The Ariel one still fits her fine. It was too big for her last season, and actually, she's finally grown into it." And here I am telling an avant-garde clothing designer that I don't want my seven-year-old turned into a fashion victim. Plus, I don't like the precedent that when Mommy says no, she can run to Granny.

"Being indulgent goes with the territory," Tulia tells me, vaguely amused. "I can't wait 'til *you're* a grandmother."

• • • • • • • • • • • •

Dear Claire, On a job. Meeting Hunks. Sand and surf and sex. Last fling of my roaring 20s. Wish you were here. Not! Say hi to Zoë. Love, Mia.

• • • • • • • • • • • •

I guess "very upset" is a relative term.

"Oh, God, she's a *shopgirl*." Nina Osborne's words sink into my gut, sending seismic waves of queasiness undulating through the rest of my body. Some people never outgrow the urge to be cruel. Playground bullies just get older, taller, fatter, balder; and their female counterparts . . . well, kittens become cats.

It's been a busy season at the Met. A couple of glitzy exhibits are packing the halls. From behind my jewelry counter in the main gift shop, I've learned to discern the true art lovers—those who have been waiting a lifetime to see a work of art in person— from the dilettantes who just want to be able to tell their friends that they saw the latest blockbuster because it's so hard to get in.

Nina Osborne, although Zoë tells me she has "real paintings"

on her walls, appears to fit neatly into the latter category; those
who collect exhibits. After I overhear the first offending remark
about my new job, she tells her companion, a moneyed matron
of the same ilk, that she'll meet her back at the gift shop in half
an hour after they "do" the Monet/Manet show. Since I'm used
to being asked questions about them, I've memorized a few
facts about each of the current exhibits. The Monet/Manet displays 186 works of art across seven rooms. If my calculations are
accurate, that leaves Nina approximately 9.6 seconds to view
each object, not factoring in travel time from the gift shop on
the first floor to the exhibit, which is tucked away in the south
wing of the second floor. Actually, according to the statistics
given by one of my art history professors, that's better than the
average viewing time of eight seconds per object.

I guess my own little brand of snobbery is kicking in, as a
form of private revenge for Nina's rude comment. A *shopgirl*
indeed!

After Nina and her friend have "done" the Monet/Manet,
they approach my counter. I've never been made to feel smaller
in my life. Or poorer. They want to see the most expensive
items in the case; and while it's true that the stuff is costume
jewelry, some of the reproductions cost several hundred dollars.

Nina is torn between an eighteen-carat gold necklace and the
vermeil version of it, which is only slightly cheaper, but it's the
color that makes the difference. She spends countless minutes
examining the two pieces side by side, probably much longer
than she took to enjoy any of the masterworks upstairs, some of
which are so breathtaking they bring tears to my eyes. "Claire?
Which would you choose if you could afford them?"

I feel my blood begin to bubble and boil. I want to sink into
the floor and evaporate. One of us is going to die. I briefly wonder if I were to reach across the counter and strangle Nina with
one of the necklaces, whether I would get fired. Probably so. But
it would be worth it. If I didn't worry about having to take care

of a small child, it might even be worth going to jail for. The only way I can survive this encounter is to fantasize, Walter Mitty-style, about revenge. I am a modern-day Medea (except for the infanticide thing), and the necklace is poison, but Nina doesn't know it. She politely asks me for help with the difficult clasp. I cinch it closed and it sears her neck and throat. She becomes unable to speak, the circular burn mark reddening and deepening the more she struggles to say something nasty to me. She begs me to remove the choker, but, *oops*, I am powerless. Once the clasp has been fastened, the black magic is out of my hands.

I catch my supervisor watching me. *Can't try any funny stuff, Claire.* "Which one would I select?" I repeat. I smile sweetly and point to the one with the vermeil finish. "If I were you, of course, I would choose this one, no question. It's much more mature-looking." *You bat.*

She pushes it away and taps the glass in front of the gold necklace, as though a fingerprint on the piece itself would mar it irrevocably. "Then I'll take *this* one. I think it does more for my tan." She turns to her friend, keeping half an eye on me. "I always think pallid skin, particularly at this time of year, tends to make people look so sickly. And after all, a bronzed complexion is a universal symbol of good health." Nina's friend must be mute, because I have not heard her utter so much as a syllable in my presence. And I don't know whether she's in concordance with any of Nina's opinions because the Botox injections (a girl can tell, okay?) have rendered her face wrinkle-free, but alarmingly impassive.

"Will that be cash or charge?" I ask.

Nina takes out a platinum card and slaps it on the counter instead of handing it to me. I run her transaction while she tells her girlfriend how much fun it is just to treat yourself to a little something now and again. I carefully box up the "little something," all $825-plus-sales-tax of it. I can't wait for this woman to leave my counter, but I wonder if *she's* wondering whether or not I work on commission and if I do, is thinking smugly that with her purchase she's just performed an act of charity.

As she leaves my counter, with the curtest words of thanks, she comments to her friend that she can't wait to tell some of the other Thackeray mothers what Claire Marsh is doing with her time these days. My supervisor catches my eye. I'm glad I have no other customers at the moment because it gives me an excuse to Windex the countertop. I am, in fact, wiping away my tears.

I get to kinder karate in time to watch the last ten minutes of the class. Zoë's earnest little face, a mask of concentration, is adorable. My Powerpuff Girl is learning how to kick butt for real. As soon as the session ends, all the students bow to the sensei, and suddenly their game faces disappear and they become little kids again, running straight into the arms of the waiting parent or nanny.

"Did you see me?" Zoë asks breathlessly.

"I sure did! I'm so proud of you." I hug her and she's all girly-girly again.

"Sensei Steve says I get to take the test for the orange belt in March!"

"Wow! That's terrific, Z!"

She mops her brow. "I'm thirsty."

I hand her a juice box from a shopping bag, then remove the rest of them from the bag and offer them around to the other kids. At least with kinder karate the parents aren't expected to bring solid food when it's their turn to supply the snack. In fact, it's discouraged. Some of the moms and dads show off by showing up with fancy drinks full of electrolytes. I don't have the time or the money to hunt down that kind of stuff. I barely made it to a Duane Reade to see what they had in their refrigeration units.

Zoë's blowing bubbles through the straw. "It makes the box jiggle! Look!" she says, and demonstrates her new discovery. "It's like science. See?"

I'm amused that she's having such a good time. She's precious when she's in such high spirits. She's also a born leader. After a minute or so, she's got half the kids in the class blowing bubbles into their juice boxes.

One of the mothers pulls her kid aside and takes the box out of her hand, tossing it into the trash. I can see that she's digging her nails into the little girl's arms. I bet the child can feel it right through the heavy cotton sleeves of her ghi. The mother shoots me a dirty look and turns back to her pinioned daughter. "I don't want you to do that, Emily. It's not nice. Ladies don't play with their food."

I glare back at Emily's mother. If blowing bubbles in your juice is such a crime, God help Emily if she ever commits a genuinely major infraction. "Why don't you go change?" I suggest to Zoë, who had stopped drinking her juice as soon as Emily's mother began to scold her daughter.

Zoë heads off to get out of her ghi and into her street clothes, so I take the opportunity to get as far away from the other moms as possible. I review the flyers on the bulletin board. Out of curiosity, I pick up a trifolded brochure that contains the dojo's schedule of classes. "You thinking of joining us?" asks Zoë's teacher, Sensei Steve, a thirty-something Jewish guy with fuzzy red hair. Behind us, a number of adults, their ages easily spanning two or three generations, are just coming in for the next class.

I blush and stick the brochure back into its holder. "I'd love to, but I don't have the time. Not to take a class myself . . . unless you've got parent-child classes. Two birds . . . one stone . . . you know? That would be just about the only way it might work out." I chuckle. "Or *I* might work out." Actually, there's a parent-child class offered by the bikram yoga studio Zoë goes to, but it's too darn hot in that room for me.

Steve laughs. "We don't have mommy-and-me classes yet, but that's a good idea! I'm always looking for ways to grow the business and serve the community." He tells me that Zoë has taken to karate with remarkable acuity, which is why she is progressing so swiftly. Her ballet classes have also contributed to her ability, combining training in grace as well as strength and discipline. However, he says, uncharacteristically shuffling his feet and averting his gaze—which, up to this point has been direct—my daughter, he tells me, often has the tendency to wander.

"Around the room?" I ask. "That sounds like a great way to end up getting kicked in the head by mistake."

"No, no, no. Mentally," he says. "She . . ." He's reaching for the right words, and I can sense that he's tiptoeing around what he may really want to say because he's afraid it might not land well and he could lose our patronage. Finally, the muscles in his face stop working so hard and he settles into a smile. "Zoë . . . has the tendency to stray from the ritual poses. From their order. She . . . *choreographs*."

Before I can say something, Sensei Steve hastens to add that he finds her attitude somewhat charming. But it can be distracting to the rest of the class. And of course, part of the study of martial arts is discipline. I explain that her ballet teacher, Miss Gloo, consigns the final ten minutes of class to improvisation, allowing her little charges the chance to dance around the room on their own, incorporating the steps they practiced that day. Not that Zoë should be making up her own moves instead of following the instructor, but I can see why she thinks it's okay to improvise, since a precedent has been set in another program.

I tell the sensei that I understand that his karate class is structured very differently from ballet and promise that before her next session, I will speak with Zoë about the importance of following directions.

"Don't be too hard on her, though," he cautions. "In some ways, she may have the right idea."

I'm puzzled. "What do you mean?"

Sensei Steve grins and shrugs. "Well, her improvisational skills may act to her detriment in a classroom situation. But if she ever got into a real-life fight, I wouldn't want to be her opponent!"

In the front hall I drop the mail on the table by the door, help Zoë off with her parka, scarf, mittens, and snow boots, and then follow her into her bedroom so I can put away her karate gear. How I envy Mia, whom I spoke to for all of two seconds last week, when she called to tell me, breathlessly, that she had just returned from a fabulous gig in California, doing the makeup for a calendar shoot on Catalina Island with a pod of Navy SEALs. What I wouldn't give for a break. At this point, even an afternoon nap is a luxury.

"What happened in here?" I gasp, surveying the wreck that is my child's room. It had become increasingly messy over the past couple of days, and I'd urged Zoë to straighten it up; but now it looks like a thief demolished the joint in search of priceless treasure. "Zoë, what have I told you about keeping your room clean?"

"It's not my fault."

"It's not . . . what? Whose 'fault' do you think it is?" She looks around, eyeing the mess. Just a few days ago, the room was in pretty good shape. "Zoë, I'm talking to you." She's pulling off her socks and adding them to the pile, acting as though my words are nothing more than the vaguely annoying hum of a mosquito.

"It's Dobby's fault."

"Dobby's?"

"Dobby's supposed to clean up my room."

"Nice try, Z. Very clever. But the last time I checked, we

didn't have a house elf. And I seem to recall that Dobby *causes* more messes than he cleans up."

"That's what I mean," she says, pretending to look as annoyed as I truly feel. "Dobby made it look like this and he's supposed to clean it up."

"Mommy doesn't have very much patience for this right now, Zoë. Mommy's had a long day." *And a particularly lousy one.* After my encounter this afternoon with Nina Osborne and the nasty glances from the kinder karate mom, it won't take much to really push me over the edge.

"I've had a long day, too," she insists. "And I still have to do homework. We're supposed to draw a picture of our favorite sound."

"Well, get out your crayons because the only sound you're about to hear is me getting very angry."

"You're already very angry. And that's not my favorite sound. My favorite sound is macaroni pouring into the pot of boiling water."

I grab her arm and turn her so that she is forced to witness the disaster area that is her bedroom.

"We need to talk about discipline," I tell her. "First of all, I'm the mommy around here and the mommy is the boss."

"Ouch. You're hurting me."

I doubt it, but I relax my grip. "I'm sorry. Now, you may not like everything I have to say, but as long as you live here, Mommy makes the rules."

She wriggles out of my grasp and throws herself on a pile of clothes and toys that, I believe, are on top of where her bed used to be. I'm assuming it's still under the avalanche. "Then I don't want to live here anymore." She begins to cry and I bite my tongue before I suggest that she might be happier with Scott and Serena. It's a subject I wouldn't touch right now with the proverbial ten-foot pole.

I perch on the edge of the bed, shoving aside a bunch of

stuff that suspiciously resembles the clothes I just laundered for her last night. Thank God I've got a small washer/dryer in the room off the kitchen that was originally designed as a maid's room. Otherwise I would live at the laundromat. "Hilda doesn't help us anymore, Z, so you've got to take care of your own things. We've talked about this before." I'm beginning to wonder if the state of my daughter's bedroom isn't a metaphor for some form of maternal neglect. "I know it's been very hard for you since Daddy left. But it's been hard for me, too. And I don't know what to tell you . . . other than I'm doing the best I can right now." Zoë looks up from the pile, her face red and tearstained. "But I need you to do the best job *you* can do, too."

"I *am*," she insists, snuffling. I look around the room for a box of tissues, can't locate one at first glance, and run into the bathroom for some paper so she doesn't snivel all over her recently washed and newly wrinkled clothes.

"Zoë, look at this room. It wasn't like this a couple of days ago. I know it wasn't. Don't tell me you're doing the best you can."

"I told you, it's not my fault!" she says stubbornly, raising her voice. "It's Dobby's!!"

"Stop it, Zoë! It's not funny anymore. I'm just about at my wit's end today. Now clean up this mess and then get started on your homework."

"What's your 'witzend'?"

"Wit's end. It means I've run out of patience. Don't push me, or we're both going to be sorry."

"Why?"

"All right! If you can't appreciate your things, I'll find a little girl who does." I grab Baa by the neck and start to walk out of the room with him.

"Okay. I'm going, I'm going." She begins to sort through the mess with a minimal amount of diligence.

"I'm counting to ten. One . . . two . . . three . . ."

She begins to pick up speed. By "five," she's almost at a normal pace. "Six . . . seven . . ."

"I told you, I'm doing it!" she yells.

"Don't yell at your mother!" I yell back. "I want this room completely cleaned up in twenty minutes. Do you hear me? I'm coming back in here in *twenty minutes*. Then we'll start on your homework." I turn to leave the room and trip over her yellow knapsack. Exasperated, I grab it from the floor and desperately look for a place to put it where it will cease to be a hazard in an obstacle course.

"I need that," Zoë says.

"You wouldn't have even found it until you cleaned up. We just got home and already it ended up buried." I place Baa on her desk and hand her the bag.

She rifles through its deep center compartment. "I have a note for you."

Oh, no. Now what?

"Don't worry, it's nothing bad," she says reassuringly, having noticed my panicked expression. "It's a permission slip." She forks over a crinkled sheet of paper. "We're going on a class trip to the firehouse next Friday and you have to give your permission. You have to sign it and I have to bring it back before the end of the week." I read it over while she continues to hunt through the bag for something.

The permission slip is a pro forma thing. I find a green magic marker—on the floor—sign the paper and hand it back to her. "Here. Put this where you'll remember to give it to Mrs. Hennepin tomorrow. Do we need to make a reminder?" We have a calendar posted on the inside of Zoë's bedroom door, another dry-erase board where she can write down important things.

"I'll do it," she says, presenting me with an envelope retrieved from the knapsack and going to the board. "You have to be class parent in February. That's what the other paper is about. They sent it in the mail, too, just in case."

I'm sure it's sitting out on the hall table. I noticed a Thackeray envelope in today's stack of letters and bills. I peruse the note, which assigns me parental duty on Valentine's Week. Essentially, class parents provide a much-needed extra pair of hands to the teacher and the special subjects instructors. The Thackeray moms and dads like to know how their tuition dollars are being spent, so a week of unpaid servitude was the academy's solution. If I'm unable to discharge my duties—I think of Miss America finalists—I can arrange to swap weeks with another parent. At this point, one week is as rotten as any other. I've just started the job at the Met gift shop and now I'll need to ask for time off. It won't be easy on the wallet, either. The Thackeray Academy assumes that parents have both the time and the income to devote to participating firsthand in their children's education. And, in my case, once upon a time they were right.

I watch Zoë, who knows I've got my eye on her, her face in a determined pout, putting away her clothes and books and games and toys, doggedly cleaning up the chaos.

And suddenly I recognize—too well—that, though it may be an unpleasant task, it's time for Claire Marsh to get her own house in order.

· · · · · · · · · · · ·

My Trip To the Firehouse

by Zoë Marsh Franklin

Yesterday our whole class went on a trip to the firehouse because we are learning in school all about how our city works. The first fireman we saw was a man named Jim. He is the chief at that firehouse and he is like the boss of all the firemen. He has a big tummy and a big mustache. Fireman Jim said hello to all of us and then he said he was having a very busy day so he introduced us to another fireman, Fireman Dennis, who was going to give us our tour.

Fireman Dennis isn't roly-poly like Fireman Jim. And he doesn't have gray hair like Fireman Jim. Fireman Dennis has brown hair and he was more friendly than Fireman Jim. He liked talking to our class a lot, I think. I don't think Fireman Jim really wanted to talk to us. But Fireman Dennis was having fun with us. He said there are a few firewomen too, but they didn't have any at their firehouse.

When Fireman Dennis showed us how they slide down the pole when they have to race to a fire I didn't know how Fireman Jim could get through the hole in the ceiling to slide down the pole because his tummy is big. Fireman Dennis even made a funny joke about Fireman Jim's big belly. Fireman Dennis told us that the firemen work some days in a row and then they have days off in a row. When they have days off they go home to their own houses. And when they are working they sleep in the firehouse up-stairs, which is why they have to slide down the pole to the fire truck, which is in the garage. The pole is faster than taking the stairs. Fireman Dennis showed us the upstairs part of the fire-house where the firemen sleep. It looked like the Annie movie where all of the orphans' beds were in one big room.

And then Fireman Dennis asked who wanted to slide down the pole and we all raised our hands. But he said we couldn't all do it, so there could be one boy and one girl from each second-grade class. He picked me as the girl from Mrs. Hennepin's class and Bram got picked as the boy. Xander got angry because he didn't get picked and he started to throw a temper tantrum and Fireman Dennis made a funny joke because he said Xander was acting like a mean old dog and did he know what happens to mean old dogs? And Xander said no and Fireman Dennis said that they turn a fire hose on mean old dogs and get them all wet and splash them and that makes them quiet really fast. Xander didn't think it was funny, but I did.

I loved sliding down the pole. It was even more fun than the slide at the playground. And Fireman Dennis let us climb up on the hook-and-ladder truck and on the pumper truck and I got to ring the silver bell, too. Ashley said I was being a hog because I got to do lots of things at the firehouse, but I don't think I was being a hog and some of the times it was because Fireman Dennis picked me.

Then Fireman Dennis showed us the big kitchen and told us what kinds of things firemen like to eat for dinner. He said they like chili a lot and he was the winner of a lot of contests between firehouses to see which one had the best homemade chili. I had chili once when Mommy made it. It was too spicy. Some of the boys in my class thought it was a sissy thing to do, to cook. Fireman Dennis doesn't look like a sissy. He looks very brave and a little bit like Prince Eric in The Little Mermaid. *His mouth looks nice when he smiles.*

We learned all about what happens inside the firehouse after someone pulls a fire alarm somewhere and how the firemen know what house to go to and how fast they can get ready. And Fireman Dennis told us how bad it was for somebody to call a false alarm. Because it's really dangerous because if there's a real fire when the firemen are off answering a false alarm, then they can't get to the real fire fast enough sometimes, and it means that people could die. When I was little I used to be scared of fire truck sirens because I thought the fire was in my house or maybe next door. And I was especially scared when the sirens ~~waked~~ *woke me up in the middle of the night because I thought maybe our house was burning down.*

And I learned that being a fireman is a very dangerous job because fires are so hot and because of what is burning, sometimes things explode during the fire or ceilings fall down on top of firemen while they're trying to put out the fire. Or floors fall in, and the firemen fall down all the way to the next floor.

Fireman Dennis said that all firefighters are like brothers of each other even if they aren't really relatives. He showed us the pictures on the wall of the firemen from his fire house who died fighting fires. He said it's called the Wall of Heroes. And there is a purple-and-black swish of fabric on the wall above the pictures that is what firemen are supposed to put up when a fireman dies. There were I think nine pictures on the wall of firemen who died, all of them from Fireman Dennis's firehouse. I asked if seeing the pictures every day was scary. Fireman Dennis said that it was a little bit scary because it was a reminder of the danger of being a fireman. And then I asked him if seeing the pictures every day made him sad, and he said that looking at the pictures did make him sad—he even sounded sad when he was saying it to our class—because they were all his good friends and almost like his real-life brothers. But then he said that he loved being a fireman and his best friends died doing what they loved to do best, which was helping people and it wasn't going to change his mind about being a fireman and that it was the best job in the whole world.

Chapter 14

I'm not a joiner—that's not my thing—but like the right-handed diamond, the singleton's statement that she doesn't need to get a guy to get a rock, everybody's doing it. Turning thirty and letting the world know about it. *The New York Times* now has a word for us. Trigenerians. The celebration's like a wedding for singles, a sweet sixteen for grown-ups. Trends. This is everything *Claire* is trying to get away from. The big bash. Keeping up with the Joneses. Or the Silver-Katzes. Pay to play. But I had a breakthrough after I got back from Catalina. Okay, so I'm hitting the three-oh; I have no choice about it, obviously. But I chose to stop moping about it, and underline it in big pink neon streaks instead.

I can't decide where to have it or what to do, but I think I'll ask everyone I know to join me. I'm torn between all-out black-tie elegance somewhere or tequila shots and PB & J sandwiches at my favorite East Village bar. It'll be way past Zoë's bedtime, but I want her there.

There's more to this, too. Mia Marsh is saying bye-bye to an old life. I'm fed up with relationships that aren't much more than multi-night stands. I looked at that Excel chart I made. One bottom line was that none of the guys were in it for the long haul. I'm sick of that. Over it. And I noticed that a lot of the guys didn't have real jobs. Or steady ones. And I never gave a shit about that because *I* had a job. A great one. And made good bucks and didn't care what they did, as long as they seemed to be happy doing it.

But I think the commitment thing has to factor into every part of your life in order for it to work. You make the choice to commit to a job you love, as much as to a guy or girl you love. Do what you want, but do it a hundred percent. Hal, for instance, was a slacker. Luca went with the flow. He was mostly into the *idea* of Beauty in all its forms. Cowboy was . . . well, Cowboy was a disaster. Mia's Big Mistake. And Robert Osborne was more committed to himself than anyone else. I can't believe I just had a split second of pity for Nina. And then there's Chris, the Navy SEAL I just spent a weekend with, who's not much for maintaining even a post-coital correspondence.

Valentine's Day looms large and lacy and pink and red on the calendar's horizon. And I don't expect so much as a card from any of the guys who've been in my life for the past several months. This sucks. What happened to true love?

When Claire and I were young, Thackeray had no rules about giving out Valentines. In other words, if you had a crush on one kid, you could act on it—if you were brave enough—and not have to bother about bringing a Valentine for each guy in the class. Not anymore, evidently. Nowadays, you bring one, you'd better bring ten. It kind of dilutes the purpose if you tell *everyone* you love them. Makes you sound either promiscuous or like you're proselytizing for Jesus.

So, I'm looking at being loveless on Valentine's Day and dateless on my birthday. I called Claire to commiserate and she didn't want to hear it. No one's beating down *her* door, either. But Zoë's gotten Valentines mailed to the house and Claire says the kid has a secret admirer. Seems like the *Finding Nemo* generation is having a much better time than the finding *me* generation.

· · · · · · · · · · · ·

Dear Diary:

Valentine's Day is going to be so fun! Mommy is class parent this week and so she gets to be at the Valentine's class party and we get to go to school together. Mrs. Heinie-face is not very nice to Mommy the way she is to the other class parents when it's their turn. Mommy says she feels like she's back in second grade for real again.

We made Valentine heart cookies when I got home from school today. We used a cookie cutter that's shaped like a heart and we have more than one and they are different sizes so we can cut out one heart and put it on top of the other one. Mommy even let me help roll the dough. Before we put them in the oven, we sprinkled them with red sugar and then the sugar melted on purpose because the oven is so hot. Some of the cookies we didn't put sugar on. We left them naked. And when they came out of the oven and they cooled off, we put icing on them. Mommy made pink icing but I don't want to give the boys in school pink because it's a girl color. I put the ~~bestest~~ best cookies in a little box and I'm going to give it to Xander when no one else is looking. He likes cookies a lot.

Mommy told me that when she and MiMi were little they used to give valentines at school and Mommy got a lot of valentines always but sometimes MiMi didn't get any. And then Mommy said one Valentine's Day MiMi didn't want to go to school because she thought everyone was going to get lots of valentines and she wasn't going to get any ones and it would mean that nobody loved her. So she pretended to be sick so she would have to stay home and miss school.

Mr. Kiplinger made a rule that for tomorrow because it's Valentine's Day we don't have to wear our uniforms. So I have a new dress that I am going to wear to school tomorrow. It's bright pink and Granny Tulia made it just for me. It has long sleeves and a red heart on one of the sleeves. And it has a big pocket that's shaped like a heart and I can put my valentines inside the pocket. And it has a special purse that matches it and it's a big red heart, too. I have hair barrettes that look like hearts. Mommy said I could wear my Dorothy ruby slippers to school.

I can't wait for tomorrow. I was supposed to go to sleep at 7:30 because it's a school night but I wasn't tired after my bath. I'm still not tired. I thought writing in my diary would make me tired. My HAND is tired, but I'M not.

• • • • • • • • • • • •

"It's not the function of the class parent to offer an opinion," Mrs. Hennepin tells me. "You're here to help maintain and ensure their daily routine. And, of course, to experience, firsthand, how your child is being educated."

I figure if Thackeray expects me to participate, even if only for a week, in the quotidian conducting of lessons, I should do more than bear witness to them. I should become *involved*. So, as an example, for the past two days I've encouraged—or let's just say I haven't *dis*couraged—some of Zoë's classmates from coloring their homemade valentines in any hue they wish, not just in the traditional spectrum of red to pink. One kid made his heart a lurid shade of purple. Mrs. Hennepin confronted him and asked him to redo it. The brave child defended his creation and told the old bat that "there are, too, purple hearts," because his grandfather got one in Vietnam.

I've done a lot more than come home coated with flour after accompanying the kids to a cooking class (blueberry muffins) run by the Industrial Arts teacher. A lot more than helping them safely handle scissors and palette knives in art class; more than ending up with clay caked under my nails and dried paint in my hair. More than troubleshooting during math, English, and social studies and being startled out of my skin when I suddenly found myself holding Iggy, the school's iguana, so the science teacher, Mrs. Peabo, could demonstrate something that I'm still too freaked out to remember.

This is the third consecutive day that I've borne witness to Mrs. Hennepin's attempts to squelch their creativity and young imaginations. I can feel my blood seething in my veins. Zoë writes "I love you" in *script* and the old witch glares at her. Privately I wonder about the identity of the future recipient of my daughter's valentine card. Me? Her father? MiMi? Xander? I have a guess about the identity of her "secret admirer." I've caught Bram Siborsky looking at her, spaniel-eyed, on more than one occasion.

"What kind of message are you sending these children?" I demand of Mrs. Hennepin. "Love comes in all colors, not just pink and red."

She sighs, exasperated with me, clearly counting the minutes until Monday, when a new class parent, preferably someone far less difficult, fulfills the obligation.

It's stifling in here; and not just because the classroom is overheated. I find that I can't wait for recess. The air is cold and crisp today, with the promise of spring around the corner. The groundhog didn't see his shadow this year, but I can't remember what that means. Either way, according to the calendar, there's six more weeks of winter after February 2. Four weeks and change still to go.

In the winter when the weather is clear, the kids are allowed to have recess on the roof, an uninspiring, black-topped, fenced-in affair overlooking Central Park. There's room enough up there for games of tag or an organized sport like kickball or basketball, or to play hide-and-go-seek—or make out if you're a hormonal adolescent—in the science shed, which houses off-season or additional equipment like microscopes and gardening tools.

So here we all are on the roof (I am refereeing a game of poison ball) when Zoë runs up to me sobbing and blubbering all down the front of her parka. She hurls herself into my arms, spreading snot and tears along the lapels of my camel-hair coat. "What happened, sweetheart? Did you get hurt?"

It takes a few moments before she can regain her composure enough to tell me her tale of woe. "I gave . . . I gave . . . I gave . . ." I hand her a crumpled but clean Kleenex from my coat pocket. She accepts it and does a lousy job of wiping her nose. "I gave the cookies to Xander, and . . . and . . . and . . ." More hysterical tears.

I stroke her hair and hold her, trying to calm her down. "What's the matter? Didn't he like them?"

"He crumbled them up and he gave them to the pigeons!" she bawls. "And then he threw some of them through the fence to see if he could hit people on the street."

"My poor baby," I whisper. Men. Maybe we females were raised all wrong. The way to a man's heart isn't through his stomach at all. I'm no radical feminist, but an ice pick would be a far more effective method in some cases. How dare that brat break my little girl's heart! And someone ought to tell him it's not nice to pelt pedestrians with baked goods. Do I bring this to Mrs. Hennepin's attention? Or to Mr. Mendel and Mr. Kiplinger? Should I go straight to his mother; or dare I take disciplinary matters into my own hands?

"Did he eat *any* of them?" I ask Zoë.

"Uh-huh," she admits, still snuffling. "He had one and he said it was good, but then he said he had more fun giving them to the birds. Or seeing how far he could throw them. And we worked so *hard*," she sobs. I stop myself from saying that Xander Osborne may, alas, be the first in a long line of inattentive, undeserving guys for whom Zoë will extend herself, only to find her tender feelings smashed, her little heart crushed. Maybe, I tell myself, with crossed fingers, *her* destiny will be different. Happy Valentine's Day? Bah, humbug.

The forty-five-minute recess period ends and the kids are shuttled back downstairs to the classroom, where it's time for social studies. They're covering a unit on "Our City and How It Works," which I find amusing, wondering if the students will get to navigate a murky, labyrinthine section on municipal bureaucracy, including: Getting Off Jury Duty, Beating a Parking Ticket, and What to Do If Your Noisy Neighbors Still Won't Keep It Down after 3 A.M.

I'm sitting in the back of the room, listening to Mrs. Hennepin recap last week's lesson on the fire department, which encompassed the recent class trip to the local firehouse. I'm hoping the section on sanitation won't entail an off-campus excursion to a landfill.

Perhaps it's just the power of suggestion, but I smell smoke. *Couldn't* be. Could it? I'd insisted on opening the windows this morning because it was too stuffy in the classroom and the kids were getting logy. Now I watch an acrid curlicue the color of burlap spiral past a windowpane. I may be paranoid but I'm not nuts.

I leave my class parent post on the uncomfortable gunmetal-colored folding chair and stroll to the front of the room where Mrs. Hennepin is talking about why recycling is important. I hope Zoë remembers this, because I can never recall, with the frequently shifting rules being handed down by our mayor, what we recycle and when. I hate to seem cynical about it, but yesterday's news ends up as roofing material in China.

In the calmest voice I can manage, I whisper into the teacher's ear that I think the school is on fire. She gives me a startled look, bug-eyed with alarm, then inhales deeply and sniffs the air. She is inclined, however much she may personally dislike me, to agree.

Mrs. Hennepin claps her hands and commands the children to grab their coats and line up along the wall by the door. "We're all going to go downstairs to the sidewalk and across the street," she announces.

A chorus of whys is answered by the increasingly powerful smell of smoke. No doubt about it, now, something, somewhere close, is burning. I step outside the classroom into the hallway, crack the glass on the little red box affixed to the wall and pull the alarm, which alerts the other classes as well as the fire department.

There is a shuffling of feet, a scuffling of students to make it to the stairwells in an orderly fashion. Fourteen grades—pre-K through twelfth—must be safely evacuated. We get to the street and I help Mrs. Hennepin do a head count of our charges.

Shit. One missing.

She knows the roll backwards and forwards, not I, but I do know enough of Zoë's classmates by name and appearance to do my own mental tally. Smoke is now billowing off the roof, fueled by the winter breeze and whatever combustibles are burning.

Xander Osborne is not here. Come to think of it, I'm pretty sure he never returned to the classroom after recess, and somehow, his absence eluded our notice.

The fire department has arrived and the men start to enter the building with their hoses. A cherry picker is being unfolded toward the rooftop in a zigzag of metal framework.

I remove my heavy coat and thrust it into the surprised hands of Mrs. Hennepin. Then I make a mad dash across the street, which has just been closed off to vehicular traffic, and into the building.

"Mommy!" Zoë screams. "Where are you going?" A chorus of adult voices echoes the same.

But I know where Xander is; I couldn't be more sure of it. And because I know I know this and the firefighters don't, I believe, in this very instant, that I can get to him before they can. I'm not lugging heavy equipment and, for once, there's a payoff for my misspent youth. The only thing that would burn in such a concentrated location on the Thackeray Academy's roof is the only structure on it: the science shed.

What I haven't taken into account is that the roiling smoke, now beginning to fill the central stairwell, has rendered it difficult to breathe without proper ventilation equipment; and, in these conditions, I have a hard time seeing where I'm going.

I've made it to the second floor landing—I think.

As sure as the sun sets in the west, I am certain that Xander Osborne, seven-year-old arsonist—I'm sure of this, now, too—is somewhere near the science shed, if not inside it—in which case, it could be too late.

Third floor. I'm still ahead of the firefighters.

I'm counting the landings in my head, trying to keep track of them. I yank my sweater over my head and bring it to my mouth, using the wool as a filter.

I'm on the fourth landing. I need to get down the corridor and locate the door that leads up the stairs to the roof. It feels like I've swallowed a sharp object that's pushing against the walls of my throat. Behind me I hear the heavy footsteps of the firefighters and the rattle and thud of lifesaving equipment. They are shouting to one another but the sound is no more than a series of guttural grunts to my ears. I have a single focus: to find that door and make it one more flight to the roof.

I've climbed the final staircase. One barrier remains. The metal door is hot as hell. I burn my fingers on its handle and on the knob that must be twisted to release the lock. I have the same kind of lock on my apartment door. My fingers should know it, but the surface is too hot. The sleeve of my pullover becomes an erstwhile "potholder." I throw my less-than-significant weight against the door. Adrenaline tells my body it doesn't feel the searing when it makes contact with the steel.

I'm now out on the roof, making choking sounds that I hope sound like "Xander!" In one of my recurring nightmares, one I've suffered since childhood, I'm being attacked and I open my mouth to scream, but no sound will come out. I feel like I'm living it now. Where is this kid? I make my way toward the burning science shed and then I think I glimpse him through the billows of black, just outside the shed, tented underneath his hooded parka. I can't tell if he's moving. Behind me, the firemen have made it to the roof. Do they see us? I don't know. If they don't, we're in the direct line of fire of their hoses. The force of the water could injure us—or worse.

I reach Xander. He's unconscious, I think, but breathing. I don't know what to do, don't remember any of the lessons we're all supposed to memorize, except "stop, drop, and roll." Since his body is not on fire, the mnemonic is moot.

"Xander, wake up!" I shake him. Try to get a response. "Wake up, goddamn you!" I'm flinging the crumpled heap of child back and forth as though he's a Raggedy Andy. "You have to go, now," I insist. "You have to go downstairs."

Through some miracle I manage to rouse him. And through the charcoal denseness, I can make out the figures of two, maybe three firefighters coming toward us.

Xander's eyes open, but the smoke is stinging them. He shuts them again and clings to me. "You have to go, sweetie. Crawl on your belly. That's it. Pretend you're a snake. Crawl on your belly toward the door." But he doesn't want to let go of me. I manipulate his little body into a prostrate position and try to pull him along with me. Who knows what the hell is really stored in that shed? Could be heat-sensitive chemicals. I've got to get him back to the stairway before there's a Jerry Bruckheimer-style explosion.

I hear a voice, muffled, filtered through an oxygen mask. "We've got you now, ma'am. Is the boy okay?"

"He's alive. Take him," I say.

I don't remember what happened next.

"Well, look at that, your eyes are blue." I have just opened my eyes—I think. I'm on the sidewalk outside the school, surrounded by a crowd of adults. I think I see an ambulance amid the jumble of emergency vehicles. I am peering into the concerned, carbon-smudged, sweating face of a firefighter.

"Happy Valentine's Day," he says. "Welcome back." He removes an oxygen mask from my face. I have no idea how long I'd had it on.

"How's . . . ?"

"The little boy? He's gonna be all right. We're going to send him to the hospital, though, just to be sure. His mom is on her way over here."

"That's good. Thank God." I close my eyes again.

"Nuh-uh. No Sleeping Beauty act. We need you awake right now. I don't want you slipping back under."

"I want . . . where's Zoë?"

"Who's Zoë?" the firefighter asks me. His eyes are the color of bittersweet chocolate.

"My daughter. My little girl." My own voice sounds unfamiliar to me. "I want her to know her mommy's okay. I'm okay . . . right?"

The fireman nods. "You're better than okay. You're pretty fucking—excuse my language—pretty damn brave." He chuckles. "I guess 'damn's' not much better than 'fucking.' " Is he blushing under that soot? "Brave, but maybe a little nuts. Running into a burning building to save a little kid. You're going to do me right out of job, Mrs . . . ?"

"Marsh. *Ms.* Marsh. Claire. Call me Claire. I'm . . . did . . . ? Did you give me mouth-to-mouth resuscitation?"

He nods again but doesn't elaborate. "You were saying something, just before you asked me . . . about the mouth-to-mouth."

His dark eyes seem to flicker with interest. Or maybe it's just a fleck of soot and I'm imagining things in my new glad-to-be-not-dead state of semi-consciousness.

"I was? What was I saying?"

The fireman looks embarrassed. "A *Ms*. You were saying that you were a *Ms*., Not a *Mrs*."

"I'm divorced." Which reminds me . . . "Where's my daughter? I need to see her." With my hero's help, I raise my head and look around. All the kids are still on the sidewalk. The rest of the firemen are leaving the building, starting to pack up their gear. I guess they'll give the word when it's safe to bring everyone back inside. "Zoë. Zoë Marsh Franklin. Can you find her for me, please?"

The fireman doesn't leave my side, but calls to one of his colleagues to find a seven-year-old kid named Zoë Marsh Franklin. "Tell her her mom's okay and wants to see her!" Fuzzily, I guess that they must have kept the kids away from me in case I wasn't going to be all right. That would have been a terrible thing for small children to witness.

"Mommy!" Zoë hurls herself between me and the fireman, throwing her body over mine. "You're Fireman Dennis!" she says, looking at him.

"You two know each other?" I ask.

"We met him when we went to see the firehouse," Zoë says. "Remember when you signed my permission slip? He gave us the tour. And I wrote all about him in my report for class, remember? He showed us how they slide down the pole and everything. And how to cook chili. And I got to sit on the fire truck and ring the bell and even slide down the pole, too. Did you save my mommy's life?" she asks him.

"I think I might have helped," he says, his manner slightly "aw-shucks."

"Wow," Zoë breathes. She looks like she wants to hug him but thinks twice when she gets a closer look at his grime-coated exterior.

"I think what we both mean is 'thank you,' " I say. "Thank you very much, Fireman Dennis." I hold Zoë close, very, very happy to be alive. "So," I begin awkwardly, realizing I'm nervous, "so . . . my mother taught me that the proper way to say thank you is to write a note. Although she was never quite clear on the protocol involved when someone saves your life. So, I guess what I'm asking is . . . to whom should I address it? My note. Fireman Dennis . . . ?"

"McIntyre." He extends his hand. My own looks tiny in the palm of it. "Dennis McIntyre. And *my mother* taught me never to stand on ceremony. So, if it's okay with you, Zoë, your mom doesn't need to write a letter. She can thank me in person." Dennis puts his hands on my daughter's shoulders and looks directly into her shining eyes. "Can I take your mom out for dinner next week? And maybe a movie?"

"Are . . . are you . . . are you trying to pick me up?" I ask.

"I already did that." He smiles. "Claire. So, if it's all right with you, I'm ready to move on to step two."

Chapter 15

 Dear Diary:

Mommy's different. I was so scared when she went into the school the day it caught fire. And Mrs. Hennepin wouldn't let me go to see if she was okay when the firemen brought her out. So I was even more scared then. But Fireman Dennis saved her life and now she doesn't get mad at me so much anymore. She used to get mad at me sometimes if I didn't finish my dinner and when I picked at my food. Fireman Dennis asked her on a date. Mommy wanted to know what I thought about that. I told her I think it's good because he's very nice. Mommy said she doesn't know how she feels about that. She and Fireman Dennis have been talking on the telephone and they talk for a long time and she's happy when she talks to him. Maybe he could be my new daddy. I don't think my real daddy will come back. I used to think that but I don't think it anymore. I think he is happy being with Serena. Daddy went away in June and it's February now. That's . . . July, August, September, October, November, December, January and part of February. That's really a long time. If he was going to come back to live with Mommy and me he would do it. So I don't think he's coming back. Maybe

Mommy thinks that too. Maybe that's why she is talking to Fire-man Dennis a lot.

They are going to go on a date but Mommy is busy with her job and Fireman Dennis is busy with his job and we have my homework every day except on weekends and my yoga and ballet and Museum Adventures and kinder karate, and if she goes out without me Mommy won't let me stay home alone so we have to get a baby-sitter and MiMi said she would baby-sit me but she has been busy too.

MiMi is going to have a big birthday party at nighttime and I'm going to get to go and be with the grown-ups. She came to visit us and asked Mommy if she could borrow Mommy's wedding dress to wear at her birthday party because she said it would be fun to wear a wedding dress on her birthday. Mommy didn't have a fancy wedding dress because she and Daddy didn't have a big party. She did wear a long white dress but it is not fancy like a bride's dress with a big skirt like a princess. Well, it's a little bit fancy. The back of it stretches on the floor a little and if you get too close, you'll step on it. Mommy said MiMi could borrow it if she wanted to but maybe it was bad luck because Mommy and Daddy didn't stay married.

• • • • • • • • • • • •

I can't believe Claire met a guy! That didn't come out right. I *can* believe it; she's gorgeous, sweet, and funny. What guy wouldn't fall for her? But if he hadn't dragged her off a burning rooftop and given her mouth-to-mouth, chances are they wouldn't have been introduced.

Maybe one of these days they'll actually go out on a date. I invited him to my birthday bash, so she'll see him again at least once. Between his schedule and hers—and Zoë's—they're having a hard time getting it together. Zoë actually seems pretty okay with it. That kind of surprised me, I think. In fact, she seems more cool with it than Claire does. It's a bad pun, but I think my sister is afraid of getting burned again. I don't want to see her hurt. On the other hand I can't watch her deny herself, out of fear, a second shot at love. If all goes well, I'll get to meet Dennis tonight. I think she's sick of my calling him her "hot date." My birthday won't exactly be a cozy setting, but at least they'll get to spend a bit of time together. And he gets to meet the whole Marsh family in one shot. Talk about trial by fire.

I'd better quit while I'm ahead, here.

I stepped into The Corner Bar, which is exactly what it sounds like. A local place located at an intersection. Dark. Used to be smoky. If you bury your nose in a banquette and inhale deeply, you can still get enough of a whiff of stale cigarette smoke to satisfy most nic-fits. The only glitch is the jukebox, which plays kitsch like Olivia Newton-John and Weird Al Yankovic.

Jake, the guy who owns The Corner, is a thirty-something who treats the bar like his pride and joy, which makes it a cool place to hang out, toss back a few, and shoot some pool. A couple of weeks ago, when I broached the subject of renting out the place for a private party, he got really into it. Jake, in fact, was the one who talked me into getting my guests to go whole hog and do the black-tie thing. Since his music is an acquired taste, he agreed to supplement the jukebox selections by cranking up his stereo. I agreed to supply some tunes.

I wanted to talk to Jake just to be sure that everything was cool for tonight. The Corner had just opened. Jake was wiping down the tabletops and talking to a curly-haired, good-looking guy in a suit who was leaning against the edge of the bar.

"Hey, girlfriend!" He dropped his rag on a table and gave me a hug. "Happy Birthday, Sweet Pea!"

"When'd you get a girlfriend?!" the suit wanted to know. If you know Jake well, the man's in love with his saloon.

"Figure of speech, man." Jake slung his arm over my shoulder and brought me over to the suit. "Owen, this is Mia. The birthday girl. Miss three-oh."

"Congratulations. I did it myself not too long ago." He grinned and winked at me. Nice smile. Even nicer eyes. "Trust me, you'll survive." The suit extended his hand. "Owen Michaels."

"Mia Marsh. What brings you to The Corner in a three-piece suit at . . ." I looked at my watch. "Eleven A.M. on a Saturday?"

Jake poured Owen a glass of O.J.

"Business meeting in an hour. With a potential client. I believe you've got to look the part if you want to inspire confidence."

Fair enough. "Does he?" I asked Jake. "Inspire confidence?"

"You're looking at one satisfied customer. Actually, it's Owen who should be satisfied. The Corner has been a great ROI for him."

"ROI?"

"Return on investment. Owen and I went to Colgate together. You know how some kids want to be astronauts or firemen when they grow up? I always wanted a bar. Now, this guy," he said, pointing at Owen, "Mr. MBA, here, has the Midas touch when it comes to investing. He can play the stock market like it's a Stradivarius. Knows when to jump in and when to bail out."

"Awww, shucks, Jake," Owen drawled comically.

"Jump in? Bail out? That sounds more like playing the Hokey Pokey," I quipped.

"Mia? O.J.?" Jake asked me. I nodded. He poured. "Want anything special in it?"

I shook my head. "I'd better not start this early. I'm in a party mood and I'm shitty at pacing myself. So, what are you going to put in a 'Mi♥amore'?"

"What's a 'Mi♥amore'?" Owen wanted to know.

"A specialty drink I asked Jake to come up with for my birthday. It's the name of the cosmetics line I want to start up. Eventually. My pipe dream. I'm a makeup artist."

"I haven't tried it yet but I was thinking of floating Chambord on top of a glass of Muscatel. It will be sweet as hell. Just like you," Jake teased. "We'll try it now, if you want, so I make sure the Chambord will actually float for a bit."

I frowned. I had a mental image of what Jake's idea would look like. Blood and plasma. Ugh. "Tell you what. I pass. Think up something else. What about making it deep pink? I don't know, vodka, Chambord, and pink lemonade. Not to shatter your rosy illusions, Jake, but sweet and tart is closer to who I really am. It's probably a drink already, but we can rename it for tonight."

It was Jake's turn to frown. "Sounds awfully *girly*, but it's *your* birthday, Mia."

"I think you should have whatever drink you want. And I like the name," Owen said helpfully.

I stuck out my tongue at Jake. "Hah! See? And I think you're swell," I said, turning to Owen. "I know it's short notice, but if your tux is clean, you're welcome to stop by tonight. Any time after eight." I liked this guy. Okay, so he was wearing a suit before lunch on Saturday, but there was something about him I couldn't quite pinpoint that made me like him right away. I don't know . . . he was friendly, direct, confident, without being a showman about any of it. Like, "yeah, well, so I'm good at making money." No big deal.

"Thanks for the invite, Mia. I'd like that," Owen said. "I'll try to make it."

To my ears, it was kind of noncommittal. Like "sounds cool, but don't count on me." Story of my life so far. Oh, well. I've got more to worry about than whether a near stranger I've just spent all of ten minutes with will show up later. More pressing, in fact, is figuring out what I'm going to wear. I thought I had it all mapped out, but I've changed my mind fifty times already.

By 10 P.M. the party was in full swing. Most of my friends are night owls. I was surprised that Zoë was still going strong. My niece was wearing an adorable party dress with ruffles and flounces. She looked like a little princess.

If I didn't know that Claire had far less spare time than the mayor, I'd swear she looked rested. She was radiant. I think her new guy has something to do with it. Dennis McIntyre is not only a hunk, he's attentive, warm, and seems great with Zoë. He also hasn't turned and run after maximum exposure to three more Marshes. He'll really be one of New York's Bravest if he makes it through the night unscathed. Some first date. Poor guy. Actually, our family's not rude or mean or anything—just eccentric.

"So, have you kissed him?" I whispered in Claire's ear.

She laughed. "Mouth-to-mouth. So, yeah, I guess. But I wasn't conscious, so I don't think it counts!"

"Do you think it'll go anywhere?"

"My fingers are crossed. At least he understands my crazy life. I've had to cancel dates because of Zoë's schedule and he's had to break them to go put out fires."

"How can he make a date with you on a day that he's working?" I'm confused.

"No. They call him in on a day off sometimes."

"Isn't it scary, dating a fireman?"

"We haven't *had* a date yet. This is *it*, remember? You know, I didn't think about it until this minute, but it's scary being a mother every day, too. I'm not a paranoid person—except in playgrounds—but you just never know what can happen."

"Let me get you a drink," I offered, and pushed my way to the crowded bar. The Corner was packed. I'm a lucky woman, to have so many dear friends. Apart from Owen—who had just walked in, looking mighty tasty in his tux—there wasn't a casual acquaintance in the bunch. I asked Jake to fix a Mi♥amore for Claire, and one for Dennis, who has sidled up beside me, perched his butt on a bar stool, and asked if there's anything he could do to help.

"Be good to my sister," I said. "That's not a suggestion. It's a threat." I laughed, but we both knew I was dead serious.

"If she can find time to let me, I'll do my best," he assured me.

"She's been badly burned," I told him. "Relationship-wise. Burns can take a long time to heal. And there's almost always scar tissue. I expect you know that."

"I'm a patient man."

Zoë came over and rested her chin on his knee. "And my parents got divorced when I was a kid, too. I've been where this one is," Dennis said, gently patting Zoë's back. "You hungry?" he asked her. "Your Aunt Mia is serving PB & J sandwiches."

"Uh-hunh."

I could see that she was beginning to get sleepy.

"Let's go find the food, then." Dennis stood up and steered Zoë toward the buffet table. "Thanks for the drink!" he said, turning back to me. He'd declined the shocking pink Mi♥amore in favor of a bottle of Bud.

Lucky Sixpence was dancing by the jukebox with my mother and some of my other gay friends. I had to do something about this music. Lucky had punched up the title song to *Grease* the movie. "Grease Is the Word" or whatever it's called.

"Where are my CDs?" I asked Jake.

He took a look behind the bar. The pile next to the stereo system was his own. "I don't think you ever brought them over."

"Fuck. I'll be right back, then."

"Where are you off to?" Owen asked me. "You can't skip out on your own party. Besides, I just got here!"

"Come with me then," I suggested. "I need to run home for a minute. I forgot to bring my tunes and I can't stand Jake's juke." We walked out into the East Village night, coatless, Owen in his Armani tux, me in Claire's wedding gown. It had been my original wardrobe choice for tonight; and after trying on every other gown in my own closet, I decided to stick with my first instincts.

"Your sister must have had a June wedding, judging from that dress. Aren't you cold?"

"We don't have far to go. I just live down the street."

Owen slipped off his jacket. "Take it anyway. You're shivering."

"No, I'm not," I lied, hiking up the skirt so I could walk faster.

"Mia, you're the most stubborn woman I've met . . . today. It's February, for God's sake. If you're going to hang out with me, you're going to stay warm. I'm as stubborn as you are."

"You're no gentleman!" I teased, as he insisted, despite my protests, on draping his jacket over my shoulders.

"On the contrary. No gentleman would *not* give up his coat to a damsel in that dress on a winter night."

"You're real funny." We arrived at my apartment building. "It's not fancy," I warned him. "And get ready to climb a few flights."

"Don't worry. I work out."

"But I love the neighborhood. And I've got exposed brick and a lot of sunlight, so it's pretty homey for what is, basically, an apartment in a renovated tenement."

"You don't have to apologize for where you live, Mia. I'm not a judgmental person. And even if I were, it would be none of my damn business."

I looked him in the eyes. "I like it that you're direct."

"Thanks. Here. Do you need help with this?" He lifted the slight train at the back of my dress. "Wait. There's a loop here." He handed it to me. "Even though Claire got divorced, she probably would still be pissed at you if you dragged the hem of her wedding dress up four flights of stairs."

We started climbing. "Where'd you learn this? You're not . . . ?"

"I'm as straight as a yardstick. I've got three sisters. All married already." He laughed. "They'd shit a brick if they could see *us*, now!"

"Why?"

"Look at us! We just met this morning and here we are, standing side by side, looking like two dolls on a wedding cake."

"Fuck. You're right. It is pretty funny." Something weird was going on. Something was off. Not with Owen, though that was weird enough. Something was wrong with my front door. I know I locked it. I always lock it. I live in the East Village, not in Kansas. "Does that look jimmied to you?" I asked Owen.

He inspected the door, the handle, the locks, making muttering guy-noises. Then he gently pushed the door and it opened. "Holy Christ, Mia! You told me not to think too much of your place, but you didn't say you were such a lousy housekeeper!"

"I'm not! In fact I'm—"

Fuck. Fuck! FUCK! Someone had broken in. The hallway, the living room, the kitchen, my bedroom, bathroom, closets—everything had been trashed. It didn't take more than a few seconds to realize that they'd gotten my stereo, my TV, VCR and DVD player, my cameras, and my laptop—that has my whole fucking life on it.

Rice Krispies and Cocoa Puffs had been dumped all over the kitchen countertops, the eat-in island, and the floor.

"What the . . . !?" I began to tremble.

Owen drew me into his arms. Just being protective, not coming on to me. "They were looking for jewelry or cash. A lot of people hide stuff like that in cereal boxes."

Shit! I went into the bedroom. Every drawer had been yanked out and overturned. My underwear was all over the floor in colorful heaps. At least it was clean. All my jewelry was gone, including some good costume stuff—vintage pieces, and things that belonged to my mom and grandmothers. All gone. I felt so violated. My *underwear*, for fuck's sake! And my laptop had everything on it. My appointment schedule for the next several weeks. My business plans for *Mi♥amore Makeup*. My banking information. Saved passwords for all sorts of websites. My Excel "eligibility" spreadsheets. Those contained a shitload of personal information.

Well, no point in looking for the CDs I was going to bring back to The Corner. Those had been taken, too. They must have thrown my things into big laundry bags. "We've got to go back to the bar and form a search party!" I said, hysterical. Owen was already on the phone with the cops. Taking charge. I was grateful and relieved for that, since I couldn't think straight.

Some fucking thirtieth birthday. Someone had insured that it was one I'd never forget.

"The cops are on their way over to get a statement," he told me.

"A fat lot of good it will do. Look, the best way to deal with this right now is to get everyone at the bar to come with me down to Astor Place. Fan out. Find my stuff before it's sold or fenced." Owen gave me a strange look. "The Thieves' Market. That's what they call that stretch across the street from Cooper Union. Most of the time stuff gets stolen in this neighborhood, it ends up there first. Trust me. I once went through this with someone." Charles had been robbed a few years ago and we combed the Thieves' Market for his possessions and ended up finding a lot of it. But you have to get there fast. These people don't want your *stuff*. They want *cash*. ASAP. For drugs mostly. One of the best times to burglarize my nabe is on a Saturday night because you've got a lot of young people, partygoers, clubbers, who won't be home and the thieves need the darkness to provide cover. But the pawn shops aren't open until Monday morning, and they need to ditch the loot and get a fix.

"You talk to the cops if you want," I said. "I'm going down to The Corner. Tick-tock! The clock is running!" I hiked Claire's wedding dress up to my knees and raced down the stairs.

I met a pair of them as I fled down the stoop. "Are you here for Mia Marsh? Apartment 4A that just got robbed tonight?"

They nodded. That was fast. I'm impressed. "Can we talk to you for a few minutes?"

I wanted to say yes; I wanted to say no. "Look. I'm going to get a posse of my friends and go down to Eighth Street. The Thieves Market. You're welcome to join me. If you want to go upstairs, be my guest. There's a guy named Owen Michaels up there. He'll show you around."

"Is that your . . . ?"

"You authorized him to be in your apartment?" the other cop asks.

"Yes. He's a Good Samaritan. That's all." I explained the situation; my birthday party, et cetera, and how we ended up dressed like a bridal couple, why we went back to my place— probably way more information than they really needed, but I didn't want them to think I was any weirder than I am. I ran through a quick list of the stuff that I knew off the bat was missing.

"We'll need a statement from you, Ms. Marsh."

"Then one of you can tag along with me."

"We're not allowed to split up," they explained.

"Then meet me down by Astor Place in fifteen minutes. Believe me, I'll be there!" *I* don't really believe that there's too much the cops can do for me. I'm pretty sure that participating in a search party goes beyond their job description. I need my stuff back *now*, if I can find it. I can always go down to the precinct tomorrow or Monday and give them a statement. They just want it for the record. It's not like they really *do* anything with it. I'll believe otherwise when they catch the perps.

I ran down to The Corner and announced to my guests that my place had been robbed and I needed their help. You should have seen the motley crew that raced over to Eighth Street with me. Lucky Sixpence and a handful of other cross-dressers, a bunch of more "normal" people I know from the fashion world, Charles, Celestia, my parents, Claire, Dennis, and Zoë; and finally, Jake, who locked up the bar and joined us.

We were met by Owen, who had gotten a written complaint number from the cops. Since he was as much an eyewitness as I was to the devastation in my apartment, he'd given his statement. "You'll have to go in to the station with an itemized list of what's missing. And photos of your stuff, if you have them. If you don't, from now on, you should take Polaroids of all your valuables and keep them in a safe place. And on Monday, call your insurance company, too, to report the theft."

"How can I take fucking Polaroids when they stole my fucking camera?!" I demanded. "And what do you suggest is a 'safe place,' since they turned my whole fucking apartment fucking upside down!?" I apologized to my mother, not for my language, but because they got her jewelry and trashed some of her best designs. The garments were one-offs, too. "By the way," I said to Owen. "You don't even know me. Why are you doing all this?"

"Because he's a mensch," Jake said. He was scouring the jumble of stolen stuff laid out on blankets along the sidewalk for anything that might be mine, asking me about an item when he thought he'd found something. "I've known him since we weren't even old enough to drink and he always knew I wanted to own a bar. He's an investment banker—that's his background."

"Sorry about that," Owen said to me.

"Eek!" I stepped back and made the sign of the cross. "Shit, you *are* a grown-up!"

Jake laughed. "Yeah, but someone's gotta be. Owen started up a nonprofit with a bunch of other dweeby men and women who wear suits on weekends. They're called the Dream Makers. They work with young entrepreneurs on start-ups. They help with business plans, five-year forecasts, venture capital, all that stuff. He provided the venture capital for The Corner."

Charles's ears pricked up like a pointer's. "Hey, Mia, maybe he can help you with *Mi♥amore Makeup*."

"I can't even think about it right now," I told him. "Let's just try to get back my stuff first."

"Hey, Mia, is this you?" Owen was holding a fistful of 8x10 glossy prints.

"Oh, my God!" I snatched them from his hand.

"I guess that's a yes."

Luca's photos. The prints he had given me way back when. If

these were here, then chances are, we'd find some of the rest of my things.

"Wait!" Owen reached for the pics. "Mia, you're amazing-looking."

I quickly handed them off to my mother, who stuffed them into her large purse. "No way. We don't know each other well enough for you to see me naked yet."

"Well, that's a first," Claire teased, whispering into my ear.

"Fuck you, Clairey."

"I told you, you'd never know where those photos would end up. That they'd come back to haunt you."

"Yeah, but Luca has nothing to do with it. Unless these aren't *my* copies of the prints. There's always that possibility." I turned to one of the "vendors," sitting on his blanket, smoking a joint, totally confident that there wasn't a cop in sight. "How much were you charging for those photos, by the way?"

The guy was so stoned he didn't even seem to process that I was the model or that we had just reclaimed them from his array of contraband. "One dollar each one."

"That's all?! Fuck!"

"You're worth much more than that," Owen assured me.

"Gee, thanks."

"Although they do a better job of capturing your body than your essence."

"My essence? How good a look did you *get* at them?!"

"Hey, don't pick a fight with me. I'm just trying to cheer you up."

"Well, don't think I'm ungrateful or anything, but the best way to do it would be to find my laptop, for starters." How did such a non-techie as me become so totally dependent on a computer within a matter of months? There's a good argument for being a Luddite.

"Oooh, this is pretty, MiMi!" Zoë was on her hands and knees, picking through things. She held up a sparkly object. "This is yours! You let me play dress-up with it when we were at your house."

She's right. "Keep going, Zoë. Great job! Find some more stuff."

Claire kept an eagle eye on her. After a minute or so, she knelt down beside Zoë. "We've got some more pieces, Mia!"

The "proprietor" clasped his hand over Claire's. "Hey—you can't just take that. You've got to buy it."

"I'm not paying you for my sister's stolen jewelry, you jerk. Now, let go of me."

In a moment, Dennis had materialized, stepping across the blanket to face the guy. "I think you're going to want to let the lady alone." He drew back his fist.

"Don't hit me!" the guy pled.

"Then you let us find her stuff," he said, pointing to me. "And maybe you'll want to tell me where the rest of it might be."

By now, Claire and Zoë had found a few more pieces of my jewelry. A fawn-colored sedan, the kind that looks like an unmarked cop car, pulled up to the curb.

Two guys got out, but they didn't look like detectives, even the undercover kind. They opened the trunk and started to unpack its contents. I screamed. "That's my TV set!" The guy holding it started to run. Owen and Dennis gave chase. Half a block east, the guy dropped the TV—*bang, crash, tinkle*—and kept running, pursued by our impromptu vigilantes.

My father and Charles approached the other guy, but he pulled a knife and held them at bay. Claire whipped out her cell phone to dial 911. I hoped I wasn't telegraphing my surprise to the kid with the knife. Lucky Sixpence and our other cross-dressing and trans-gendered pals had used their ability to blend in (believe me!) with the local crowd and had come up behind him, surrounding him in a semi-circle.

Then, as though she'd hopped off a springboard, Lucky jumped the kid, landing on his back like they were playing chicken. She yanked the kid's hair and reached, with her long, manicured talons, for the kid's eyes.

The kid screamed bloody murder and dropped the knife. Jake grabbed it, flipped it shut, and stuck it in his pocket. Lucky stood there, in the middle of Astor Place in her size twelve pumps, with her stiletto heel firmly placed on the back of the kid's neck.

A police car skidded to a stop, turning off its siren. The two uniforms who got out were the same guys who had come over to my place almost an hour ago. They cuffed the kid and Jake turned over the blade. We went through the stuff in the trunk of the sedan, finding most of my electronic equipment. Two of my cameras were still missing, but my laptop was there. I opened it and proved to the cops that it was mine, but they said I couldn't have my other items back until they had been taken to the precinct and inventoried. And I'd have to show them that they were mine as well.

By now, Dennis and Owen had returned, empty-handed, from their pursuit of the other perp. "From now on, you should write down the serial numbers of all your equipment and store it someplace safe, so that if this ever happens again you'll be able to go right to your list and it'll be a cinch to prove the stuff is really yours," Owen counseled.

"Organize my whole life, why don't you?"

"Mia, be nice," my mother said. "Owen's just trying to be helpful." She formally introduced herself and the rest of the Marshes. Zoë was still crawling around on the blanket, hunting for sparkly things, her patent leather Mary Janes shining in the streetlight's amber glow.

The cops didn't seem to want to do the paperwork, but Owen thought we should take a field trip to the station house to give statements. After all, more than two dozen of us had ID'd the thieves. The one we'd nabbed would turn in his accomplice, most likely. And I sure as hell was going to prosecute.

"Before we go, we've got a little ceremony to attend to," my father said. He launched into his little speech about the Marsh tradition of annual birthday poems.

"But her birthday cake is back at the bar," Zoë said. "She has to blow out the candles."

Charles went across the street to Starbucks. He returned with a giant muffin. "This is just for show. A stand-in. We'll go back and do this for real later." He'd made me an amazing cake. There was no way we were going to forget to eat it. Even if it would end up being one in the morning and no longer my thirtieth birthday. He found a votive in an ugly glass that had been sitting on one of the Thieves' Market blankets, took out the candle, and shoved it into the top of the muffin.

"Wait, you can't light it until Grandpa Brendan has read the poem," Zoë insisted. "It's tradition. And anyway, the candle is so big that the muffin could catch fire while MiMi is holding it waiting to make her wish."

"Yeah, and then we'll have to call the fire department," Claire added, looking at Dennis. Her face was glowing.

My father pulled a sheet of paper from his jacket pocket. What a spectacle we all made. Charles scrounged up a few more beat-up candles from the Thieves Market and my friends and family stood around, holding them. We looked like a bunch of Christmas carolers who had gone seriously astray.

Dad cleared his throat. "For My Older Daughter (who chose to dress up like a bride on her birthday)," he added parenthetically. "On Turning Thirty."

Elf or gamine, woman, child,
Feminine, by love beguiled,
Wistful wraith or working wench,
Who dares say in what dimensh
Your carefree heart and mind abide
Or where your secret dreams reside.
Wherever they may choose to rest,
On this day may they all be blessed,

Sublime, delightful, worry-free
For now and all eternity.

"Blessed, huh?" I interrupted. I gestured at the mess surrounding us.

"You are blessed. You got most of your stuff back," Claire said.

"You've got all of us," Charles said. "Don't forget."

My father gave us a dirty look and told us that he'd just delivered only the first stanza.

"Oops. Sorry, Daddy."

He shook his head and chuckled, then resumed reading.

Youth's a time that's yours for spending,
As you walk along life's ramble,
Rising sun to sun's descending
Every moment is a gamble.

Any dream with heart behind it
Could be that big, solid winner,
Life could be as you designed it
(with the luck of a beginner).

Youth was given you for spending,
A fortune's all you've got to lose,
What the years may hold is pending.
Youth is when you pay your dues.

Dennis used his lighter to fire up the muffin votive and they all sang Happy Birthday. I made a wish—without saying it out loud of course—that my life could indeed, be as I designed it, from now on.

Chapter 16

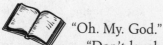 "Oh. My. God."

"Don't laugh at me!" I warn Mia. It's bad enough as it is. She stops hawing into the phone as though she's turned off a faucet. "That laugh of yours can sound pretty mocking sometimes, you know? Have men ever told you that?"

She's given herself the hiccups. "Wait. I can't talk until I can . . . breathe."

"You did it to yourself. At my expense. So I can't feel sorry for you." All I did was call her up and beg for some sisterly advice. I'm about to embark on my first one-on-one date since . . . well, literally since high school, and I'm terrified. And she thinks it's hysterical. "Honestly, Mia, I don't know what to do. I've gotten myself completely stressed out over it. Do I offer to pay, at least for my part of dinner? If he pays for dinner, should I offer to pay for the movie? Should I not offer, but just take out my wallet and pay for the movie tickets? And the Sex Question."

"First of all, you do know I'm ecstatically happy for you, right? I'm just having fun giving you grief 'cause you sound so wired. And you know, you've gone from asking about first date rules to a hop in the sack in, like, less than one sentence."

"Fuck you!"

She tsk-tsks. "Language, Claire!"

"And I know you're making fun of me, but don't get all prudish all of a sudden. Given our histories, it doesn't suit either one of us."

"Where's Zoë? She's not in the room with you, is she?"

"Would I be using the S-word—let alone the F-word—if she were? She's in her room, working quietly . . ." I cock my head for a moment. Maybe too quietly. "She's supposed to be working on a special St. Patrick's Day project for school. In addition to their usual curriculum, this month Mrs. Hennepin is giving them all-Ireland, all the time. Kind of like an immersion course for second graders. I'm sure if the hag knew Gaelic, Zoë would be coming home bilingual."

"So, when are you finally having The Big Date?" Mia wants to know.

"In a perfect world, Saturday night. So I've got six more days to panic. I got a baby-sitter from Thackeray, a fifth-former named Annabel Rosenbaum, whose references are terrific. You know there's a bulletin board now where the kids can post Help Wanted ads. There are a couple of entrepreneurial computer-geek kids offering their services if you need additional hardware or a new program installed. And they're not cheap! But I guess they know their market. Anyway," I add, feeling the butterflies rise in my stomach, even though I'm only speaking to my older sister, "things were great between us at your birthday party, but I'm freaked about being alone with Dennis. I mean not *freaked* freaked. Just . . . freaked. It's like being a virgin again or something."

I confess to Mia that I need the scoop on the Sex issue because I want to know what the rules are these days. After all, it's been nearly eight years since I've been on a date, and Scott and

I didn't exactly have a traditional ritual courtship. It all happened pretty fast. Well . . . do I want to jump Dennis's bones and fuck his brains out, she asks me in exactly those words.

"On Saturday? Or at all?" I ponder my own questions. "Well, this definitely isn't a mercy date. I mean if I weren't attracted to Dennis, I would have said 'Zoë and I thank you very much for saving my life,' and then he would have given a Gary Cooper shrug and said, 'Aw, shucks, ma'am, I was just doing my job,' which is more or less what he said anyway, before he obtained Zoë's permission to ask me out, and we would have left it at that."

I cover the phone and listen again to ascertain whether Zoë is all right. I hear sounds of activity in her room, and she seems to be having a conversation with the imaginary Wendy, so I guess everything is still copasetic down there.

"He kissed me good night after your birthday party," I tell Mia. "So, we're past that hurdle. Although, since he gave me mouth-to-mouth when he rescued me, that probably counts as the first kiss. Sort of. Even though I can't remember a thing about it. The good-night kiss was really good, though. His lips were very soft and he tasted like chocolate. So you can tell Happy Chef that your birthday cake was an aphrodisiac." I realize I'm about to chew my hair. "Listen to me, I sound like a tenth grader. It's like my dating growth is stunted."

"Stop panicking," Mia says. "Let go a little. And stop playing with your hair."

"How did you know . . . ?"

"I've known you since you were born, remember? You asked me for advice, I've got three words, okay? It. Never. Changes. I hate to say it, but the puppy-love crushes at Zoë's age, teen angst, adult second-guessing—it's all the same. First, we used to count daisy petals and made those stupid folded fortune things and asked the Magic 8-Ball . . . you know, 'Sorry, forecast hazy,' and stuff like that; then we sat by the phone and waited for it to ring. Now, we just stay online all day and wait for today's three magic words: 'You've Got Mail.' "

Zoë wanders into my bedroom. "Mommy, I need help." She's holding a can of Play-Doh. "It's all hard and it has white stuff on it," she frets.

It looks like we have a craft emergency. "Mia, I need to run. Zoë needs me for something. But thanks, anyway. At least I know my fear is normal." I get off the phone, not much wiser or more enlightened about current dating protocol than I was half an hour ago.

I examine the crusty yellow Play-Doh. "I don't think we can resurrect this, sweetheart. Do you have other colors you can use?"

"What's res-sur-wreck?"

"Resurrect means bring back to life. I think this can is about as dead as Play-Doh gets."

"But I need yellow. You can't mix other colors to get yellow. And you need yellow to get green." She tugs at my hand. "We need new Play-Doh. Now. Or I can't finish my project." She pulls me into her room. On her giant pad of newsprint she's drawn a big picture of an old-fashioned village, with thatch-roofed houses that remind me of the illustrations in some of her books. On top of a hill stands a man holding a stick. Usually, her portraits of male figures tend to resemble her father, inasmuch as a child her age can create that kind of likeness. The man with the stick looks like someone else. It might be my imagination, but there's a bit of a resemblance to a certain fireman who has charmed his way into our collective hearts.

"This is ain-shen Ireland," she explains, pointing to the picture.

"What?" For a moment, I think she really *is* speaking Gaelic.

"Ain-shen. It means old."

I correct her pronunciation. She tells me she learned the word in school, so I guess she's parroting what she thought she heard. I wish Mrs. Hennepin, for all her devoted attention to de-

tail, would write the new words on the board when she introduces them in contexts apart from spelling vocabulary.

"So what do you plan to do with the Play-Doh?" I ask her.
From the looks of it, the homework project will be a mixed-
media extravaganza. We may need to back the flimsy newsprint
with cardboard or foam core; I can see that now.

"Don't you know about Ireland and St. Patrick?" she asks me.
She looks confounded that Mommy seems so uneducated. "I
need the Play-Doh because I'm making snakes."

I can't wait for Mrs. Hennepin's reaction to this!

"So we need to get Play-Doh *now*. Before the store closes. So
I can finish it because I have to hand it in tomorrow. If I don't
I'll get in trouble and I *need* the Play-Doh to *finish* it."

"Why is this the first I've heard about this assignment, Zoë?
And don't whine. It's not the way to get what you want."

"But I *neeed* it."

"Don't just tell me to do something. It's not polite."

"But you tell me to do stuff all the time. So *you're* not polite."

"I'm the Mommy. I get to tell you to do things, because it's
part of my job. And I do usually ask you nicely, in fact. The first
three times, anyway."

She starts to put her shoes on. "So, can we go?"

"Let me get my jacket and my purse. Get your coat on and
ring for the elevator." I was going to sit in the breakfast nook and
do my nails while she was finishing up her assignment, but I
guess they'll have to wait. I examine my hands. Not dreadful.
Not a total, embarrassing, pressing emergency. I'd just wanted to
take a little me-time.

We run into a friend of Zoë's at Child's Play, the chi-chi little neighborhood toy store. New York is much worse for the
demise of five-and-ten-cent stores like Woolworth's and
Lamston's—the urban equivalents of Kmart, where you could
go to pick up just about anything for less than you'd pay in an
art store or toy shop. Lissa Arden is my daughter's friend from

her Museum Adventures program. The two of them do artsy-craftsy projects after school, like go to Our Name Is Mud and make and decorate pottery. Lissa's mom, Melissa, is a charming Englishwoman. They're looking for goody bag treats for Lissa's upcoming birthday party.

While Zoë tracks down her Play-Doh and the little girls ooh and ahh over half the items in the store, Melissa tells me how difficult it is to find the appropriate birthday venue, the right party favors, unusual invitations—the works. I commiserate. "I'm really in a twist about all of this," Melissa confesses. "We discovered this marvelous little place over on Eighty-third Street; a bead shop that does children's parties. But their space is limited, so I can't possibly invite all of her friends, let alone Lissa's entire class at Ethical Culture. And we're bound to end up ostracized for it."

Melissa's woes strike a chord. Suddenly I realize that our social circle isn't much more than a twenty-first-century version of the Regency *ton*. Women like Nina Osborne and Jennifer Silver-Katz set the standards by which everyone else is harshly judged. And if you flout convention, whether deliberately or accidentally, you are "cut," and your child suffers for it. I share my epiphany with Melissa and she agrees. "Of course, they think my accent is charming," she chuckles, "so I can squeak by, sometimes. But it really is dreadful. There are days when Lissa comes home in tears because the snack I provided has too many carbohydrates in it. Would you believe no one in her class eats Nutella? The first time it happened, the mothers forgave me because I was 'European,' but of course when my husband Simon goes to pick her up from her programs with wrapped cheese slices or a box of Yodels, they're practically gagging for him."

I wonder why I'd never noticed before that Melissa Arden and I are so simpatico. I suppose it's because Zoë and Lissa interact mostly through the Museum Adventures program. The two of them have never had a play date, one-on-one. I feel a bit regretful that I haven't gotten to know Melissa better. Although her situation is considerably different from mine because she's married, perhaps her friendship might have made me feel a bit less like I was bucking the trends alone. I seize the moment and suggest that we set up a play date, as much for myself as for Zoë. To my delight, Melissa accepts with alacrity.

We catch up with the girls, who are busy choosing party hats for Lissa's big day. Lissa is modeling a paper tiara that says "birthday girl" on it in silver script. "I want one, too," Zoë says, and grabs a yellow one.

"But that says 'birthday girl' on it, see!" Lissa says, snatching the yellow crown away from Zoë. "And it's for *my* birthday, not yours." She tosses it back into the bin.

Zoë starts to cry and Lissa picks up a package of conically shaped hats. She hands them to her mother.

I squat down and look Zoë squarely in the eye. "Z, you're overreacting," I say in a stage whisper. "Remember what that means?" She nods and the water faucet behind her tear ducts miraculously shuts off. I look at the party hats they've placed in Melissa's portable shopping basket. "Ever notice how the birthday girl gets a crown and those in her thrall are given dunce caps?" I remark to Melissa, under my breath.

She gives me a funny look, then bursts out laughing. "Crikey, you're right. It's positively medieval! And dreadful for their self-esteem, when you think about it." She turns to her daughter. "Darling, what do you say about finding crowns for the other little girls that don't say anything on them? That way they can be princesses, too, but you get to be the Birthday Princess." She places the offensive pointed hats back on the shelf.

Lissa shrugs, which her mum takes as a sign of acquiescence. They begin to sort through the bin of unlettered tiaras.

"I want a yellow one," Zoë insists and grabs for the only yellow one, the one that says "birthday girl."

How do I tell her that we don't even know if she'll be invited to Lissa's party? I give Melissa a strained, embarrassed look, which I hope conveys my question.

"You're not acting like a very big girl today," I say, through gritted teeth. "Now, let's pay for your Play-Doh and get home so you can finish your art project." I try to remove the yellow crown, but she slaps her hand over mine and clutches the tiara to her head.

"She seems a bit knackered," Melissa observes.

"I'm what?"

"Knackered," Melissa repeats.

"What's that mean?"

"Tired," I tell her.

"You talk funny," she tells Melissa bluntly.

"That's not a very polite thing to say, Zoë. It's not nice to make fun of other people."

"I wasn't. I just said she talks funny."

"I don't think so. Colorful, maybe. But that's a good thing, don't you think?" She doesn't reply.

Melissa reaches for the yellow tiara. "I think I need that, Zoë," she says. "Tell me, do you know anything about *Alice in Wonderland*?"

"I saw the video," she says. "It's a Disney movie."

Melissa smiles. "Then you know that one can celebrate *un*-birthdays, too. Well, I think I need this crown so I can make it into an *un*birthday girl tiara for one of the guests at Lissa's birthday party." I get it and give Melissa a look that is both relieved and grateful. But Zoë looks confused. "I s'pose I'd better spell it out, then. Zoë, Lissa will be inviting you to her birthday party. And we're going to save this coronet for you to wear when you get there. So, may I have it, please?"

My daughter relinquishes the crown. A crisis averted, thanks to a quick-thinking mommy (not me), and our emergency shopping trip completed, we return home to spend the evening hand-rolling pencil-thin Play-Doh snakes.

*   *   *

"Moooommmmy, we have to go. We're going to be late."

"I know, I know. Believe me, I know. Just a minute, sweetheart." I've been running back and forth to the bathroom all morning. It's a case of nerves, that's all, but they're getting the better of my body. I was up before dawn stressing over my date with Dennis tonight, making lists of lists of everything I have to do before seven this evening, the first of which is to get Zoë to her 10 A.M. bikram yoga class. Once I get her settled there, I've got forty-five minutes to pick up the dry-cleaning, run to the drugstore, and have a professional manicure before it's time to pick her up. I figure I'll treat myself to a little pampering and a better job than I can do myself; hopefully it will relax me a little. I'm as wound up as Zoë's little jumping frog toy, bouncing all over the apartment, bumping into the furniture. As my Gran used to say, "If your head weren't attached, you'd forget to take it with you."

At least there's the promise of spring in the air. If the weather man is right, we can leave our winter coats at home this morning and get away with wearing sweatshirts or windbreakers.

We trot over to the yoga studio, which is just a few blocks from our apartment. Zoë prefers to wear her exercise clothes to class; she hates locker rooms. If we have nowhere else to be after class I don't mind, and I shuttle her home to shower post-haste. Bikram yoga is, literally, one of the hottest fitness trends, known for the sweltering studio conditions. People exit the class smelling pretty rank, in my opinion.

From the moment I kiss her goodbye and tell her I'll be back within the hour, I feel like my old Thackeray gym teacher, Ms. Schumacher, is standing over me with her sky blue cardigan, her stopwatch, and her whistle. Time for a wind sprint through the neighborhood.

I ransom my dress from the dry-cleaners, grab some shampoo, soap, and aspirin at the drugstore, and head over to the nail salon. Each time a customer comes through the door, the ladies look up and greet them by name. I'm impressed. I've been in here only a handful of times in the past year and they chorus "Hello Claire! Manicure?"

"Usual color?" one asks, reaching for the sheer shade I tend to favor for its "subtlety," meaning that my manicure can last for two to three weeks if no one looks too closely.

The array of colors entices me as much as if I were Zoë in a candy store. Everything looks appealing. "No . . ." I say hesitantly, second-guessing myself. "Tonight's a special night. A big change. So I want something different." I opt for a bright spring-y pink. A real bubblegum hue.

By the time the manicurist is finished with my nails, I have less than ten minutes to spare before I need to return to the yoga studio. "You want Quick Dry?" she asks me. I agree that I'd better go for it, because I don't have the time to sit under the air dryer. "Dollar fifty," she says. Who knew they charged more for that? Since the stuff is called "Quick Dry" and not "Immediate Dry," I point to my purse, asking her to fish out the wallet and remove the money.

Seven minutes. As I rush up the stairs, plastic dry-cleaning bag flapping in the breeze, I am assaulted by my own biology. Oh, no. No, it can't be. It's not due until Tuesday, I think. Four days early. It's nerves. That's what did it. I know I have nothing in my purse. And a quick fix in the ladies' room won't do the trick since my body has decided to entertain me with its impression of the Nile. Actually, the Nile flows *up*. Never mind.

I rush down the two narrow flights of stairs and dash back to the corner drugstore. As I dig for my wallet in order to pay for my purchase—*fuck*! There goes the fresh manicure. The nails on my right hand are a smudgy mess. Plus, there's a bright pink smear along the inside of my pocketbook. Shit. Well, nothing I can do about it now. Or probably ever without ruining the bag.

Back up to the yoga studio and straight for the ladies' room before I really mess up my clothes and embarrass the hell out of myself. I hang the dress inside the stall and take care of business.

I hear the door open, followed by the sound of voices. "When she was a stay-at-home, her daughter never acted that way. You know, she and Ashley are very close." It's Jennifer Silver-Katz. "Zoë was a much more cooperative child. Much better mannered. Even until a few months ago. But now that she's working, I think Claire's really lost touch with what's going on with her daughter on a day-to-day basis."

Oh, my God. She's talking about me.

"I'm not entirely sure I agree with you, Jenny," the other mom says. Her voice sounds familiar, which tells me Zoë must know her kid. "*I'm* a working mother. I've always worked and I don't think Ben is any the worse for it. Being out in the world enables you to bring some of that world into the home. He's certainly not going to get that from his father. From his father, he has a built-in rabbi to give him bar-mitzvah instruction when the time comes."

I realize it's Sarah Ephraim, whose son Ben was assaulted by Xander during musical chairs at Zoë's birthday party. Ben's the geeky kid whose bash was held at the planetarium last year.

"Leonard lives in such an insular world. It's like a fishbowl. If *I* didn't work outside the home, who else would there be to bring the secular world—outside of his classroom, I mean—into Ben's life?"

"Of course *I* could *never* do it. It's just not me. I wouldn't feel right about it. My children need me; if you're going to make the decision to be a mother, it's self-centered to try to have a career. I used to work, of course, but that was before I married Aaron and had the girls. Nina Osborne and I were talking about that just the other day. In our household, my husband provides us with the lifestyle, I furnish the nurture, and Ashley's teacher, Mrs. Hennepin, supplies the structure. She's so good with structure. Ashley adores her. And Tennyson's teacher, Mr. Clay, is a dream. But, Sarah, *you* have a better argument for the working mom than Claire Marsh does. You're in advertising. *You're* using your brain. Your job is rewarding, and you've got something to share. Claire's a *shopgirl*. At a nonprofit, yet. So, you tell me how a working mother like that is able to give a developing child the attention she needs. What do you think of this lipstick? It's the new Nars color."

"I think it makes you look too old. If I were you, I'd ask for your twenty-five dollars back."

A cell phone rings. Jennifer answers it. "Hi, Tenny, what's up, sweetheart? What? I thought you said this morning you didn't want to go! Yes, but don't you have a test on Monday? . . . . .Sweetie? Don't you have—. . . . . .I know, but I thought you have a test Monday. In health. . . . . .Do you have a health test Monday? Because if you're not going this afternoon, you should be . . . Oh, I see. Yes. No. Oh, in science?? You have a science test?. . . . . .I thought you had a health test. . . . . You have two tests Monday? Back to back? Then I think you had better get cracking, young lady. Yes. Yes. Yes. That's what I said, Tennyson. Stay home and skip kick-boxing and study for the— . . . . .You can spar with your sister later if you want to practice. Just don't kick her in the head. You remember what happened last time. . . . . .Yes, I know, but you also have a little chest cold. . . . . .No, I *don't* think it's so bad that you'll be sick on Monday. I know where you're going with that, Tenny. You can't fool me. Sweetie, do you need help studying? No . . . No. No . . . No, I can't sweetie. Mommy has a facial. She can't help you today. No. No. I can't change it. Tomorrow? Mrs. Osborne and I are playing tennis, sweetie. You know, Mommy needs some 'me time,' too. No. No . . . . .No, what did I just say to you? I *can't* help you when I get home. After I drop off your sister, I'll need to run. What? Ask Maribelle. *Maribelle*. That's one of the things we pay her for. I know you don't know anything about photosynthesis, Tenny, but Mommy doesn't either. Maribelle should be able to figure it out, and if she can't, then go online to the teacher help site. It's bookmarked. I'll see you in half an hour. Love you! Bye." I hear the phone snap shut and Jennifer sighs.

"And of course, you miss so much when you have a job," she continues, without skipping a beat. "Claire wasn't a working mom at the time, but she was in *school* when Zoë had most of her 'firsts.' She was much more hands-on between college and her divorce. But since Claire went to work, Zoë acts out much more when she's on play dates. She doesn't play nice sometimes. I hate to discipline someone else's child, but honestly, half the time I feel like the kid's surrogate mother. Claire is always asking me to do a favor here, a favor there."

I'm in shock. I feel like I've just been slapped in the face. The heat and color rise in my cheeks as though the sting is actual. I unfurl some paper and dry my eyes.

I flush the toilet and unlock the door. Then I head straight for the sinks with my head held high. The room is as quiet as a mausoleum. No way for them to weasel out of anything I overheard. Still, I can't look these women directly in the eye; I'm not that brave. I collect my dress from the stall and summon my courage. "You needn't feel so put out in the future," I tell Jennifer Silver-Katz. "Don't worry; I won't ask you for any more 'favors.' "

Chapter 17

Bleh. The temperature in the room is over a hundred degrees. While the kids are storing their mats, Zoë's yoga instructor Sarita, a slender honey blonde whose real name is Cameron, approaches me. She cocks her head as though she's studying my features in order to paint a portrait. Then she takes both my hands, straightens up and looks deeply into my eyes. "Zoë seemed a little hostile today. Is everything all right at home?"

She continues to discuss Zoë's behavior in her soft, good-karma voice, offering her suggestions for better-balanced chakras. I start to explain that what Zoë might be reacting to is that tonight I'm going out on my first real date since her dad and I divorced. However, I hasten to add, I thought she seemed to be taking it very well. Has been excited about it, in fact. Then I listen to myself for a moment. "Ummm, wait a minute," I say to Sarita, feeling my heart quicken, my ire increase. "You see Zoë, what, once a week for forty-five minutes in a classroom context with twenty other children? And you presume to tell me how to parent?" She starts to reply, her mouth a big round O of surprise. "You know, I've think I've had enough of that already this morning, thank you very much."

I collect Zoë, who has been talking to Ben. His mother gives me an uncomfortable look as we scoot past them.

"Are you okay, Mommy?" she asks, as we descend the stairs.

"No, sweetie. No, I'm not."

"What's the matter?"

"Nothing. Never mind." I know better than to ask her if I'm a good mommy. There's only one answer I want to hear right now and I don't want it either prefaced or followed by qualifications and caveats. "I'm just a little scared about tonight."

"Is that what you're going to wear?" she asks me, eyeing the dry-cleaned dress.

"Yes. . . ." She doesn't look too sold. "Why?"

She shrugs. "Nothing. It's just boring. That's all."

In the past fifteen minutes or so, the temperature has dropped about twenty degrees. What began as a bright and sunny late winter Saturday is now damp, gloomy, and windy. "I'm cold," Zoë says, after walking a couple of blocks. I can see her shivering. After sweating up a storm in that yoga class, and refusing to change clothes in the locker room, her exercise things must now feel cool and wet against her little body. I yank my sweatshirt over my head and put it on over her windbreaker. She looks a bit ridiculous because it fits her like a nightgown, but it's the best way of keeping her warm right now.

"Aren't *you* cold, now?" my little girl asks solicitously.

"I'm okay. We don't have far to go anymore."

"Your nails are smushy."

"I know. Let's hope Dennis doesn't notice."

"It's okay, Mommy. I don't think he cares about nail polish."

"So, little miss fashion coordinator, you have a problem with my dress?"

Zoë wrinkles her nose. "It's plain."

I defend my wardrobe selection to a seven-year-old. "It's simple, not plain. And black is considered very chic."

She shakes her head emphatically. "But you look like a grown-up in it."

"That's the point. I *am* a grown-up, Zoë. What do you think I am?"

"I don't like the black dress. You'll look like Xander's mommy. Old. You should wear a party dress. Something sparkly."

I'm past explaining to a little girl with her head full of fairy princesses that something sparkly would be a bit over the top for a quiet dinner at a modestly priced local bistro, followed by a movie, if we can agree on one. Dennis doesn't want to see a chick flick, despite my defending them as "date movies," and I refuse to see anything where more footage is devoted to destroying property than to character development.

As soon as we walk in the door, I insist she get out of her damp, smelly yoga clothes and into a hot bath right away.

After lunch, she follows me into my bedroom brandishing her star-tipped wand. "I'm the Fairy Godmother and you're Cinderella," she announces, then insists on vetting every single thing I'm going to wear this evening. So, I agree to something more colorful than my original choice, and I also acquiesce to my daughter's directive to wear a dress—"not pants!" But I found a rip in it, so I had to stitch it up. Then I had to hunt for more-or-less matching accessories, while Zoë, who seems to have tired of playing Carson Kressley, goes into her room to play.

It's now after six. Dennis is supposed to be here in forty-five minutes. Our reservation is for 7 P.M.

I'm in the process of microwaving something for Zoë's dinner so that Annabel doesn't have to feed her, when she wanders into the kitchen. Her face is pale. She's dripping with sweat.

"Mommy, I don't feel so good."

I kneel and hold her, touching my cheek to her forehead. She's burning up. I hope she didn't catch a chill on the way home from yoga this morning. "Let's go."

"Where?"

"To take your temperature. Get into bed. I'll be right in." No need to panic—yet, I tell myself.

She's running a 102-degree fever.

Now panic.

It's six fifteen. I give her a spoonful of ElixSure, tuck her in, and call Annabel. She lives only a couple of blocks away, so she wouldn't have left her house yet. "Zoë's just come down with something," I tell her. "So, obviously, since I'm not going anywhere tonight, I'll have to cancel." Annabel is very sweet about it. She sounds neither relieved nor put out by this news, which makes me feel confident that I can call on her again to request her baby-sitting services.

Oh, God, Dennis will be here any minute. I try to reach him, realizing that by now he's left his apartment. I leave a regretful message on his answering machine, explaining the situation. I don't know why I did. He's in transit anyway. I call his cell phone, and get the voice mail feature. He's probably down in the subway.

I cancel the dinner reservation, then unzip my dress and toss on a pair of jeans and a shirt. No point in staying all gussied up, particularly since Zoë can't "decide" whether or not she "needs" to throw up.

Six thirty.

"Do you want me to fix you some soup, or do you want to go back to sleep?" I ask Zoë. "You should be able to keep down the broth." She hasn't eaten anything since lunch.

"Orange sherbet."

"I don't think we have any, sweetie. Do you have a second choice?"

"Orange sherbet," she repeats, her voice at once stubborn, tired, and forlorn.

At 6:44, the doorman buzzes my apartment to see if he should send up Mr. McIntyre. Zoë and I spend the next thirty seconds arguing on whether she should go back to bed (my idea), or (hers) cling to my waist and greet Fireman Dennis at the front door. She gives her best imitation of some suction-cupped sea creature and I am unable to extricate her limbs from my person before the doorbell rings.

I swear to God, my heart really is fluttering. I'm excited that there are only a couple of inches of painted steel between us, yet I can't remember if I've ever felt so nervous. I unlock the door. Dennis is dressed very nicely in slacks, polo shirt, and sportcoat, accessorized with a pretty bouquet. He assesses my outfit and his face falls a bit.

"I'm sorry . . ." I begin. I look down at my daughter. "Zoë developed a high fever."

"Hi, Fireman Dennis!"

"Zoë, go back to bed now. You said hello. Mommy will be in, in a few minutes."

Reluctantly, she shuffles off toward her room.

"Feel better, Zoë," Dennis calls after her.

It's so awkward. He's standing there, sort of one foot over the threshold. "Please, come inside," I offer. "I . . . um . . . I was dressed better than this a few minutes ago. You'll just have to believe me." Nervously, I rake my hand through my hair and Dennis presents me with the bouquet. I thank him, admire them, then inhale. Where did he find blossoms in New York City that are so fragrant? "Listen . . . I'm so sorry. I was really looking forward to this. But when she's running a fever . . . obviously, I can't leave Zoë with a new sitter—with any sitter—just to go out and have fun. I don't feel right about that kind of thing. I'm sure there are mothers who do it, but I'm afraid I'm not one of them."

"Hey, there's nothing to apologize for," Dennis says. "I don't know if . . . I don't know how you feel about this, and it's fine if you send me right home, and we'll just do this another time . . . but, would you mind terribly if I stayed for a little while? Before I get back on the subway? I could go out and get a pizza or pick up some Chinese food, or we could order in . . . ?" He leaves the proposal hanging.

"Just a minute," I say, I holding up my index finger. I go into Zoë's bedroom and ask her how she feels about my reconfigured date. She thinks it's a fine idea—on two conditions. I return to the foyer where Dennis stands expectantly waiting.

I greet him with a smile. "For the price of one bedtime story of modest length with no skipping pages, and a pint of orange sherbet—not to be confused with sorbet, ice cream, gelato, or frozen yogurt—you've got yourself a date."

"I'll be back within a half hour," he says. "And as long as I'm taking a field trip, what's your preference—Chinese or pizza?" I present him with the take-out menus from the best local places. It takes us longer to agree on what to eat for dinner than it probably will take for the restaurant to cook it. I'm not too crazy about pepperoni; he doesn't eat mushrooms. He loves Hunan and Szechuan—the hotter the better; I prefer the milder Cantonese and Mandarin dishes. And we know that our taste in movies diverges radically. It's our first date without a crowd around and already we're a Cole Porter song. If Dennis weren't so handsome, kind, and charming, I'd be singing "Let's call the whole thing off."

"Half pepperoni and sausage, half mushroom," he says, thrusting the hot, flat pizza box into my hands. "Do you have any idea how hard it was to keep the sherbet from melting while I carried this?"

"You poor baby," I tsk-tsk.

"Not to mention how difficult it is to find *sherbet* in this neighborhood!" He hands me a bag containing the sherbet and some Coke.

"I didn't send you off to capture the Golden Fleece, you know!"

"Okay, okay, you can stop giving me grief," he says good-naturedly. He points to the pizza. "You might want to keep that in the oven—but take it out of the box—"

"Duh!"

"—while we take care of the sherbet and bedtime story issue," he adds, cheerfully ignoring my editorial comment.

I follow his suggestion and spoon out some sherbet while he watches me, leaning against the kitchen counter like he's as familiar with my apartment as any of my old friends—who I haven't exactly had time to see in months, so maybe that's a bad analogy. "Did I tell you about the time Zoë spent nearly a month refusing to eat any food that wasn't orange?" I say, freezing the sherbet container.

He nods. "I would venture a guess . . . that in all the time we've spent on the phone with one another, I've probably received a play-by-play account of her life ever since your obstetrician smacked her on the butt." I can tell he's teasing. Although it's true that over the course of all our phone calls and e-mails, we've pretty much gotten full biographical histories of each other and every close relative. I've stopped him, though, whenever he invokes the name of an old girlfriend. I don't understand why guys don't think it's a big deal to mention old girlfriend stuff to the woman they're currently with. Are there really women out there who aren't bothered by this? Because I sure as heck am, and I don't know any of my female friends who aren't.

And the guys are always, like, "Well, I'm with *you* now." They don't get it. They claim not to be bothered when an old boyfriend or ex-husband thing comes up. I don't get *that*. I try to keep the ghosts out of the room, unless there's a real reason for summoning them. Like telling Dennis why Scott and I got divorced.

"You're like my sister that way," he said, the first time I *unh-unh-ed* him from discussing the time he was on vacation with one of his exes.

"Which sister? The beauty queen or the paralegal?"

"Megan. The beauty queen. And she was Miss Teen New York State, so I don't know how much that counts."

"Of course it counts! What, she has to be Miss Universe and appear in a pageant in Singapore or something, and not Schenectady, for it to count with you?"

We do tease each other a lot, Dennis and I. When we fall back into our familiar banter in my kitchen, I feel less nervous somehow about the fact that he's actually here, in the really appealing flesh. That this evening we're able, for the first time, to do a whole lot more than listen to each other's voice or tap away on a keyboard.

"Let's go, Mr. Lifesaver," I say, leading the way to Zoë's bedroom.

"Here you are," I say, placing the tray on her lap. She's sitting up in bed, reading one of her kid-craft type magazines. "Can we do this for St. Patrick's Day?" she asks, pointing to a page.

"Do what, sweetheart?"

"Make those cupcakes. And I could bring them to school like I did with the heart cookies on Valentine's Day. We're supposed to bring something Irish to school on March seventeenth."

I look at the page she's referring to. It's a recipe and decorating directions for leprechaun cupcakes, a complicated design. They're actually ice-cream-cone cupcakes, with the flat-bottomed cones tinted green, forming the leprechauns' hats.

"I'll think about it, okay? We've still got a few days to go. Let's tackle one thing at a time. How are you feeling?"

"Yucky." She pulls a book from the folds of her bedclothes. "Can you read me two chapters from this, please?" she says sweetly, thrusting the book at Dennis.

"*Charlotte's Web*. That's pretty grown-up stuff, isn't it?" he asks her.

My reaction is somewhere between a snicker and a chuckle. "You'd be surprised what kids her age are reading these days.

Believe me. Welcome to the world of fast-track grammar schoolers."

"Hey! I *am* an uncle, you know! I don't think my nieces and nephews read such advanced stuff at Zoë's age, though." Dennis leans in to whisper to me. "However . . . if I recall correctly, this book has a really sad *e—n—d—i—n—g*."

"Why is the ending sad?" Zoë asks.

"If you spell it out, you'll give away the plot," I warn.

"It's okay," she assures him. "I've read sad stuff before. And I've seen sad movies. *Dumbo*'s really sad in parts. And scary, too, when the house catches fire and he's trapped inside. And *Bambi*'s reeeeeeeally sad."

"Um . . . Z? Isn't reading *Charlotte's Web* a homework assignment?" She tilts her head coyly. That's a "yes." She's putting on her best I'm-sick-but-irresistibly-adorable face. "Then you're doing us *both* a favor by reading these chapters," I tell Dennis. "She's got more homework in second grade than I think I had in sixth."

"I love bedtime stories," Zoë says. "And sometimes I like Mommy to read me something different, but when it's *homework*, it . . . it . . . it goes faster when someone else reads it out loud because I can't read so fast. But it's the same words," she offers, as a rationalization.

"You'd better watch it or she might become a lawyer," he cautions, grinning. I shudder.

"I want to be an astronaut." She tucks into her sherbet as Dennis begins to read. I'm charmed, and for some reason I feel *proud* that he reads the material so well, acting out all the parts with the skill of an old Irish raconteur. Maybe it's a cultural thing; storytelling runs through his veins. Of course, that ability has nothing whatsoever to do with the fact that he's the man I think I would like to be my boyfriend, but it does indeed make me proud. And Zoë is very picky when it comes to reading aloud. She can be quite a scathing critic.

I find myself noticing Dennis's mouth as he reads, wanting to kiss him, remembering how soft his lips were the first time we kissed and wondering what he might taste like this time. The fact that he's got a flair for reading and is so good with Zoë is also a turn-on

"Okay, that's two chapters and no skipped pages," he says, closing the book. "There'll be a quiz in the morning."

She takes this literally. "Will you be here to give it to me?"

Dennis and I exchange an awkward glance. "I don't think so, sweetie," I tell her, although I'm certainly thinking about it. He's pretty irresistible right now.

"Oh." She pauses momentarily before switching gears. "Do I have to go to sleep now?"

"That's usually why it's called a bedtime story, Z. Say thank you to Fireman Dennis for reading to you and for doing such a good job."

"Thank you Fireman Dennis for reading to me and for doing such a good job," she parrots. "And you can do it again some-time, if you want."

"The pleasure will be mine. Goodnight, Zoë. Feel better, now, okay?"

"I don't feel better now, but I will in the morning, maybe."

"Why don't you go check on the pizza situation?" I suggest. Dennis leaves the room and I lean in to kiss my daughter good-night. "I'm glad you enjoyed your bedtime story. Didn't Fireman Dennis do a good job?" I take the sherbet bowl and tray away.

She beams, then sighs, like a lovestruck maiden. "Yeaaaaah. I like Fireman Dennis a lot. He doesn't talk to me like a little kid."

"I'll pass along your compliment." I give her a kiss and turn off the light.

"She's a good kid," Dennis remarks, happily accepting my grateful embrace. He tastes like cinnamon red-hots. Dennis has already set the table in the breakfast nook and found all the appropriate dishes and utensils. Rather than feel at all offended or violated by the fact that he's obviously given himself a tour of my drawers and cabinets, I'm relieved that he doesn't act like he wants—or expects—to be waited on, when I've got a sick child to deal with. "I hope you don't mind that I went ahead and did this," he adds, gesturing at his handiwork. "Kitchens are kitchens. A firehouse isn't *that* much different than a lady's home." In a gentlemanly gesture he pulls the chair out for me, and his hands graze my shoulders when he seats me. It feels delicious.

"No, it's great. Thanks. You did a very thorough job. I'm surprised you didn't find the pornography." I wink, making sure he realizes I'm kidding.

He laughs. "Ooh, there's pornography?" He slides his chair away from the table and heads straight to one of the higher cabinets.

"Come back and sit down." He does, and then I pop up. The porno joke lightened the mood, but made me even more aware of the sexual tension in the air, and I'm not sure how to deal with it. "I've got a bottle of red wine here somewhere." I locate the Beaujolais and pour a glass for each of us.

"To . . ." Dennis raises his glass to toast. "I'm not very good at this, I'm afraid."

"I don't believe it! I thought you Irishmen are legendary for your toasts. You know . . . 'May the wind be at your back and the road rise up to meet you' and all that."

"You're not supposed to combine those two, I don't think. Anyway, cheers. To Zoë's speedy recovery."

Our less-than-glamorous dinner is punctuated by the sharing of childhood reminiscences, much laughter, Dennis's spirited defense of Terminator movies, and the occasional awkward silence. It seems pretty clear that we're both interested in taking whatever has been going on between us over countless phone calls and e-mails to another, physical level.

He reaches for my hand across the table. "Hey, your nails are smudgy."

"Aaah! Zoë and I were hoping you wouldn't notice."

"I noticed," he says, "but I don't care, in case you're concerned about it. You haven't offended my . . . my . . . *manicurial* sensibilities."

He's got me smiling. "It fits better when you're not wearing those big Kevlar gloves," I say, enjoying the feel of our clasped hands. Mine in his.

"About Zoë's question . . ." he begins.

"Which one?" I realize we're both whispering.

"The one about me being around tomorrow to quiz her on the *Charlotte's Web* chapters I read to her."

"Oh, that one."

"Claire, you're blushing."

"So are you." There are a few moments of heavy silence. A real pregnant pause. "I don't think it's a good idea . . . tonight, I mean . . . but . . . but . . ." I'm scared to say this. More than just nervous. Really scared. I haven't been with another guy, apart from Scott, since I was a senior in high school. And Scott was only the second man I ever made love with. And what if Dennis isn't thinking the same thing . . . I mean, I think he is . . . but what if . . . ? "I really do want to, though. Eventually. And I don't mean too far away eventually. Soon eventually."

"I understand." He doesn't sound pissed off or rejected. *Whew.*

"It's just that with Zoë . . . and this is only a first date, such as it is, and all . . ."

He's watching me dither, a confused muddle of words that are meant to express my current state of womanhood and motherhood and longing and desire and fear.

"It's okay, Claire. I understand," he repeats. "I really do. I'm not bullshitting. I don't do that. There's no reason for us to force anything, or feel we've got a timetable here. If it's okay with you, I'm not going anywhere." He chuckles. "I mean, except home tonight."

We clean up the kitchen together, and then he says he thinks he'd better start heading back.

I'm a little disappointed. "So soon?"

"Yeah, I think so. Because if I don't leave now . . ."

It's my turn to understand. "It's okay. Can I kiss you good night?" Dennis takes me in his arms. At first his mouth just brushes mine. Then he truly claims it, deepening the kiss with a passionate urgency. He hugs me to him, caressing my back, shoulders, and neck, and it's quite a while before we come up for air. I love the way it feels to be held by him, the softness of his lips, the scent of his skin. "You taste like pizza," I whisper.

"Then maybe next time, you'll try the pepperoni," he breathes into my mouth, then pulls away and starts laughing at what I might be taking for a dreadful double entendre.

I give him a playful smack on the upper arm. "That's terrible!"

"I didn't mean it that way, I swear I didn't!" We're both laughing hard now, and fall into each other's arms. "You do believe me, don't you?" he says, kissing me again.

"Oh, yeah, sure, of I course I do," I giggle. "And I *do* want to try the pepperoni."

Chapter 18

For the first time in my life, I'm scared to live here. I mean, after the break-in, I don't feel like my apartment is safe. I threw out half the clothes they dumped on the floor; I was too skeeved to touch them again. Not the nicest reason to buy new underwear. Charles helped me put the place back together and we got a locksmith to put so much hardware on the door, I feel like *I'm* the one who's in jail every time I get home and flip all the locks. The guys who broke in are waiting for their trial. I've heard they've both got rap sheets a mile long. If convicted—which they'd better be—they're probably looking at a long time in the can. And one of them violated his parole when he robbed me. Dickhead.

"You need an alarm system," the locksmith told me. I figured he was just trying to sell me more stuff.

But Charles thought he had a point. "You don't have to get something traditional," he said. "My friends John and Maria don't have a bell or some horrible noisy thing like those car alarms, which always make *me* want to take a crowbar to the cars. They have two dogs instead. And they bark like crazy when anyone is anywhere they're not supposed to be."

"But what if the thieves ignore the barking and go for it anyway?"

Charles licked his lips. "They're dinner."

"Well, this much I know," I told him, as we took a walk to a local pet store. "A burglar alarm can't stomp roaches or reach my light fixtures to change a bulb. And a dog needs to be walked at least twice a day. Can you honestly see me doing that? And we all know I am *not* a morning person. Any dog I'd get would have to learn to walk himself!"

We passed the pet store and decided to head to a bar instead. "And," I added, "I get my most creative ideas when I'm shopping or screwing, so it's a wise career move in the long run."

Charles gave me a funny look. "Mia, you just made some sort of leap that went too fast for my fragile little masculine synapses. *What's* a wise career move in the long run?"

Oh. Had I not made myself clear? "A husband."

"Aaaaand . . . where are we going to find such an item?"

I looked around the bar. No prospects there. At least, not now. "Will you help me go over my Excel sheets?" I just happened to have them in my purse. Since they contain such personal details, I got weirded out about having them around the house after the robbery. As long as my bag doesn't get snatched. Charles knows about the spreadsheets and finds them wildly amusing. In fact, he thought he might try the same technique. Besides, it's cheaper than therapy. Maybe I could start a trend. A self-help psychotherapy/dating/computer skills combo. You know, "Learn and master a popular software package while understanding why you're such a fuck-up as a lover!"

Spring is, like, in a few days. Didn't Celestia say my love life was supposed to look up around now?

Charles ordered two apple martinis. The waitress looked at us like we were tourists. "This is a real shot and beer place," I whispered to him.

"Does that mean I have to drink them?" he said peevishly. "And if she gives us attitude, I give her a shitty tip."

"Sounds a bit harsh."

"It's the same give and take in the cutthroat world of guiding. Just ask your sister."

Charles and I don't see eye to eye on this kind of thing. Yeah, I know the place is empty, more or less, so in his view, there's no reason for her to cop a 'tude just because we asked for green girl-drinks. But I always tend to think there's more than the obvious going on. Maybe she got dumped by her man last night. Maybe her dog died. Maybe she's PMSing. Of course, Charles could be right; maybe she's just a bitch!

I laid out the charts on the small table. I have the pages taped like sheet music so it's one long chart that folds out, accordion-style. "My, God, you've dated more men than I have!" Charles exclaimed. He looked at my categories. "Oral?"

"Sex."

"Duh. I already guessed that. I didn't think it was their favorite toothbrush brand." He threw up his hands. "That's too vague, Mia. You're giving me nothing here. Does that mean they like you to do it to them or they like to do it to you, or both?"

I gave him a look. "*I'm* the common denominator here. Figure it out."

"Oh. Right. But it doesn't say whether they were good at it, and if so, how good. I mean if it's an important enough factor to have on the chart, I think there should be some kind of a rating system. Don't just have Y or N. Make it a Y on a scale of one to ten, or one to a hundred." He pointed to another category. "What's DB?"

"Dresses badly."

"Again, not detailed enough. What's 'dresses badly' *mean*? Mismatched socks? Blue with brown? T-shirts that say stupid things?"

"All of the above."

Charles unfolded my Guy Chart section by section, skimmed it, and sighed like a Jewish grandmother. Our drinks came. From the way she looked over his shoulder, the waitress seemed intrigued by my somewhat scientific autobiographical presentation. You'd think, from her hawklike look, that she'd dated some of the same guys.

"Okay," he said, entwining his fingers around the *V* of his martini glass. "You've got a lot of Peter Pans here. And how you *act* is what you *attract*." He looked pleased with his little aphorism.

"You sound like a gay, white Johnnie Cochran."

"I'll ignore that pathetic attempt at humor. You want to make a real stab at commitment, you need to make a serious effort to present that to the world."

"You mean act predatory?"

"Well, no. And yes. If you're clear—in your head—that you feel it's time to quit dating fly-by-night guys who make you feel good—not that there's anything *wrong* with that—and become interested in spending your increasingly precious dating hours only with men who have a future that includes marriage—and kids, if that's what you want, too—then that will be the kind of person who will gravitate to you. If you go on acting like the good-time gal that you are, you'll only attract good-time guys."

"Are you saying I'm not supposed to have fun? Not be me?"

"No. And yes."

"You're driving me crazy with that, you know." I dipped my fingers into my water glass and flicked a few drops in his face. Charles flinched. You'd think he was the Wicked Witch of the West. "Afraid of water, are you?" I teased.

"It's a matter of commitment," he replied, totally ignoring me. "Committing to being committed. Ever since you hit adolescence—and I've been there every step of the way, remember—you've put out vibes that you really don't care too much about the long run. You're into the here and now. You're a creature of the moment. Which is a really cool thing, don't get me wrong—it's one of the parts of you I love the best—but what it means is that men pick up on that vibe, sugar." He pointed at the chart. "Every one of these guys supports my theory. They're all grasshoppers. We need to find you an ant."

I slid his green martini toward my side of the table. "I think you've drunk enough of this bug juice. I have no idea what the fuck you're talking about."

Charles reclaimed his cocktail. "The Aesop's fable. You know, the grasshopper lives for the here and now, while the ant stores up for the winter."

"I don't think that's a very exact analogy."

"Okay, maybe not. But you know what I mean." He flipped through the Excel chart. "Hey, you know who's not on here?"

"The President and the Dalai Lama?"

"Them, too. The guy from your birthday party."

"What guy?"

"The one who owns the bar."

"Jake? *I* never went out with Jake!"

"No, the other guy. Mr. Capital Gains or Investment Capital . . . you know—curly brown hair, Armani tux, good grooming."

"Oh. Umm . . . Owen Michaels, his name was. I didn't go out with him, either. He played Good Samaritan when my place was robbed and then I got a birthday kiss at the end of the night. In fact, he played about the same role you did that night, except he looked a bit slimmer in his tux," I teased.

"He's an example, on paper, anyway—which is where you should put him," Charles said, poking at a page of the chart for emphasis. "So you have a sample—of the kind of man you should be considering from now on. Remember how he sort of took charge after you realized you'd been burglarized? If *you* didn't find that sexy, Mia, *I* did." He put on his sanctimonious face. "You know, Miss Control Freak, even the most take-charge people like to be taken care of sometimes."

I did want to call Owen, actually. I've got his card someplace; I'm not sure where I put it. I want to talk to him about my ideas for *Mi♥amore Makeup*. I've got some money socked away—

maybe I *am* an *ant*, after all—and Celestia did say that these days the stars would be on my side in the business sphere. "Yeah, I guess a phone call won't hurt," I said to Charles. "I could, like, sound him out about my start-up, in a real low-pressure way. We've got a mutual friend in Jake, so maybe I could see if Owen plans to go over to the bar on Saint Paddy's day." Jake always does a big thing that night. So if a conversation with Owen— either personal or professional—went south fast, the stakes would be really low and we could still enjoy the night by hanging and talking with other people.

I'm not sure this is a very committed way to commit to committing.

············

Dear Diary:

Happy St. Patrick's Day! You can tell in this diary that it's St. Patrick's day anyway because I drew a four-leaf clover and a snake. Mrs. Heinie-face did not like my snakes from last week. She said they were disgusting. I said that I know snakes are disgusting and that everyone thinks snakes are disgusting, so it was a good thing that St. Patrick made them go away from Ireland. I made my project so you could put the snakes in Ireland and then take them away, because I just drew a picture and that was Ireland. And the snakes were made out of Play-Doh and I put plastic wrap on them after Mommy and me made them so they wouldn't get hard. So they were still sticky on their tummies and you could stick them to the drawing or unstick them and take them away. Xander said he liked the snakes a lot and that made me happy.

Mrs. Heinie-face called my mommy and Mommy said that just because Mrs. Heinie-face said that she thinks snakes are disgusting, if she gives me a U because of that, she will make a big com-

*plaint about it. Mrs. Heinie-face gave me an S after all. I think
my Ireland project was better than Satisfactory. I think I should
have gotten an E. I can't wait until third grade and no more Mrs.
Heinie-face. June, when we have our graduation is really, really
far away.*

*Mommy said we could make the leprechaun cupcakes for
school but she didn't want to make them from scratch like it said
in my magazine. But the magazine said that if you want to use a
cake mix, you could do that, too.*

*But we didn't have a lot of the ingredients. Mommy was tired
from work when she said we could make the cupcakes because I
said "remember I need to bring something Irish to school tomorrow" and then she said okay, but then we had to go to the grocery
store because we needed to buy all the ice cream cones and the
cake mixes and we had to get the icing and the special candies to
decorate them and we had to buy a lot of bags of gum drops so
we would have enough of the right colors because they have to
look exactly the same as the picture in the magazine.*

*I stayed up extra late to help because I wanted to do the deco-
rations and that was my favorite part but we had to wait for the
cupcakes to cool off before we could decorate them. From the directions we had to paint the cones with green food coloring because
the cones are the leprechaun hats. And we had to put vanilla
icing on the cake part because those were the heads and the faces
and then we had to put candy on it to make the eyes and the nose
and the mouth and the beard. But we couldn't do that unless we
turned the cupcakes upside down. Which was really right side up
so they would look like leprechauns.*

*While we were waiting for the cupcakes to be finished baking,
Mommy helped me with my homework. We have math that I
don't understand. We have to add numbers that are three numbers big to other numbers that are three numbers big and I keep
getting confused. I keep forgetting about carrying numbers.
Mommy said that if I'm going to be an astronaut when I grow up*

*then I have to know how to do math. Maybe I won't be an astro-
naut. I don't think Rockettes have to know math. And that's my
second choice.*

*When we took the cupcakes out of the oven, most of them
spilled out over the sides of the cones and they were all gloppy. I
think it was because Mommy filled them too much, but the recipe
said halfway and that's what she did. I saw her. Mommy said
maybe it would be okay when they cooled off. But then some of
them flopped out of the cones when we turned them upside down
and then others of them, when Mommy tried to cut off the parts
that glopped over, they just got all crumbly.*

*Some of them were okay, but because of the messy ones and the
broken ones we won't have enough for one for each of my class. And
then I was crying because we wouldn't have enough and it was a
lot past my bedtime, so Mommy said I should go to sleep and we
would wake up extra early and decorate them in the morning, because even the good ones were still too hot to put the icing on.*

*But in the morning, the cones got all mushy during the night
and it made the leprechaun hats all smushy and you couldn't
hold them by the hat to eat them because they were too mushy
and the cupcake part squooshed out. So we couldn't decorate
them and I wanted Mommy to make new ones but she said we
didn't have enough time to start all over again from scratch. I
said we weren't doing it from scratch. We were using cake mixes
but then she said she meant that we didn't have enough time to
start all over again at all. And she made me add up the numbers
like math class. 10 minutes to put all the ingredients together and
mix them up and 30 minutes to bake them and then to be extra
sure they would be cool so we could decorate them it would be 30
more minutes to wait and then it might take a whole hour just to
decorate all of them.*

*And then Mommy saw what I was wearing to school because
we didn't have to wear our uniforms again today because it's a
special day. She said, "Aren't you supposed to be wearing St.*

Patrick's Day colors?" And I said yes, we could wear green or
white or orange or we could put the colors together. I was wearing
a yellow dress that Granny Tulia made for me that has bright
pink pockets. Mommy said that she didn't think I was following
the rules. And I said yes I WAS following the rules because Mrs.
Hennepin said you could put the colors together and yellow and
bright pink makes a kind of orange and orange is one of the St.
Patrick's colors. Mommy thought I should wear something green
instead because she said Mrs. Hennepin likes it when people follow the rules. And that she knew Mrs. Hennepin was going to be
unhappy with both Mommy and me because I wasn't following
the rules. But I didn't want to change clothes.

 And I was crying because I didn't want to change and because
the cupcakes didn't come out and because I have to bring something Irish to school and now I don't have anything and I would
get a U for the whole St. Patrick's Day. I asked Mommy if I could
just be sick today from school. But she said no and that I was
sick for real last week and already missed a day of school and it
wasn't good to pretend to be sick just 'cause something bad happened.

 Mommy told me to stop crying and she got a smile on her face
and she said she wasn't going to make me any promises but she
had an idea. So she went to the telephone and she made a call
and then when the other person picked up the phone she said "Hi,
Dennis, it's me. Is today still a day off for you?" And I heard her
listening. And she smiled even more and she said, "I want to
know if you can do Zoë and me a big BIG favor? Can you go to
school with her today?"

 So Fireman Dennis came to school with me and he talked to
our whole class about being Irish and he told us stories that his
granny used to tell him when he was a little boy my age about the
Little People and the banshees and it was so fun! And Mrs. Hennepin gave me an Excellent for bringing something Irish to class.

She said that it was a wonderful surprise. And THAT was the biggest surprise. That I got an E.

Oh. I forgot. Mrs. Hennepin said I didn't follow the rules with my yellow and pink dress because everybody else was wearing green or orange. And she didn't understand when I explained it. That I WAS wearing orange. So in art class today I asked Ms. Bland if I was right that yellow and bright pink make orange and she said they make peach which is a shade of orange. And Mrs. Hennepin didn't like it that I asked Ms. Bland. So I had the best time when Fireman Dennis came to class with me but I had the worst time when I got in trouble for my dress. I don't think Mrs. Hennepin will EVER like me. She IS a Heinie-face!

Chapter 19

APRIL

"Claire, are you sitting down? I'm getting married!"

"Oh—wow—oh my God, Mia, that's amazing! I mean—who's the guy?"

"April Fools!!"

"You witch!"

I laughed. "I could always get you, you know? I've been waiting for this for weeks." Some people look forward to Christmas. Me, I can't wait for April Fool's Day to roll around. I was a real prankster at Thackeray, back in the old days. Senior year, sixth form, we dressed like commandos and "liberated" the student body. I think we were trying to reenact the invasion of Grenada or something. I had Claire, who was only in second form then, posted as a lookout. She was pissed at me because we wouldn't let her do more. I was all for it; I knew she was as good as any of us, but the boys outvoted me. The guys, dressed in camouflage fatigues and toting pretty authentic-looking black plastic machine guns, staged a distraction with "explosives" (baking soda and water in plastic 35mm film canisters) strategically placed in trash cans throughout Thackeray's halls and classrooms. Then our ringleader nailed Kiplinger with a water balloon and he surrendered immediately. After all, "boys will be boys."

"Okay, you got me—for the nine zillionth time since I was born," Claire admitted. "But something must have made you pick that 'gotcha!' " I could *hear* her smiling. Her voice took on a sweet, probing quality.

"That Owen Michaels is a pretty cool guy, after all." Oh, God, I just got an all-gooey face, I'm sure of it. Good thing I don't have picture phone. I'm so embarrassed. "But, Claire, he's a DB! On my Excel charts. Charles made me add him, even before Owen and I went out. And he looked like a total keeper on paper, until our actual date, and then I had to add him to the DB category. Although, to be fair, he's a DB with a star."

"Don't be so judgmental. You can be picky about the stupidest things, you know that, Mia? You're just as bad as your friend Gina with that Adam-Sandler–movies guy. And what do you mean by 'he's a *pretty* cool guy after all'?" Claire quizzed. "He was *mighty* cool at your birthday. And that's the only time I met him, but he didn't come across as an uncool guy at all. Not to me, anyway."

I told her about our date.

On St. Patrick's Day, I'd run into Owen accidentally-on-purpose at The Corner Bar, like I'd more or less planned to. Charles came with me, in case I had to bail. That wasn't the "date," though. That was just hanging out with a lot of other people around, kind of like my birthday. And Owen had just come from meeting a client, so he was dressed in a suit again, like the first time we'd met. Two smart-ass, ex-dot-com guys who'd gone to Yale, went through job re-training or whatever they call it, something Claire's ex should have tried. Anyway, these savvy MBAs, seeing all the construction always being done in New York, figured they'd cash in. On the other end. Since there's no empty land around here, you've got to demolish the old structure first. So they went to Owen to help them start up Edifice Wrecks. I told him that just 'cause of the name alone, I'd hire them anytime I had a building I wanted to knock down.

We spent most of the evening talking business, since the atmosphere in the bar was not exactly romantic. Owen listened to my *Mi♥amore Makeup* pitch and was genuinely interested. It was so loud in The Corner that it was really hard to chat, but he seemed pleased to see me. He said he'd been thinking about me a lot since my birthday, but he'd gone out of town on business, and was swamped when he got back. He told me he was glad he'd run into me, complimented my green mini-dress, and asked me out.

This was cool. Him asking me out, I mean. Very cool. I feel a connection with this guy. I can't explain it. He's so different from me. So not my type. But he's so easy to talk to. It's like I've always known him or something. I have to ask Celestia. Maybe I *have* known him and it's some past-life thing. I hope we were never siblings. That would completely skeeve me.

We set up a real date for the following Saturday night.

He rang the bell at six o'clock and I buzzed him in. When I opened my door, I could have died. It, like, wasn't the same guy. I mean, he can't dress! I'd seen him in a suit and then a tux and then a suit again. And all three times he looked great. Like James Bond. But he must have a sartorial blind spot for dressing down.

Owen picked up on my reaction immediately. "Is there anything wrong, Mia? You said to dress casual."

"*Caszh* isn't really your thing, is it?" I said, too bluntly. I felt like shit as soon as the words were out of my mouth. His face went all red. "I am *so* sorry, Owen. I'm an asshole. Please don't go away. What can I do?" I started to run around the apartment, panicky, picking up a pair of wine stems, looking for a bottle of good stuff. Anything to appease. "Truth told, I'm scared shitless about fucking up this date, and, hey, look! That's what I did as soon as you showed up! Appearance isn't everything. It's nothing, in fact," I continued to blather.

I uncorked the wine and poured. "Now you'll think I'm the most shallow bitch in New York, if not on Earth."

Owen took a glass from my hand. "Slow down, Mia. Calm down. Deep cleansing breaths. All that." He steered me to my couch and we sat, side by side. "Actually, I dressed this way on purpose." He was wearing a Harris Tweed herringbone over a brown and orange argyle cashmere V-neck over a blue and yellow tattersall-patterned sportshirt. "I mean not on-purpose badly. This is the kind of thing I always wear when I go casual and I get ribbed about it all the time, but no one wants to tell me why. They're too busy laughing at me, or else they don't say anything. Even my sisters refuse to help. They're all sparing my feelings, I guess."

"You can't do anything about your kin, but maybe you need to find yourself some new friends. Including me, probably, after what I said to you a few minutes ago."

"Well, knowing the way you are, a real shoot-from-the-hip kind of person, I figured you'd be honest about it. I realize I need some help, here. But it's like getting a math problem wrong, and you acknowledge that, okay, you got it *wrong*, but no one shows you *how* to get the *right* answer."

"Honey, you need more than me. You need the Fab Five."

"Oh, I'm not *that* bad," he chuckled. "I'm a stickler for good grooming and you could eat off my bathroom floor. If you had really a mind to."

"I think I'll pass. But I believe you." I laughed.

He raised his glass. "Cheers." We took our first sips. "I'm okay with everything else, clothes-wise. I know how to dress up. You've seen it. Three times already. So you know it's not an accident." He chuckled at his own expense. "I guess it's a good thing I went into a white-collar profession."

"How are your comedic skills? Because, with this," I said, gesturing to his outfit, "you might get hired by Barnum and Bailey."

"I *was* a clown, actually. Back in college. I did kids' birthday parties. I more or less sucked at it," he added. "That's when I decided that business school was a better bet for me."

"I don't want to spend our first date giving you wardrobe pointers," I said. "But here's a quick tip. Lose the sweater for now. 'Cause the jacket and shirt actually coordinate pretty well."

"But I'm going to need it for where we're going."

"Which is . . . ?"

"A night cruise. The food may not be four-star, but it's good enough. The view, however, can't be beat."

I love boats. "You made a good choice. I mean it. It doesn't have to be a dinner cruise to get me revved up. We could paddle around Manhattan in a kayak with a couple of ham and cheese sandwiches and a few cold beers and it would be a great date."

Owen slipped his arm around my shoulder. "I'll remember that for next time."

I snuggled against him on the couch. "I wasn't kidding. You may not think it to look at me," I added, indicating my leather pants, vintage top, and stiletto heels, "but I can be outdoorsy. Depending on what it is. Just don't ask me to go bungee-jumping."

"What about diving?" Owen asked, letting his fingers do the walking through my hair. "I've been certified for years—I love it."

"Never did it. But I'd be up for it, I guess—after I took a class or ten. I love water. I'm a Pisces, remember?"

And then the next thing I knew I was on his lap, straddling him, my knees digging into the couch cushions. I don't know who "put" me there—me or him—it was just an urge—and I couldn't stop kissing him. He tasted like toothpaste and Merlot. I could have kissed him for hours, though I figured it might be best to wait until after dinner to suggest a remedy for his multiple fashion *faux pas*.

On second thought . . . "What time is our reservation?" I whispered.

"There's only one sailing," Owen whispered back. His fingers traced a line along my collarbone. "Should I cancel it?"

I weighed our options. "No. Let's go. It'll be cool. We . . . can pick this up when we get back . . . if you want."

"I want. I very *much* want, Mia." We straightened out our limbs and clothes. "Unless you think it's too soon, and this was just a heat-of-the—in which case, that's totally okay."

I looked at him. Who knew he'd press all my buttons, ring all my gooey bells? And what a nice guy. I saw that when we first met. And how sweet he'd been on my birthday, being such a knight. That was long before I started to think about his lips. "The way I see stuff, there's no set pace. Everyone's—each situation is one-of-a-kind, right?" No need to tell him that I do tend to move faster than most chicks I know. Always have. It's not a crime. Truth told, I've spent more time talking with Owen and seeing him, just as a person, not a lover, than with nearly every other guy I can think of. Before I went to bed with them, I mean. In a Mia-way, this is a first.

"Well, you can't dress down, but at least you don't eat weird," I said to Owen after dinner. We strolled on the deck. It was kind of cold. Maybe that's one reason he picked it. If you wanted the full effect of the view, you had to snuggle to stay warm.

"Eat weird?" he asked.

I explained the Serena thing. "We Marshes don't trust people who eat weird. Except when *we* decide to do it." I told him about my niece and the orange food month.

"You are a stunning woman, Mia," he said, happy to change the subject.

"Ah, it's all artifice," I teased, mocking myself. "The makeup makes me magically youthful." Suddenly I thought of Lucky Charms.

"Hardly," he laughed. "I mean the makeup is nice and all, but what's this about you and age? You're only thirty. I was there, re-member?"

"And a good thing, too!" I cuddled into him. "I wouldn't have been half as good at handling all that."

"Nah. I bet you would have." We kissed. His mouth felt soft on mine. Our lips touched, just gently, for a long time. "It's one of the things that attracts me to you. Your ability to go with the flow. To not freak out under pressure."

"You didn't think I freaked out when we found out I was robbed?"

"That was nothing, compared to just about every other woman I've ever known. Including the ones I'm related to. My sisters are very girly-girls."

I pulled away and smacked him on the butt. Playfully, but pretty hard. "And I'm not? I'm insulted, you know that?" I was only half kidding.

"Oh, boy," Owen sighed. "Talk about finding yourself between a rock and a hard place. I'm damned either way, right?"

"Yeah. You are."

"Mia, you are *very* feminine. You have nothing to worry about on that score, believe me. There is no doubt in my mind, or in the minds of all the other guys I've noticed noticing you. At Jake's, on your birthday—"

"That may have been because I was running around the East Village in a strapless wedding gown in the middle of February."

Owen pretended to think about that. "Okay, maybe you've got a point. But after the initial shock value, believe me, it was all about how you looked in it." He brought me close and tipped my chin with his finger, tilting my face towards his. "Which was . . ." he said, right before we kissed for about two straight minutes, "breathtaking. Spectacular."

"You're not so bad yourself! Look!" I pointed to the Brooklyn Bridge. "Now, *that's* breathtaking and spectacular. The lights look like diamond necklaces, don't they?"

"Oh, yeah, you're a hundred percent *girly-girl*, all right. I give you a kiss and a compliment and the very next thing you talk about is diamonds!"

"Nuh-unh," I said nuzzling him. "You're wrong, my sentimental friend. I gave you a compliment back. First."

After Owen brought me home, we made out some more on the couch. We both stood up and I was about to lead him to the bedroom, but something made me stop. I turned back and told him, "Please don't think I'm a cock-tease because of this. Because, trust me, I'm not. No way. But . . . I can't even believe I'm saying this after such a great date . . . and you . . . you're so great . . . and maybe it's because you're so great and because I have such a piss-poor track record that I want this to be different. For me, anyway. Can . . . can we wait a bit?"

He took me in his arms. "Of course we can, you nut! You don't need to get yourself so worked up over this."

"Oh, yes. I do," I said. "Wait 'til you get to know me better. I *do*. Trust me on that, too."

"No big deal, Mia. Whenever you're ready."

"You sure?"

"Of course I'm sure. I'm not just saying that because I think it's what you want to hear."

"You sure about that, too? Because guys say they're sure and they don't really mean they're sure. What they really mean is, 'I can't fucking believe I didn't get laid tonight. And I bought dinner and everything!' "

Owen started to laugh. "That might be true in your experience, but I am not 'guys.' And I can only speak for myself, not these nameless, faceless, generic 'guys,' but I promise you Mia, that when I say something I mean it. So, take your time, and I'd love to see you again, if that's okay."

"It's very okay." I kissed him and walked him to the door. "I had a blast tonight."

"Me, too."

"Thanks, Owen." We shared another kiss at the door. "I'll call you soon."

I closed the door and went back to the couch. I liked the slight dent in the soft cushion where his ass had been. A goofy memento of his presence. I wondered if it still was warm. The cushion, not his ass. He'd probably hailed a cab when he got downstairs. Owen Michaels didn't strike me as the kind of guy who took mass transit at 11 P.M., just to save a few bucks. I went to the phone and dialed his cell.

"Hey. It's me. I hope you don't have plans for Monday morning, 'cause, if it's all right with you, tomorrow might turn into kind of a late night. And I promise to give you a real lesson in how to dress down." His answer made me smile.

• • • • • • • • • • • •

Dear Diary:

Ashley's not my best friend anymore. She came over to my house after school for a play date yesterday. That's how it started. MiMi picked us up from school because Mommy was working and she gave us a snack and Ashley said she didn't like the snack because she doesn't like cheese and MiMi said that Mommy told her she was supposed to give us something healthy and Ashley didn't want anything that MiMi said was good for us.

Aunt MiMi was getting mad, I think, because Ashley didn't want to eat any of the things that MiMi said we could have. And MiMi opened the cabinet where we keep the cookies and she took the box of Oreos and she threw it on the table and she said, "Here! I don't care what you eat. You're a spoiled brat!"

And I didn't think that was nice for MiMi to say that to Ashley because she's my best friend. And Ashley started to cry and told MiMi that cookies are junk and HER Mommy never lets her have cookies for snack after school. And then Mommy came home from work and wanted to know why I was crying. I said I was crying because MiMi was mean to Ashley. And Mommy asked why Ashley was crying and Ashley said it was because Aunt MiMi said she was a spoiled brat because of the Oreos and because she didn't want to eat any of the food that MiMi said we could have for a snack.

And Mommy looked like she was trying hard not to laugh and to be very serious. And MiMi put her hands in the air and said to Mommy, "I don't envy you!" I asked Mommy what envy means. She said envy is being jealous of somebody. I used to be jealous of Ashley because she has a summer house with ponies and a real movie theater but I'm not anymore, because I wouldn't want to have a mommy who wouldn't let me eat cookies.

Mommy was still wearing her spring coat and had her pocketbook on her shoulder, but she made us fruit cup with fresh fruit from scratch not out of a can. And then she said when we finished our snack we should start our homework even though tomorrow is a weekend. Mommy always likes it when we do my homework on Friday after school so we can both play on the weekend but we don't always finish it on Friday. Like my big projects. We have to design a city. But Mrs. Hennepin said that we have all of Easter vacation to do it. We have to build a diorama and we have to pick what kind of government we have and who is in it and make a budget and say how much money it will take to pay the firemen and the policemen and the teachers and all the people who will be working for the city to make it run.

Mommy sat at the table and helped Ashley and me with our homework. We have a lot of math and it's really hard. I'm still confused. Sometimes I get the right answers but I don't know why they're right. I figure it out on my fingers even though I'm not supposed to. And we have spelling words to practice, too. When we took out our homework Mommy said something really quietly about being a hands-on mom. After she said it she looked at

MiMi and MiMi made one of her funny faces where she rolls her eyes around. Tennyson, Ashley's sister, makes a face like that all the time when she thinks someone is being stupid, which is a word Mommy doesn't like me to use. She says it's not nice and I should say silly instead.

After we did our homework I asked if we could play while Mommy was making dinner. So Ashley and me went into my room and we played dress-up. And I took out my Disney princess dresses that Granny Tulia and Grandpa Brendan got for me and I was going to be Belle because her yellow dress is my favorite and Ashley was going to be Cinderella and as soon as I said I was going to be Belle then Ashley said SHE wanted to be Belle and she tried to take the dress away from me and I was holding onto it really tight and part of it ripped. And I got really mad at Ashley and I yelled at her and said that I "called" the Belle dress first and she picked Cinderella. Then she yelled back at me and she pulled my hair and I tried to pull her hair back.

And Mommy and MiMi ran into my room and wanted to know why we were fighting and why was it that there was so much crying this afternoon and she said she thought we were best friends. And I said I thought Ashley was my best friend too, but then she wanted to dress up as Belle and she tore my dress. And Ashley said she didn't tear it. She said I tore it MYSELF. And I said she MADE me tear it because she was trying to take it away from me and I didn't let her and that's why it tore. And I don't think it can be fixed because it's the floaty part that tore.

And then the telephone rang and I think it was Fireman Dennis because Mommy called the person "sweetheart." She told the person, "I can't talk now, sweetheart, I'm breaking up a fight."

Ashley said she wanted to go home. So Mommy asked Ashley if she meant that for real and if she should call Ashley's mommy and ask her to take Ashley home. And Ashley said that her mommy and daddy were going to dinner and to a Broadway show so they weren't home and that was why we were having a sleep-over. Because her mommy and daddy wouldn't be home until really late at night, past our bedtimes. And her nanny wasn't there at night and Tennyson was sleeping at a friend's house too.

We had dinner and Ashley and I weren't fighting so much. We played Barbies and watched a video and then we went to sleep. But we didn't sleep right away. We were talking a lot. And Ashley said she was sorry for tearing my Belle dress. She didn't sound a lot like she meant it for real.

But we had an uh-oh in the morning because Ashley's mommy and daddy were supposed to pick her up at eleven o'clock but they called Mommy on the telephone to say that they couldn't do it until the afternoon. And the uh-oh is that Mommy and I are going to Lissa's birthday party at Bruce Frank Beads at twelve o'clock and I know that Ashley wasn't invited because Lissa doesn't know her so she couldn't invite her if she doesn't know her. And I went into Mommy's room and I told her what are we going to do? Then Mommy talked to Lissa's mommy and Lissa's mommy said that it sounded like there was nothing Mommy could do because she couldn't leave Ashley alone, so Ashley could come to the party because another little girl had canceled because she had a sore throat so there would be enough places at the table. And Mommy called Ashley's mommy and told her where Bruce Frank Beads is and that the birthday party ends at two o'clock.

And then Fireman Dennis called again and Mommy said she was getting ready to take me and a friend to a party so she couldn't talk a lot and she would see him tonight. He calls a lot when Mommy and me are doing stuff and she always has to say I'm sorry, can we talk later?

Chapter 20

It's like pirate treasure! I can't speak for Zoë, but it's definitely the best kid birthday party *I've* attended in ages. I'm impressed. Melissa Arden might have had to winnow the quantity, in terms of her guest selection process—as she said, the venue is modest in size—but she certainly didn't skimp on quality. To save time, she pre-selected the beads, and there are little cups set out all over the big oak table, overflowing with vintage and semiprecious stones, Venetian glass, and glittering, funky findings. A bunch of seven- and eight-year-old little girls and their mommies are going to be taught over the next two hours to make necklaces, bracelets, and earrings from (among non-mineral media as well) peridot, coral, amethyst, carnelian, turquoise, garnet, and jade. I'm sure the mothers who are keeping score have already toted up what Melissa and Simon have laid out for the beads alone.

The Bruce Frank staffer is a friendly blonde named Casey. She must do the kids' parties a lot because she's got a great way with small girls who don't seem to want to wait for instruction. They can't wait to get started, and I can't say I blame them. The mommies get to use the pointy pliers and wire cutters and we're taught how to make loops and connect them. And with two long "head pins," a few beads, and a pair of pre-made ear wires, it only takes about five minutes to make a really cool, totally unique pair of earrings. I find myself wanting to try all the different colors, and to experiment with mixing and matching media. We get a mini-class in knotting and the little girls are more adept with the needle and stringing paraphernalia than they are with the metal stuff.

I watch Zoë fashion a necklace with colorful glass beads and admire her aesthetics. She's pretty good with the materials. Some of the children are having trouble with the smaller findings; although the pieces are kid-size, it's a coordination issue. Casey suggests they make something out of the larger, nugget-sized stones. The whole point of the party is that every guest will go home with at least one piece of wearable jewelry that she made all by herself.

All the mommies and daughters sitting around the table makes me think of quilting bees. I compliment Melissa on choosing such a delightful venue. What a treat for us big and little girls to sit around a table for two hours—with time out for birthday cake, of course—and create pretty things together, as opposed to sitting around the dining table helping them with their homework—or, more specifically—using carrot and stick to coax, cajole, and coerce them into sitting down for more than ten minutes at a stretch to do something that has all the allure—for both of us—of a vaccination.

The subject of homework presses everyone's hot buttons. Fractions introduced in preschool; math problems assigned to fifth graders that our generation didn't see until junior high; science projects you need a B.S. to competently complete.

Melissa Arden bites a string, instead of clipping it with the scissors. "Lissa's brother Will, who's in sixth grade over at Ethical Culture, is supposed to redesign the New York City subway system by Monday."

"Well, I'm sure he'll do a better job of it than what we've got now," I say, "particularly with the signage."

Lissa sighs. "The really crazy part is that things like the sub-way project don't get our knickers in a twist anymore. Simon and I have grown accustomed to the insanity of our children's assignments. It's appalling—the pressure the schools claim to be under to force-feed them overachievement. Last semester, Will had to publish a newspaper. Daily. For two straight weeks. With no cartoons, crosswords, or horoscopes."

It's as though a floodgate has been opened. My sisters in sor-row, even the quiet ones, are no longer shy about contributing to the discussion.

One of them, whose daughter is at Trinity, bubbles over with bile. "You wouldn't believe what Cosette came home with the other day! They have to illustrate the Seven Deadly Sins. Isn't that a little *advanced* for a *second grader*?"

"No!" chorus three other women.

"What *are* the Seven Deadly Sins?" Zoë asks.

Cosette herself is too focused on her necklace to respond, nor does she seem to evince interest in anything but the most in-tense concentration on stringing it together.

I expect an adult to begin to define or explain the concept of the sins for her, but some of the mommies start to list them. Soon, the table resembles a bunch of contestants on a game show, trying to come up with the right answers for the adult version of a Seven Dwarves or Eight Reindeer question.

"Sloth," says Ariadne Bernstein's mom, Andrea.

Zoë looks quizzical. "What's that mean?"

"Laziness," Andrea says.

"Mommy would you finish this for me?" Laurel Browning asks, turning to the parent on her right. "I don't want to do it anymore."

"Like that! *That's* Sloth!" I joke, and we all laugh. Laurel blushes and picks up her bracelet again.

"Avarice," says Melissa. "Don't you like that word? I mean how it sounds." She repeats it, savoring it, and the last syllable sounds like Pop Rocks exploding on her tongue.

"What's *that* one?"

"Avarice? It's the same thing as greed," I tell Zoë.

Ashley starts arguing with Juliet, the child to her left. "But I want some of the purple ones. You're hogging them all!"

"I'm using them now. They're mine," Juliet insists, pulling the dish of amethysts closer to her beading board.

"Juliet, all of the beads are for everybody to share," Melissa says gently. I wish I could master her tone of voice. Juliet immediately gives in. I can never get a kid to do that. Maybe it's Melissa's accent. Whatever it is, it produces results.

Zoë stands up and whispers in my ear. "Was that 'Avarice'? Juliet hogging the purple ones?" I nod.

"And there's Pride, that's another one," says Molly O'Brien's mother, Shoshana.

"And Envy. You know what that one means, Z. You just learned it yesterday."

"And Lust," adds Shoshana.

"Lust is not a sin," says Melissa. She winks at me. There's a dead silence. "Humor, people, humor." Melissa and I burst out laughing. I think the woman is wonderful. A true kindred spirit. I am, however, grateful that my seven-year-old's attention span, being mercifully short, and easily distracted, relieves me from the necessity of defining the word.

Casey announces that it's nearly time to put away our jewelry things so we can clear the table and make room for the cake. She and Melissa begin to pack up all the unused and leftover materials that Melissa had purchased for the party.

I remove the store-bought accessories I arrived in and bedeck myself with some of my newly minted ornaments. Blue topaz and antique silver beads.

"Look at all the pretty things you made, Mommy!" Zoë exclaims as I start to sort out my baubles, categorizing them by item: necklaces, bracelets, and earrings. "What are you going to do with them?"

"Wear them. Maybe save some as birthday gifts for people."

"MiMi would love the one you made with the orange beads and the thing hanging from it. It would go with what she wore to Granny Tulia's house on Thanksgiving. Remember?"

"Unh-huh, I do remember. The 'thing' is called a medallion." Melissa had selected a number of unusual medallions; some had a religious orientation, others were jade or faux tortoise shell and had a very Eastern, Indian feel to them.

Casey comes over to examine the jewelry I'm now wearing. "You have a real talent for this, Claire. And speed," she adds with amazement, looking at the number of pieces I've made in the past ninety minutes.

"My mommy makes a lot of jewelry from scratch," Zoë says proudly. "She makes pretty things that are *fun*, too, like she made me an Ariel necklace for Halloween with blue beads and Goldfish crackers. But she put shiny stuff on the Goldfish first so they'll never go bad or get eaten by bugs, except that *people* can't eat them anymore, because the shiny stuff is like clear paint."

"You could probably make a living at this, if you wanted to," Casey tells me. "And I'm not just saying that to get a new customer. Though we do have frequent beader discount cards."

"*I'd* buy one of your designs," Melissa says. "You were doing something with garnets that was quite stunning, actually. It's my birthstone, so I always tend to gravitate to them, usually with my mouth hanging open like a salivating dog. Simon says it's dreadful. I told him he should consider himself lucky I wasn't born in April. *This* is the diamond month, right?"

I wasn't sure if Melissa was being sweet or serious. "You're . . . kidding, right?" I ask her. "About buying my jewelry?"

She shakes her head. "Not a bit. And I know some other women who might fancy the kind of things you were making today. I'd be happy to introduce you if you're interested."

"Melissa's right. You're good at this, Claire. *I* liked the peridot earrings with the silver beads," Shoshana says. "I was watching you the whole time. You put us all to shame. I felt like, you know, a normal person who has to play basketball with Michael Jordan."

I laugh and feel my face grow warm. "You give me *way* too much credit!"

The table is now laid for the birthday treats. Rather than a single sheet cake, Melissa has opted for cupcakes, iced in jewel tones, topped with sprinkles to make them look "sparkly." They have been arranged like a giant necklace. The display elicits *oooooooohs* from the little girls. She hands out the crowns, and Zoë practically jumps out of her seat when her yellow "unbirthday" tiara is restored to her little hands. I don't understand the dark cloud that crosses her face a few moments later.

"What's the matter, Z?" I whisper to her.

Apparently, Zoë is concerned that Lissa won't get her birthday wish because there are no candles for her to blow out.

"Oh, God, thanks for reminding me!" Melissa goes to her purse and locates a little bag containing a box of birthday candles. "I always forget something," she chuckles. "Half the time I think I'd forget my head if it weren't screwed on." At Zoë's instruction, candles are inserted into nine of the cupcakes—eight plus one to grow on—and Lissa is given the opportunity to make her birthday wish come true.

"Whew!" Zoë says, when her friend extinguishes them on a single breath. My daughter is genuinely superstitious about this kind of thing. And she's big on rules. In Zoë-land, if the "rule" is that you "have to" have candles on a birthday cake, deviation— whether for creative or accidental reasons—rankles her. Come to think of it, my mother is very much the same way.

Jennifer Silver-Katz, with Nina Osborne in tow, shows up a few minutes early to claim Ashley. Both women are sporting designer track suits, tennis racquets slung over their shoulders.

When Jennifer sees all the mommies and little girls wearing their new jewelry, she looks a little jealous. I try very hard not to be pleased about this. Ashley proudly displays her two bracelets to her mother, then drags her over to me to say, "Look what Zoë's mommy made!"

Jennifer has been eating crow ever since that little incident in the ladies room at the bikram yoga studio. In her embarrassment, she's bent over backwards to try to be nice to me. She inspects my new accessories. "You did that this afternoon? The earrings, too?"

I nod. "I guess I kind of got on a roll."

"She made zillions of stuff," Zoë says, holding up my Baggies. "She could make it even . . . even . . . even more fast than the elves in the hollow tree make cookies!"

"They're really niiiiice," Jennifer says, fingering my drop earrings. Her slight nasal whine is the tone in which she customarily delivers compliments, so I know she means it.

"They're real stones, too, aren't they?" Nina asks, somewhat suspicious.

I nod. "Yes, indeed. They're not plastic, if that's what you wanted to know."

Nina leans toward me with the predatory glance of a woman who believes herself to be the first to have spotted a true bargain. She glances from the semi-precious gems I'm wearing to the colorful horde stashed in the little plastic bags. "Are you selling?" she whispers conspiratorially.

A famous movie line flashes across my brain like a bolt of lightning. *If you build it, they will come*. "Why, yes, I am!" I reply, in the same low tone, aware, in a similar inspirational epiphany, that the Ninas and Jennifers of my world are seduced by the notion of exclusivity. "But not here," I add, surreptitiously touching my finger to my lips.

"Of course," she says, *sotto voce*. "I'll call you."

As the party breaks up and all the thank-yous are exchanged, Melissa asks if I have time to wait a few minutes, until the other mommies leave. While the other guests depart, Zoë and I admire the Asian crafts and sculptures that adorn the room. "Sorry you had to wait," Melissa says apologetically, "but I wanted to ask you something." She and Casey are completing the task of storing the remaining beads in little plastic-lidded cups. "Look," she says, "I've already paid for all this stuff. And once we unspooled the wire, it can't be returned, and there's nothing I plan to do with it, except throw it in a box in case Lissa or Will need it for a homework assignment to counterfeit the Crown Jewels. I'd sort of assumed we'd use up all the beads, and I really don't relish counting out each one with Casey in order to get a store credit against my initial purchase. It's honestly not worth my time to go through all that, and it's really a bit ridiculous for me to bring it home, when it can go to better use."

She places the shoe box of extra beads and craft materials into my hands. "Knock yourself silly." She laughs, for which I am grateful, as it keeps me from bursting into tears. "Just remember the 'little people' when Claire Marsh Originals are as valuable as a Miriam Haskell or a Kenneth J. Lane!"

I laugh. "Good God! Their pieces are *vintage* now, so by the time I have the chance to reflect upon my 'humble beginnings,' I'll be about a hundred and ten!"

Annabel Rosenbaum, the baby-sitter, a sweet-faced eleventh-grader whose short brunette locks look like she chops them herself using a butter knife and no mirror, swings by at six o'clock. She looks like she's coming to stay for the weekend. "What *is* all that stuff?" I ask.

"SATs," she moans. "Studying. I took them once already but I think I can do better." She rolls her eyes. "*My parents* think I can do better, actually. So I'm taking them again in two weeks." She shrugs the knapsack off her shoulders and looks visibly relieved. The poor child will have scoliosis by the time she's eighteen if she carries this kind of weight every day. The bag hits my foyer floor with a resounding thud.

I call Zoë, who comes bounding out of her room dressed like Tinker Bell.

"Hey, Tink!" Annabel immediately starts to applaud. "I do believe in fairies," she chants. Zoë is enchanted. Words cannot express my sense of relief that these two have instantly bonded. I give Annabel a tour of the apartment, point out the emergency numbers on the dry-erase board in the kitchen, explain what kind of snack Zoë is allowed to have, if she wants one—I'd already fed her dinner—and ask the teen if she would kindly help Zoë with any homework questions she might have. Mrs. Hennepin has been loading on the math lately and Zoë and I didn't get to finish all of it before the weekend, as Ashley was over here last night and I had to help both of them.

I make it clear to Annabel that Zoë doesn't *have* to do any homework tonight, but that maybe ten minutes' worth wouldn't be a bad idea, since she still has assignments to be completed that are due on Monday.

This is something I don't understand. The teachers see these seven-year-olds five days a week. Unless the educators are totally clueless, they must realize how short the kids' attention spans are, particularly for subjects like math which are so rarely made interesting to them, even in a sophisticated curriculum like Thackeray's. It's nearly impossible for Zoë to focus on a single task for more than fifteen or twenty minutes without needing a break. Her mind wanders if her body's not allowed to. She needs to leave the table to get up and jump around, or she disappears into another room to play pirates and princesses for a while, or stages a Barbie fashion show.

I feel like I'm leaving my little girl in good hands with Annabel. One less thing to be nervous about before my second attempt at a "real" date with Dennis.

. . . .

Dear Diary:

I have a new friend. Her name is Annabel and she goes to Thackeray too, but she'll be going to college after next year. She came to baby-sit me tonight because Mommy and Fireman Dennis went to a restaurant to have dinner. She has even more homework than me. She said we could play so we played Peter Pan and I was Tinker Bell and I pretended I was really sick and she clapped her hands and said she believed in fairies and then I got all better. And then I wanted to be Peter and I said Annabel had to be Captain Hook and we were fighting with swords but they're only made of plastic and they're not sharp or even really pointy. Mommy got them at the Disney store. And I won because I was Peter and Peter always wins and Annabel had to end up in the water with the crocodile. Annabel is very good at playing pretend. I like her a lot.

Then, after we played, we had a snack and then Annabel said let's do homework together. Because she said it wouldn't be so yucky if we were both doing it. I said I didn't like math and Annabel said we should do the things we don't like first because that will get it out of the way so we could do the more fun subjects. I like writing and I like it when we get art projects even if they're not for art class with Ms. Bland, like when Mrs. Hennepin gives us homework that has art things in it like when we had to do Ireland and I drew the picture and I made the snakes with Play-Doh. And I like spelling because I'm good at it.

I couldn't understand my math homework so I didn't want to do it anymore. And Annabel asked if she could look at it because maybe she could help me. So I showed her and said I had 20 problems to do and I could only figure out some of them. And she made such a funny face. She said, HOW old are you? And I said I'm a little bit older than seven and one quarter. And she said she never had math problems that were so hard when she was in second grade. She didn't have Mrs. Hennepin. She had a nice teacher who isn't there anymore. Annabel said that the nice teacher got married and she moved away, all the way to California, so the school had to get a new teacher. Annabel is in fifth form, which is the same as eleventh grade. At school, after sixth grade, they start calling the grades forms instead of grades but they start from one all over again. So seventh grade is first form. We have pre-K and kindergarten and then we have six grades and then we have six forms. I'm going to be in school forever.

Annabel said my homework was really hard and she said she already forgot how to do some of the problems. We started with fractions and I'm stuck and Annabel was having a hard time helping me. She said she felt really bad because she WANTED to help me. I wished she could help too. I wished it a lot, because if Annabel doesn't know how to help me with my homework maybe Mommy won't ask her to come to stay with me anymore when she goes on a date with Fireman Dennis. Annabel is my favorite baby-sitter I ever had even though I haven't had a lot of baby-sitters.

• • • • • • • • • • • •

"These are nice," Dennis remarks, nibbling my ear. Whenever he does this, I fear we'll be arrested because I become sexually uncontrollable. I have warned him that I am not to be held responsible for my actions following this erotic gesture, no matter where we are, what time of day it is, or who might be watching. We're now walking in Battery Park, after a lovely meal at a restaurant overlooking the water. For a few moments, we pause to lean against the railing of the fence and gaze at the Statue of Liberty and Ellis Island.

"Thanks. I made them today. At the birthday party I took Zoë to."

"I meant your ears," he whispers into the right one.

"Oh." I'm embarrassed. Of *course* he's not interested in the *jewelry*. He's a *straight man*!

Dennis tickles me in the ribs. "I'm teasing you, Claire. I did mean your earrings. They're nice. Your *ears* are more than 'nice.' They're adorable."

I turn to him and give him a kiss. "Thank you. And thanks for dinner. Good choice! So . . . you think anyone would want to buy something like this?" I ask, giving an earring a gentle push so it begins to swing a bit.

"Yeah, why not? I mean, not that I know anything about that sort of stuff, so my opinion is probably kind of worthless, but, yeah, I don't see why not." He slips his hand in mine. "Can we take a walk?"

"I thought that's what we're doing," I giggle.

"You know what I mean. I mean *keep* walking. I want to walk *to* someplace." His fingers lightly caress the top of my hand, and the gesture has a way of easing my mind. Despite my attempt to respond with a light heart, to my ears the words, "can we take a walk" have the same uh-oh effect as "we need to talk."

We stroll along the promenade by the Hudson River. "You know this used to be called the *North* River," I tell Dennis.

"Really?" The corners of his mouth have a way of curling up when he's curious about something, so I know he's actually intrigued.

"Occupational hazard. Or, former occupational hazard, I should say. It's a tour-guide thing. It was on the test they make you take. File under Useless Trivia—more or less. But I kind of like that sort of . . . minutiae. I think it's cool."

Dennis slides his arm around my waist and pulls me toward his body as we continue to walk. "You're a history geek!"

"We history geeks prefer the word 'buff,' thank you very much."

He pretends to think about it. " 'Buff' is a good word. Very good word."

"Speaking of which, Zoë asked me the other day if you and I were going to have a sleep-over."

"And what did you tell her?"

"I reminded her that Easter break or spring break or whatever they're calling it this year is right around the corner, and perhaps she might like to spend a couple of days with her grandparents out in Sag Harbor. Of course that means I have to get her all the way out there. Or they've got to come into New York to pick her up, only to drive right back."

"Or they could come in and stay at your place for a couple of days while you stay at mine." We pause to kiss. "Why are you smiling?" he asks.

"Why do you think? I like kissing you. And I like the way you kiss with your eyes open. You do that a lot. I just . . . it's . . . nothing. It's just nice. I like it."

"I like to look at you when I kiss you. You always look like you're having fun."

"I always *am* having fun. Remember the day you rescued me and you wouldn't let me close my eyes?"

"I couldn't let you slip back under. There we were, outside a school, and you know how teachers are always talking about the three R's. Well, to me, as a firefighter, The three R's are Risk, Rescue, and Reward. That day, I got an extra reward. When Zoë said I could ask you out!"

"You're such a softie!"

"I beg your pardon, young lady. I have abs of steel!"

I roll my eyes. "What a comedian."

We pass the marina outside the World Financial Center and admire the yachts. Mia would love them. Through the enormous windows of the restored Winter Garden atrium we can see a band playing a free concert. We walk through the room, skirting its edges, pausing to sit on the sweeping staircase for a few minutes, listening to the music. It's entertaining, but not great. "Enough" hits each of us at the same moment and we give one another the kind of mutually understood signal that it takes most couples years to develop.

Stepping out of the easternmost exit of the Financial Center, we find ourselves nearly at Ground Zero. Dennis releases his hand from mine, drawn closer to the site, as though a giant magnet is pulling him forward from the heart. Whatever he needs to do right now must be done alone.

"Have you . . . ? Have you rescued people before? Before me, I mean?" I ask softly. I'm not sure what to say because I realize what he's feeling at this moment is big stuff for him. It's a subject that, for all our conversations, has never been raised. I've been afraid to—and I suppose he's had his reasons for not to wanting to discuss it.

Dennis doesn't reply.

"You were down here, weren't you?"

Silence.

"Don't get the wrong idea," he says finally. He's still facing the site, refusing to speak directly to me, to let me see his eyes. "If you're thinking that I've never talked about that day because I ran away or something . . . did something cowardly, or something I should be ashamed of."

"I'm not . . . Dennis, I'm not. Why would you think that would even occur to me?" I watch his back hunch, his shoulders shrug.

"No one becomes a firefighter to get rich. A lot of us do it because our fathers and grandfathers and uncles were firefighters. It's like going into the family business or something." He made a sound that was not quite a chuckle, not quite a snicker. "Of course, not every family business has such high risks. It's true about it being a brotherhood. And those of us who made it out that day lost three hundred and forty-three of our brothers. You stand here years later and it's like it was yesterday."

Dennis turns around. He looks stricken, like he's aged fifteen years in the past five minutes. He won't let me come any closer.

"And the thing is . . ." he continues with difficulty. "The thing is . . . that . . . it's what we do. You don't think twice about it. Rescuing. If another plane hit a building tomorrow morning . . . I'd be there. No doubt in my mind." His voice becomes choked up. "So . . . before we go any further with things . . . you and I . . . past that point of no return . . . that *sleep-over*—if you don't want to continue to see me . . . now that you know what you're getting yourself into—what I'm saying is—what I'm saying is . . . I'd understand."

I don't know whether he wants to be touched, to be held. I can't tell. I want to give him what he needs but I don't know what that is. I do know this: that I'm going to stick around to find out. And that I would be a fool to ever let this man go.

Chapter 21

If someone wanted to give me a gift, completely out of the blue—or if I could make a single wish within the bounds of reason—at this point, I don't know whether I would ask for a weeklong nap, a serious full-body massage, or a housekeeper with the talent and speed of Mary Poppins.

Until Mrs. Hennepin gave her class the homework assignment from hell—to build their own city—I'd fantasized about using the Easter vacation time to crawl into bed for a week. I don't mean seven days of lovemaking. I mean a put-your-head-under-the-covers, "Go away world!" kind of break. By the time Dennis and I were able to organize our "sleep-over," *sleep* was about the only thing I felt like doing. Dennis, bless his patient heart, has been very understanding.

Zoë is reading *Peter Pan* and keeps asking me if we're going to do Spring Cleaning. If. If there were world enough and time, I might actually be able to tackle the items that have been on my domestic to-do list since before the divorce. With each school vacation, I think, foolishly, that I might actually get to them. The rugs need a thorough shampooing; the drapes have to be taken down and dry-cleaned, the upholstered furniture could use a good steam cleaning, the hardwood floors should be buffed and polished, the contents of my kitchen cabinets can be much better organized, my closets need the Fab Five and a dump truck, and I can't even think about the bathrooms. Zoë's outgrown a lot of her clothes and there's no point in holding on to them, but as long as this will necessitate a trip to the thrift shop, I might as well comb through my own things as well, so I only schlep once. Those are the big things. Then there are the weekly household chores—the laundry, grocery shopping, vacuuming, dusting, ironing.

I am so burned out, so on edge. And because I've never been good about expressing anger, I just seem to seethe internally. Zoë and I have been discussing camp for her this summer. My parents have offered to make it their treat and I've acquiesced, although I'm not comfortable accepting so much financial aid from them; and Zoë seems so young for a sleep-away venue. But camp, any camp, won't begin until July, which right now seems like a lifetime away, a distant dream floating hazily in the future. I can fantasize about six weeks of quiet Claire-time, but it doesn't solve my current problems or soothe my immediate woes. It's more like the daydream equivalent of a bubble bath. In the meantime, I need to cast a villain.

Enter Regina Hennepin, stage left. She grins maniacally, unable to conceal her glee at having devised a unique method of torture designed to test her second graders' accumulated knowledge and retention of virtually every subject they've studied thus far this year—history, math, science, civics, art—and to try the patience of every parent who thought spring *break* would be just that.

But of course Rome wasn't built in a day.

Therefore, in her magnanimity, Mrs. Hennepin has allowed her students a full week to design and construct their cities, to invent a workable budget that is supposed to be as sturdy as the structures themselves (pretending, naturally, that the buildings are constructed of brick and stone, steel and glass, as opposed to egg cartons and cellophane).

I hear rumors that some parents—those who have had out-of-town excursions planned for this week have actually hired others to fulfill the assignment while their child enjoys a week of Kinder-Spa treatments in Palm Beach. I don't suppose Mrs. Hennepin has taught the kids about the 1863 draft riots.

This, to the rest of us who, gosh-darnit, just aren't going to be able to make it to our time-share in Martinique, is not only un-affordable, but immoral. Although at this point, I am ready to throw ethics to the winds. I wonder if Annabel could use a lit-tle extra cash, so I can use the city-planning time to take a nap.

In the meantime, whenever I can steal a moment for myself—which is usually around 2 A.M., when I am kept awake worrying about how little time I have to accomplish a never-ending string of tasks with ever-increasing levels of difficulty—I've been de-signing and making jewelry, making use of Melissa Arden's ex-travagant gift. It relaxes me while enervating my spirit and sparking my imagination. I enjoy playing with color, delighting in its power to excite or soothe; and to achieve a different mood or look with every individual piece or suite—matching neck-lace, bracelet, and earrings—that I create.

I've gotten a number of phone calls about my designs. Nina Osborne and Jennifer Silver-Katz called me within hours of Lissa Arden's birthday party. Melissa bought the garnets—she insisted on paying me, and I felt terrible about charging her after she'd been so generous and supportive, so I sold them to her for just a few dollars. Shoshana O'Brien snapped up the peridot earrings and placed an order for a matching necklace. I fulfill my handful of special orders in the middle of the night. With my tiny cottage industry, I feel like the mutant love child of Santa Claus and Mrs. Fields.

For mommy-daughter fun-time this week, Zoë and I dye and decorate Easter eggs. We select the ingredients for family Easter baskets during one of our many shopping excursions for arts and crafts supplies for Zoë-land, her city-queendom. By the end of a particularly long day we're both so cranky and exhausted that I allow her to eat three fistfuls of jelly beans, two Peeps, and a mid-sized chocolate bunny for dinner. They're the same *colors* as veggies, a starch, and a portion of meat; and one meal made of sugar won't kill her. It might even keep her awake while we tackle her math and spelling homework and put the finishing touches on Zoë-land—which will need a team of construction workers to cart it over to Thackeray next Monday.

I put Zoë's temporary, sugar-rush-induced burst of energy to good use with the spelling. I call out the words and she does jumping jacks or some sort of interpretive dance while she spells them aloud. Each word takes on a rhythm and mood in her imagination. She's good at it, which pleases me, and it's terrific for her self-esteem, since the math continues to freak her out.

And she's bored with her city-queendom by now. We've been doing a little bit every day this week, but she's long been ready to move on to something else. City planning takes time, I try to explain, with thinning patience. Where's Robert Moses when you need him?

Perhaps these insanely time-consuming homework assignments are designed to stimulate a child's imagination. Up to a point, I believe that to be true. My daughter has a wellspring of fancies and fantasies. But a limited attention span.

It seems to help if she plays dress-up while we work, although I've warned her that if she gets paint or glue on one of her Disney princess outfits, chances are we won't be able to wash it out properly.

"Okay, Tinker Bell," I say, "let's pretend I'm a visitor to Zoë-land. Why don't you give me a tour of your city, okay?" Zoë doesn't realize it, but this is a dress rehearsal—minus the fairy costume—for the oral presentation Mrs. Hennepin expects of her.

"Okay!" she says, then runs out of the room.

"Hey! Where'd you go?" No response. "Zoë? I thought you're going to give me a tour of your city!" I'm tired, and I want to be sure this project from hell is finally done. Besides, I can't wait to get my dining room back. My parents' mahogany table has more or less been transformed into Crafts Central.

Zoë skips back into the dining area with one of her dolls. "Barbie is going to give the tour. Oh, it costs a dollar."

Zoë takes me by surprise with this one. "Well . . . I'm not so sure the person who financed the construction of the entire city should also have to pay for the tour."

"Nuh-uh," she insists, "because . . . because . . . because it's like if you build a museum, even if you builded it, you still have to pay to go see the pictures because the soldiers who guard the pictures so nobody steals them have to be paid so they can feed their families and you have to pay people to keep it clean and take the tickets and work in the gift shop like you do."

As far as I'm concerned, she's just aced the assignment with this little speech. I hope Mrs. Heinie-face is as dazzled as I am that Zoë Marsh Franklin has developed such a mature grasp of economics. Maybe she should forget the astronaut thing for a while and run for Congress. I locate my purse and pony up the dollar.

With a little help from her owner, the mini-skirted Barbie steps onto the giant slab of foam core and begins her tour. "Welcome to Zoë-land. Zoë-land is a city that's ruled by a queen. The queen's name is Zoë. There is a king and his name is Xander—" Zoë drops the higher-pitched Barbie voice and looks me earnestly in the eye. "But that part's a secret," she warns me. "King Xander isn't here right now. He's fighting a war with the wicked witch who lives in the next city."

"What's the witch's name, Z? I mean—Barbie?"

"Evil Witch Heinie-face. But that part's a secret, too. But you get to learn the secrets because you paid to build the city. But *only you* get to know them!"

She points to the double-decker central area with one large, fancy building, surrounded by smaller, modestly designed structures. The buildings on the upper level rest on another piece of foam core supported by dowels and former toilet-tissue cardboard cylinders. "This is where the main things happen in the city. This is the palace where the queen lives and these are the buildings where her favorite subjects live and all the people live who work for the queen and the city like the policemen and the firemen. Because they have to live right in the middle of the city so they can get someplace fast in case there's an emergency. But there are hardly ever emergencies because everybody likes each other and there isn't any fighting or stealing. But just in case."

Zoë raises Barbie's arm and has her point to the lower level. "And where the buildings are, in the middle of the city, if it gets really, really, really, cold outside, and like if it's snowing or it's raining, the people can walk underneath the city so they don't have to get cold." She pauses for a moment. "See, I was going to make the weather warm the whole time but I like it when the leaves change colors a lot and I like it when it snows, too, except not when it snows too much unless it means we get a snow day. So I had to make my city so you didn't have to go outside when the weather was yucky, but you could still go places that were important and that you had to go to, like school or to your job."

I'm so impressed. Really overwhelmed by all the thought she's put into this. True, I've helped her build a lot of it, but she hasn't really shared the ideas behind the construction concept with me until now. Just a few short months ago, this child was in hysterics because I had to get a job and go off to work. And now look at her! How aware she is of mommies and daddies who need to work to feed their families. Her urban planning even takes them into account in the event of inclement weather.

Barbie finishes the tour of Zoë-land, and I congratulate both of them on such a terrific achievement. Certainly worthy of a celebration that calls for a glass of pink lemonade. If Mrs. Hennepin doesn't give my little girl an E, I am personally going to strangle the woman with her stretchy white headband.

Unfortunately, I can't let Zoë rest on her laurels, because there are still forty math problems to solve before classes begin again tomorrow. And it's 8 P.M. We're both totally spent. This is nuts. She should be taking her bath and getting into bed, so she can get a good night's sleep before the grind begins anew—like it ever stopped—in the morning. Neither one of us have had much of anything that can be called a vacation during the past week. I don't remember getting assignments during the breaks when I was Zoë's age. I know my parents would have been furious over it, if I had. Whatever happened to vacations as extended blocks of time so kids can, well, be kids? And so the *parents* could get some much-needed relief from all the homework, too!

Zoë and Barbie have danced off. I follow my daughter into her room and remind her that we've got to do her math. She's getting out of her Tinker Bell costume and into the blue Cinderella gown.

"I can't do it. I'm going to the ball now."

"Zoë, don't make me into a meanie over this. You know you have to do your math homework."

"But I've been working so hard," she moans.

"I know you have, sweetheart. And you've done such a good job. With your city and your spelling words. But I hate to say it . . . we still have the math to do."

"I hate math!"

"I'm not so crazy about it either. But math is a necessary evil."

"What's that mean?"

"A 'necessary evil' is something that you have to do because it's important for your development, even if it's unpleasant. Like having to eat vegetables or drink a glass of milk with every meal when you're a little girl, or doing math homework so you can learn arithmetic, which you'll need to know when you want to buy things. So, please don't make me yell at you. C'mon, let's go."

"Cinderella will do five problems."

Well, it's a start. I lead her by the hand to the table in the breakfast nook, where the math worksheet has been sitting for the entire week of vacation. No sooner does her tush hit the chair than she bounces up like she's just sat on a tack.

"Zoë, where are you going?" I call after her.

"I forgot my crown," she yells from the other end of the apartment.

She returns to the table four times as slowly as she left it. We start to tackle the first problem. "Okay, Z, we've got one hundred and sixty-five plus three hundred and forty-seven. So, we start with the column all the way on the right. Five plus seven is . . . what?"

Bang! She's off again. "What is it now?!"

"I need my wand!"

She dances back into the room a few moments later.

"Sit. Please."

"Okayyyyyy," she whines.

"Let's pick up where we left off."

"I can't do it without my wand."

"Fine. But there's no need to whine about it. So, let's make the answer appear like magic. The right hand column. Five plus seven. Wave the wand over it. What's five plus seven?" She counts it out on her fingers. I don't think this is how they're supposed to be learning to add three-digit numbers.

"Twelve."

"Good! Good girl! So, how do you indicate that?" She regards me like I'm speaking in tongues. Finally she writes a twelve below the sum line. "Well . . . sort of. A twelve is a one and a two, right? Right?"

She's nestling her chin in her clasped hands. Her folded arms rest on the tabletop. Her eyes are bleary. "Zoë, please pay attention," I beg. "We're only on the first problem. After this one, we've got thirty-nine more to go. We've had a whole week to do these; we could have done a few of them every day, but you kept putting it off. Now, five plus seven is twelve. So you put the two part of the twelve at the bottom . . ." I draw a two, mimicking her handwriting. "And you put the one part of the twelve on top of the next column over to the left. It's called 'carrying.' So in this case, you write the two and you *carry* the one over to the next column and you write it—in smaller handwriting, enough so you remember it needs to be there—just above the six, which is the top number on the second column. Are you with me?"

"Yes." Her voice is so sleepy. Despite my extreme frustration, I still feel sorry for her.

"Okay, then. Watch what I'm doing, so you can figure it out all by yourself on the next one. So, you've *carried* the one over, and written it above the six. Now, you have *three* numbers in that column because you have the one that you just carried over and you have the six that's the middle digit of the first big number and you have the four that's the middle digit of the second big number. That's one plus six plus four—which is how much?"

Cinderella is sound asleep over the breakfast table, her right arm now outstretched, still clutching her magic wand.

I slide my chair away from the table as silently as I can manage. I'm about to make a deal with the Devil; it sets a dangerous precedent and goes against every ethical bone in my body. But the alternative is to inflict mental as well as parental cruelty on my child. It's nearly 9 P.M. on a school night. She's seven years old. She has to be awake at six tomorrow morning. How can I possibly *force* Zoë to stay awake long enough to do thirty-nine and a half math problems, when she can't even understand this one and her concentration was kaput at least an hour ago?

I open the kitchen utility drawer and remove the calculator, then tiptoe back to my chair. I pick up Zoë's number-2 pencil. I'm familiar enough with her handwriting not to need a sample in front of me, but just in case, I take a look at her last completed worksheet. By nine thirty, the new set of problems has been solved, thanks to the calculator. I slip the worksheet into Zoë's math book and zip her backpack closed.

My daughter sleeps the sleep of the innocent.

I, on the other hand, am a forger.

Chapter 22

 Dear Diary:

Mommy and MiMi are fighting again. And it's because I got
an E on my city. Actually, I got an E-minus. Mrs. Hennepin
gave me an E for my presentation but she made it a minus because it started to fall apart but it wasn't my fault. Mommy
helped me carry it to the school but there was a thunderstorm.
And we had my city covered up with big plastic bags like we
use for garbage and we taped them to the bottom of the big
board so my city wouldn't get all wet. But some rain must
have got in it anyway because it was really windy and when I
got my city inside and I pulled off the plastic bags, some of the
paint ~~runned~~ ran a little bit and some of the glue got unsticky
and some of the cardboard poles got sort of mushy so they
didn't hold up the top level as good anymore. June Miller,
April and May's mommy, was the class parent on the week
when we had to hand in our cities and when she saw that
mine got a little smushy from the thunderstorm she said I
shouldn't worry. She said the mushy parts looked like it was a

picture in a Dr. Seuss book. But Mrs. Heinie-face wasn't nice about it like June was.

Lily Pei got an E-plus. She had moving sidewalks for people to walk on that really moved! She showed me how it worked. The sidewalk was like a fat black rubber band and underneath her city was a motor that made the rubber band go around and around. She said it was called a belt but it didn't look like the kind of belt you put on to hold up your pants or to make your dress look prettier.

Xander got an E on his city and it wasn't as good as mine was. I think all the teachers are nicer to him because he gets angry and throws tantrums when he doesn't like something. Ashley thinks so too. She's my best friend again. Her mommy and Xander's mommy told their friends about the pretty jewelry Mommy made and they all want to have some and they all want to be her friend. Before she started making jewelry, Mommy wasn't really friends with them the way she is with some of my other friends' mommies like with June and with Mrs. Arden, Lissa's mommy.

Our cities were on show at the school in the cafeteria for two whole weeks. When Mrs. Hennepin gave them back, some of the kids wanted to keep them because we worked really hard to make them. But Xander and some of the other boys didn't care and they threw them in one of the garbage cans outside the school but they were too big and they took up the whole can and they stuck out from the top. Xander said, "I know how to make them fit," and he took matches out of his pocket and he lit the top city on fire. I thought we would have to call Fireman Dennis but Mr. Spiros, the shop teacher, was outside and he saw it and he and two of the other teachers got fire extinguishers from off the walls of the school and they put it out by themselves. Then the teachers took the boys to Mr. Kiplinger's office. I think they got in big trouble.

I brought my city home because I worked so hard on it that I didn't want to throw it away. It's in my room now but it's so big that it's hard to walk around it. It doesn't look pretty anymore. I think we have to take it to the garbage in our building after all.

Mommy said I could have a treat because I got an E (she said she wasn't going to count the minus part). And Aunt MiMi keeps saying that she promises to take me to a fashion show for grown-ups because I play dress-up with her when I come over to her house to play and I always ask her if I can go with her to her job and see a REAL fashion show with models and lights and hair-styles and everything. And she's always saying I can go sometime but sometime is never. I said the treat I wanted was to go with MiMi and MiMi said the reason she didn't bring me with her ever is because I have to be in school when the fashion shows go on because they go on in the daytime. And Mommy won't let me miss school to go to a fashion show with MiMi. She said I can't go because Mrs. Hennepin gives so much homework that some-times it's more than we can finish in one night and if I miss school even for one day then I will have to catch up on TWO days of homework and Mommy said it's too much to get me to do all in one night and if I don't do it then I get U's and then we will both get in trouble with Mrs. Hennepin.

Mommy said that the summer will be coming soon and maybe MiMi can take me to a fashion show then, because school will be over. But MiMi said they don't have fashion shows in the sum-mertime.

MiMi said it was just for one time and it would be a different kind of education than school. I don't know what that means but I want to go!!! And MiMi said to Mommy that she needs to relax a little bit and bend the rules. And Mommy told MiMi you're not a Mommy and you have to make rules for kids because it's im-portant and if MiMi were a mommy, she would know that. Mommy said that MiMi was acting as much like a little kid as I was because she was getting all upset. But I AM a kid.

And then MiMi got REALLY mad at Mommy and said that Mommy and her rules were just as bad as Mrs. Hennepin and

*HER rules. And she said she was going to ask her new boyfriend
Owen to meet with Mommy about her jewelry-making but now
that Mommy was being a pain in the tushie (MiMi didn't say
tushie—and she said the F-word before she said the pain in the
other-word-for-tushie part) she was thinking about changing her
mind and not saying to Owen that he should help Mommy.*

*And then Mommy said that MiMi was being extra-babyish be-
cause Owen is a person and not a toy that MiMi plays with in
the sandbox. And they were yelling at each other and Mommy
was yelling "I hate yelling!" And she said to MiMi that now she
had a really bad, bad headache and MiMi could do whatever she
wanted. She yelled "FINE!" really really really loud and she said
if MiMi wanted to take me out of school for the day to go to the
fashion show, it would be okay because she was too tired to talk
about it anymore and she didn't want to fight with MiMi.*

*So next week on Thursday I get to go to a fashion show with
my Aunt MiMi. I CAN'T WAIT!*

・・・・・・・・・・・・

Who would have thought my job would be relaxing? By
comparison, I mean. Zoë has been sounding like a broken record
all week. Nonstop chatter about this Lucky Sixpence fashion
show that Mia is taking her to this afternoon. It's like living with
a magpie. I could have sent Zoë to school for the morning, with
an excuse to leave at lunchtime and not return for the rest of
the afternoon, but I felt it would be more disruptive for her, not
to mention hell on both my schedule and Mia's, than for Zoë to
miss the entire school day.

My feet are a little sore from standing for so many hours in
new shoes, but it's been a quiet day here at the Met so far.
Mother's Day is around the corner. So where are all the men
buying jewelry? Not at the museum, evidently. Most of my customers are women, treating themselves or buying gifts for oth-

ers. Lately I've begun to examine the museum reproductions with a more discerning eye, checking to see how a piece is put together, wondering if I can create a similar design of my own.

Apparently, great—and I use the word facetiously—minds think alike. As I daydream about starting my own jewelry business while simultaneously attempting to appear alert and approachable, Nina Osborne strolls up to my counter. I feel my stomach seize, remembering with exquisite clarity the last time Nina stood on the other side of this glass case, the humiliating sting of her words, and how the experience made me want to crawl under the covers for a week.

"Did you enjoy the sculpture exhibit today?" I ask her with forced effervescence, figuring she'd paid us a visit while Xander was in school, in order to "do" the current blockbuster. *The Naked Form: From Rodin to Brancusi* is drawing the visitors like a magnet. Even the venerable Metropolitan Museum is aware that very little attracts a crowd as much as a whiff of sex.

"I saw it during the members' preview," she replies dismissively. I notice she's wearing a pair of my earrings; onyx and gold electroplate with two shades of coral. She points to a coral bead necklace in the case and asks me to show it to her. She flips over the price tag. Three hundred and ninety-five dollars. I permit her to try it on, and she assesses her appearance in the counter-top's freestanding mirror.

"It matches the earrings pretty well," I volunteer. "And although the design is quite simple, the price is a fair one, for the workmanship. I mean—it's not a rip-off."

Nina nods, frowns, then purses her lips and frowns more deeply. "Can *you* make something like this?"

"I have the tools; I'd just have to get hold of the stones." I examine the necklace more closely. "Something like this wouldn't be very hard at all." I lean over the counter, in as ladylike a manner as possible, so I can lower my voice. "See, this necklace *is* what it *is* because it's a reasonable contemporary facsimile of the necklace that Madame LaFrontiere is wearing in the Sargent portrait on the second floor. If you saw this piece in a jewelry store, it probably wouldn't catch your eye." I lay the necklace across my palm. "If were up to me to design something, not just copy it, I'd really have fun with these. You could make the same strand with malachite or turquoise, citrine, peridot, carnelian— whatever gemstones you were into in the entire spectrum from garnet to amethyst—and then create it so that you could wear more than one strand together. A single keeps it simple, but you could also mix and match cool tones or warm ones, or twist all six for a rainbow choker." I was really getting into it.

I pause to help another customer, and Nina, in her nosy way, informs the woman that I'm a jewelry designer and that she should be the first on her block to own one of my originals. "Give her a card," Nina prompts. I'm not sure whether this kind of help is a blessing or a curse. I work on commission for the museum and could probably get canned for touting my own wares instead. Besides, I really have no jewelry design business. What is Nina thinking? *And* I have no business cards! Is this a further attempt at humiliation? I give her a wide-eyed stare.

"Claire just had a trunk show on Saturday. She must be all out of them," Nina says smoothly. "See?" she says, showing off her ear drops to the bewildered woman. "Claire made these. Stunning, aren't they?"

I catch my supervisor checking me out suspiciously. "So, which pin were you interested in?" I ask loudly. The unusual ambush thwarted for the time being, my customer is clearly re- lieved. She points to one of the museum's bestsellers and asks me to gift wrap it.

"Are you trying to get me fired?" I hiss at Nina, after the woman has departed with her blue hippopotamus.

"Trying to get you out of here," she counters.

"Same thing!"

"But if you'd rather squander your talents as a shopgirl for—

what do you make here—minimum wage? Then don't let me stop you."

"You really can be such a bitch," I mutter under my breath.

Nina Osborne's hearing is excellent. "But I'm a bitch who can spot a winner." Her laser-whitened teeth look even brighter against her perpetual tan. "I don't usually do this," she says, prefacing the removal of a jewel-encrusted Judith Leiber card case from her purse. She hands me a business card with the Barneys department store logo embossed in one corner. "Laura Sloan is their jewelry buyer for the high-end costume pieces. She's a friend of mine; we both sit on the advisory board of the Helena Rubenstein Foundation. Laura's always looking for something new. No guarantees, of course, and I'm sure you'll need a lot more samples, since Jennifer and I bought more than half of them last week. And you'll want to have a business strategy as well. Laura's been burned by flaky fly-by-nights."

Nina turns to leave, then retraces a step or two, realizing she's left the LaFrontiere reproduction sitting on the counter. "Oh, and I don't want the coral necklace," she says, pointing to the museum reproduction. "I like your idea better."

"This is *so* weird," Mia says, biting into a breadstick. Owen discreetly points out that she's dribbled a few crumbs down her shirt and she dusts herself off with her napkin. I love to watch someone taking care of my older sister. It actually does make me feel warm and fuzzy all over.

"It *is* a first," I admit. "Gentlemen, this is the first time—as far as I can remember, anyway—no, it *has* to be the first time, because I got married right out of high school—that Mia and I have ever double-dated."

"History is being made," Dennis says solemnly, then breaks into a grin. "And you're both surviving it. Beautifully, I might add."

"We're very impressed," Owen contributes. The men are evidently sharing some sort of secret communication. It's not a sleazy thought; that's not their style. It's just some mysterious guy-thing we'll probably never get.

Suddenly, Mia claps a hand to her mouth. She leans over to whisper to me, "Isn't this the restaurant that Seinfeld called the 'break-up' place? You know, where a guy takes a girl when he wants to break up with her?" Her face bears a look of horror.

I regard our dinner companions, who, after three months, appear to have remained as smitten with us as we are by them. "Maybe that's where *he* took women for their last mutual supper," I suggest. "But every time I've ever come here, I've had a very pleasant experience." Pomodoro is a popular neighborhood destination and, as our Uncle Seymour used to say about restaurants, "If you can get in, don't go."

"Try the lobster ravioli," I insist. "I always get that when I'm here. You'll think you died and went to heaven." Pasta in a cream sauce is the last thing my waistline needs, but as long as I'm going out to dinner, I might as well splurge. Leaving room for dessert, of course.

"You know all the food is dead here," Mia teases.

I laugh and explain Serena Eden to Owen. Dennis knows all about her by now.

"And I heard," Mia adds with relish, lowering her voice, conspiratorially, "that Serena and Scott are on the rocks."

"No way!"

"Way, Clairey! Or headed there, anyway."

There's no need to suppress my surprise, but it's harder to shelve the glee. "How do you know these things? You don't see them—do you?" I would consider that an act of betrayal. Normally, so would Mia, but you never know.

"Eden's Garden is in my neighborhood, remember? I ran into a chick on the street who I recognized as the waitress from last December when Zoë and I stopped in there. So I just asked her how it's going. Out of curiosity, you know? And she remembered Zoë, and mentioned the Serena-and-Scott thing. I got the sense she's one of those girls who just likes to dish at the drop of a hat."

Dennis, who'd been resting his hand on my thigh, rubs my leg affectionately. "So, how do you feel about that?" he asks. The question, spoken softly and with some trepidation, is only for me, not for the table.

"I'd say . . . it's none of my business, really."

"That's very mature of you. What a grown-up!" he remarks.

"I'm getting there," I smile. "Slowly but surely, I'm getting there." I bestow a gentle kiss on his lips. "You have nothing to worry about, my darling," I murmur, aware that Owen and Mia are enjoying the show. Except I don't care. Dennis needs to know this. "In a way, we have Scott to thank for our getting together. If I were still married to him, my life would be different, of course, and I probably wouldn't have met you. And even if I had, I wouldn't have been able to do anything about it." I raise my wineglass. "So, here's to Scott, without whom I would not have met Dennis McIntyre."

"To Scott," the others toast.

"Who would ever have thought we'd be doing this?" Mia observes. "The 'what-ifs' can be really wild sometimes, can't they?" She slips her hand into Owen's. He looks at her with evident admiration and my heart is ready to burst for them. "I mean, for God's sake, here I am, sitting next to a man in a Brooks Brothers' suit! A man who doesn't throw paint at canvases tacked to a tenement floor in Alphabet City or play an electronic instrument, take photographs of semi-clad women, or is a hero by profession—though *you* actually ended up with one of those, Clairey!" She snuggles against her boyfriend. "But he's *my* hero. Fuck PC-ness, you know?! He definitely rescued *me*!"

"So, I'm everything you never dreamed of," Owen teases.

"Kind of, yeah," Mia admits. "Talk about being a grown-up. He's kicking me in the ass to turn my *Mi♥amore* concept into reality—and—*da-dummm*!" She drums her fingers on the table. "Owen's made a capital investment in the project!"

"Brava!" I cheer, brimming with happiness for her. We clink glasses.

"That's fantastic! Congratulations, Mia," Dennis adds.

"And, Claire, I'd like to extend my financial participation to another family venture," Owen says. "Mia thinks the world of your jewelry designs and told me you're already establishing an elite clientele."

"Yes, my burgeoning cottage industry," I chuckle. "Private-school moms seem to like my designs."

Owen raises his glass to me. "It's a good start, Claire. You may not be taking yourself seriously, but it's an *excellent* start. Those women have money, taste, and influence. And anytime you want to set up a meeting to talk with me, my checkbook is open."

I feel my cheeks flush and my eyes begin to water. "Oh . . . oh, my God. I . . . I feel like Cinderella. Thank you."

"I know what you're thinking," Mia tells me. "And you're *not* a charity case, and Owen is willing to make an investment in Claire Marsh Originals not because we're sharing a bed and I make him very happy. So get over that, in case you're hung up on it. Not the bed part, the charity part. You've got talent, a small core of clients even now, and an entré at Barneys when you're ready. That's not totally small potatoes."

I swirl my wine in the goblet. "So," I say, a bit giddy about all this, "my God, we're about to plant our own flags on the beauty planet. Who would have guessed that both of us would be *so* taking after Mommy?" I chuckle.

"Well, in some ways, anyway." Mia looks at our guys. "In other respects, she got it right the first time. Its taken us a lot longer to find our One True Love."

Chapter 23

Why the hell did I say I'd do this?! Backstage at a fashion show is a fucking three-ring circus. And this afternoon, I mean it literally. Lucky Sixpence's fall "Big Top" collection (so named because of the trapeze silhouette of most of the garments) is being paraded at Madison Square Garden. When Lucky found out that the Ringling Bros. and Barnum & Bailey people would permit her to stage her fashion show on their circus set, her dream venue for this collection, she was in seventh heaven.

Zoë's been bugging me for ages to take her to a show, and Lucky Sixpence is kind of like a big kid herself—most times she looks like a cross between a live Raggedy Ann doll and a clown, so I figured this gig would be the most child-friendly one on my schedule. Two more pluses are that Lucky's a personal friend—whereas my other clients aren't—in fact Zoë met her at my birthday party, and Lucky loves the idea of little girls being into dress-up. "You're reaaallly tall for a girl!" she'd told Lucky. It was not the time to explain transgendering.

It was kind of weird getting to the backstage area. The whole maze of hallways below the Garden's arena smelled like anything *but*. More like fertilizer, since that's where they house all the circus animals during the Ringling Bros. run.

"It smells like poopy in here," Zoë remarked. "I don't want my sandwich anymore because it's going to smell like poopy, too." She clutched a brown bag in which Claire had packed her lunch since I told her there was no way I would get a break to feed Zoë.

"Yup, it's animal poopy from the circus," I told her. "But it won't smell like that upstairs where they'll have the fashion show." I lied. You can't really get the smell of lions and tigers and bears (oh, my!), as well as elephants, out of the building until the circus packs up and leaves town. Months ago, when she'd set this gig up, I'd asked Lucky if she was sure she wanted to go through with it. "Buyers will gag," I warned her. She pooh-poohed me and said they'd be having too much fun to care. And she reasoned that her models, even the plus-size ones, who are a lot svelter than real plus-size chicks, never eat anyway, so they'd have nothing to puke in case the faint stench of manure got to them.

One of the large dressing rooms was set up for makeup. At least I had professional lighting ringing the mirrors. I was afraid there'd be fluorescents down here, which would have been a nightmare.

Lucky and I had a final powwow about the look she was going for. She wanted lots of bold color. Real glitter on the eyes and cheekbones, and lips as slick as red patent leather.

Most of her models are larger chicks. Because that's Lucky's clientele; size fourteen and up. "Larger" is a relative thing, though. Lucky's plus-size models wear a twelve. That's *normal* in *real life*. She does have a few girls, though, who are the usual sticks, like Dalit, a real sabra—Lucky calls her "True Grit"—and Yelena, a platinum blonde Ukrainian who speaks only two words of English: "Diet Coke." Her mother follows her everywhere to translate everything else. Actually, last time I saw Yelena was at another show and she had learned three more words of American: "Marlboro Light, please."

Lucky hired ten girls for the show, Yelena, Dalit, and eight plus-sizes. I explained to Zoë that each of them would model a dozen outfits on the catwalk, which in today's case, is the rim of the center circus ring, specially widened for the fashion show. Zoë will get to see it all from the front row. The plan is for Lucky to send down two girls at once, one heading clockwise, one counter, and they'll meet in the middle at "six o'clock," stop, pose, and finish the circle, passing one another until they both meet again at "midnight" and dash offstage to change into their next outfits.

"What if they bump into each other and fall into the sawdust?" Zoë asked.

"Let's hope they don't!" I said. "All of these shows are timed with split-second precision," I told her. "And all hell always breaks loose, no matter how carefully choreographed you get."

"What if they put on the wrong thing?" she wanted to know.

"Well, that could happen by mistake, but to try to prevent that, they take pictures in advance, so each of the models knows what she's supposed to wear in what order." I showed her how the Polaroids of each girl in every one of her outfits are taped to the cinder-block wall. The outfits are numbered and arranged in order on a rack so the girl can find them right away; and the dressers, who are as fast as any Indy 500 pit crew, can strip them of what they've got on and slap on the next getup.

"Why is it called a 'catwalk'?"

"I don't know, Zoë."

"Can you find out?"

"Yes, I'll find out. But not today, okay?"

What I did find was a folding chair for Zoë, placed it right by my makeup chair, and asked her to stay there, sit still, and watch. Gently, I warned her not to get up and run around because things would get really hectic and she could not be underfoot. Although I frequently work solo, for a large show like this I hire assistants. So I assigned my two elves to various girls, to start working on their foundations. Once base was blended and applied to every face, I'd talk to them about how and where—and what—colors I wanted on their eyes, lips, and cheekbones. I was short one elf this afternoon. Who the fuck knew where she was? She'd never even bothered to call. I hate that. I seethe just thinking about it. So many kids want to get into fashion for the glitz and the strobes, but they haven't a fucking clue how to act like a responsible employee. I always want to grab them by the shoulders and shake them and say, "This is a *real job*, folks! Either *do it*, or get out of here and go play with your trust fund."

I hadn't been working on the first face for ten minutes when there was a catfight. They work the same shows all the time so you'd think they could deal with it, but there's no love lost between Yelena and Dalit. The mutual malice is a cultural thing. Dalit thinks Yelena is a provincial anti-Semite; Yelena thinks Dalit is an arrogant Jew. Unfortunately, they're both right. And just then they were both giving Antonio, the lead hair stylist, heart palpitations, tearing at each other's coiffures like a couple of junior high schoolers.

"They're naked!" Zoë exclaimed.

Did I mention that models do tend to run around naked backstage? Nobody blinks. It's a booty call that no one hears. Given the demographics of fashion show personnel, no one cares that your usually nonexistent tits and scrawny butt are hanging out. Actually, Lucky's girls are often better looking in the buff than most models, because they have some meat on them. But Dalit and Yelena are your average human clothes hangers.

"Why are they fighting?" Zoë asked me. She was totally fascinated by these two nude foreigners trying to claw each other to death.

It was an incredibly vocal display, though none of us understood any of it.

Then two of the plus-size girls got into it, trying to pull Dalit and Yelena apart. The whole room stopped to watch. It was like a bunch of six-foot-tall Powerpuff Girls kicking bare butt.

Yelena's mother had just joined the action, whacking away at Dalit's back with her purse, when Lucky entered the makeup room. "What the fuck is happening?" she demanded. "Girls, girls, please!" She clapped her large hands together like a grammar-school teacher outgunned at a playground brawl: an outrageous-looking Miss Jean Brodie whose charges have disobeyed her.

Zoë pointed to Lucky. "MiMi, she said the F-word!"

"She's gonna say a lot worse if they don't cut it out," I told her. "I thought you wanted to watch me do Delilah's face?"

"I do." I started to apply traffic-light green glitter to the model's eyelids. "That's pretty. She looks like a fairy. Will you do *my* face, too?"

"Not today, Zoë. What I'm doing today can be a lot of fun, but it's still my job. So even though it's a treat for *me* that you're here this afternoon, I have to work, okay? I'll do your face, I promise, but it will have to be at my house."

My niece didn't look too thrilled. But there's not much I could do about it. By now Dalit and Yelena had been separated and had gone off to sulk in two different corners of the room. "So what the hell was that about?" I asked Lucky.

"Dalit stole Yelena's boyfriend and Yelena called her a slut," Lucky said, savoring the words like a juicy mango.

"She called her a slut? Yelena speaks no English!"

Lucky, though pissed off at the girls' unprofessional behavior, couldn't resist dishing. "*Dalit* speaks *Russian*, darling," she trilled in her Scottish burr. "Along with five or six other languages. And she understands the word 'slut' in all of them."

"What's a slut?" Zoë asked.

"A bad word," I told her.

"What kind of bad word?"

"One you don't need to learn for another ten years."

"Mommy always tells me what words mean when I ask her."

I tried not to let on that I was getting fed up with her constant barrage of questions, and needed to focus. "Zoë, sweetie, MiMi really needs to work now. Are you hungry? Do you want to eat some of your lunch?"

"No," she said, a bit grumpy.

I knew this hadn't been a great idea to begin with.

"I'm bored," she said after about another fifteen minutes. She'd seen me finish three faces and supervise my assistants through three more.

The pace was picking up backstage. Runners with racks were getting the garments rolled into place. Lucky's fall collection embraced color with ferocity. "Paisley is the new Black," she'd proclaimed in *W* magazine last month, sending the department stores' top buyers into a tizzy. "New York is just an itty-bitty island," she'd continued boldly, in a pronouncement that threatened to alienate Seventh Avenue. "Darlings, the *rest* of America craves color and pattern. Joy, people! They want Joy!" On the hangers, her clothes looked like Holly Hobbie meets Romanian gypsy, with a dash of Audrey Hepburn thrown in for shits and giggles. The tops and dresses, throwbacks to the seventies, were paired with peg-leg pants in solid brights and jewel tones in every fabric from panné stretch velvet to Thai silk to denim.

With about an hour to go before showtime, Lucky Sixpence began to suffer her usual case of the jitters.

"I'm breaking out in hives, people!" she announced in a ringing singsong. "It's too dead back here; you're making me nervous. Let me see some *energy*!" She cranked up the sound on the backstage stereo equipment. I love loud music but I wasn't in the mood. Of the two assistants who *had* shown up to work with me today, one had become, uncharacteristically, all thumbs, and I had to redo everything she'd done. My other elf was doing a fine job, but was slow as hell, which meant I'd have to finish his faces, too, or the girls would never make it to the catwalk on time.

It's not easy to be ten places at once.

"See, Zoë, here's a lesson you won't learn in school. From the outside, fashion shows look very glamorous, but it's not like that behind the scenes, right?" I was focused on fixing a face, so I didn't hear her answer. "Right, Zoë?" I asked again.

I looked up when she didn't respond the second time.

The folding chair was empty.

"Zoë!" I looked around the room and didn't see her. "Hey, has anybody seen my niece?!" I yelled. My stomach acid shot up into my throat; I had a sour taste in my mouth. "Yo, people!" No one could hear a fucking thing over the pounding hip-hop blasting out of the speakers. I located the stereo and turned it off.

"Hey!" Lucky said. "We need that!"

"Hey, yourself. I need just two seconds of quiet. Look, folks, has anybody seen my niece, Zoë? Little blonde girl—you all met her an hour or so ago? Is she in here?"

It was like watching a film go from normal speed to slow motion. All action, all talk, ground to a halt to look around the room for Zoë.

Delilah was being helped into her first outfit, a few tucks being strategically taken to make the blouse hang a little differently. "I don't see her, Mia," she shouted.

"She was just here a minute ago," said Coco, one of the other models.

"Zoë! Zoë!" We chorused her name, first in unison; then it began to sound like a round. Show preparations were put on hold while we fanned out, the girls forming a half-dressed search party. Most of the doors on our level were locked, so there was no way she could have entered what was behind them. Lucky raced upstairs to the arena level, dashed back and reported no sign of her on the floor of the Garden. None of the people up there had seen her either.

Oh, God, what if she got up to the street and is wandering around Manhattan? Or worse. The show was due to start in under an hour. After fifteen minutes of an all-hands-on-deck search, and coming up Zoë-less, I made the phone call I'd been dreading.

Claire answered her cell right away. "Mia, I told you not to call me at work—" I gave her the news. "Mia . . . I—I—how . . . how the hell could you lose her?!" she shouted into the phone. I was sure the entire Met Museum had paused to stare at her.

"I don't know. But I did, okay? She was here one minute and gone the next. I'm sorry! But scolding me isn't going to find her any faster."

"Be right there!" she said and hung up.

"I called the cops," Claire said, bursting into the makeup room, "and they immediately entered Zoë into their missing persons system. They said they can't issue an Amber Alert though, unless we believe she's been abducted." Her body was shaking like she'd just been pulled from a frozen lake. She was too stressed to cry. "I had a bad feeling about this from the beginning, Mia. I just—I just knew something was going to happen. I felt it. How do you lose a child when she's sitting under your nose?!"

I couldn't help feeling defensive. "Because she's a human being with legs and she used those legs to get up and walk away. Look around you, Claire. It's a madhouse in here. Which is actually par for the course, but it's worse than usual today. I'm understaffed, I've got a ticking clock, and I can't have my eyes on Zoë one hundred percent of the time when I'm trying to make up a face. I've got a job to do here. I told her to sit right there," I said, pointing to the metal folding chair, "and not to wander off." Then I remembered she had said she was bored. But what was I supposed to do about it?

"You were in charge of her," Claire insisted. "If you're taking care of a child, you have to have eyes in the back of your head and learn to multitask." She continued to berate me at ninety miles per hour.

Over the headset, Lucky spoke to the stage managers upstairs on the Garden floor and told them that we were running behind schedule. "It happens all the time," she reminded them. "Just stall the press, and don't let the doors open to guests until I give the go-ahead."

"Well, here's the high energy you asked for," I said to Lucky cynically. I felt as badly as Claire did, perhaps worse, but we have different ways of dealing with panic. I get caustic; she gets voluble.

She refused to phone our parents right away. When she called Dennis to tell him about Zoë, Claire was practically ranting incoherently. Unfortunately there wasn't much the NYFD could do to help in any official capacity. And since he was on duty, he couldn't even come down to the Garden to at least lend us some moral support.

"Where? Where would you go if you were a seven-year-old little girl?" Claire asked rhetorically. We all tried to get inside Zoë's head.

"She said she was bored," I repeated. "Where would a kid go if she was bored?"

"I'm just afraid she decided to try to go home by herself," Claire said. "She could be anywhere out there. Wandering the streets." She began to tremble violently again. "Or worse. God-*damnit*, Mia!"

We paired people up and sent them out to search again. Claire and I headed off in the same direction. "How far could she have gotten?" I wondered aloud. The maze of underground walkways reminded me of some kind of modern-day catacombs.

"It stinks down here," Claire said.

"Well, the circus is in town," I reminded her. "I'm told it doesn't smell so bad upstairs, but I don't believe it."

"Christ! The circus! That's right!" Claire stopped dead in her tracks. "Wait—" I was about to say something but she held up her hand like a traffic cop. "There's something . . . I have no idea if I'm right . . . but it's just a thought. Zoë—Zoë wrote this essay for Mrs. Hennepin at the beginning of the school year. It was—it was about a favorite memory. And it was about one of the times Scott and I took her to the circus. And she met this elephant named Lizzie."

She grabbed my hand and began to drag me down one of the corridors. "It could be a long shot, but follow that smell!"

The sub-basement was a ghost town. The circus performers wouldn't be in the building for a few more hours yet. There was no one around, so we really did allow ourselves to be led by the nose.

"Menagerie," Claire kept muttering. "Menagerie. Where the hell do they keep the menagerie?"

The *click-click* of our heels on the cement floors echoed off the cinder-block walls. It was eerily quiet. We had no more clues. Claire yanked my arm so hard it hurt. She pulled us to a standstill. "Listen," she said. "Let's just listen."

"What am I—?"

"*Shhhh.* Just listen." She cocked her head. "Hear that?"

"No."

Claire grabbed my wrist and set us both in motion. "I think that was a roar."

The animal smell was getting even stronger, so I figured we were now on the right track—or at least the track Claire wanted to be on.

We rounded a corner. "Tigers!" Claire exclaimed. "Look!"

Half a dozen of the beasts were pacing restlessly behind a huge metal gate. They didn't look happy. Outside the cage a guy dozed, slouching on a folding chair, his hat pulled halfway over his eyes. "Excuse me," I said, waking him. "Have you seen a little girl?" He gave me an uncomprehending look, so I repeated the question a couple more times.

"I don't think he speaks English," Claire said. "But I wonder what he *does* speak." We couldn't guess the man's nationality. Could have been anything from South American to Mediterranean to Balkan. After exhausting our command of French and Spanish, with no success, we gave up speech and resorted to sign language and wild semaphoring.

"Fuck! We're getting nowhere," I said.

"Is anyone here?" Claire shouted. "Is anyone here? Has anyone seen a little girl?" She paused to wait for a reply. None came. "Okay, okay, okay, I know she's down here somewhere," my sister babbled. "I feel it. I can't be wrong. I'm a mother. And a mother knows these things. Oh, God," she added, turning to look at me, "what if—what if she—I don't know—what if she *got eaten* or something. Or mauled. Like Roy. Or that guy up in Harlem a while back who kept a pet tiger and lied and said he'd gotten bitten by a pit bull."

I tried reason. "I doubt she got eaten by a tiger, Claire. Okay? We just passed their cage and I think if something had happened to Zoë, even though the guy didn't speak any English, there'd be a whole bunch of people around, and—"

"Elephants! Remember? Where do you think they keep the elephants? It's got to be either elephants or clowns. Those are the two things Zoë mentioned in her essay. Oh, wait—I think there was something about dogs, too. A dog act."

"I don't think we're going to find any clowns down here, Claire. Only the animal trainers seem to be on this level. And there isn't a performance for hours, so why would the clowns be here anyway?"

"How would Zoë know that? It wouldn't stop her from looking for them. Zoë! Zoë! It's Mommy. It's Mommy and MiMi. Zoë, baby, are you down here?"

"I don't see any dog acts, Claire."

"*Sh-shhhhh*. Hold on a sec. Hear it? She's crying. At least I hope it's her."

There was a little dogleg of a turn in the maze. It led to a cul-de-sac, where, huddled just outside the steel bars that separated a mommy and baby elephant from human traffic, was Zoë, sobbing and clutching her knees to her chest. There was a rip in her tights at the knee. Beside her sat the remains of her lunch: a half-eaten apple and part of a jelly sandwich.

"Zoë!" Claire raced over to her. "Oh, my God! Sweetheart, are you okay?" Zoë looked up and threw her arms around her mother's neck. "It's all right. Mommy's here," Claire soothed. "Mommy's here. What happened? Did you get hurt? Who hurt you?" Claire was hugging Zoë so tightly, the kid couldn't even squeeze out a word. "What happened? How'd you get so far away from MiMi?" Now that Zoë seemed unharmed, Claire allowed herself, through hysterical tears, to express her anger as well. "Didn't MiMi tell you to stay in one place and not to wander off?"

"I had to pee," Zoë said, her voice sounding small, forlorn, and slightly guilty. From the expression on her face it looked like she might have done it in her pants by accident. Claire fished in her purse for a tissue and began to wipe away her daughter's tears. The front of her blouse was now splotched with her own.

"Why didn't you tell me that?" I asked Zoë. "That you needed to pee? All you said was that you were bored."

"You said you were busy. And you *were* really busy . . ."

"Zoë, I could have taken five minutes to go to the ladies' room with you."

She looked so helpless, even with her mother beside her. "I got lost," she said finally. "I went to look for a bathroom but everything looks the same and I couldn't find it and I was trying to get back to the room where you were, but I couldn't find it, either."

"Is that how you ended up here?" Claire said.

Zoë nodded. "But by accident. Because I wasn't looking for the animals. I was looking for the bathroom." She started to cry again. "I found one with a picture of a lady on the door but it was locked." She buried her face in Claire's shoulder, embarrassed.

I looked into the cage behind her. I could swear the elephants looked solicitous. "Where's the elephant man, as it were?"

"I don't know. I didn't see anybody," Zoë said. "But I saw the elephants and I wished I had peanuts to give them, but I didn't have any. I wanted to feed them, especially the baby because he looked hungry. So I was giving him my apple, but then he touched my hand too much and I got scared. And then when I got scared I jumped away, and when I jumped, the *elephant* got scared and then the mommy elephant made a big noise, and then the noise made me more scared and I tried to run away but I tripped on the bump in the floor," she said, pointing to an uneven patch of painted cement. "And I fell down, and my tights broke." She showed us her skinned knee. "And I hurt myself and then I was lost and I didn't know how to get back and find you. And I didn't know if you could find me and I was hungry so I ate some of my sandwich but it smelled like poopy so I couldn't finish it and I was still hungry . . . but I couldn't eat my apple because the baby elephant ate part of it first and I didn't want it after that."

Claire cupped Zoë's face in her hands. "But you're okay, sweetie? Apart from the skinned knee, right?"

"Unh-huh. Except I peed in my pants. But it was an accident," she whispered.

"It's okay," Claire said gently. "It's okay. We'll just throw them in the laundry when we get home. Do you want to stand up now?" Zoë shook her head. "Okay, then we'll just sit here for a while until you're ready to go, all right?" She sat beside Zoë on the floor, cradling her in her arms.

"You're my favorite person, Mommy," she whimpered.

"Really?" Claire burst into tears again. "Because I know I

haven't been around as much as I used to be. And we haven't had too much special time together in a long time . . . I mean to do fun things, not 'homework time' or running back and forth to school and to all your activities. And sometimes, when I get upset with you, I feel like I'm being such a meanie that *I* don't even want to be around me! And I know you think that all I ever seem to do some days is tell you what you have to do, or what you're not allowed to do and I have to make you sit down and do your schoolwork when you'd rather be playing. But somebody has to be in charge of things like that, and it's just me, now. And it's really hard having to be the boring old mommy, sometimes."

Zoë's tearstained face looked up into Claire's. "But you'll always be my mommy. No matter what." I watched the elephants watching them.

"That's right." Claire hugged her daughter. "And you'll always be my baby. You can't ever get rid of me," she joked.

"And you're not *so* boring. I just don't like it when you make me do my math homework. And when you get mad at me."

"I've got news for you, kiddo. I don't like to get mad at you. Or anyone else. Except maybe Mrs. Hennepin. I'm finally beginning to enjoy that, actually. Although it's a good thing that we only have a month or so to go until we won't have to deal with her anymore. But I'll make a bargain with you."

"What?"

"I know I haven't been a lot of fun lately. Maybe not even since last summer. You know, Z, it's been tough for me, too, adjusting to things without Daddy. And having to take care of a lot more stuff than I used to do when he was around. And having to get a job, so I'm not always able to spend the kind of time with you that I'd like to. I know I'm not as fun for you as MiMi. And I haven't been able to take you for treats and special outings and things like MiMi does. So, if you'll be a little bit patient with me, I promise you I will try really, really hard to be 'fun' again." She gave Zoë a squeeze. "So, whaddya say?"

I'd been hanging back, letting them have the space to re-unite—without me. For a woman who was bubbling over with apologies to her kid for not having her act together, Claire was the most together mom I'd seen. More than ours, even. Maybe *she* didn't realize this, but I did: Claire had not only risen to, but met—squarely in the face—every challenge she'd been faced with since Scott walked out the door last year. I think I'd been kidding myself, too. Thinking I was maybe ready to handle a child for more than a few hours at a time. The time I spend with Zoë makes me sure I want to have a kid . . . just not yet. I don't know how to do the things Claire does. *She* might think she lacks patience, but, compared to me, she's got it in spades. From where I stand, not just right this minute, but all the time, observing, watching her to see how she does it, Claire's a total pro at motherhood. In Zoë's mind, maybe I'm the "fun" one, but I'm a rank dilettante at knowing what to say to a kid and when to say it. *How* to say it. And maybe it won't be 'til I have one of my own that I'll learn.

Zoë looked at me before answering her mother. From the look on her face, I felt like I'd failed her. Claire had taken a Wash'n Dri out of her purse and was cleansing Zoë's skinned knee. When she finished, she put a Band-aid over the wound, kissed it, and pronounced the boo-boo all better. Zoë kept her eyes on me. I felt miserable, but I knew this little life lesson had to be learned, as much as it hurt both of us. For all the high heels and the dressing up and the glitter, MiMi isn't really the Fairy Godmother who will always show up at the darkest hour and make the slight or the scrape go away with a graceful wave of her magic wand.

"So, what about my promise, Z? Think your tired old mother can learn to have fun again?" Claire stood, then helped Zoë to her feet. Zoë wrapped her arms around Claire's waist. "I'm taking that as a yes," she said.

I looked at my watch. "I should be getting back—"

"Now I wish we'd left a trail of bread crumbs," Claire joked. "I wasn't paying too much attention to what turns we took."

"Tell you what, Zoë," I said. "As soon as we get to the makeup room and I make sure all the faces are done, and you get the chance to wash up, I'll tell Lucky we're good to go. So, do you still want to go upstairs to watch the fashion show? Or would you rather go home?"

She looked at me like I was nuts. "Upstairs!"

I came over and hugged her. "That's my girl! Way to go! So let's all find our way back. While I finish the makeup, your mom can run out and buy a pack of new undies and a fresh pair of tights at the drugstore. There's got to be a Duane Reade within spitting distance. After you change clothes, I'll get you both a special escort to take you upstairs to the front row. So you can't get lost again, all right?"

I dashed ahead of them, but I could hear Claire's voice resonating in the narrow corridor. She was telling Zoë, "Let's call it a do-over. You and me, okay?"

"Okay," Zoë agreed.

"And you know something?" Claire added.

"What, Mommy?"

"This could be the start of a beautiful friendship."

Chapter 24

June is a lot like Christmastime. Everything winds down and heats up at the same time. Zoë is counting the minutes until school ends, and—I have to admit—so am I. The dry-erase board in the kitchen resembles some kind of Command Central. We've got Zoë's year-end ballet recital, her final presentation for kinder karate, and parent day at bikram yoga, where the mommies and daddies are encouraged to sweat out their bad karma alongside their offspring. I've been finding a million excuses not to participate, but I've run dry of them. So, there goes a perfectly splendid Saturday morning in June.

Then we've got the round of graduation parties. Nina Osborne has already invited the class—and their parents—to a Yankees game. Box seats, naturally.

I suppose I should heave a huge sigh of relief at the fact that at least we have no double bookings or other end-of-term scheduling conflicts this time around. The prospect of summer camp hovers enticingly before me like the twinkly orb that announces the arrival of Glinda the Good Witch.

Although, ironically, just as Zoë and I are beginning to set off on surer footing together and have a whole summer in which to hit our stride, she'll be going off to camp for a month. But we both need the break. Zoë, particularly, needs to have the opportunity to run around outdoors, to chase butterflies, and to learn to sleep through the night after hearing a ghost story.

I'm sitting on a bench in Central Park anxiously watching her cavort on the monkey bars. Part of my new promise to be more "fun" was to agree to these playground excursions. The clever minx had proposed a compromise. "You can talk to the mommies about your jewelry," she said, "while I play."

A couple of weeks ago, we started making kid-jewelry, daughter versions of the mommy pieces, but with plastic and glass beads instead of semi-precious gemstones. Actually, Zoë helped design a number of prototypes, which I then whipped up. We've got three collections now: the adult jewelry, a Mommy and Me line, and a Completely Kids collection, comprised of the kind of stuff I created for her birthday party goody bags and for her Ariel Halloween costume—the mermaid necklace of blue and green beads and shellacked Goldfish crackers.

I continue making pieces well into every night, long after Zoë has gone to sleep. She thinks I should peddle my wares in the playground, going from bench to bench with my sample case. I've been very hesitant about this approach, but I give it a try today, and net one immediate sale, two special orders, and four nannies who ask for my business card.

As I wrap up my transactions, Zoë demands my attention. She's now sitting in the mud, playing with, I believe, earthworms. It rained last night and the ground is still very damp in patches.

"Mommy, come look!" she says. I join her, juggling my purse

as well as the sample case. "No, closer!" I bend over. "No, you have to *kneel down*."

"Zoë, sweetie, this afternoon I came straight from work to pick you up, and I'm dressed all nicely. And there's no clean place to put my bags. I can see very well. It's okay."

She sighs, fed up with me, and realizes she's lost this round. Now she knows how *I* feel most of the time. She's using a twig to cut the worms in half. I only hope she learned this in science class and not from Xander Osborne. When she bisects them, the two halves wiggle independently. "See! When you cut a worm's tushie off, it makes it come alive again!" She's delighted with her discovery. I hate creepy-crawly things and I feel, somehow, like an accessory to murder.

"Do you have a jar?" she asks. "I want to take some of them home with me."

I finish our bottle of Snapple. "Will this do the trick, Z?"

She regards it, frowning. "A mayonnaise jar would be better, see, because it's fatter."

"Well, you're welcome to give it a shot, but my best guess is that you won't find any of the nannies or mommies out here who happens to have an empty mayonnaise jar in her purse, so we'll have to make do with this, okay?"

"Okay," she sighs, with all the regret of an NIH scientist forced to make do with inferior materials. She rinses the bottle in the water fountain, a freestanding structure that always looks to me like a sandpaper-coated birdbath, then yanks a few leaves off a low branch and stuffs them into the bottle. Satisfied with their feng shui, she then drops three earthworms in after them.

I look at the inert bodies lying on top of the leaves. "Z? They're not moving."

She studies her new pets for a few moments. "They're just sleeping," she says, in a teacher voice. "They haven't gotten up yet." Her focus is distracted when something near the edge of the playground catches her eye. She runs over to a landscaped patch of grass and plucks a buttercup. "They need a flower to decorate their room," she announces, an expert in interior design now. Carefully, lovingly, she washes the yellow petals in the water fountain, then introduces the flower into her makeshift terrarium.

"We have to punch holes in the cover so they can breathe, Mommy."

The corkscrew element of my Swiss army knife may never be the same after this.

"So, are we done with the playground for today?" I ask her.

She nods. As we start to head home, she mentions that her year-end ballet recital will be given in the park, instead of at Miss Gloo's studio. "We are celebrating the coming of summer, because June twenty-first is the . . . it's the . . . the . . ." She searches her memory for the phrase the ballet mistress must have used.

"Solstice?"

"Yes! It's the summer sol-stitz, so we're going to be like the lady who used to dance in scarves—"

Dance in scarves? "Not Salome?"

Zoë gives me a funny look. "No! Who's *Salo*-may?"

"A lady who danced in scarves. Or without them, actually."

"Not Salo-may. Another lady. We're going to wear white costumes like Greek statues. Like she wore."

"Aha! Do you mean Isadora Duncan?"

"Yes, her! And we're going to do a worship-nature dance. And also in June it's Arbor Day, which celebrates trees, so it's for Arbor Day, too. Not just the sol-stitz. Miss Gloo said that in the olden days, like when Granny Tulia and Grandpa Brendan were little, we celebrated Arbor Day like other holidays, like we celebrate the Fourth of July, but we don't do that anymore."

I slip my arm around Zoë's shoulder and draw her towards me as we continue to walk. "And it's a real shame, too."

"I think we should all celebrate Arbor Day again, just like we do on Thanksgiving," Zoë says. "Because we have a lot to thank the trees for."

Zoë is in her room reading and I'm taking five minutes to relax in the tub, soaking away sore muscles and the day's emotional tensions. Busy mothers should never underestimate the power of a few drops of aromatherapy. Maybe not as mood altering as a hit of peyote or an LSD tab, but certainly safer.

My daughter knocks on the bathroom door and enters without waiting for permission. "Can you make me this dress?" she asks, showing me an illustration in her storybook. "In the *exact* same colors."

"Sweetheart, Mommy's taking a bath now. You can see that. I can't make you a dress—*that* dress or *any other* dress—*right* this very *minute*. Now you *know* that."

"Okay," she says and shuffles out of the room.

"Close the door, please!" I call after her. She takes a long time, at least a minute, before she obliges. I lean back in the tub and inhale the lavender. In my flight of fantasy I am floating on the water amid fragrant petals, like Elaine, the Lily Maid of Astolat, in the Arthurian legends—except I'm not dead, of course. My hair spreads and splays over the surface like a mermaid's golden tresses. The water supports my weight like a strong pair of unseen magic hands, an aqueous lover caressing me.

The door opens once more and my eyes spring open as well, my idyll interrupted. I sit bolt upright. My wet hair splashes the tiles and the little throw rug before settling lankly around my shoulders.

Zoë brings her book tubside again. "Then can *Granny Tulia* make me this dress?"

I slide back into the water; a total immersion.

....

Dear Diary:

Mommy was a good sport, today. She went to my yoga class with
me in the morning and in the afternoon she watched my kinder
karate demonstration.

   Grown-ups get to go to the grown-up yoga classes when they
feel like it but kids have to sign up for a bunch of classes at a time
and because this morning was the last class, we were supposed to
bring our mommies or our daddies. Mommy said to me that
MiMi might like the yoga and maybe she should go with me in-
stead, but I told Mommy how much I wanted her to come with
me and do the yoga with me, so she went. Mommy likes exercising
but she likes to do it outdoors. She doesn't like to do it indoors at
all because she says there's not enough air and it makes her feel
like she wants to throw up.

   Even though there were a lot of people in the room which made
it even more hot and squashy I think Mommy didn't have such a
bad time after all. She got all sweaty and she said to me that she
saw how it needed to be so warm in the room because it was eas-
ier that way to turn yourself into a pretzel. Afterward, she said
she was really hungry, so she took me to E.J.'s Luncheonette and
we had pancakes for lunch. That was a treat because we never
have pancakes for lunch, only for breakfast.

   Then we went back home and Mommy said I had to take a bath
before we went outside again to go to kinder karate for my group's
big demonstration. I was excited and a little bit scared about it.

   Sensei Steve told us we should just have fun and concentrate
like it's a regular class but he unfolded the bleachers so people
could have a place to sit and watch. I didn't tell Mommy, but
part of the demonstration was like a test to see what level we
are. The levels in karate are called kyus. I started kinder karate
last September in the 10th kyu which is the very bottom one

and you get a white belt. Every three months I took another test and I passed them, so I got a yellow belt and then I got an orange belt. There were two different tests I could take today. If I took the easy test I would still be an orange belt but I would get a new belt with a stripe on it, which makes it a little bit more special. The hard test is the one where I could get a green belt, which is the next one up after orange in Sensei Steve's dojo. But he said if I felt scared about doing it in front of a lot of people that I could take the easier test and I could wait until September to take the harder one as long as I kept practicing over the summer.

I like getting a new color belt for passing the tests. It's like getting a present. And I wanted to make Mommy really proud of me and take the harder test because she talked to me back in the winter because Sensei Steve said to her that I needed to work harder on concentrating and on paying attention when I'm in class and I can't make up my own steps during class time. I have to practice the katas exactly the way he shows them to us.

Mommy was the only one from our family who came to watch the karate presentation. Daddy told us that he had to work at the restaurant so he couldn't come. MiMi and Owen couldn't come and Fireman Dennis had to work today. And Granny Tulia and Grandpa Brendan live far away in Sag Harbor. But they are coming to the city for my ballet recital and EVERYBODY is coming for my graduation. I didn't tell Mommy this either. Mrs. Hennepin asked me to write out the program for graduation in script. She wouldn't let me write in script all year in class because the other kids hadn't learned how yet but she knew I was practicing at home because on my projects, like on my memorial and on my city, I would write in script. So, now, FINALLY, I get to write in script. I want it to be a surprise when Mommy sees it. Mrs. Hennepin is going to tell me everything that is going to happen at graduation and I will write it all out pretty and she will take it to be copied at the school office and there will be a program put on

every chair on graduation day. I can't wait for Mommy to see it.
It's SO hard for me to keep it a secret. I think maybe because
school is almost over and Mrs. Hennepin won't have to teach me
anymore that it makes her happy and so being happy makes her
be nice to me.

I tried to concentrate really hard in the karate demonstration
and to pay really careful attention to when Sensei Steve called the
moves. Sometimes I start to do it before he finishes calling it and
that's not good so I tried this time to wait until he said it and
then I did it. When it works right everybody does the move at the
same time like the Rockettes. And I pretended that it was just like
a regular class and none of the people were watching me.

After the demonstration, Sensei Steve gave out the new belts to
the students who passed their test to get to the next kyu. I was so
happy when he gave me my green belt, and Mommy was crying
and she took a picture of it, and she said she would put the pic-
ture on the computer and e-mail it to Daddy and Granny Tulia
and Grandpa Brendan and MiMi and Fireman Dennis. Fireman
Dennis knows karate, too. We sparred once and he let me knock
him down. He was showing Mommy that karate is self-defense
and how a girl can protect herself even if her opponent is bigger
than her.

Sensei Steve said right in front of Mommy how proud he was
of me. He told Mommy that all the concentrating and listening I
have been working on really showed. And he said that the lessons
I learn in karate are good for the rest of life, too. Sensei Steve told
us that he hoped I would come back to kinder karate after the
summer. I asked Mommy if I could and she said she would think
about it, which is what she says when she really means yes.

• • • • • • • • • • • •

What a day! I traded shifts with a museum coworker so I
could make it to Zoë's ballet recital. Miss Gloo obtained a

permit from the parks department to stage her year-end presentation in Central Park—but where? The map that Zoë gave me was fanciful at best. It's not her fault; it was hand-drawn by Miss Gloo, and no matter which way I turn the paper, I think I have a better chance of ending up somewhere in Middle Earth than in the secluded glade that the ballet mistress has chosen as the performance venue for her mini-Isadorables.

I'm running late, and I'm running in heels and I'm running in circles.

I phone my father's cell and ask him to be a human GPS. Brendan has a flawless sense of direction and a photographic memory. He talks me over hill and dale, and just as I round the crest of a gentle, grassy, rise, I hear Miss Gloo's voice over a portable sound system, announcing the program. Zoë had told me that her class's dance is right near the beginning of the recital, and I know that the piece is only set to run about ten minutes, tops. If I miss it, I might as well have not tried at all.

I hadn't thought about my shoes when I got dressed this morning. They look very smart at the museum, even though I'm behind a counter all day so no one really sees them, but they were not designed to be taken, quite literally, on field trips. The spike heels are sinking into the soft earth as I race down the slope. I have visions of catching one of them in the damp ground and tumbling, like a nursery-rhyme character, right down into a phalanx of folding chairs.

Almost there. I'm panting, sweating—I need to exercise more. My body isn't supposed to act like this! I'm still in my twenties! For my own peace of mind, I decide to blame the pointy-toed slingbacks and my narrow skirt—which is certainly a contributing factor as well, in hobbling my momentum and progress.

As I near the rows of chairs and blankets, arranged as if this is an impromptu concert at Tanglewood, I see Zoë, dressed like a little wood nymph, stepping onto one of the platforms that form the small raised stage. I can't tell whether or not she notices where I'm standing when she scans the audience, searching for her family. By now, I'm close enough to see her disappointment, fearing her mommy is not in the house. I raise my hand high above my head and wave to her, a giant semaphore. The movement catches her eye and she glances in my direction. I hope she realizes it's me.

Despite the earnestness of the Duncan-esque choreography, her face breaks into the biggest smile I have ever seen cross her lips. She's positively glowing. My eyes brim with tears and my heart is ready to leap out of my chest. My baby. I wonder if she will remember this moment decades from now. I am positive that I will never forget it. In fact, I would have walked through fire and crawled though quicksand to see that smile.

I'd been hoping that Zoë's graduation would be a triumph as well. Along with each child's diploma, the Thackeray administrators hand them an envelope containing the name of their teacher for the upcoming year. Third grade has a "good teacher" and a "bad teacher," too. And I had decided to attempt to circumvent a graduation-day disaster by making an appointment with Mr. Kiplinger, during which I intended to make a formal request for Ryan King, the "good teacher." Ryan's a relaxed, sweaters-and-corduroys kind of guy, who sort of reminds me of a younger version of my father. The "bad" third-grade teacher is a very young woman named Audrey Pennywhistle. Even her name gives me a headache. She's peppier than Barney the Dinosaur on speed, and in her earnestness to prove—mostly to the parents—that she can handle her job responsibilities despite her extreme youth, in my view she goes overboard and tries too hard. Her reputation for assigning Herculean homework projects has assumed mythical proportions.

Dennis was a sweetheart. When I told him about my mission, he wanted to know if I could use some company.

"You mean some muscle?" I'd teased. "You're adorable. But since you wouldn't be appearing in any official capacity, it would probably confound them."

"Just thought I'd establish a presence is all."

Wow. I let his words hang in the air for a while, enjoying their weight. Then I said thank you, kissed him, and let the matter drop.

I attended the meeting alone, the upshot of which was that Kiplinger would give me no guarantees, but intimated that he would look forward, with much alacrity, to fewer visits from me in the coming year.

On graduation morning I go to my closet and remove something I haven't worn in a year. Zoë has specifically requested that I put on the same pink suit I wore to her first-grade graduation. As I slip into the skirt, I realize it's missing the button on the waistband, then remember that the button had popped off just as I was running out the door last year, and I never did get the chance to stitch it back on. I'm a bit amazed that I can actually recall where I'd put it. I open my jewelry box, locate the pink button, and start to hunt for some thread in a color that won't clash horrifically.

At the moment, the apartment resembles an open house. Everyone has begun to gather here before heading over to Thackeray. My parents have arrived, after getting up before dawn to make it into Manhattan this early, and my mother is helping Zoë with her hair. Tulia made the dress that Zoë had so coveted from her storybook, and she resembles a Kate Greenaway illustration in a flounced white "frock" with wide pink sash—not yellow, surprisingly—and golden curls. My father is, naturally, checking out my library, remaining unruffled by all the commotion around him. I've taken a personal day. Mia cleared her calendar weeks ago. Dennis is off work today. And even Owen made sure to keep this morning free of client meetings.

The graduation ceremonies begin at 10 A.M. We leave the house at nine o'clock to walk over to the school. Our little procession somehow reminds me of the village weddings in Jane Austen novels.

"Why do they call them graduation *exercises?*" Zoë wants to know.

"Ask Grandpa Brendan," I reply, figuring it will give him something both useful and enjoyable to do.

Zoë repeats her question.

"Well," my father says with such mock authority that *I* know he's putting her on, even if Zoë doesn't realize it, "exercises are things you repeat, right? Nobody does just one push-up . . ."

"Yeah . . . ?" She's waiting for the other shoe to drop, as are we all. I just love to hear the kind of stuff Brendan will come up with. He plays with words like they're modeling clay.

"And every year you graduate from one grade into another. So it's an exercise, because you have to repeat the graduation process, year after year."

"Says you," Mia sasses under her breath. She and Owen are walking hand in hand. They slow down so he can whisper something to her. She actually blushes. I'm dying to know what he said.

Zoë breaks into a grin. "I don't believe you!" she says to her grandpa.

"You're getting too smart for me, kiddo," he teases.

"Look at this," Dennis says, nodding at Mia and Owen. He turns to glance at my parents, who still look like they're in love after over thirty years of marriage. His own arm is slipped around my waist. Zoë has left her grandfather's side and is now holding Dennis's other hand.

Seven truly happy people—some of them *related*—walking up Central Park West and it's not even Thanksgiving.

Dennis knows what I'm thinking. "Yeah," he says, agreeing with my unvoiced words. "How cool is that?"

"*Pretty* special," I nod. "Not only that, I actually found five free minutes to sew on a button this morning!"

Chapter 25

Once we get to the Thackeray auditorium, I ask my family to find us some seats while I take Zoë to join her class. Several rows at the front of the theater have been reserved for the students. Grammar schoolers graduate in the morning, and the afternoon is reserved for the middle and high school students. Back in my day, we only had two graduations: sixth grade and sixth form. I guess graduating each grade is one way of showing parents what they're paying for. Like Sensei Steve and his revenue rainbow of karate levels and corresponding colored belts. After locating Mrs. Hennepin's section I give Zoë a kiss and wish her good luck.

I look for the rest of the Marsh clan. My mother is standing in the aisle waving her program, although her hat is such a scene-stealer that it would be hard to miss her. "You might want to take that off, so whoever sits behind you can see the stage," I suggest.

I slide into the row and take the program off my seat, turning to the second grade's page. I do a double take when I see that the order of events for their commencement exercises is hand-lettered in a penmanship I recognize very well. Mrs. Hennepin, seized by the spirit of something, has finally permitted

Zoë an outlet in which to show off her cursive writing. I'm amazed and delighted. Maybe she's visited Oz, where the Wizard gave her a heart. Or had some pre-graduation Scrooge-like epiphany. It's been a whole year in coming, but better late than never, my mother remarks. I'm so proud of my kid, I'm sure everyone in the auditorium can see me glow.

The lights dim and Mr. Kiplinger strides majestically to the podium, playing his headmaster role to the hilt. He welcomes the teachers, school administrators, students, and their parents and explains the morning's schedule, as more fully delineated in our printed programs.

We all rise to sing the school song, a creaky old chestnut with Latin lyrics that, for the past hundred and eighteen years of Thackeray history, no one has ever known how to translate properly. Then the grades are graduated, starting with pre-kindergarten, each grade having their chance to climb the four steps to the stage, where the kids line up alphabetically and upon hearing their name announced, receive their diploma from Mr. Kiplinger. Instead of the traditional scroll, the Thackeray diplomas are flat certificates inserted into elegant burgundy leather folders.

Amid much pomp and a good deal of singing, pre-K, kindergarten, and first grade are graduated. Then it's time for the second graders to have their place in the sun. On behalf of both second-grade teachers, Mrs. Hennepin approaches the podium and says a few words about the past year. Her speech is intended to be nostalgic and vaguely humorous.

"Here at Thackeray, precocity among the students is as common as April showers," she says, "and of course that's just one of the things that makes our academy such a special place to learn. But sometimes we feel it's in the best interests of the *class* if we give the occasional tug on those precocious reins, so the rest of the students have the chance to catch up with our little fast-trackers."

"Where's she going with this?" Mia whispers in my ear.

"I'm not too sure. She sounds like such a dimwit," I reply.

"This year, one of our little speed-demons was Zoë Marsh Franklin."

Dennis squeezes my hand. There's a bit of a commotion at the far end of the row; for a moment, I look toward the disruption. My ex, Scott, is standing in the aisle, pointing to the only empty seat. He's always late. I was concerned that he might not even make it in time. I watch while people pull their legs in, to better accommodate his swift-as-possible progress to the vacant chair. My mother shoots me a look, which silently asks how I feel about Scott's arrival. *He's her father*, I mouth, then shrug. He's also a former faculty member. And he's here alone. Which is interesting. Maybe there is some truth to the rumor Mia heard last month.

Mrs. Hennepin is continuing her little preamble. "The Marsh girls have always been well known to Thackeray faculty and administrators for insisting on getting their way, and one of this year's members of the outgoing second-grade class is no exception. At the beginning of the fall term, Zoë ably demonstrated her advanced aptitude to write in cursive, but we felt it was inappropriate to encourage her to use this skill in the classroom when the other students were not yet at her level. Of course," Mrs. Hennepin adds with a little smirk, "we went to the mat over that. However, 'all's well that ends well,' as Shakespeare said, so this year we decided to pay a little bit of homage to old traditions, and give a prize for exemplary penmanship to one of our second graders. I am very pleased to say that the first recipient of this new award is Zoë Marsh Franklin, whose handiwork can be seen in your commencement programs on the second-grade page."

My mouth falls open into a shocked O. My relatives and our significant others take a split second to laugh at my reaction before jumping to their feet. On the stage, Zoë looks totally caught by surprise. Her eyes widen like Orphan Annie's. Standing to her immediate left, April and May Miller jump up and down and congratulate her as though they're runners-up in a beauty pageant. Mrs. Hennepin beckons Zoë to the podium and she steps out of the line to accept a blue ribbon from Mr. Kiplinger. I go from imagining *Miss America* to thinking *County Fair*. Still, I am so proud of my little girl, despite Mrs. Hennepin's inelegant swipe at my family.

To a round of applause, Mrs. Hennepin pins the blue ribbon to Zoë's new dress. Zoë steps back into line, and then, starting with the A's, one by one the second graders are called by name to receive their diplomas. After the last child, Chelsea WuDunn, returns to the line, all forty-four soon-to-be third graders take a bow and pose for a wide-angle photo-op. Then the music teacher Mr. Wisdom—yes, that really is his name—raises his baton and they sing, inexplicably, John Denver's song "Leaving on a Jet Plane," after which they wait for their applause and return to their reserved rows in the auditorium.

Finally, after the sixth-grade commencement program draws to a close, the house lights are brought back up and it's mayhem as all the relatives attempt to reunite with their kids.

As we head down the aisle to greet Zoë, she's swamped by a sea of friends who stop her on the way out to get a better look at her blue ribbon. She's the center of attention and seems overwhelmed. Ordinarily my daughter adores being fussed over, but like me, she hates crowds. They tend to freak her out a bit.

"Zoë!" When she hears me call her name, she looks up the aisle to see where my voice is coming from. She attempts to extricate herself from her cluster of admirers while I elbow a few adults who seem deaf to the words "excuse me." We navigate through the crush and meet the rest of our family right outside the auditorium. Out on the landing, the air is cooler and there's room to breathe.

"Hey, show us your diploma!" I say to her and she opens the

leather folder for all of us to ooh and ahh over. Mia continues to snap photos with her digital camera. "You know what this is, don't you?" I ask Zoë, removing the sealed envelope.

She nods. "But I'm too scared to look."

"May I?"

"Okay." She winces and closes her eyes as I open the envelope containing the name of her third-grade teacher.

I give Dennis the thumbs-up sign, then turn back to Zoë. "You've got nothing to worry about, Z. Here, read it for yourself." I hand her the letter.

"I got Mr. King!" she announces, jumping up and down. "He's the *good* third-grade teacher," she explains to her grandparents. Suddenly, she becomes distracted, and I follow her gaze. Scott is standing near the wall, hanging back, like he's waiting for an invitation to join us.

It's an awkward moment, which all of us, even Zoë, keenly feel. Forced cheer, under the circumstances, would be even more so. I take Zoë by the hand and step away from the family, bringing her to him.

"Congratulations, Zo! I'm so *proud* of my best girl!" he says, kneeling down to give her a big embrace, and I feel a stab of regret over the nuclear family that isn't. The moment is bittersweet. Scott's moving on had destroyed that nucleus. Now, *I've* moved on and I'm in a much better place. For me. Certainly a much better place than I've ever been since the divorce. Still, that awareness doesn't soften the pang of sorrow I just felt, not to mention the weird sensations of guilt over being happy with Dennis as I watch my ex-husband hugging our daughter.

"You're looking beautiful, Claire," Scott says, releasing Zoë. He stands up and looks at me, unsure whether to give me a hug or to shake my hand and we end up in a clumsy hybrid of the two that embarrasses both of us.

"Thanks. Thanks very much." I feel like I'm speaking underwater. It's so surreal, talking with my former husband about our daughter while my relatively new boyfriend chats with my family, trying bravely not to appear discomfited by any of this. I realize it will be very strange to introduce the two of them, but ruder not to.

"Scott," I say, steering him to the rest of the relations, "this . . . this is Dennis McIntyre, my boyfriend. Dennis, this is my ex-husband, Scott Franklin." They shake hands, perfect gentlemen, but don't seem particularly inclined to converse. Small talk *would* seem a bit silly, I suppose.

"Well . . . I'll . . . I'll be heading back home, now," Scott says. He gives Zoë another hug and tells her he'll take her for a special graduation treat at her earliest convenience. She's very excited about that, and starts talking nonstop about pony rides someplace.

"I'll phone you with her schedule," I tell him.

"Great."

What else is there to say?

"Wonderful to see you again, Claire," he says, and heads down the stairs. He looks so alone—lonely really—nearly, though not quite, slinking off.

I need to turn away, so I walk to the corner of the landing and face the wall. I want to be alone for a minute. How can I be so happy in so many ways today and yet . . . ? If my heart were made of porcelain, it would just have developed a visible crack. I feel compassion for Scott, actually. Out of the corner of my eye, I see Mia start to follow me, but it's Dennis who gently places his hand on her arm and stops her. The fact that he "gets it" makes me love him even more.

Zoë seems less affected by what just transpired with her father. Or maybe she's dealing with it differently, I don't know. She's busy jumping up and down and telling my parents what she wants for a graduation present. And she's over the moon about getting Mr. King for her teacher next year. Mr. Kiplinger was right; the assignment should save me a lot of trips to the headmaster's office.

On the way down the stairs, we run into the Silver-Katzes. Ashley will be in Audrey Pennywhistle's class next year. "We're so lucky," Jennifer says. "Miss Pennywhistle has even more energy than the kids. There's not a minute of wasted time in her classroom!"

She tells me she'd like to host a jewelry party later in the month. That kind of thing is very "in" these days. Chic moms love to "discover" hot accessories designers and have them do a private trunk show for all their equally chic friends. It's a very good way to get word-of-mouth out there and costs the designers nothing but a couple of hours of their time and a negotiated give-back to the hostess, usually in the form of a commission on pieces sold or ordered during the party.

"Sounds terrific," I tell Jennifer, and looking at Owen, I add, "I'll discuss it with my business manager." Her eyes widen as it dawns on her that perhaps I'm not such a charity case after all.

• • • • • • • • • • • •

"Claire, are you sitting down? I'm getting married!" I heard my sister gasp on the other end of the phone line.

"What?!"

I bet she was looking at the calendar. "No, April has not come twice this year. It's still June." There's silence from her end. "Aren't you going to congratulate me?"

"I—I am! I'm just . . . oh, my God, Mia, this is *wonderful*! I'm so happy for you! It *is* Owen, isn't it?"

"Duuuh!"

"Just checking." Claire was laughing and crying at the same time.

"I'm marrying a man who wears suits every day. Can you believe it?" My own voice sounded higher than usual, hysterical, even—but in a good way. I thought of it as the giddy sound of a woman wildly, madly, in love.

"Have you . . . have you set a date?"

"September, if we can swing it that fast." It takes several months to properly plan a wedding, especially in New York, and September is a popular time of year. "But I don't think we'll do it at the Plaza or anywhere like that. Not a big hotel. It's too impersonal. Someplace different. We met at The Corner Bar, but I don't think Mom and Dad will go for that!"

"You'd be surprised. Hey, what about their house? It's simple, classy, homey—"

"And it's their house."

"Good point. So, when did this happen? Tell me all about it." Claire has always been such a romantic. She loves hearing proposal stories. She used to say to me that happy endings are like favorite sweaters. You just want to wrap yourself up in them and curl up like a contented cat.

"Last night. In the middle of the Hudson River. Looking at the Statue of Liberty, actually. Total schmaltz—but it was wonderful. Just the way it's *supposed* to be, right? What little girls fantasize about. Remember, Owen and I had our first date on a cruise around the city? So, he suggested we do it again. And there we were, leaning against the rail and looking at Lady Liberty, and I said something about freedom and he asked me if being free, to me, meant being alone. And I had no idea where he was going with that. I said, 'No, of course not.'

" 'So, you don't look at marriage as giving up your freedom?' he asked, like he was fishing.

"And I just looked at him and said, 'Not if you're marrying the right person.' And I swear, right there on the deck of the boat in the middle of the harbor cruise, he got down on one knee and proposed to me!"

My sister made a funny sound.

"Claire? Clairey, you're squealing!"

"I know. I'm sorry. You know it's one of my 'happy noises.' "

"Believe me, I know. You've been making that sound since you this afternoon and then you can go out to dinner with him tomorrow?"

I pretend to consider it. "I think that would be all right."

She actually says "Yippee!" and bounces around the breakfast nook as though she's on her invisible pogo stick.

"How about calming down a bit, huh? You're acting like you're already on a sugar high." I reach for the phone. "I'll call Annabel, and see if she can sit tomorrow night. I don't think she's headed off to Italy yet." Annabel plans to spend half the summer on a backpacking tour in Tuscany. She's been studying Italian at home with an interactive CD-ROM.

"You know, there's a chance there may be nothing to celebrate," I tell Dennis, as I wait for the call to connect. "Laura Sloan might not offer me a contract."

"There *is* that possibility," Dennis admits, "but it doesn't change the need for a celebration. Look how much you've accomplished in just a couple of months! We're celebrating *you*, Claire."

How cool is that? I feel a blush spread from the apples of my cheeks all the way into my hairline.

The following morning, as I pass Zoë's bedroom door, I overhear her telling Wendy, her imaginary friend, all about her trip to Dylan's yesterday. "You couldn't go because Dennis doesn't know you very well yet," she informs Wendy. "But you could share some of my Jelly Bellies."

I knock on the door. "Hey, Z. I have a question for you." She looks up, somewhat confused. What could Mommy possibly need to know that she, Zoë, would have the answer to? "I was wondering if you'd like to come with me to Barneys this morning. That is . . . of course, unless you'd rather go straight to Lissa's house."

She scrambles to her feet. "I can go with you?"

I nod.

were pre-verbal. We're going ring shopping tomorrow. Can you believe it? It's so . . . conventional!"

"So un-Marsh-like," Claire agreed.

"Clairey, I know you know this because you've been married, but it's a first for me, relationship-wise. It's *so* cool! *The* guy, as opposed to *a* guy, I mean. It's like the difference between going to—like when you have a stiff neck or muscle spasms or something, and you stop into one of those Asian nail salons to get a ten-minute back-rub. Even a twenty-minute one, let's say. And it feels good at the time, but really, the effect is so temporary. I mean, you lean forward on one of those chairs—you don't even lie down—and they massage you through your clothes, so how can they do it properly—or really well? And they never ask if you have any specific medical problems or anything, like the professional massage therapists do when you go to a spa or something and have it done right. You know, at a spa, you get naked and you lie down and they pay attention to your whole body. For an hour. Not just ten minutes. And the massage is just for you—*your* muscles—*your* limbs—it's *nothing* like some quickie you get in a storefront."

Claire was quick on the uptake. "So, all the other guys you've dated over the years were the nail salon massages. And Owen is the spa."

I was laughing my butt off. "You'd better believe it, sister!"

•••••••••••

I give Dennis Mia's good news. He's in the kitchen frying bacon and the apartment smells like a "home."

Zoë comes into the room just as she hears her aunt's name mentioned. "What about MiMi?"

"She and Owen are getting married!" I tell her. "Isn't that wonderful?" I watch her process this. She doesn't share my boundless enthusiasm. Her wheels are spinning elsewhere.

"Are you and Fireman Dennis going to get married?" she bluntly asks, aware that Dennis is not five feet away from her.

Things like double weddings, particularly where both brides are sisters, don't often happen in real life. It's the stuff of Restoration comedy. Dennis and I exchange glances. "Well . . ." I begin, completely unsure of how my sentence will end.

"Well, not as soon as September," Dennis tells Zoë, "but I wouldn't be surprised if it happened eventually."

How can he sound so matter-of-fact, when my heart has just leaped out of my chest and landed on the counter next to the pancake batter?

"Would you like that?" he adds, speaking directly to her.

"Yes," she says, dragging out the word. "Can we have *real* maple syrup with the pancakes? The one in the can that looks like a house? I don't like the kind in the plastic bottle."

I wonder at what stage in our lives, or at what age, "really big stuff" becomes "really big stuff." There's much more than a generation gap between myself and my seven-year-old daughter. There's a reaction gap. "I didn't hear you asking if *I'd* like that," I say to the bacon fryer.

"Any objections?" he asks, kissing my nose. I shake my head. "We're getting there," he whispers in my ear. His lips graze my neck. It tickles. "I definitely think we're getting there."

"Careful," I warn, my voice low enough for Zoë not to hear. "I hate nasty surprises."

"Not to worry. I don't anticipate any. Now, how about fresh-squeezed orange juice? That's a perfect way to start a Sunday."

I look at the two loves of my life, so at peace with things, so at ease around each other, like they've been doing it for the past seven and a half years, and not just for the last few months. A year ago, could I have imagined this? I think not.

"I've got an appointment with Laura Sloan over at Barneys tomorrow," I tell Dennis, deciding it's time to change the sub-

ject. "I'm showing her all three collections, including the kids' stuff and the Mommy and Me jewelry."

"That calls for a celebration," he says. "What do you say I take you to dinner afterwards?"

"Me, too?" Zoë asks.

"Tell you what," Dennis proposes, "how about I take *you* out for a celebration today and I'll take your Mommy out for a post-Barneys dinner tomorrow?"

"Where will you take me?" Zoë demands.

"I don't know . . . I didn't really think about that yet. Where would you like to go? I understand you like to play with worms, so how about the natural history museum? Or maybe the planetarium? How does that sound?"

"My daddy takes me to the planetarium."

This is a collective uh-oh. The room falls silent for a few moments.

"Oh. Well, then maybe that should be your special place that you go to with your daddy," Dennis says diplomatically. "We'll think up some other place to go."

"It's okay . . . I guess you could take me to the planetarium, too," Zoë replies, as if she's doing Dennis a favor.

"Then maybe we'll do that someday," he says, giving her all the space she needs for such an excursion to become her own idea, if ever. And if not, that's okay, too. "I don't know about you, Zoë, but I have a real craving for something sweet."

"We're having pancakes," she says helpfully.

"That's true. But I was thinking jelly beans. And gummi bears. And red licorice. And caramels." The way he lets each sweet roll off his tongue, he's making my mouth water. "I don't know if you're interested—maybe you're not—in coming with me to Dylan's Candy Bar this afternoon."

Zoë lights up like Times Square. "Ooh, yeah! Can we? Mommy, can I go to Dylan's Candy Bar with Fireman Dennis

"Really?"

"Really. After all, some of the jewelry designs were your idea. What do you say?" Zoë scampers over to me and throws her arms around my waist. "You're welcome."

I remind her that she'll have to act very grown-up during our excursion, and she practically bounces off the furniture in an overzealous effort to choose the perfect ensemble. "This is going to be *so* fun!" We select an outfit for her and she compliments my own choice of wardrobe, which is a big deal for both of us, since she's so judgmental about everything I wear.

"I'm so glad you let me get dressed without you."

"Well, you look fun today. More like MiMi. So it's okay. Oh, can MiMi come with us, too?"

"MiMi's got her own plans today, sweetie. She and Owen are going to pick out her engagement ring. Besides, I thought this might be something we could enjoy together. Just the two of us." I call Melissa Arden to see if I can bring Zoë over for her play date with Lissa a bit later than we'd previously scheduled. Melissa tells me it won't be a problem, they'll be home all day, and they wish us both good luck at Barneys.

I introduce Zoë to Laura Sloan and explain that some of the concepts for the kids' jewelry were hers. Our meeting is going very well. Laura thinks it's neat that I brought my daughter with me. "You're really very entrepreneurial, Claire, and that sets a good example for her." Then she tells me that Nina Osborne has high praise for me—as a designer, as a mom, and as a person. I try very hard to disguise my surprise over the source of such compliments. "Oh, yes," Laura says, as I realize I haven't been able to mask it at all, "she told me how you ran up to the roof of the school and saved Xander's life."

"She *helped* save him," Zoë corrects, interrupting Laura. "Fireman Dennis and his friends *actually* saved Xander. And Fireman Dennis saved *Mommy*, too. And now he's her boyfriend."

Laura's hand flies to her heart. "Ohh, that is so sweet. Is that true?" I smile sheepishly.

"And they might even get married one day soon and I'd have a new daddy. Well, I'd still have my old daddy because he's my real daddy, but—"

Gently, I place my hand on Zoë's knee. "I think Laura gets it," I whisper to her.

"So," Laura says, ready to change the subject and get back to business, "I love your designs. They're whimsical, original, well made. The only question I have for you is how fast can you make them?"

"She's *really* fast!" Zoë tells her. If she doesn't decide to be an astronaut when she grows up, my daughter could have a real future as an agent.

I explain how much time it makes to craft each piece, assuming I'm giving it my full attention, and don't have to stop what I'm doing to attend to some domestic emergency or put it aside for eight hours while I go off to work at the museum.

"Well, the point is for you not to have to go back to the museum," Laura says. "The jewelry design should be your job. Not your job—your *career*. And as long as you can deliver the pieces on schedule, it's none of Barneys' business when you complete them. So your time is as flexible as you need it to be. Based on everything you've shown me today I'm prepared to offer you a contract."

My cheeks grow warm and my eyes begin to water. "That's . . . that's wonderful!" I can hardly believe the good news.

"There's something else I want you to consider. We're not stupid or naïve. We know that there are other high-end department stores and hundreds of boutiques in New York which you could interest in your designs. Barneys, of course, enjoys a certain cachet and our customers welcome its exclusivity when it comes to a number of the goods and services and products we offer them. So, we're prepared to offer *you* a sweet-enough deal

financially, provided that Claire Marsh Originals are sold only at
Barneys."

It sounds fantastic. But I don't know enough about the business world to figure out if this is really the best deal I can get.
Something inside me says, *Don't jump at the first chance. They
know you're green and they know you're hungry.* "You'll give me
all of this in writing, won't you?" I ask Laura.

"I've got it right here," she says, opening the manila folder on
her desk. She hands me an unsigned contract.

Clearly, if Laura fell in love with my designs, they had the paperwork all set to go. The numbers look good. This should indeed mean that I can give the Metropolitan Museum my notice.
It's all very exciting. Still, I wasn't born yesterday and I know
that their contract has been drawn up to inure to Barneys' benefit. I think it's a good idea to get a professional opinion before
signing my name. "I'd like to review this with my business manager," I tell Laura, knowing I'll probably dial Owen from my cell
phone as soon as Zoë and I are back on Madison Avenue.

Laura stands and extends her hand to me. "Of course. It's not
a problem. If you can get back to me by the beginning of next
week, though, I'd appreciate it. And . . . I look forward to doing
business with you. So . . . is there anything else you'd like to ask
me before you go?"

"*I* have a question," Zoë says. "Why is your store named for a
dinosaur?"

"Hey, hey, no running on ahead," I caution Zoë, as we head
for the exit. Every little thing on the main floor catches her eye,
particularly the jewelry displays.

"I want to see if it's as good as yours is, Mommy." I catch up
with her and clasp her hand. "You could make stuff like that if
you wanted to. Easy. But your jewelry is a lot prettier."

I've got a contract in my purse, a flexible new career, a happy
child, a man who adores me, a sister who's finally in a fulfilling

relationship after at least thirteen years of bad luck, and a pair of parents who still enjoy communicating with each other. The air in midtown Manhattan suddenly smells sweet and the sky is the saturated shade of turquoise-blue you see only in digitally enhanced picture postcards and Magritte paintings.

"Zoë, would you like to go on a play date with me? Right now?"

She beams at me. "Yeah! Where?"

"We're just a block or so from the Plaza Hotel," I tell her. "How 'bout we go have lunch with Eloise?"

Being New York, no one even pauses to notice two blondes, one a miniature version of the other, holding hands and actually *skipping* toward Fifth Avenue.

Want More?

Turn the page to enter
Avon's Little Black Book—

the dish, the scoop and the
cherry on top from
LESLIE CARROLL

Celebrity Magazine: *Who's Hot*

This month, Celebrity *freelance writer Leslie Carroll contributes to our "Who's Hot" column, profiling Claire Marsh, jewelry designer to the stars.*

Dateline: Hollywood, California.
Sometime in the near future.

The pre-Oscar buzz this year isn't about who will take home the coveted golden statuettes. Richard Dreyfuss and Alec Baldwin appear to be locks in their respective categories, Madonna is a surefire shoo-in for Best Director for her own biopic, Meryl Streep is looking to break all Academy records for number of awards taken home—she must have several sets of bookends by now—and a newcomer named Alice Finnegan (who used to be a legal secretary) is the odds-on favorite to win the Best Actress nod for her remarkably brave portrayal of an adulterous prostitute opposite tall, dark, and hunky heartthrob Jon Santos.

Here in tinseltown, the talk is all about the tinsel itself that will accessorize the glitterati on the red carpet and in the plushy seats of the Kodak Theatre. With near-meteoric speed, jewelry maven Claire Marsh has rocketed her way into the hearts and homes of Hollywood's A-list celebs. They can't seem to get enough of the young designer's unique creations. Nicole Kidman, in fact, was photographed for a recent cover of *Vanity Fair* clad in nothing but Claire Marsh Originals, as the baubles' line is known.

We caught up with Claire—and her young daughter Zoë—in their spacious home in Manhattan, overlooking Central Park.

CELEBRITY: *First of all, thanks for meeting with us this afternoon.*

MARSH: Not at all, I'm always delighted to talk to the press.

CELEBRITY: *I have to say that I'm surprised that all this Hollywood hype hasn't induced you to chuck it all and move out there.*

MARSH: Not on your life. In fact, I think that living in New York keeps me grounded, despite the fact that we're actually several stories above street level here. New York is where I grew up and where I prefer to raise Zoë. The pulse of the city is in our blood. I can't imagine what we'd do in L.A., in fact.

ZOË MARSH: Swim a lot.

CELEBRITY: *So you like to swim, Zoë?*

ZOË: Uh-huh.

MARSH: Speak in real words, please, Zoë.

ZOË: Yes. I like to swim a lot. And in California we would have a lot of sunshine. But all my friends are here and so is my Aunt MiMi.

CELEBRITY: *But your Aunt MiMi—Mia Marsh—has become something of a Hollywood darling herself of late, hasn't she?*

MARSH: Yes, her own cosmetics line took off like a shot, too. So between that and her film gigs, it's true, she's out in L.A. a lot. She just finished designing the special-effects makeup for *Halloween XXVI* and she's about to start on *Titanic 2: Let's Haul Her Up* for James Cameron. But she's still pretty much a newlywed and her husband adores New York. Mia's a real East Villager at heart. I think her brain would atrophy in Hollywood.

CELEBRITY: *And yours?*

MARSH: My brain? [she laughs]. I'm kind of a culture vulture, I must admit.

ZOË: What's a culture vulture?

MARSH: Somebody who likes art and ballet and museums and theater . . .

ZOË: You never go to the theater. Well, hardly ever. [she turns to the interviewer]. She used to work in a museum, though. That's how she got discovered. Sort of.

CELEBRITY: *Why don't you talk about that a bit, Claire?*

MARSH: I think I need to set the scene. Any single mom can attest to the fact that if you need to work for a living, doing so while raising and caring for a child can make you feel like a hamster in a cage. That wheel just never stops turning. After my divorce, I needed to find a job that was flexible enough to bend into the pretzel that was Zoë's schedule. Believe me, her social life was much more exciting than mine. And affording professional, even paraprofessional, child care was a complete non-option. In fact, I'd like to thank my parents in print for contributing to our upkeep. If it weren't for them, Zoë and I would have been living in a cardboard refrigerator box in Central Park.

ZOË: It would have been a cool view, though.

MARSH: Zoë, why don't you start your homework now?

ZOË: I can't.

MARSH: Why?

ZOË: I need your help. We have to redesign the solar system because of the new planet they discovered. I need Styrofoam balls, too, and we don't have any.

MARSH: Why don't we walk over to the Rose Center [the planetarium affiliated with the New York City Museum of Natural History] and see what they came up with?

ZOË: We're not allowed to do that. That's copying.

CELEBRITY: *[laughing]. We're getting a little off track here. Claire, you were telling me about how you worked in a museum when you got your start as a jewelry designer.*

MARSH: Sorry about the digression there. So I had a day job at one of the reproduction jewelry counters at the Metropolitan Museum of Art and when I had a little time on my hands, I started to look at some of the pieces to see how they were made, and thought I could do at least as good a job. I always designed jewelry as a hobby when I was younger . . .

CELEBRITY: *You're still pretty young now! If you don't mind my asking, how old are you?*

MARSH: I do mind. As Oscar Wilde said—and I paraphrase, "A woman who will tell someone her age will tell them anything."

CELEBRITY: *[coyly] Then how* young *are you?*

MARSH: As Oscar Wilde said—actually he has Cecily Cardew say it in *The Importance of Being Earnest,* "I admit to twenty at dinner parties."

CELEBRITY: *I give up.*

MARSH: Good. I never understood this mania people have, particularly the press, for needing to know someone's age. Honestly, who the %@$*^* cares?

ZOË: Mommy, you used the F-word!

MARSH: Anyway, one afternoon I had a rather fortuitous visit from a customer who happened to be the mother of one of Zoë's classmates. Actually, before that, Zoë and I had attended another classmate's birthday party—

ZOË: Lissa isn't a classmate. She's in my Museum Adventures after-school program.

MARSH: I stand corrected. Lissa had a jewelry-making party— you know, all the kids' parties are themed these days—last year we went to one in an O.R. at Mount Sinai because the kid wants to be a doctor when she grows up. I swear, all the kids were in scrubs and watched a liver transplant. Sorry about that. Back to the jewelry party. My designs were a big hit among the other moms, and it spawned a cottage industry. Shortly after that, Nina Osborne—the woman I referred to a minute ago—visited me at the Met Museum and gave me the business card of a friend of hers who happens to be a buyer at Barney's. I went to see her, she gave me a contract, and the rest, as they say, is history.

CELEBRITY: *Actually, it was your sister, wasn't it, who got your designs into the consciousness of the Hollywood cognoscenti?*

MARSH: Definitely. I wear Mia's makeup exclusively and she wears all my jewelry designs. The Marsh family has always encouraged cooperation over competition, so there was never any major sibling rivalry between Mia and myself.

ZOË: That's not what you and MiMi used to tell me.

MARSH: Zoë, I baked some Kahlua brownies and left the plate in the kitchen. Why don't you run in and bring it out for our guest?

ZOË: Okay. [she leaves]

CELEBRITY: *You were saying . . .*

MARSH: Right. So Mia was working on *Taste Me* with Sharon Stone, and Stone admired Mia's jewelry. She was the first Hollywood star to buy one of my pieces. And she's always been a style setter. She loves to go for that classic Hollywood but with a twist look. Remember the time she wore a Gap tee-shirt with a long skirt to the Oscars? Well, several of my pieces combine that eclecticism, so she really took to them. Then of course Catherine Zeta-Jones had to have one. Arnold bought a few pieces to appease Maria after some sort of domestic squabble, I was told. Mel wanted me to design a unique pendant for Monica Bellucci to wear as Mary Magdalene in *The Second Coming,* his sequel to *The Passion of the Christ,* but I said it was a no-go unless he donated five million dollars to the Simon Wiesenthal Center.

CELEBRITY: *And now all of Hollywood—well, except Mel—is wearing Claire Marsh Originals! How does that make you feel?*

MARSH: That's kind of a silly question, Leslie. I mean, it's the obverse of asking a grieving mother how it feels to find out her kid was killed in Iraq. How does it make me feel to have a multimillion-dollar jewelry business within such a short space of time? It feels $%)^&^$%$) fantastic.

ZOË: [reentering the room precipitously balancing a large platter of the aforementioned brownies] You said the F-word again, Mommy. You never use the F-word and you used it two times today. You sound like MiMi. [to the interviewer] My Aunt MiMi uses the F-word a lot, even though Mommy always tells her that she knows lots of other words and she could use more variety in her enthusiasm.

CELEBRITY: *[to Marsh]. You really said that?*

MARSH: [blushing a little]. Well, maybe not in so many words.

ZOË: Yes, those words, Mommy, that's how I know them.

MARSH: Why don't you offer Leslie a brownie, Zoë?

CELEBRITY: *[taking a brief break to scarf down a brownie].*
These are delicious.

MARSH: Thanks. They're a secret family recipe.

CELEBRITY: *So, not to change the subject or anything, but which*
celebrities will you accessorize on the red carpet next
week?

MARSH: Nicole, certainly. Catherine and Sharon, of course. I
hear that Meryl has asked to see two different pieces that I
designed based on Fabergé eggs, since she's nominated for
her performance as Catherine the Great. Haley Joel
Osment's date will be wearing my earrings. Oh, and Alice
Finnegan—she's a new client—couldn't be a nicer
woman—she's become a real friend—she promised to
wear something as well. She dropped a hint that she's
always wanted to wear a tiara, and I've never done one, so
this could be new territory for both of us. She wants to
conjure the image of old-fashioned Hollywood glamour,
particularly since she had to look like such a wreck
through most of her film.

CELEBRITY: *As long as she doesn't end up looking like the*
Queen of England.

MARSH: That's not likely to happen with my pieces. It's funny,
isn't it?

CELEBRITY: *What is?*

MARSH: That the actresses who have to ugly up or dress down in
their pictures are the ones who win the Oscar that year.

CELEBRITY: *Are you saying that it's Alice Finnegan's wardrobe*
and makeup that should win the Academy Award?

MARSH: Hell, no! And don't make me look like that's what I was
saying. That's another thing you journalists love to do. Put
words in our mouths and make us look catty or stupid.

CELEBRITY: *We would never . . . !*

MARSH: No, you blame it on your editors for cutting out the
parts that reflected what we really said!

CELEBRITY: *I'll ignore that. So . . . you've got a thriving new* *business that seems to know no limit. Do you ever run out of ideas?*

MARSH: Are you asking if my creative wells run dry? Sure. I think that's got to be true of any artist. But you know who my main inspiration is? Zoë.

ZOË: Me?

MARSH: You, kiddo. When you're lucky enough to have an inquisitive young child and you try to experience life through their eyes, where every day is filled with myriad delightful discoveries, it tends to recharge your artistic batteries.

ZOË: Would you like another brownie, Miss . . . I forgot your name.

CELEBRITY: *Carroll. Ms. Carroll. But you can call me Leslie.*

ZOË: Do you want another brownie, Leslie? [interviewer helps herself to a second brownie.] Do you have a boyfriend?

CELEBRITY: *Newspaper writers get to* ask *the questions, they don't have to* answer *them.*

ZOË: Oh. My mommy has a boyfriend. His name is Dennis. I think they're going to get married like my Aunt MiMi did. I have a new uncle now. His name is Owen. He's very nice. MiMi taught him how to dress nice, too, because I think he was color blond.

CELEBRITY: *Excuse me?*

MARSH: Color *blind,* Zoë. And I don't think Owen is. I think he was just sartorially confused.

ZOË: What's "sartorially" mean?

MARSH: It means pertaining to someone's clothing or sense of style, or the way they dress.

ZOË: Oh. [to interviewer]. You're sartorially nice. I like miniskirts, too. And your shoes are really pretty. Mommy won't let me wear high heels like that.

MARSH: Because you're still in grammar school. And will be for quite some time.

CELEBRITY: *Thank you, Zoë. So, Claire, tell us about Dennis.*

MARSH: He's a New York City fireman—

ZOË: My mommy is dating a hero.

MARSH: [blushing]. I don't think Dennis thinks of himself that way. [she lowers her voice to a near whisper.] He was down at the World Trade Center on 9/11. Lost a lot of buddies from his engine company.

CELEBRITY: *Wow. That must still be very hard on him.*

MARSH: I think it is.

CELEBRITY: *Zoë seems to think there may be wedding bells in your future.*

MARSH: I don't like to jinx anything. The problem with giving an interview to you tabloids is that you blow stuff way out of proportion and then gloat like crazy when you do a follow-up report on the celebrity dust-up. Dennis and I are both very happy right now and we hope that continues to be the case. I refuse to give you any reasons to indulge in preliminary schadenfreüde.

ZOË: What's—?

MARSH: Gleefully enjoying other people's misery.

ZOË: It sounds like a kind of ice cream. Like Häagen-Dazs.

MARSH: It's colder. You know, Leslie, there's a funny thing about a personal life. See, it's personal.

CELEBRITY: *Then I'm running out of questions, here.*

MARSH: I can tell.

CELEBRITY: *Now that Claire Marsh Originals has become an enormous undertaking, how do you juggle the demands of career and motherhood? Do you still have the kind of flexibility you had when you started up as a cottage industry? You worked right out of this apartment, didn't you?*

MARSH: I did most of my beading right in there, on the table in the breakfast nook. In the mornings the room is just flooded with light. Believe it or not, I still design and make each piece by myself. I don't consign any of the work to a subcontractor or rent my name to another designer who creates the jewelry for me. It's all still me, and I'm very proud of that. Because the pieces are now regarded as high-end, part of that territory is exclusivity—which in fact translates to building *fewer* pieces as my business grows. I find that if I budget my time well, I can manage to meet all of my production demands and still work around Zoë's social calendar.

CELEBRITY: *And you still haven't hired an* au pair*? You can afford one now, you know.*

MARSH: Yes, I know. But Zoë and I are a good team, and we get along so well—most of the time—that I always fear introducing another person into the mix will end up being a detriment and not a benefit. However, I have hired a housekeeper to do the cleaning. I have always hated housework—*detest* it—with a passion, and not having to deal with laundry and vacuuming and scrubbing floors and changing beds and all that is the biggest blessing in the world. I think it's even better than having a masseuse on call.

CELEBRITY: *Then you have that now?*

MARSH: The masseuse? [laughs]. I wish! I'm a spa slut. I do take time to unwind at Bliss or someplace like that a couple of times a month, usually when Zoë's with her father, so I have a long stretch of time to myself.

CELEBRITY: *Speaking of Zoë's father, how does he feel about your stunning success with Claire Marsh Originals? I bet he's kicking himself for screwing up your marriage.*

MARSH: At the risk of sounding like my sister Mia, I no longer have an interest in checking out Scott's butt to see if it's bruised.

CELEBRITY: *You may be the only woman I can think of whose husband left her for an* older *woman. How did you handle that?*

MARSH: Badly.

CELEBRITY: *They do say that living well is the best revenge. And you certainly have managed to do that.*

MARSH: Yes, I have, but that's not exactly why I did it. I didn't set out to get revenge on my adulterous husband. I'm not Clytemnestra.

CELEBRITY: *You tend to pepper your conversation with esoterica, don't you?*

MARSH: I'm well educated. I have absolutely no reason to apologize for that or to dumb down my vocabulary for people who haven't read Oscar Wilde or Greek mythology. You may not know this, but my father, Brendan Marsh, was poet laureate of New York for a time. He was also a professor of literature up at Columbia. So Mia and I grew up in a kind of rarefied atmosphere when it came to that sort of thing.

CELEBRITY: *And yet you girls didn't go right on to college yourselves.*

CLAIRE: Our parents wanted us to feel free to explore our own avenues, to follow our blisses, as it were, without a timetable. It was so different for the two of us compared to the way kids are raised nowadays. Actually, who am I kidding? Mia and I were even weird among our peers. We were super-dorks for the longest time because our mom, Tulia, made us into her guinea pigs and sent us off to school in her one-off clothing designs. We were teased mercilessly.

CELEBRITY: *What was it you started to say about raising kids today?*

MARSH: They're like video games. They're totally overprogrammed. There is such an insane emphasis on getting into Harvard from the time the umbilicus is sealed that there isn't a minute for kids to have time to explore and wonder. They're not even allowed to make mistakes, which are a natural part of the learning process. What is it they say— the ubiquitous "they"—about Edison taking ten thousand tries before he got the lightbulb right? If little Tommy Alva were growing up on the Upper West Side today, right in this neighborhood, or even worse, across the park on the East Side, we'd be conducting this interview by gaslight because he never would have been allowed to fail even once, let alone ten thousand times. Zoë, remember when you were in second grade and Mrs. Hennepin gave you an Unsatisfactory on one of your projects because she said it looked like a child did it? I mean, a child DID do it! What the heck was she thinking?! And that's the prevailing mentality, and the private schools and the parents encourage it.

I would transfer Zoë to a public school, but the ones in this area are not exactly stellar and Thackeray is actually a relatively progressive school with excellent academics, despite a few wacko teachers, like Mrs. Hennepin. At least they still have the funds for the arts classes, which I think are an absolute necessity. Even the best public schools in Manhattan have had to slice and dice, if not totally abandon, their arts curriculum. I'm on my soapbox here, but where would any culture be without its freedom of expression? Honestly, I think the worst thing that can happen to kids today is to have no background in music and art and no opportunity to express it in the schools, since opportunities at home are probably even more limited for most families. So that's one reason why I keep Zoë in that inordinately expensive private school.

CELEBRITY: *But now you can afford it without your parents' support.*

MARSH: True, but it's still obscene. I think my tuition at Columbia was less than Zoë's at Thackeray.

CELEBRITY: *You mentioned earlier about the overprogramming of kids. How do you feel about all those after-school activities?*

MARSH: It's a double-edged sword. First of all, if the kid shows no interest in participating in an activity, the parents ought to be flogged for pushing him into it. That's really a form of child abuse. If parents are trying to create a resumé for their child, that's nuts. But if the parents and the kids use the after-school and weekend programs to broaden the child's horizons in a way that isn't offered in school or is something the kid is really into doing, then the activities can be wonderful, and great venues for them to learn things like cooperation and teamwork as well as karate or ballet or swimming. You want to raise well-rounded kids, not neurotic ones.

CELEBRITY: *Do you think you're a good mom?*

MARSH: I'm not the right person to answer that. I think we need to ask the person my "mom-dom" most affects.

CELEBRITY: *Zoë, is your mother a good mom?*

ZOË: Yes.

CELEBRITY: *That's it? Just "yes"?*

ZOË: Yes. Except I still have to clean up my room and I don't like doing that. Especially since now we have a housekeeper to clean the apartment.

CELEBRITY: *Maybe your mommy doesn't want you to grow up to act like a princess and not know how to do anything for yourself. If your mommy hadn't learned how to do things for herself, then where do you think you would be today?*

ZOË: [looking at her mother] Living in a cardboard refrigerator box in Central Park. [she giggles.]

CELEBRITY: *So, learning how to be independent can be a very good thing, right?*

ZOË: Uh-hunh. I mean yes.

CELEBRITY: *Are you proud of your mommy? I know she's proud of you.*

ZOË: Well . . . after my daddy left us we didn't used to always get along but when she started her jewelry-making business and she met Fireman Dennis, she got really happy and then we got along better. When Mommy is happy, that makes me happy too. When I grow up I want to be just like her.

CELEBRITY: *Well, thank you both for sharing your time and airing your views with* Celebrity. *And we'll look forward to the upcoming Oscar telecast for a veritable fashion show of Claire Marsh Originals. Just one last question, Claire. Do you worry about what Joan Rivers will say about your pieces?*

MARSH: Not a bit. She'll be wearing them herself.

Ron Rinaldi

Native New Yorker **LESLIE CARROLL** is also a professional actress, dramatist, and journalist. She is the author of the novel *Temporary Insanity,* as well as two contemporary romantic comedies. Leslie has worked more temp jobs than she cares to remember, in politics, advertising, public relations, and—far too frequently—law. Visit Leslie's web page at *www.tlt.com/ authors/lesliecarroll.htm.*

LESLIE CARROLL

AVON TRADE... because every great bag deserves a great book!

HELP WANTED, Desperately
Any position will do...
ARIEL HORN
Paperback $12.95
($17.95 Can.)
ISBN 0-06-058958-2

Claire Voyant
(clair-vol-änt) n.
1. a straight-to-video actress who can see clearly that her life is going nowhere. 2. a daughter who wonders how she could possibly be related to her family (or is she?). 3. a reluctant bridesmaid who asks: If a funeral can be planned in two days, why not a wedding? 4. the hilarious, heartfelt new novel by
Saralee Rosenberg
Author of A Little Help from Above
Paperback $12.95
($17.95 Can.)
ISBN 0-06-058441-6

kissing in technicolor
Sometimes it's bigger than the big screen
jane mendle
Paperback $12.95
($17.95 Can.)
ISBN 0-06-059568-X

USA Today bestselling author of The Sweetest Taboo
CAROLE MATTHEWS
THE SCENT OF SCANDAL
"Matthews' will charm any bridget Jones's fans with this novel... A Library Journal"
Paperback $12.95
ISBN 0-06-059563-9

#1 NEW YORK TIMES BESTSELLING AUTHOR
MEG CABOT
author of The Boy Next Door
"Cabot's fans will devour this fluffy, fun urban fairy tale."
—Publishers Weekly
Every Boy's Got One
Paperback $12.95
($17.95 Can.)
ISBN 0-06-008546-0

PLAY DATES
It's not all fun and games
LESLIE CARROLL
author of Temporary Insanity
Paperback $12.95
($17.95 Can.)
ISBN 0-06-059606-6

Don't miss the next book by your favorite author.
Sign up for AuthorTracker by visiting *www.AuthorTracker.com*.

Available wherever books are sold, or call 1-800-331-3761 to order.

ATP 0205